GOB'S GRIEF

Selected by the *New Yorker* as one of the '20 Under 40', CHRIS ADRIAN is the author of *The Children's Hospital*, *A Better Angel*, and *The Great Night*. He lives in New York, where he works as a paediatrician.

ALSO BY CHRIS ADRIAN

The Children's Hospital

A Better Angel

The Great Night

GOB'S GRIEF

CHRIS ADRIAN

GRANTA

Granta Publications, 12 Addison Avenue, London W11 4QR

First published in Great Britain by Granta Books, 2013
This paperback edition published by Granta Books, 2014
First published in the United States by Vintage Books, a division of Random House, Inc., New York

A CIP catalogue record for this book is available from the British Library.

1 3 5 7 9 10 8 6 4 2

ISBN 978 1 84708 582 5

Offset by M Rules

Printed and bound by CPI Group (UK) Ltd, Croydon, CR0 4YY

For my brother

GOB'S GRIEF

THOMAS JEFFERSON WOODHULL WAS ELEVEN YEARS OLD when he ran away from home to join the Union army. One night in August of 1863, he sprinted down a white road that seemed to bloom out of the darkness as a bright moon climbed higher and higher in the sky above him. He was in a hurry to catch the train that passed a mile east of the shack where he lived with his brother, his mama, and her family, the notorious Claflins of Homer, Ohio.

The train was halfway gone when he got to the tracks. Tomo ran alongside the boxcars, cursing at the top of his voice. "You shit for a train won't you just *stop?*" He would have been grateful for just a bit of slowing. But the train moved on speedy and serene. He wished he had a gun to shoot it with.

Glancing back, Tomo saw that the caboose was coming up fast. He cursed again, louder and fiercer, the curses escalating into a wordless howl as he threw himself up at an open boxcar, managing a precarious grip, which he knew he must lose in a moment because he was not strong enough to hold on. He had resigned himself to slipping away, and launched a final "Shit on you!" at the train, when suddenly a set of pale hands came out from within the car and hauled him up and in.

"Why are you making all that racket?" asked his savior, who was just a dark shape until he put Tomo down and turned up a lamp. The man had brown hair and bright blue eyes, and fat lips so red that they seemed stolen from a girl. "Why are you being so noisy? Do you know I was trying to sleep?" He spoke, like Tomo's grandmother, with a heavy German accent.

"I didn't think I was going to make it," said Tomo.

"Where are you going, that you call a train a shit and wake a poor soldier from his sweet dreams?"

"To the war," said Tomo.

"The war? I think you had better go home to your mama, little Fenzmaus." His fellow passenger started to push Tomo toward the door, telling him to roll when he hit the ground. Tomo spun away, out of the man's grip, and threw himself to his knees on the rough floor of the car.

"She's dead!" Tomo cried. "My mama's dead, with my papa and my brother and my aunts, my uncle and my granny and grampy! We all got the typhoid and I ought've died too, but I didn't, 'cause I'm the damned unluckiest boy who ever breathed a breath. Throw me out! Go on! I don't care. It's all shit anyhow. I'll just lie down by the tracks and *die*." Tomo dropped down on his stomach with his head on his arms, and wept with great drama, peeping up a little to see the man standing above him with both hands on his head, as if holding a hat down against a high wind. It was all a lie. Tomo's family were sleeping peacefully in the falling-down shack they called home. His twin brother ought to have been with him, but he wasn't. He'd stayed in Homer for the sake of cowardice. Tomo pounded his fist against the floor in imitation of despair, but really it was rage against his brother that moved his hand.

"I . . ." the man said, kneeling down to touch Tomo on the shoulder. He stood up and crossed the car, then came back to kneel again, and push something gritty against Tomo's wet cheek. "Would you like a cookie?" he asked. "My little Frieda baked them, so I could take them back to my Niners. Do you see? Do you see the nine?"

Tomo sat up and took the thing. It was a molasses cookie, fully half the size of his head, and stamped like a coin with the number nine in the center. Still crying his false tears, Tomo bit, chewed, and swallowed.

"Do you like it?" asked the man.

Tomo nodded.

"Children and soldiers, they both love cookies. Poor Fenzmaus. Haven't you got anybody to watch over you?"

"Don't need nobody," said Tomo.

"No family. Not anywhere?"

"Just Betty."

"Betty? Is that your sister?"

Tomo shook his head. "My horn," he said, indicating the bugle that hung at his side. He put her to his lips and blew, not a military tune, but something sad and angry that he made up on the spot. The man leaned back on his heels and covered his eyes with his hands. "I know camp music, too," Tomo said, and played "Boots and Saddles." Tomo was a splendid little bugler—he knew all the drill calls, be they for bugle or fife, for cavalry, infantry, or artillery. He could play anything if he heard it once.

"So pretty!" declared the man. "Play me another."

Tomo played and played, until it was almost dawn, and the man said it was time for them to go to bed. They had become acquainted, between songs. The man's name was Aaron Stanz. He was a private on French leave from the Ninth Ohio Volunteers, who were camped in Tennessee, awaiting orders from General Rosecrans. In a contest of lots Stanz had won the privilege of visiting his young wife, whom he had not seen since he kissed her goodbye at Camp Harrison in the summer of '61. "How long can a man and his wife be apart?" he asked Tomo, who said, "Always," because he was thinking of his mama and papa, divorced since before the war.

The Ninth, as it happened, was short on field musicians. And Company C, from which Aaron Stanz hailed, had only a drummer; their fifer had died at Hoover's Gap. Tomo closed his eyes and had a brief vision of departing horses—it had been his hope to bugle for a cavalry regiment—but then he said he felt it was divinely sanctioned that he go and bugle for Company C. Aaron Stanz said he did not believe in God, but admitted the convenience of the arrangement. It would not be traditional or entirely in accord with regulations, having a bugler instead of a fifer, but he was sure Captain Schroeder would agree that Tomo must do in this pinch. Anyhow, though there were no angels except in the minds of men deranged by their religion, Tomo blew like one, and Aaron Stanz could not imagine that the Captain would resist the charms of Tomo's bugling.

When it was time for bed, Tomo lay down on Aaron Stanz's rubber blanket, and tried to sleep with his head pillowed on that man's arm. He complained that it was too bright to sleep, and that he wanted to go look at green Kentucky passing by outside the door. Aaron Stanz put his cap over Tomo's face, and called him Fenzmaus again, which was pipsqueak—Tomo's grandmother Anna called him and his brother that sometimes, though never with such gentle affection as Aaron Stanz invested in the word. Eventually, Tomo drifted to sleep, lulled by the steady noise of the train, but shortly woke with a start from a dream of falling. The cap fell from his face, and he cried out softly. Tomo reached around him for his brother, away from whom he had never spent a single night. But then he remembered how Gob was back in Homer, afraid of the war and the great wide world.

The journey south was uneventful, except for a stop in Tullahoma, where a soldier poked his head into the car and made a perfunctory search while Tomo and his new friend hid behind stacked barrels of salt pork. "He wouldn't understand my special arrangement," said Aaron Stanz.

They arrived at Camp Thomas, after rolling from the train near Winchester and walking for some five miles, during which time Aaron Stanz was always supremely certain of his way. He was welcomed in camp not like a technical deserter, but like a hero. Stanz's welcome had to do with his popularity—it was immediately obvious to Tomo that he had had the good fortune to fall in with the best-liked fellow in his company—and with the gifts he brought back. In addition to his wife's molasses cookies, he'd brought two sacks stuffed with roast turkeys and soft bread, new boots for three men (each boot filled with candy and chewing gum), and best of all a small barrel of cool beer. The Ninth Ohio was an all-German regiment, and every man in Company C greatly missed his beer. There was little opportunity to get any in the wilds of Tennessee.

That evening, they had a little party. Though the company had died back to half its original strength of one hundred and two, there was only enough beer for every man to have a few swallows directly from the tap. Fortunately every third turkey was stuffed with a bottle of whiskey. Aaron Stanz called it oil of gladness and poured a cup for Tomo, who took it behind a wedge-tent and did not drink it, but only held it under his nose, and thought of his papa, because when they were very small he and Gob had snuggled up to him, sometimes, after he'd drunk himself senseless.

While Tomo was savoring his cup of whiskey, another boy came up and accosted him rudely. The boy was about Tomo's age, and very fair; blond as a broom straw and white as a grub. Without so much as a how-do-you-do he knocked Tomo's tin whiskey cup from his hand, then kicked him over and sat on Tomo's belly. The boy pulled out a set of drumsticks and played a brutal little number on Tomo's head.

"Looky here," said the boy. "There's only one drummer in this regiment, and it ain't you." He raised his sticks again, but Tomo had grabbed his cup out of the dirt, and he crushed it against the boy's face before he could bring his sticks down. The boy fell over to the side, and in a moment Tomo was straddling his chest. Tomo took the sticks and drove them into the ground on either side of the boy's head.

"I got nothing to do with drumming, I'm a bugler," Tomo said, taking Betty out from under his jacket. Aaron Stanz had told him to hide her there, because he wanted to surprise his comrades with music, a last gift. Not only did Company C have no fifer, the Ninth's regimental band had been absent since September of '62, when the government had refused to salary them any longer. Tomo blew a note straight into the small white ear of his assailant. "See?" he said. "I got nothing to do with drumming."

"I can't hear a thing!" screamed the boy.

Aaron Stanz dragged Tomo off of him. The noise had attracted a swarm of men.

"He deafened me!" the boy wailed, sitting up now, and brandishing his sticks again.

"Shut up, Johnny," said Aaron Stanz. The men were looking at the bugle, glinting in the light from the torches that lined the camp streets.

"I forgot to tell you, boys. The Fenzmaus is a bugler. Isn't that a lucky thing?" The men of the company stared wordlessly at Aaron Stanz. Then there was a rush of murmuring all around the circle.

"Jesus sent me here to play for you," said Tomo. The boy called Johnny laughed cruelly.

"Also, spiel mal!" said a man, whose name, Tomo would come to know, was Raimund Herrman. He picked Tomo up and put him on one of his massive shoulders, and then pranced down the company street to a big cook fire. Tomo stood on the empty beer barrel, which some clever soldier had labeled "molasses" to confuse the authorities, and blew out tune after tune, while the men of Company C drank and danced with each other. Tomo blew marches, because they were soldiers, and vile polkas, because he knew that was the sort of music his grandmother liked, and she was the only German whose tastes and habits he knew. Men called out song names to him, begging him to play "Anna Engelke," or "Romberg Park: Elf Uhr," or "Liebe Birgit." Tomo knew none of those songs, but if they hummed a few bars he could make something up, and that seemed to satisfy them. The boy called Johnny skulked out of the darkness, with his big Eagle drum, and though he sat far away from Tomo, he offered up a friendly beat to Tomo's bugling. Men from other companies came to listen, and they danced, too, until the dancing pairs were four and five deep around the fire.

Tomo could have played all night, but the party only lasted until somebody got the idea of serenading Colonel Kammerling in his tent. A procession was formed, with Tomo and Johnny at its head. They marched the revelers across the camp, to the Colonel's tent, where they fell into rank and sang in voices that were deep and lovely and drunk.

Colonel Kammerling appeared behind an adjutant who was shouting himself hoarse trying to silence the crowd. There were cries from the men of "Speech, speech!" The Colonel stepped up to Tomo, who was still tooting merrily, snatched the bugle from his mouth, then handed it back, bell first. Tomo took it meekly, because Colonel Kammerling was a severe-looking gentleman.

"Go to bed, boys," was all he gave for a speech. He turned and went back to his tent, and the party was suddenly over. As soon as he stopped playing, Tomo felt very sleepy. He clutched Betty to his chest and followed Aaron Stanz back to his dog tent, where he slept between Stanz and another soldier, Private Frohmann. He found he could not sleep in the middle, so he rolled over Aaron Stanz, who mumbled "Frieda!" at him, and kissed the back of his head, and snored like a hog. That night, Tomo dreamed that his brother was looking for him all over their small room. Under the rickety bed, in the old wardrobe with the shrieking hinges—over and over again Gob looked in the same places, over and over again he asked of the air, "Tomo, where are you?"

Aaron Stanz shook Tomo awake at five o' clock the next morning.

"Get up, Schlaftier!" he said. "Get up, Fenzmaus! You've got your work to do!" Aaron Stanz dragged him, still half asleep, across the silent camp, and stood him on the barrel near the ashes of the previous night's great fire. Johnny the drummer boy was waiting for them. Tomo rubbed his eyes and yawned, and looked out over the slumbering camp. The air, warm and heavy, hung in low blue patches between the tents. Tomo yawned again and said, "It ain't even lightened yet." But he took a deep breath and blew the assembly. It rang out brashly through the still air. Johnny said it was too queer, the bugle and drum playing for infantry. "You won't last a week in this company!" he yelled at Tomo, then stormed off, beating angrily on his drum. "Don't you pay any mind to him," said Aaron Stanz.

Tomo played the call again, and a wave of steady grumbling washed up and down the company street. The men cried, "We ain't no hay-burners!" and "Put the bugler in the guardhouse!" and then, when Tomo played the call a third time, someone shouted, "Kill that rooster!" This last precipitated a moment of perfect silence. Then the shouter was shouted at in fast ruthless-sounding German that Tomo could not follow, for all that his grandmother had often cursed at him, fast and ruthless, in her native tongue.

Tomo and Aaron Stanz walked back to their tent against a steady flow of men headed towards the sinks. When they arrived, Aaron Stanz kicked awake his tentmate, who sat up and rubbed violently at his face. Aaron Stanz handed Tomo a cup of water, which he drank, not realizing he was supposed to wash with it. Aaron Stanz and Private Frohmann laughed until they cried, while a murderous rage built up in Tomo, and he was about to strike out at someone when Aaron Stanz picked him up and hugged him, and shook him, and hugged him again, and declared him the most precious Fenzmaus there ever was.

Tomo played Company C through its day. It was a happy day, for him and for them. It was happy for them because they had something more than dry drum music to regulate their day, and happy for Tomo because this was precisely the sort of life he had envisioned for himself, a life beyond Homer, beyond his mama's miserable humbugging world. The situation lacked only Rebs to lick, and he did not doubt that they would come. It lacked his brother, too. Tomo's anger against him was ebbing, so he was glad and not glad that Gob was not with him.

Tomo tooted reveille while the company stood at parade rest, all of the men in full uniform, though if you looked a few hundred yards away to where the Fifty-Ninth Ohio stood in rank you would see men still in various states of undress, some without coats, some without shoes, a few only in hats and shirts. Not only was the Ninth an all-German regiment, they were the sort of Germans that Tomo had never encountered before, not the crazed, superstitious sort, but the neat, hardworking sort. The regiment was famous throughout the whole army for its efficiency and bravery, pitied only because it could not keep a chaplain. But the Ninth drove away its chaplains on purpose. By and large the men were skeptics, except for a few Bavarian Catholics, who bothered the Protestant chaplains with their devoted Mariolatry.

After the reveille Company C gave Tomo a triple hurrah. The sonorous, Teutonic sound washed over him as he stood on his barrel. He played their breakfast call at six-thirty, their sick call at eight. He stood outside the hospital tent watching the invalids line up—in Company C there were only a few, and they were all genuine sick, not shirkers—and sipped the thick, bitter coffee Aaron Stanz had given him to drink in a soup can. Tomo strode up to a man in line and said, "My papa's a surgeon." The man had a green face and stank of ammonia. He said nothing to Tomo, but smiled weakly. Tomo ran back to his barrel and played fatigue call, then went and watched as Aaron Stanz helped to bury dead horses. The company had saved them up for him, a perfunctory punishment for his temporary desertion. His coworkers were two men who had stolen a pie from a sutler. The horses were ripe. Three times the two thieves took time out from the work to retire into the bushes, where they made a noise that was like hurrah! without the h.

"That grave's too shallow!" Tomo kept saying to the two, but they had no English, and weren't inclined anyway to listen to a boy. Aaron Stanz was working on his own grave, but when he came over at last to see how their work was coming along he said as much as Tomo had. There followed a brief argument, which ended when they dragged a stinking carcass over and pushed it into the hole. The legs stuck out a good two feet above the ground.

"Oh, that's spicy!" Tomo said, leaning over the grave and getting a faceful of the rotten miasma. He did not watch as the thieves went to work with saws, but ran back to his barrel to play the drill call. He tagged along the back of the line as Company C drilled in the rising heat of the morning. He fetched water for Private Frohmann, and for a pair of twin corporals named Weghorst to whom Tomo naturally gravitated.

At noon, he was back on his barrel, playing the dinner call. He took a meal to Aaron Stanz and the thieves, who had skipped drill to continue their work, but they would not eat, so Tomo split the food with Johnny the drummer boy, who was by turns sullen and friendly all through the day. Tomo played another drill call after dinner, then watched from a tree with Johnny as the battalion marched and turned on the parade ground.

At quarter to six, he blew the call to inspection and dress parade, then shaded his eyes against the bright boots and brass of the Ninth. They were a shiny bunch, and Tomo felt somewhat slovenly among them. He was glad for the dusk which hid his dirty Claflin britches, his stained shirt and patched coat. As the camp darkened he played the supper call, and later, with beans still on his breath, the assembly of guard.

He spent some time fashioning crosses from twigs and twine, while Aaron Stanz stomped down the last of the horse graves. After Tomo had planted the crosses, he went back to the barrel and played tattoo, summoning the company to the last roll call of the day. The very last name read was his own—or rather the one he had adopted. "Alphonsus Hummel!" shouted the first sergeant, but there was no response. Tomo, sitting on his barrel with his chin on his fist and his eyes closed, had fallen asleep. The whole company had a chuckle at him. Aaron Stanz carried him sleeping to the tent, but woke him later to play taps. That was Tomo's favorite tune—he always felt something settle, deep and peaceful, inside of him when he blew the last note. He heard the fifers in other companies blowing that last note, and other drummers knocking out the few final beats of the day. Johnny had overcome his distaste for bugle-infantry miscegenation and was tapping similarly next to him. Tomo stood on his barrel and watched the lighted tents go dark one by one, and then he waited in vain for another party to begin. His napping had left him wide awake, but the previous evening's revelry had been solely a function of Aaron Stanz's return, and not an every-night occurrence. So, after Johnny left him, Tomo sat next to the remains of the party-fire with a balled-up rag muffling his bugle, and he played the whole day through twice more before he retired.

"This company is cursed," said Johnny. "They lost three fifers since Shiloh. Death wants 'em. They can't keep 'em."

"I ain't a fifer," said Tomo. The boys were watching an artillery drill. Tomo wanted them to hurry up and fire the guns, but they only seemed to be dragging them haphazardly all over the field. He had been in camp a whole week and not yet heard a big gun fired.

"That's no matter," said Johnny. "Death'll gobble a bugler just as quick, if he's dumb enough to march with Company C. We ain't marched yet, though. It's early enough you could live, if you ran off now."

"You put that curse up your ass," said Tomo, and then cheered and blew a toot on Betty, because six guns had very quickly been lined up, and, in what seemed like the space of a few breaths, were loaded and fired. There came a second group of explosions as the shells burst near targets at the end of the field. One gun overshot and destroyed the top of a tree in the woods. Tomo blew a soft dirge for the departing magnolia.

"That's your song, you dead bugler, you rotting blowhard," said Johnny, but there was little venom in his voice. That first week, he had made himself Tomo's companion. Tomo did not mind him. He was lonely for Gob, and it was good to have a body around to talk to, for all that Johnny said doom when he was not bragging about how his drum had been blown up by a shell at Shiloh.

When the drill was over, they ran across the field, into the woods to look at the fallen magnolia. For a little while they played in unnaturally low branches, until Johnny ducked behind the tall stump and sat down. He told Tomo to come and sit by him.

"Time to pet my snake," he said, lifting his hips so he could pull his pants down to his knees. Tomo had seen this thing done before, but it was not something he thought he would like to do himself. Didn't he pet his snake? Johnny asked him. Didn't nobody ever show him how?

"It's only about the best thing ever," he said, tugging languidly at his member, which was even whiter and more grublike than its proprietor. "Go on," he said. "Give it a try." Tomo took down his pants and gave himself a few pulls, just to shut the boy up. "Ain't that grand?" asked Johnny. He closed his eyes and leaned his head against the tree. Tomo pulled up his pants and climbed up to the new top of the magnolia. There was a little fire there, which he patted out with his coat sleeve.

Below him, Johnny kicked his feet and bounced his hips up and down, and turned his head to kiss the tree. "Ah, Mrs. Davis, you are a fucking beauty!" he moaned, and then shouted wordlessly three times, each time louder than the last, the last so loud Tomo thought the guard must come into the woods to see who was being murdered. Johnny uttered an expansive sigh, then put his hands behind his head.

"Where are you, bugler?" he called. Tomo whistled above him. Johnny climbed up and shaded his eyes to look out over the camp, which sprawled as far as they could see.

"I think I see General Thomas," said Tomo.

Johnny said, "Pretty soon I'll start to spurt. Then I'll find a girl and have me some babies."

In another week, the Ninth marched out. Tomo played on Betty as he walked next to Aaron Stanz. They were going south and east, into Georgia, their movement part of a grand design to maneuver Bragg out of Chattanooga. "Chattanoogey," Tomo kept saying to himself, and giggling. "I never been to Chattanoogey."

"You seen one of Reb cities," said Aaron Stanz, "you seen all." But Tomo had never seen a Reb city. He imagined Chattanooga, a city full of Negroes and furious widows. He made up a song as he walked and called it "Chattanoogey."

That first day, his feet were sore and bleeding: his ill-fitting boots had pinched his toes up all funny, and he had walked the nail right off his left big toe. He shook the nail out of his boot and threw it on the cook fire. Aaron Stanz told him to make a wish on it, so Tomo wished that Gob might wander miraculously into camp, having pursued him down from Homer. And then he burned his hand snatching the nail from the fire, because it seemed to him that he had made an ill-advised wish. He didn't want his brother here. He put the nail back in the fire, wishing that a snake would crawl into the bed he had formerly shared with Gob and bite him on the ass. And then he wished he had another nail, to wish his brother to him after all.

With a tin plate balanced on his knees for a desk, he wrote a letter:

Secessia, August 23, 1863

Brother,

Well, this is the life, and you are missing out on it. No Mama and no Buck, no humbugging. Every night I eat my fill, and people here give a bugler his due. Is this what you feared, to live a good life? When you are sensible again, you can join me and see, though maybe by then Richmond will already be burned.

Yours in war,
Jigadier Brindle T. J. Woodhull

p. s. see how rapidly they have promoted me you can be my adjutant

He bought an envelope and stamp from the sutler and put the letter in his coat pocket, where it remained unmailed. From the sutler he also bought an abundance of pies, because it occurred to him that he had not yet spent a dime of the money he'd brought with him—ten whole dollars hoarded over the course of many months from the family's humbug profits. He went back to Company C with pies stacked in his arms, and was hailed by every man as a righteous pie boy. It was seven men to a pie, but somehow there seemed enough to go around.

After supper, the Weghorst twins threw down four square

crate tops to make a dance floor. Tomo and Johnny and a fiddler from the Second Minnesota played while the boys of Company C danced, not in pairs this time, but singly. Everybody had his own dancing style—Aaron Stanz kept his arms straight at his sides, his palms turned up behind him, and moved his head like a chicken while his feet skibbled furiously. The Weghorst twins kept their hands and arms above their heads, and bent from side to side at the waist, towards each other and away again. Raimund Herrman pointed his nose at the black sky, put his hands on his hips, and pedaled furiously. Tomo spun around in a circle while he played, till he got so dizzy he fell over, and thought he would lose his pie, from the dizziness and the heaving, shaking laugh that he laughed.

They marched through the Cumberland Mountains, where Tomo blew echoing notes out into misty valleys and Aaron Stanz collected late-blooming wildflowers for his wife. He pressed them into a Bible he only opened for that purpose. It was almost empty of them now, but had been stuffed full when he went home. Stanz told Tomo how he had spent a whole night laying them out for his wife on the floor of their home, naming them and telling her where he had found each flower. "Dwarf irises," he said to Tomo, tickling him under the chin with one. He asked if he wouldn't like one to send home to his mama, and then he blushed and asked Tomo to forgive him. He said he would take Tomo home with him to Cincinnati, when the fighting was all done, where sweet Frieda would bake him molasses cookies the very size and shape of a whole boy.

When they came to the place where Battle Creek empties into the Tennessee, Tomo got his first glimpse of a live Rebel. Pickets faced each other across the river. Tomo went down with Johnny, who called out across the water, "Good evening, you damned Rebels!"

"Go to hell, you damned Yankee," came the reply.

"I got newspapers," said Johnny, "and coffee, if you got smoke."

"Hold on, you son of a bitch," said the Reb. Tomo could just make him out if he squinted. It was a cloudless night, and the moon was bright, but the river was wide. The Rebel bent over the water and pushed something out. It was a little boat, made from bark and string. It sailed slowly across. Johnny caught it downstream, lifted it from the water, and walked away back towards camp, serenely ignoring the escalating curses of the Rebel, who fired blindly at them when he ran out of curses. His fire was answered by other pickets. Tomo and Johnny ran away back to Aaron Stanz's dog tent, where they wrapped themselves up in blankets and passed Aaron Stanz's long pipe, filled with Rebel tobacco, between them.

The Rebels were gone in the morning, and the brigade began to pass over the river. Company C was one of the first to cross. Tomo sat in the bow of a dugout canoe while Aaron Stanz and the Weghorst twins rowed. Tomo looked for Confederate spoor on the far shore, and found only a discarded butternut hat, which had a tear in the brim. He stomped it into the earth, then kicked it into the river.

They camped at the river for a few days, then began a slow journey over Raccoon Mountain, where Tomo saw not a single raccoon, though he was constantly on the lookout for them. Aaron Stanz had presented him with a Springfield, sawed off to fit him, and Tomo practiced loading, tearing the paper cartridge with his teeth, pouring in the powder and the minié ball, then ramming the paper down with his stubby ramrod. He fired at Rebel oaks and cedars and squirrels, and one Rebel sparrow, missing all the animals and all but two trees.

The mood of Company C was turning. Tomo played them somber music at the fire while they acquainted him with the dead of the Ninth, most famous among whom was their former colonel, the much respected Robert McCook, of the Cincinnati "fighting McCooks"—he had four brothers also at war. He was quoted before every battle by his most ardent admirers: "The Secessionists are our brothers no more. If they will not submit, then they must be exterminated." Colonel McCook was killed outside Athens, Alabama. Sick in an ambulance, he was ambushed by a Mississippi regiment, who stabbed him ten times and set his body on fire. These same Mississippians had already earned the enmity of the Ninth when they buried some Niners facedown after Shiloh. Every Niner hoped to shoot one.

Tomo's big toe hurt terribly the whole slow way over the mountains, and he was tired of walking. He wished for a horse; he wished that it had been a cavalryman fortuitously riding the train the night he departed from Homer; and he wished for a battle, finally, since that was what he had come for, after all, a chance to shoot at some Rebs.

News came as they were coming down from Raccoon Mountain that Bragg had abandoned Chattanooga. There were cheers so thunderous that it sounded to Tomo as if the dramatic landscape had itself found a voice and was proclaiming bully for the Union. Tomo sang with the rest of the Ninth:

> "Old Rosy is our man,
> Old Rosy is our man,
> He'll show us deeds, where'er he leads,
> Old Rosy is our man!"

He thought about General Rosecrans, who happened to be Homer's only famous son. It would be quite a story to tell the people back home, if Tomo ever returned; he had gotten a glimpse of Rosecrans, back at the camp, and resisted the urge to go and introduce himself as a fellow Homerite. Maybe when we get to Chattanooga, Tomo thought. Then I will tell him that I am from Homer. But I will not say that I am a Claflin. Tomo prepared himself for a triumphant march into Chattanooga, wishing he had kept that Rebel hat, because surely the Secesh widows would lean out of their windows to spit on him.

A few nights later, Tomo was sleeping comfortably and dreaming of shooting his grandfather with his new gun when Aaron Stanz shook him awake. "Go and bugle the boys into a hurry," he said. Tomo had gone to bed spry and grand, but woke with clammy hands and a feeling like he would vomit, which he did, right in the middle of a sleepy toot. He walked along next to Aaron Stanz all through the night, dropping off towards dawn, asleep on his feet but still shuffling along. Aaron Stanz picked him up and carried him like a sack of grain, and passed him to another man of the company when he got tired. Raimund Herrman took him for a while, carrying him like a bride, and the Weghorst twins passed him back and forth for a few miles. Tomo was feverish and sweaty when they stopped, for all that it was getting very cold, and his sock was soaked through with blood. But he walked stubbornly along when they started up after only a few hours, until he slept and was carried again. When he woke, it was dark again, and the company was marching through smoke. Someone had set fire to the fence rails on either side of the road, and the flames cast harsh shadows over the faces of the men, making their features grim and weird, so Tomo thought as he came awake that he was in a company of strangers.

Wherever it was they were going in such a hurry, they arrived there just after midnight. It seemed to Tomo an entirely unspecial place. Under the light of the moon, he could see fields broken up by patches of woods—it could have been Homer, and was to Tomo's mind a bad place for a battle. There were too many trees to hide behind—he wanted broad sweeping fields across which thick columns of men could pour unhindered, and upon which they could crash into each other like the fists of angry gods.

Company C was ordered to guard the supply wagons. Tomo

slept beneath one with his head on the bare ground. A faint rumble tickled his ear and woke him in the morning. He rolled out from beneath the wagon, tangled in his blankets. Looking up from where he lay, he saw Aaron Stanz standing in stark relief against the ridge that loomed in the distance behind the Union line.

"Ah, Fenzmaus, you've made a sausage of you," Aaron Stanz said as he bent down and unraveled Tomo from his blankets. All night, Tomo had been cold no matter how many covers he heaped on, and yet his shirt and coat were soaked through with sweat. Aaron Stanz told him to go and find a doctor. "You got the ague," he said, "or worse."

"Ague can't lick me," said Tomo. "Typhoid tried and I sent him home to his mama."

"Go," said Aaron Stanz, pushing him away towards the rear just as a terrific noise of guns broke out north of them, rushing south as the enemy was engaged down the line. Somebody rode up to call the Ninth away from the wagons. Aaron Stanz pushed Tomo again in the direction of the hospital tents, then ran off with the rest of his company. Tomo took three steps, then turned and followed Aaron Stanz, pausing only to grab his rifle from beneath the wagon. He had to hobble some with his toe hurting like it was, and because he really was sick, he was slow. He caught up with Company C just as Colonel Kammerling had given the order for the whole regiment to fix bayonets and charge.

Tomo had no bayonet for his little gun, but he ran along with the Ninth anyhow into a forest-ringed cornfield. He was angry again—angry at all the damned Rebels, angry that Gob was missing all the excitement, angry that he was sick and weak, angry that he was just a boy. But he wasn't afraid. When the opportunity presented itself he swung the rifle by the barrel and clipped a Rebel in the head with the stock. The Rebel—an old man with a droopy, greasy-looking mustache—was surprised to see a boy pop out of the corn with murder in his face, and did not move to defend himself until it was too late. The old man fell with his head on his outstretched arms, and so looked like he was sleeping, but there was a great and obvious concavity at his temple. Tomo turned the man's face with his boot, and watched as the white of his left eye turned to lurid angry red.

The men of the Ninth stabbed viciously at the now shy, shrinking Rebels; some of them, their guns knocked from their grip, held up their hands in demure gestures against the bright steel, as if to say, *No thank you*. It's a wonder I'm not shot, Tomo thought to himself as he stood there looking. He was keenly aware of the bullets, but felt no urge to move. He was thinking how the sound the minié balls made was very singular indeed, and quite impossible to describe, except that he thought he heard in it something of the buzzing of a bee, the mewing of a kitten, and the snapping of fingers. He left his reverie only when he noticed a Rebel threatening Raimund Herrman, tracking the big man smoothly as he ran towards a captured Union battery. Tomo was quite hidden by the corn as he ran. If the Rebel marksman had looked he might have thought some elemental of the air was rushing towards him, but he never turned. Tomo struck him in the hip just as the Rebel fired, and when he fell among the stalks, Tomo stepped up and swung his rifle over his shoulder, like an ax, and crushed the man's throat. Then Tomo ran after Raimund Herrman, who was poking his bayonet at a Rebel beside a shiny napoleon.

"This gun is ours, you shithouse sergeant!" cried the Reb.

"No," said Raimund Herrman, "this gun is *unser*." Tomo came up behind and whacked the Reb in his kidney. When he fell to his knees, Raimund Herrman stabbed him through the head. To Tomo it seemed a rude gesture, that stabbing. He would have preferred that all of them lay about them with their stocks like civilized folk, but that was not happening. All around him, the Ninth was stabbing away at the Rebs, and carrying the moment. The Rebs broke and ran as another Union regiment came up to the recaptured battery. Tomo returned to the brigade with Raimund Herrman, where the enemy was crowding in now on the left, and the Ninth charged again. They were incorrigible chargers. "Any excuse to fix bayonets!" joked other regiments, and they asked why the Ninth bothered at all with ammunition.

Tomo was not the least bit tired during the battle—there was a thrill in his blood so strong he did not think he'd ever sleep again—but it seemed like a sweet rest when he got to lie prone behind a felled tree and shoot across a field at the Rebs. Aaron Stanz had found him and scolded him, then hugged him fiercely. Now they were shooting side by side, their lips, teeth, and tongues black from tearing open cartridges. Johnny was shooting, too, cursing viciously between shots. "Jeff Davis drives the goat!" he shouted into the din. "Mrs. Lee is a crusty old whore!"

The fighting seemed to stop very suddenly. One minute Tomo was lining up a Rebel hat to shoot at, and the next the Rebs were all gone, and there was nothing to sight on but the shadows between trees. Farther up the line he could hear them still pounding away, but where the Ninth was it was all peace and quiet. The Ninth took advantage of the lull to take their first meal of the day. Tomo was so hungry he ate a half pound of unrinsed salt beef, which stung his blistered tongue, and puckered up his face so tight he could barely open his eyes. The quiet stretched on and on, into dusk, so the Ninth thought it was done for that day, but just as the sun passed over the ridge an incredible abundance of Rebels came screaming out of the woods. They charged through the field of low grass, across to the trees where the Ninth sheltered, and almost overwhelmed them.

It was then that one of the Weghorst twins died. As they rose to fall back with the rest of the company, he opened his mouth to say something to his brother, and got a bullet there, through his mouth and out through the back of his head. Tomo heard quite distinctly the noise of his shattering teeth, a terrible sound.

When he heard it, Tomo was frightened for the first time. He wanted to run, then, away from the echoing noise in his head, away from the living Weghorst's screaming, away from the charging Rebs. But Tomo wasn't Gob. He wouldn't run away to Homer and hide under the bed.

Tomo backed off slowly, loading and firing as he went, until he walked into a private of another Ohio regiment, come up with a whole division to reinforce them. The line held till full dark came. Tomo kept firing blindly into the darkness. Eventually Aaron Stanz came and put a hand on his shoulder, and pushed his arm down so his gun touched the earth.

"No more tonight, Fenzmaus," Aaron Stanz said, and then he yawned, so big Tomo thought his whole face would disappear into his mouth, and so hard his breath washed over Tomo's face. Tomo went to the rear, then, at Aaron Stanz's insistence, while the rest of the unwounded Ninth began to throw up earthworks. At the hospital tents, Tomo said he had only come to serenade the wounded, but the truth was he was feeling sicker. He was hot with his fever now, instead of cold, but that suited him fine, because it was turning out to be a frigid night. He was having strange visions, too. He supposed his brain was too hot, so he dunked his head in a basin, but still he saw a black bug crawl out of a wounded man's ear and circle his head before crawling back in, and twice he saw the moon turn into an eye and wink at him.

Tomo played sweet music for the wounded all through the night because he could not sleep. A hospital steward brought him hot food; crisp bacon and a stew of chicken and hardtack. At the bottom of the bowl was a hard-boiled egg. Tomo fished it out and ate it with great precision, nibbling away the white until he had a perfect globe of yolk pinched between his thumb and forefinger. He swallowed it like a pill. When he finished eating, he went to visit the living Weghorst twin, thinking to play him something to comfort him, but when he found him still weeping over his brother's body, all he could do was stare numbly and clutch

Betty to his chest. He thought of his mama, back in Homer. If she were there, she'd say that the dead Weghorst now inhabited the Summerland, a place where all good spirits lived.

He went and sat next to the surviving Weghorst, put his hand on the big fellow's hand, and burst so violently into tears he felt as if his whole head had exploded in a shower of salty water. Tomo cried because it is a terrible thing that brothers should be separated, and because he missed his own brother. He suffered suddenly from the unreasoning conviction that Gob was dead, that a Rebel bullet had traveled hundreds of miles up to Homer to shatter his brother's teeth and blow out the back of his head all over their bedroom wall. Tomo put his head on the dead twin's chest and wept, thinking he would keep on until he was only dry skin and bones and brittle desiccated organs. The living twin petted Tomo's hair, to comfort *him*, which was not the plan at all, and the world seemed to Tomo a place entirely mixed up and unjust before he suddenly fell very hard into sleep, as if into a deep ditch.

The next morning, Tomo woke suddenly to the noise of cannon. He had been having a dream: he was in the house at Homer, sharing a plate of pancakes with Gob, while their mama read aloud from *The Tempest*. There was a big fire built in the hearth, and Tomo was comfortable and very happy because his grandpa Buck was dead—his head was stuffed and mounted above the mantel. Tomo shoveled pancakes into his mouth: they were drenched with butter and tasted very salty. Suddenly there was a noise outside, like thunder, and his mama leaped from her chair, shrieking, "Oh Rosy, there was no hole but the one you made! Yet now truly there's a hole in our center and Longstreet has seen it!"

Somebody had put Tomo under a tent with Johnny, who slept through the artillery noise, hugging his drum. Tomo rose and poured water over his hot aching head, and drank a cup of coffee. Johnny woke up and hastily scribbled out a note with his parents' names and address, which he pinned to his coat. "Ought to have done this yesterday," he said. After a few moments' reflection, Tomo did it too. He wrote his real name, and then his mother's name: "Victoria C. Woodhull (The Great), Town of Homer, Licking County, Ohio."

Tomo and the rest of Company C were two miles north of the hole in the line into which Longstreet poured three divisions later that morning. Just after noon two-thirds of the Army of the Cumberland was in headlong flight up the road to Rossville and Chattanooga. Old Rosy was nobody's man that day; he fled to Chattanooga. Tomo did not flee there, though he still had in him a hankering to see the place. He stayed with the Ninth, who got called up, just as things were falling apart, to Snodgrass Hill, where Thomas made his famous stand.

Tomo spent the whole day up there. Twice the Rebs crested Tomo's portion of the hill and planted their colors on it; twice Tomo rushed out with the Ninth to push the colors over and bludgeon the panting Rebs. All pooped out from their run up the hill, the Rebs had very little fight in them by the time they reached the top.

A third time the Ninth charged out. The Rebs had a round of canister and grape ready for them when they rushed out from behind their works. Tomo tripped and fell on his face, and the volley passed over him. Raimund Herrman lost his head to an erroneously loaded cannonball. His big body took a few more steps and then seemed to kneel down before it fell over. A load of shot took the living Weghorst twin in the chest. Aaron Stanz, in the rear of the charge, kept running after Tomo, stranded in the front, after his comrades had turned back or flattened themselves on the ground. The artillery spent itself as Aaron Stanz ran, and did not touch him, but then he came under furious, withering rifle fire, and seemed to disappear before Tomo's eyes. Little pieces of Aaron Stanz—a finger, a portion of his hat, part of his nose—were suddenly not there, and then he proceeded to disintegrate as butterfly-sized pieces of flesh and bone flew away from him. He ran to within a few yards of Tomo before there was not sufficient body left for his will to propel.

That horror caused Tomo to experience a reversal of feeling. Now all his former battle-mindedness left him, replaced by terror, which rose up in him until he felt he could not breathe because he was drowning in it. It was so much worse than what he'd felt the day before. Now he did want to run away to Homer, to cower under the bed and not ever come out. He and Gob would have a stolen pie and a jug of cider, a candle, and a book. What else did a boy need besides all that and his brother? They could eat and read and scratch each other's back. They could look out into the darkness beyond the candle and say it together: "I'm afraid. I'm afraid to die." Overcome by fever and fear, Tomo closed his eyes and rested his head on the ground.

It was night when he woke to the noise of Rebels cheering their victory. The sound was muffled by the dead piled on top of him—one Union and three Rebel, entwined in a heavy confraternity that must have protected him from flying bullets. He emerged from under the bodies. General Thomas was gone, leaving Tomo and the dead behind him.

Tomo went west, walking, where he had to, over the soft bodies of the dead. Amid the cheers of the Rebels he heard the moans of some wounded, and he was certain his steps would elicit a groan at some point, but they never did. He kept walking towards the ridge, dodging campfires. When he heard a group of Rebs approaching him, he fled into a patch of woods, becoming quite lost there among the pine and scrub oak, where more dead lay scattered amid the smoldering underbrush. Eventually, Tomo lost sight of the ridge, lost all sense of direction, and came at last to a swift cold creek, which he passed over, sliding down one steep bank and clawing his way up the other, grateful for the chance to dunk his whole body. Tomo felt so hot now he thought he must soon burst into flame and draw the Rebs down on him like moths. Not knowing that he was completely turned around, he headed east on the far side of Chickamauga creek. "Gob," he called out softly as he walked through the dark woods. "Where are you?"

His fever visions kept up. An owl alit on a low branch and said, "Tomo! Tomo!" The moon flipped in the sky like a tossed coin. A little boy brandishing a wooden sword led a troop of headless soldiers towards the creek. And a man in an immaculate white chiton rode out from a shadow on an elephant the size of a pony.

"Thomas Jefferson Woodhull," he said. "I know you."

"I don't know you," said Tomo, sitting down and rubbing his eyes. He did know him, though. He recognized him from the stories his mama told about her enormous destiny, about all the spirits in whose shadow she walked. He began to cry.

"There," said the man. "There now. There's no need to cry. You wanted to see the elephant, didn't you? Well, here he is!"

Tomo said nothing, but only put his head in his hands and cried harder. The elephant played a friendly tune on its trunk as the man dismounted and came to sit by him. Only then did Tomo notice he'd lost Betty in the creek. The man took Tomo's hands from his face and held them in his own. His hands were cool and dry and too smooth to be made of real flesh.

"Oh my boy," he said. "Your troubles are almost over. You are very near the road home. In yonder clearing squats an officer who can send you on your way." The man in white raised a bare arm and pointed. Tomo got up and ran, not so much because he believed the fever-vision, but because he wanted to get away. Sure enough, there was a figure in the clearing, squatting next to his horse with his pants down.

Tomo's half-spoken friendly greeting turned to a howl of rage when he saw the man in the clearing was a Rebel, and a general for that matter—his stars shone very clearly in the bright moonlight. Tomo brought his gun up as he ran, but when he fired, he missed. As he neared the General, he flipped the rifle and caught it by the barrel, lifting it above his head, ready to deliver a crushing blow. The General raised his pistol and shot twice before Tomo could reach him. The first bullet went wide, but the second passed into Tomo's left eye, and killed him dead. Tomo fell down in the cool grass, and his fever began very slowly to depart from him. The General came over on his knees to better see his assailant. Already, there was noise in the trees. The General's staff was coming to look for him—his camp was not very far away.

When the General saw it was a little boy he had killed, he pounded his hand against his head and tore out a piece of his hair, cursing the Yankees that they should send children against him, and, because he happened also to be a priest and a bishop, he prayed gently and sincerely over the boy's body, pleading with God to please, please give this little one a home in Heaven.

PART ONE

Every Night for a Thousand Years

Sorrow ([illegible]) grieve sad mourn (I use) mourning mournful melancholy dismal heavy-hearted tears black sobs -ing sighing funeral rites wailing lamenting mute grief eloquent silence bewail bemoan deplore regret deeply loud lament pitiful loud weeping violent lamentation

anguish wept sore depression pain of mind passionate regret afflicted with grief cast down downcast gloomy serious Sympathy moving compassion tenderness tender-hearted full of pity obscurity partial or total darkness (as the gloom of a forest—gloom of midnight) cloudy cloudiness (cloudiness) *of mind mind sunk in gloom soul ((sunk in gloom)/ dejection dejected*

[illegible]) shades of night heavy dull-sombre sombre shades sombre(ness) affliction oppress-oppressive oppression prostration humble—humility suffering-silent suffering burdensome Distress—distressing calamity Extreme anguish (either of mind or body) Misery torture harassed weighed down trouble deep affliction plaintive Calamity disaster something that strikes down—

WALT WHITMAN
A collection of vocabulary for
"When Lilacs Last in the Dooryard Bloom'd"

1

WALT DREAMED HIS BROTHER'S DEATH AT FREDERICKSBURG. General Burnside, appearing as an angel at the foot of his bed, announced the tragedy: "The army regrets to inform you that your brother, George Washington Whitman, was shot in the head by a lewd fellow from Charleston." The general alit on the bedpost and drew his dark wings close about him, as if to console himself. Moonlight limned his strange whiskers and his hair. His voice shook as he went on. "Such a beautiful boy. I held him in my arms while his life bled out. See? His blood made this spot." He pointed at his breast, where a dark stain in the shape of a bird lay on the blue wool. "I am so very sorry," the General said, choking and weeping. Tears fell in streams from his eyes, ran over the bed and out the window, where they joined the Rappahannock, which had somehow come north to flow through Brooklyn, bearing the bodies of all the late battle's dead.

In the morning Walt read the wounded list in the *Tribune*. There it was: "First Lieutenant G. W. Whitmore." He knew from George's letters that there was nobody named Whitmore in the company. He walked through snow to his mother's house. "I'll go and find him," he told her.

Washington, Walt quickly discovered, had become a city of hospitals. He looked in half of them before a cadaverous-looking clerk told him he'd be better off looking at Falmouth, where most of the Fredericksburg wounded still lay in field hospitals. He got himself on a government boat that ran down to the landing at Aquia Creek, and went by railroad to the neighborhood of Falmouth, seeking Ferrero's Brigade and the Fifty-first New York, George's regiment. Walt stood outside a large brick mansion on the banks of the Rappahannock, somebody's splendid residence converted to a hospital, afraid to go in and find his mangled brother. He took a walk around the building, gathering his courage, and found a pile of amputated limbs, arms and legs of varying lengths, all black and blue and rotten in the chill. A thin layer of snow covered some of them. He circled the heap, thinking he must recognize his brother's hand if he saw it. He closed his eyes and considered the amputation; his brother screaming when he woke from the ether, his brother's future contracting to something bitter and small.

But George had only gotten a hole in his cheek. A piece of shell pierced his wispy beard and chipped a tooth. He had spit blood and hot metal into his hand, put the shrapnel in his pocket, and later showed it to his worried brother, who burst into tears and clutched him in a bear hug when they were reunited in Captain Francis's tent, where George sat with his feet propped on a trunk and a cigar stuck in his bandaged face.

"You shouldn't fret," said George. "I couldn't be any healthier than I am. And I've been promoted. Now you may call me *Captain* Whitman." But Walt could not help fretting, even now that he knew his brother was alive and well. A great, fretting buzz had started up in his head, inspired by the pile of limbs, and the smell of blood in the air, and by ruined Fredericksburg, all broken chimneys and crumbling walls across the river. Walt stayed in George's tent and, watching him sleep, felt a deep thrilling worry. He wandered around the camp, and as he passed by a fire in an enclosure of evergreen branches piled head high against the wind, he met a soldier. They sat down together by the fire, and the soldier told Walt hideous stories about the death of friends. "He put his head in my lap and whispered goodbye to his mama," the soldier said. "And then he turned his eyes away from me and he was dead." Walt put his face in the evergreen wall, smearing his beard with fresh sap, and thought how it smelled like Christmas.

Ten days later, Walt still couldn't leave. He stood by and watched as George moved out with the healthy troops on Christmas Day, then idled in the deserted campground, watching the interminable caravans of army wagons passing and passing into the distance. Near at hand, some stragglers crossed his line of sight—a large young man leading a mule that pulled a wagon, on top of which perched a fat man cursing in French. When all were gone, and the campground empty, Walt went up to the brick mansion and made himself useful, changing dressings, fetching for the nurses, and just sitting with the wounded boys, with the same excited worry on him as when he watched George sleep. Back in Brooklyn a deep and sinister melancholy had settled over him. For the past six months Walt had wandered the streets with a terrible feeling in him—Hell under his skull bones, death under his breast bones, and a feeling that he would like most of all to lie down under the river and sleep forever. But in the hospital that melancholy was gone, scared off, perhaps, by all the shocking misery around him, and it had been replaced by a different sort of sadness, one that was vital, not still; a feeling that did not diminish his soul, but thrilled it.

When Walt finally left Falmouth, it was to watch over a cargo of wounded as they traveled through the early-morning darkness back to Aquia Creek, where they would be loaded on a steamer bound for Washington. With every jolt and shake of the train, a chorus of horrible groans wafted through the cars. Walt thought it would drive him insane. What saved him was the singing of a boy with a leg wound. The boy's name was Hank Smith. He'd come all the way from divided Missouri, and said he had a gaggle of cousins fighting under General Beauregard. He sang "Oh, Susannah" over and over again, and no one told him to be quiet.

All the worst cases went to a hospital called Armory Square, because it was closest to the boat landing at the foot of Sixth Street.

Walt accompanied them, and kept up the service he'd begun at Falmouth—visiting, talking, reading, fetching, and helping.

And he went to other hospitals. There were certainly enough of them to keep him busy. Their names were published in the papers like a list of churches—Finley, Campbell, Carver, Harewood, Mount Pleasant, Judiciary. And then there were the public buildings, also stuffed with wounded. Even the Patent Office held them; boys on cots set up on the marble floor of the Model Room. He brought horehound candy to an eighteen-year-old from Iowa, who lay with a missing arm and a sore throat in front of the glass case which held Ben Franklin's printing press. Two boys from Brooklyn had cots in front of General Washington's camp equipment. Walt read to them from Brooklyn papers his mother sent down, every now and then looking up at the General's tents rolled neatly around their posts, his folded chairs and mess kit, his sword and cane, his washstand, his surveyor's compass, and a few feet down in a special case all to itself, the Declaration of Independence. Other wounded boys lay in front of pieces of the Atlantic Cable, beside ingenious toys, in sight of rattraps, next to the razor of Captain Cook.

Walt could not visit every place all in a day, though he tried at first. Eventually, he picked a few and stuck with those. But mostly he was at Armory Square, where Hank Smith was.

"I had my daddy's pistol with me," said Hank Smith, sprawling in his slender iron-framed bed. "That's why I got my leg still." It wasn't the first time Walt had been told how Hank had saved his own leg from the "chopping butchers" in the field hospital, but he didn't mind hearing the story again. It was spring. The leg was still bad, though not as bad as it had been. At least that was the impression that Hank gave. He never complained about his wound. He'd come down with typhoid, too, a gift from the hospital. "I want my pistol back," he said.

"I'll see what I can do." Walt always said that, but they both knew no one was going to give Hank back the pistol with which he'd threatened to blow out the brains of the surgeon who tried to take his leg. They had left him alone, then, and later another doctor had said there wasn't any need to amputate.

"Meanwhile, here's an orange," said Walt. He pulled the fruit out of his coat pocket and peeled it. Soldiers' heads began to turn in their beds as the smell drifted over the ward. Some asked if he had any for them.

" 'Course he does," said Hank. In fact, Walt had a coatful of them. He had bought them at Center Market, then walked through the misty, wet morning, over the brackish canal and across the filthy Mall. The lowing of cattle drifted towards him from the unfinished monument to General Washington as he walked along, wanting an orange for himself but afraid to eat one lest he be short when he got to the hospital. He had money for oranges, sweets, books, tobacco, and other good things from sponsors in Brooklyn and New York and elsewhere. And he had a little money for himself from a job, three hours a day as a copyist in the paymaster's office—he'd given up, for the present, on seeking a fancier appointment, put away in a drawer the letters of introduction to powerful personages from Mr. Emerson. From his desk in the paymaster's office, he had a spectacular view of Georgetown and the river, and the stones that were said to mark the watery graves of three Indian sisters. The sisters had cursed the spot: anyone who tried to cross there must drown. Walt would sit and stare at the rocks, imagining himself shedding his shirt and shoes by the riverside, trying to swim across. He imagined drowning, too, the great weight of water pressing down on him. (When he was a child, he'd nearly drowned in the sea.) Inevitably, his reverie was broken by the clump-clump of one-legged soldiers on their crutches, coming up the stairs to the office located, perversely, on the fourth floor.

After he'd distributed the oranges, Walt wrote letters on behalf of various boys until his hand ached. *Dear Sister*, he wrote for Hank, *I have been brave but wicked. Pray for me.*

* * *

Armory Square was under the command of a brilliant drunk named Canning Woodhull. Over whiskey, he explained to Walt his radical policies, which included washing hands and instruments, throwing out used sponges, and swabbing everything in sight with bitter-smelling Labarraque's solution. He had an absolute lack of faith in laudable pus.

"Nothing laudable about it," he said. "White or green, pus is pus, and either way it's bad for the boys. There are creatures in the wounds—elements of evil. They are the emissaries of Hell, sent earthward to increase our suffering, to increase death and increase grief. You can't see them except by their actions." The two men knocked glasses and drank, and Walt made a face because the whiskey was medicinal, laced with quinine. It did not seem to bother Woodhull.

"I have the information from my wife," Woodhull said, "who has great and secret knowledge. She talks to spirits. Much of what she hears is nonsense—do not tell her I said so. But this bit about the creatures in the pus—that's true."

Maybe it was. Woodhull's hospital got the worst cases and kept them alive better than any other hospital in the city, even ones that got casualties only half as severe. The doctor stayed in charge despite a reputation as a wastrel and a drunk and a nascent lunatic. A year earlier he had been removed by a coalition of his colleagues, only to be reinstated by Dr. Letterman, the medical director of the Army of the Potomac, who had been personally impressed by many visits to Armory Square. "They say General Grant is a drunk, too," Letterman said in response to the charges against Dr. Woodhull.

"The creatures are vulnerable to prayer and bromine, and whiskey and Labarraque's. Lucky for us." Woodhull downed another glass. "Ah, sir—there is the matter of the nurses. Some of them are complaining. Just last Tuesday I was in Ward E with the redoubtable Mrs. Hawley. We saw you come in at the end of the aisle and she said, 'Here comes that odious Walt Whitman to talk evil and unbelief to my boys. I think I would rather see the evil one himself—at least if he had horns and hoofs—in my ward. I shall get him out as soon as possible!' And she rushed off to do just that. And you know how she failed to eject you, how she always fails to eject you." He poured again.

"Shall I stop coming, then?"

"Heavens no. As long as old Hawley is complaining, I'll know you're doing good. God bless her pointy little head."

Two surgeons came into Woodhull's makeshift office, a corner of Ward F sectioned off by three regimental flags.

"*Assistant* Surgeon Walker is determined to kill Captain Carter," said Dr. Bliss, a dour black-eyed man from Baltimore. "She has given him opium for his diarrhea, and, very foolishly, in my opinion, withheld ipecac and calomel." Dr. Mary Walker stood next to him, looking calm, her arms folded across her chest. Her blue uniform was immaculate, a studied contrast to Woodhull's stained and threadbare greatcoat, which he wore in winter and summer alike.

"Dr. Walker is doing as I have asked her," said Woodhull. "Ipecac and calomel are to be withheld in all cases of flux and diarrhea."

"For God's sake, why?" asked Dr. Bliss, his face reddening. He was new in Armory Square. Earlier that same day Woodhull had castigated him for not cleaning a suppurating chest wound.

"Because it is for the best," said Woodhull. "Because if you do it that way, a boy will not die. Because if you do it that way, some mother's heart will not be broken."

Dr. Bliss turned redder, then paled, as if his rage had broken and ebbed. He scowled at Dr. Walker, turned sharply on his heel, and left. Dr. Walker sat down.

"Buffoon," she said. Woodhull poured whiskey for her, handed her the glass, then took a rag and began to knock the lint from her second lieutenant's shoulder straps. It was an open secret in the hospital that they were married in all but name.

"Dr. Walker," said Woodhull, "why don't you tell Mr. Whitman about your recent arrest?"

The woman sipped her whiskey and told how she'd been arrested outside of her boardinghouse for masquerading as a man. Walt only half listened to her talk. He was thinking about diarrhea. It was just about the worst thing, he had decided. He'd seen it kill more boys than all the minié balls and shrapnel, and typhoid and pneumonia, than all the other afflictions combined. He'd written to his mother: *War is nine hundred and ninety-nine parts diarrhea to one part glory. Those who like wars ought to be made to fight in them.* And sometimes, up to his neck in sickness and death, he did believe that the war was an insufferable evil, but other times it seemed to be gloriously necessary, and all the blood and carnage and misery a terrible new beginning that was somehow a relief to him.

"I did my best to resist them," said Dr. Walker, "and I shouted out, 'Congress has bestowed on me the right to wear trousers!' " She held out her cup for more whiskey, and shook her head sadly at Walt. "But it was to no avail."

In the summer, Walt saw the President almost every day. He lived on the route Mr. Lincoln took to and from his summer residence north of the city, and walking down the street, soon after leaving his rooms in the morning, he'd hear the approach of the party. Always Walt stopped and waited for them to pass. Mr. Lincoln dressed in plain black and rode a gray horse. He was surrounded by twenty-five or thirty cavalry with their sabers drawn and held up over their shoulders. They got so they would exchange bows, he and the President, Walt tipping his broad, floppy gray felt hat, Lincoln tipping his high stiff black one, and bending a little in the saddle. And every time they did this Walt had the same thought: *A sad man.*

With the coming of the hot weather Dr. Woodhull redoubled his efforts to eradicate noxious effluvia. He ordered the windows thrown open, and burned eucalyptus leaves in small bronze censers set in the four corners of each ward. The eucalyptus, combined with the omnipresent acrid reek of Labarraque's solution, gave some of the boys aching heads, for which Dr. Woodhull prescribed whiskey.

"I want a bird," Hank Smith said one day in July. Walt had brought several bottles of blackberry and cherry syrup, mixed them with ice and water, and delivered the delicious concoctions to the boys, along with the news from Gettysburg. Hank was uninspired by Meade's victory. He was in a bad mood.

"I've been here forever," he said. "And I am going to be here forever." He had been fighting a bad fever for a week. "Nonsense," Walt said, and helped him change out of his soaked shirt, then wiped him down with a cool wet towel. The shirt he took to the window, where he wrung out the sweat, watching it fall and dapple the bare ground. He laid the shirt to dry on the sill, and considered his damp, salty hands. In the distance Walt could see the Capitol, magnificent even under scaffolding.

"I want a bird," Hank said again. "When I was small, my sister got me a bird. I called it after her—Olivia. Would you help me get one?" Walt left the window and sat on a stool by the bed. The sun lit up the hair on Hank's chest, and called to Walt's mind shining fields of wheat.

"Did you read my book?" Walt asked him, because he'd finally given Hank a copy, inscribed *to my dear dear dear dear boy*. Walt had had a dream, a happy one at last. Hank, transformed by Walt's words, had leaped out of bed, wound gone, typhoid gone, had shaken Walt by his shoulders, and had shouted "Camerado!" so loud the Capitol dome rang like a bell, and all the boys all over the country had put down their guns and embraced each other in celebration of that beautiful word.

"I fingered it a little. But a bird, wouldn't that be fine?"

"I could get you a bird," Walt said after a moment. "Though I don't know where from."

"I know where," said Hank, as Walt helped him into a new shirt. With a jerk of his head Hank indicated the window. "There's plenty of birds out in the yard. You just get a rock and some string."

Walt came back the next day with rock and string, and they set a trap of breadcrumbs on the windowsill. Crouching beneath the window, Walt grabbed at whatever came for the crumbs. He missed two jays and a blackbird, but caught a beautiful cardinal by its leg. It chirped frantically and pecked at his hand. The fluttering of its wings against his wrists made him think of the odd buzz that still thrilled his soul when he was on the wards. He brought the bird to Hank, who tied the string to its leg, and the rock to the string, then set the rock down by his bed. The cardinal tried to fly for the window, but only stuck in midair, its desperate wings striking up a small breeze that Walt, kneeling near it, could feel against his face. Hank clapped and laughed.

Hank called the bird Olivia, though Walt pointed out that it was not a female bird. The female of the species was dun and dull, he said, but Hank seemed not to hear. Olivia became the ward's pet. Other boys would insist on having him near their beds. It did not take the bird long to become domesticated. Soon he was eating from Hank's hand, and sleeping at night beneath his cot. They kept him secret from the nurses and doctors, until one morning Hank was careless and fell asleep with him out in the middle of the aisle while Dr. Woodhull was making his rounds. Walt had just walked on the ward, his arms full of candy and fruit and novels.

"Who let this dirty bird into my hospital?" Woodhull asked. He very swiftly bent down and picked up the stone, then tossed it out the window. Olivia trailed helplessly behind it. Walt dropped his packages and rushed outside, where he found the bird in the dirt, struggling with a broken wing. He put him in his shirt and took him back to his room, where he died three days later, murdered by the landlady's cat. Walt told Hank that Olivia had flown away. "A person can't have anything," Hank said. He called Olivia a bad bird, and growled for a week about his faithlessness.

* * *

At Christmas, Mrs. Hawley and her cronies trimmed the wards, hanging evergreen wreaths on every pillar, and stringing garlands across the hall. At the foot of every bed, they hung a tiny stocking, hand-knitted by Washington society ladies. Walt went around stuffing them with walnuts and lemons and licorice.

Hank's leg got better and worse, better and worse. Walt cornered Dr. Woodhull and said he had a bad feeling about Hank's health. Woodhull insisted he was going to be fine; Walt's fretting was pointless.

Hank's fevers waxed and waned, too. One night, Walt came in from a blustery snowstorm, his beard full of snow. Hank insisted on pressing his face into it, saying it made him feel so much better than any medicine had, except maybe paregoric, which he found delicious, and which made him feel he was flying in his bed.

Walt read to him from the New Testament, all the portions having to do with the first Christmas. "Are you a religious man?" Hank asked him.

"Probably not, my dear, in the way that you mean." Though he did make a point of visiting the Armory Square chapel, whenever he was there. It was a little building, with a quaint, onion-shaped steeple. Walt would sit in the back and listen to the services for boys whom he'd been seeing almost every day. He wrote their names down in a small leather-bound notebook that he kept in one of his pockets. By Christmas, he had pages and pages of them. Sometimes at night he would sit in his room and read the names softly aloud by the light of a single candle.

Hank dropped off to sleep as Walt read, but Walt kept on with the story, because he could tell that Hank's new neighbor was listening attentively. His name was Oliver Barley. He had been tortured by Mosby's Rangers, staked spread-eagled to the ground with bayonets through his hands and feet. Whenever Walt came near to try and speak with him, Barley would glare at him and say, "Shush!" And sometimes if Walt and Hank were speaking too loud, he'd pelt them with bandages sopped with the exudate from his hands. It was Walt's ambition to be Barley's friend, but the boy rejected all his friendly advances. Yet now he was listening.

"Do you like this story?" Walt ventured, stopping briefly in his reading.

"Hush up," said Oliver Barley, and he turned away on his side. Walt might have gone on reading, but just then Dr. Walker came by and asked to borrow his Bible. She said she had news from the War Department.

"What's the news?" he asked her.

"Nothing good," she said. "It is dark, dark everywhere." She wanted to read some Job, she said, to cheer herself. She took Walt's Bible and walked off down the ward, putting her hand out now and then to touch a boy's leg or foot as she passed. When she opened the door to leave, some music slipped in. It seemed to be borne along to Walt's ears by a gust of frigid air. Voices were singing: "For O we stand on Jordan's strand, our friends are passing over." Walt kissed Hank's sweaty head, then followed Dr. Walker off the ward. He followed the song to an invalid chorus in Ward K, led by a young nurse who accompanied herself on a melodeon. The gas was turned down low, as if to heighten the effect of the candles held by all the singers. There were deep shadows all up and down the ward. Walt retreated into one of these, and put his head down and sang along.

Sometimes when he could not sleep, which was often, Walt would walk around the city, past the serene mansions on Lafayette Square, past the President's house, where he would stop and wonder if a light in the window implied that Mr. Lincoln was awake and agonizing. One night he saw a figure in a long, trailing black veil move, lamp in hand, past a series of windows, and he imagined it must be Mrs. Lincoln, searching forlornly for her little boy, who had died two winters previous. Walt walked past the empty market stalls, along the ever-stinking canal, where he would pause, look down into the dirty water, and see all manner of things float by: boots and bonnets, half-eaten vegetables, animals. Once there was a dead cat drifting on a little floe of ice.

Walking on, he would pass into Murder Bay, where whores uttered long, pensive hoots at him, but generally left him alone. He would peek into alleys that housed whole families of "contraband." On one occasion, a stout young girl had come out of the dark, pushing a wheelbarrow in which another girl was cuddled up with a small white dog in her lap. The little dog was yipping fearfully, but the girls were laughing. Walt traded them candy from his pocket for a gleeful ride in their wheelbarrow, the two of them pushing him along for a few yards until he fell out into the filthy road, laughing hysterically, the little dog jumping on him and catching its paws in his beard.

Walt would cut back along the canal, then across, sometimes watching the moon shine on the towers of the Smithsonian castle, and on the white roofs and white fence of Armory Square—the whole scene so expressively silent in the pale weak light. He would walk among the shrubs and trees of the Mall, sometimes getting lost on a footpath that went nowhere, but eventually he would cross the canal again and walk up to the Capitol. There was the great statue of General Washington, the one that everyone ridiculed because he was dressed in a toga. (It was said that his sword was raised in a threat to do harm to the country if his clothes were not returned.)

Walt liked the statue. He would crawl up into its lap and sprawl out, Pietà-like, or else put his arms around the thick marble neck and have a good wrenching cry. At dawn, Walt would stand outside the Capitol, writing his name in the snow with his urine, and he could smell the bread baking in the basement. He had a friend in the bakery who loaded him down with countless hot loaves. Walt would walk back to Armory Square, warmed by the bread in his coat, and sometimes he'd have enough so that every full-diet boy in a ward would wake with a still-warm loaf on his chest.

* * *

"They want to take my leg," Hank told him. It was early May, and still cold. "I ain't going to let them. You've got to get me a gun."

"Hush," said Walt. "They won't take your leg." In fact, it looked like they would have to. Just when Hank had seemed on the verge of good health, just when he had beaten the typhoid, the leg had flared up again and deteriorated rapidly. Dr. Woodhull cleaned the wound, prayed over it, swabbed it with whiskey, all to no avail. A hideous, stinking infection had taken root, and was spreading.

"I saw my brother last week," Walt told Hank. "Marching with Burnside's army. It was on Fourteenth Street. I watched for three hours before the Fifty-first came along. I joined him just before they came to where the President and General Burnside were standing on a balcony, and the interest of seeing me made George forget to notice the President and salute him!"

"Hush up!" said Oliver Barley.

Hank raised his voice a little. "They'll take his leg, too. Or both his legs. He had better keep a good watch on them."

"Yes," said Walt. "The Ninth Corps made a very fine show indeed." Hank gave a harrumph, and turned over on his side, clearly not wanting to talk anymore. Walt went looking for Dr. Woodhull, to discuss Hank's condition, but couldn't find him in his office. There was a pall of silence and gloom over all the wards. News of the horrible casualties accrued by General Grant in his Wilderness campaign had reached the hospital. Dr. Bliss and Mrs. Hawley were having a loud discussion as she changed dressings.

"Trust a drunk not to give a fig for our boys' lives," said Mrs. Hawley.

"He spends them like pennies," said Dr. Bliss. "This war is an enterprise dominated by inebriates, charlatans, and fools." Bliss gave Walt a mean look.

Walt asked if either of them had seen Dr. Woodhull. Neither of them replied, but the young man whose dressings were being changed told Walt that Dr. Woodhull had gone out to the dead house.

Walt found him there, among the bodies. There were only a few, just the dead from the last week. Dr. Woodhull was weeping over a shrouded form, Dr. Walker standing next to him, her hand on his shoulder. Even from across the room, even with decay thick in the air, the smell of whiskey that emanated from Woodhull's body was overpowering.

"I knew him not," Woodhull was saying, "but I knew him well!"

"Canning," said Dr. Walker. "They'll be sending us more boys. You need to come back, now."

"Oh, Vicky," he said, dropping tears on the head of the shroud, so that the features of the dead boy became slowly visible beneath the wet cloth. The boy had a thick mustache, and a mole on his cheek. "There's such an awful lot of blood. You'd think they could do something with all that blood. A great work. Oughtn't something great to be coming?"

Dr. Walker noticed Walt standing by the door. "Mr. Whitman," she said. "If you would assist me?" Walt put his arm around Dr. Woodhull and bore him up, away from the body and out of the dead house. They put the doctor in an empty cot, in a half-empty ward.

"Oh, darling," said Woodhull, "I don't even want to think about it." He turned over on his side and began to breathe deeply and evenly.

Dr. Walker took a watch from her pocket and looked at it. "A wire has come," she said. "They're moving a thousand boys from the field hospitals." Then she leaned down close to Woodhull's snoring face and said, "You had better be well and awake in five hours, sir." She straightened up, adjusted her hat on her head, and uttered an explosive sigh. "General Stuart has died," she said to Walt. "Did you know that? Shot by a lowly infantryman. I had a dream once that Stuart came for me on his horse, with garish feathers in his hat. 'Come along with me, Mary,' he said. 'Not by your red beard, General

Satan,' said I. 'Get thee behind me.' " She paused a moment, and they stood together looking down at the serene Dr. Woodhull. "Do you suppose I did the right thing? Would you have gone with him?"

"No," Walt said, "of course not." But really he thought that he might have. He pictured himself riding west with General Stuart, to a place where the war could not touch them. He imagined the tickly feeling the General's feathers would make in his nose as they rode to the extreme edge of the continent. And he thought of the two of them riding shirtless through sunny California, of reaching out their hands as they passed through vineyards, and of picking fat grapes from heavy vines.

"I got to get out," said Hank. A week had passed, and the wounded from Spotsylvania had stuffed Armory Square to the gills. Hank's leg was scheduled to come off in two days. In the dead house, a pile of limbs edged towards the ceiling.

"Settle down," said Walt. "There's no cause for alarm."

"I won't let them have it. You got to help me get out. I won't make it if they take my leg. I know I won't." Hank had a raging fever, and tended to sink into delirium with the sunset.

"Dr. Walker is said to wield the fastest knife in the army. You'll be asleep. You won't feel it."

"Ha!" said Hank. He gave Walt a long, wild look. "Ha!" He put his face in his pillow and wouldn't talk anymore. Walt walked around the wards, meeting the new boys, then went to the chapel, where there were many services.

That night, unable to sleep, Walt made his usual tour of the city, stopping for a long time outside of Armory Square. He found himself outside of Hank's window, and then inside, next to his bed. Hank was sleeping, his arm thrown up above his head, his sheet thrown off and his shirt riding up his hairy belly. Walt reached out and touched his shoulder.

"All right," Walt said. "Let's go."

It was not a difficult escape. The hardest part was getting Hank's trousers on. It was very painful for Hank to bend his knee, and he was feverish and disoriented. The night attendants were in another ward; they saw no one on their way out except Oliver Barley, who glared at them and then rolled over in his bed, but raised no alarm. They stole a crutch for Hank, but he fell on the Mall, and the crutch broke under him. He wept softly with his mouth in the grass. Walt picked him up and carried him on his back, towards the canal and over it, then into Murder Bay, where Hank cried to be put down. They rested on a trash heap teeming with small, crawling things.

"I think I want to sleep," said Hank. "I'm so tired."

"Go ahead, my dear," said Walt. "I shall take care of you."

"I would like to go home," Hank said as he put his head against Walt's shoulder. "Take me back to Hollow Vale. I want to see my sister." Hank slowly fell asleep, still mumbling under his breath. They sat there for a little while.

If this heap were a horse, thought Walt, we could ride to California. "Never mind General Stuart," Walt said aloud, taking Hank's wet hand in his own. "In California there is no sickness. Neither is there death. On their fifth birthday, every child is made a gift of a pony." He looked at Hank's drawn face glowing eerily in the moonlight—he looked dead and returned from the dead. "In California, if you plant a dead boy under an oak tree, in just five days' time a living hand will emerge from the soil. If you grasp that hand and pull with the heart of a true friend, a living body will come out of the earth. Thus in California death never separates true friends." Walt looked awhile longer into Hank's face. His eyes were darting wildly under the lids. Walt said, "Well, if we are going to get to California soon, we had best leave now." But when eventually Walt picked him up he brought Hank back to the hospital.

"You will wash that beard before you come into my surgery," said Dr. Woodhull. Walt stank of garbage. He went to a basin and Dr.

Walker helped him scrub his beard with creosote, potassium permanganate, and Labarraque's solution. Walt held a sponge soaked with chloroform under Hank's nose, even though he hadn't woken since falling asleep on the heap. He kept his hand on Hank's head the whole time, but he could not watch as Dr. Walker cut in and Dr. Woodhull tied off the arteries. He looked down and saw blood seeping across the floor, into mounds of sawdust.

"That is America's choicest blood on the floor," Walt said to Dr. Woodhull, but he and Dr. Walker were too intent on their task to hear him. Walt fixed his attention on a lithograph on the far wall. It was torn from some book of antiquities, a depiction of reclining sick under the care of the priests of Aesclepius, whose statue dominated the temple. There was a snake-entwined staff in his hand, and a large friendly-looking stone dog at his feet. *Every night for a thousand years*, it said, *the sick and despairing sought healing and dreams at the temples of Aesclepius*. Walt closed his eyes and listened to the saw squeaking against Hank's bones. He put his hand on Hank's head and thought, Live, live, live.

Hank woke briefly.

"They got my leg," he said. "You let them take it."

"No," said Walt. "I've got it right here." The limb was in his lap, bundled in two clean white sheets. He would not let the nurses take it to the dead room. Walt passed it to Hank, who hugged it tight against his chest.

"I don't want to die," Hank said.

Walt packed his bag and sat on it, waiting at the station for the train that would take him back to Brooklyn. When it finally arrived, Walt stayed sitting on his bag, not even looking up at the train when it sat waiting noisily by the platform, and when the conductor asked him if he would board, he said nothing. When the train was gone again, he got up and went back to Armory Square. It was night. Hank's bed was still empty. He sat down on it and rummaged in his coat for a pen and paper. He wrote in the dark:

Dear Friends,

I thought it would be soothing to you to have a few lines about the last days of your son, Henry Smith, of Company E of the 14th Missouri Volunteers. I write in haste, but I have no doubt anything about Hank will be welcome.

From the time he came into Armory Square Hospital until he died there was hardly a day but I was with him a portion of the time—if not in the day then at night—(I am merely a friend visiting the wounded and sick soldiers). From almost the first I feared somehow that Hank was in danger, or at least he was much worse than they supposed in the hospital. He had a grievous wound in his leg, and the typhoid, but as he made no complaint they thought him nothing so bad. He was a brave boy. I told the doctor of the ward over and over again he was a very sick boy, but he took it lightly and said he would certainly recover; he said, "I know more about these cases than you do—he looks very sick to you, but I shall bring him out all right." Probably the doctor did his best—at any rate about a week before Hank died he got really alarmed, and after that all the doctors tried to help him but it was too late. Very possibly it would not have made any difference.

I believe he came here about January of '63—I took to him. He was a quiet young man, behaved always so correct and decent. I used to sit on the side of his bed. We talked together. When he was bad with the typhoid I used to sit by the side of his bed generally silent, he was oppressed for breath and with the heat, and I would fan him—occasionally he would want a drink—some days he dozed a great deal—sometimes when I would come in he would reach out his hand and pat my hair and beard as I sat on the bed and leaned over him—it was painful to see the working of his throat to breathe.

Some nights I sat by his cot far into the night, the lights would be put out and I sat there silently hour after hour—he seemed to like to have me sit there. I shall never forget those nights in the dark hospital, it was a curious and solemn scene, the sick and the wounded lying around and this dear young man close by me, lying on what proved to be his death bed. I did not know his past life so much, but what I saw and know of he behaved like a noble boy—Farewell, deary boy, it was my opportunity to be with you in your last days, I had no chance to do much for you, nothing could be done, only you did not lie there among strangers without having one near who loved you dearly, and to whom you gave your dying kiss.

Mr. and Mrs. Smith, I have thus written rapidly whatever came up about Hank, and must now close. Though we are strangers and shall probably never see each other, I send you all Hank's brothers and sister Olivia my love. I live when at home in Brooklyn, New York, in Portland Avenue, fourth floor, north of Myrtle.

Walt folded up the letter and put it in his shirt, then lay down on his side on the bed. In a while, a nurse came by with fresh sheets. He thought she might scold him and tell him to leave, but when she looked in his face she turned and hurried off. He watched the moon come up in the window, listening to the wounded and sick stirring in the beds around him. It seemed to him, as he watched the moon shine down on the Capitol, that the war would never end. He thought, *In the morning I will rise and leave this place.* And then he thought, *I will never leave this place.* He slept briefly and had a dream of reaching into Hank's dark grave, hoping and fearing that somebody would take his groping hand.

He woke with the moon still shining in his face, and started to weep, deep racking sobs which he tried to muffle in the pillow that still smelled powerfully of Hank's shining hair. Someone touched his shoulder, and when he looked up he saw Oliver Barley kneeling by the bed, haloed in moonlight from the window, with his hands, still wrapped in bandages, raised before him. He reached out again to touch Walt's shoulder, but this time he struck him hard, a shove that must have made his wounds ache wildly. "Be quiet, you," he said. "Just hush up."

2

EVERY YEAR AFTER THE WAR ENDED, DREAMS OF THE LATE PRESident would arrive with the spring. Just before the weather changed, Mr. Lincoln would visit Walt in his sleep, stepping out of a bright mist, with lilacs clutched in his hands and the odor of lilacs on his person. That was always the first dream—the groundhog dream, Walt called it, the harbinger of winter's end. Others followed: a dream of wrestling with a Lincoln graced with enormous black wings; a dream of building a bed for him and Mr. Lincoln to sleep in, a very long bed indeed; and a dream where Walt stood with the late President on a wooden platform overlooking Pennsylvania Avenue and watched a grand review.

The two men looked on as solid ranks of soldiers—twenty or twenty-five abreast—came marching steady down the avenue, one regiment after another. For an hour, there would be nothing but cavalry, walking slowly on exhausted gray horses with bleeding eyes—the cavalrymen swung their sabers around in salute to Mr. Lincoln and his companion. Then came batteries of ruined cannon, with gunners sitting up sharply on top of broken caissons. And then, the infantry again, Negro and white, Union and Confederate, turning their faces in a crisp motion to behold Lincoln and salute him. They marched as dusk gently fell on them, and a sign lit up on a building across from the stand. Someone had arranged a series of gaslights to spell out "How are you, Lee?" Walt peered into the gloom, trying to recognize his brother George among the marchers. But then he realized that George was not among them because this was a parade of the dead.

"Quite a spectacle," said the late President.

"They are very many," said Walt.

"Yes. It would crush me, I think, but death has eroded my cares a little."

"I have friends among them," Walt said. He went to the rail and leaned over it, looking hard at the faces as they passed by.

"Sweet Henry Smith," said Lincoln.

"Do you know him?"

"I know them all. Aren't they my boys, every one of them, just as they were yours? They want to come back. Listen to them—they are crying to come back." Walt listened—he closed his eyes and realized that the parade was going by in perfect silence.

"I hear nothing," he said.

Mr. Lincoln shook his head. "The dead are not silent," he said, and turned his back on Walt, so Walt could see his wound, gaping just behind his ear. "Go on," he said. "You may probe it, if you like." It seemed suddenly to Walt that he must do just that. It was enormously necessary to put his finger in that hole. *I have been waiting so long*, Walt thought as he reached out his finger, *to do this*. His finger sank into the wound as if into a sucking mouth. There came a deafening roar from the soldiers. Walt felt a shock all over his body, as if he'd fallen from a tree onto hard ground, and woke in his bed with his limbs splayed out around him like a startled baby.

It was May of 1868. Walt was still in Washington, making a comfortable salary as a clerk in the office of the Attorney General. He lay in bed, panting because this dream always left him feeling exhausted, and listening to the noise of migrating birds outside his window. He liked the smell of this hour—he thought it must be around five in the morning—and he liked to lie and listen to the big song, and picture the immense flock. He listened carefully, trying to identify species. As he lay with his eyes closed, listening so hard, he heard Hank's voice speaking softly into his ear. He always sounded so close—close enough to kiss. Walt had been hearing him, not since his death, but since Mr. Lincoln's, since the first time he'd dreamed of the reviewing stand, since the first time he'd put his finger in the great wound and felt the exuberant, electric whack. At first, Walt had thought it was his brother Andrew speaking to him. He'd died of tuberculosis, just after Hank died, and Walt thought he'd come back to haunt him, to chide him for not attending his funeral, for grieving less for a brother than he did for Hank, or, indeed, for Mr. Lincoln. But the voice he heard was Hank speaking, in his sweet Missouri accent, a soft voice out of the boundless west that was made elegant and articulate by death. *Bobolink, tanager, Wilson's thrush,* he said. *White-crowned sparrow. It's rare music, isn't it, Walt?*

Walt had been in New York when he heard of Lincoln's death. That Saturday, he'd sat at the breakfast table with his mother, neither of them eating anything, neither of them speaking. He'd crossed the river to Manhattan, and walked all day in the strangely quiet and subdued city. Every shop was closed, except the ones selling the equipment of grief. Walt stopped and bought crepe for the mournification of his mother's house, and a motto for her door: *O the pity of it, Iago, the pity of it!*

All week long, he went out to observe the progress of mourning. From Bowling Green to Union Square, every store, house, and hotel on Broadway was alive with the national colors in celebration of Appomattox, and over all these hung black cloth. In the harbor, black pennants flew over the flags at half-mast, and the private signals of captains and owners were draped in black. All over the city, the folds of crepe grew darker, denser, and more numerous as the week went on, until Walt thought that the sky would be blotted out by a low hanging belly of crepe, settling so thick and deep over every street and building that Manhattan might be hidden forevermore from the world.

When the President's body came to New York, Walt stood in the immense crowds around City Hall and waited his turn to see it. From the west gate of the park, people were lined up twenty across and three blocks deep down Murray Street. All across Printing House Square the crowd stretched, away up Chatham to Mulberry Street. Batteries were sounding every minute, and bells were ringing all over the city. Outside City Hall, a group of Germans was singing Schumann's "Chorus of the Spirits."

Inside City Hall, the fabulous catafalque was waiting for Walt. The coffin lay under a twenty-foot-high arch topped with a silver eagle whose head drooped sadly, and whose wings were folded shyly against its body. Very slowly, the line moved forward, until at last Walt got a good long stare at the dead man, at the coffin of wood and lead and silver and velvet, at the flowers—scarlet azaleas and double nasturtiums, white japonicas and orange blossoms and lilacs. The body had been out for many hours by the time Walt saw it. The face had begun to show wear—perhaps, Walt thought, from the pressure of all those thousands and thousands of pairs of eyes that had beheld it. The jaw had dropped, the lips had fallen open slightly to reveal the teeth. An undertaker leaned forward next to Walt and discreetly dusted the face, but this only made it look worse.

Walt stared and stared, holding up the line, fascinated by the dead gray face. A lady behind him gave a polite shove. Her child, horrified by the disagreeable face, was weeping, and she wished to move on. Walt gave her a slight bow, but as he turned to walk away he heard a voice calling his name, *Walt, Walt, Walt*. He turned back to the lady.

"Did you speak?" he asked her, though it wasn't a lady's voice he'd heard. She shook her head no, and motioned again for him to please move on. Walt looked once more at the late President's face, at the lips hanging open. As he walked away he heard the voice, plaintive now, *Walt!*

For weeks the voice would only speak his name. Back in Washington, it would call to him as he sat at his desk in the Patent Office. He'd had a new job since January, working as a clerk in the Department of the Interior. *Walt*, the voice would say, and he would look up at the Indians waiting serenely to see some undersecretary, sitting lofty and remote in their necklaces and feathers and paint. "Did you speak?" Walt would ask them.

The voice kept calling Walt's name, all through the summer, and after. It called to him at his job in the Attorney General's office, procured for him by a friend after he was fired (for the sake of his *Leaves*) from the Department of the Interior. Day and night he heard it, waking, sleeping, and dreaming, and he thought it was his brother until he knew it was Hank, and he named it Hank, and then it spoke to him sweetly and at length, no longer just calling his name. And until he named it, it was his fear that the voice was a symptom of a sick mind, but this concern slowly melted away, until it did not matter to him if his mind was decaying into madness, so long as the voice kept speaking. *What did you think?* the voice asked him. *Did you think I would leave you?*

It was one of Hank's virtues that he never told Walt what to do. The living Hank had been a great and incessant demander—Walt, fetch me some ice; Walt, I got an itch on my back, roll me over and see to it; get me a pipe; get me a bird; get me a picture of a French girl, naked. But Hank's voice never asked for anything. It offered salutations in the morning. It commented on the beauty of a beautiful day. Death had changed Hank's appreciation of Walt's poetry—the voice spoke Walt's own words back to him, or offered him new ones, a generous muse. But it never asked for anything, it never once gave a command until the autumn of '68, when Walt was in New York, having a sort of vacation.

In Manhattan, if it was very pleasant outside, Walt would take a trip on a stage. Nearly all the Broadway drivers were his personal friends. They'd let him ride for free if he didn't insist on paying—he'd ride for hours and hours and pay multiple fares. *You see everything*, Hank said the first time they took such a trip together. It was true—there were shops and splendid buildings and great vast windows, sidewalks crowded with richly dressed women and men, superior in style and looks to those seen anywhere else. It was a perfect stream of people.

One day in October, Walt took Hank for a ride on the Belt Line. They got on in the early afternoon and rode round and round along its course, circumnavigating the lower reaches of Manhattan, going down along the Hudson River docks, up along the East River front, and then across Fifty-ninth Street to start the ride all over again. The day was dusty and warm. Walt rested his head against the window and watched the sun striking through ship's flags. *A great day*, Hank said, and Walt wondered, not for the first time, if he ought to pay double the fare since Hank was with him.

Lost in the sunstruck flags, Walt hardly noticed the passengers as they came and went, until, at Fulton Market, there boarded a man who demanded Walt's attention. He tripped on the platform and fell into the car, catching his hand on the driver's strap and giving it a mighty tug. The driver (his name was Carl, he was a friend of Walt's) dropped a curse down on him. The fellow reached his hand up to squeeze the driver's calf where it hung down in view of all the passengers.

"Sorry," he said. "I am so sorry."

A muffled reply came down from the driver on his perch. Walt looked away as the fellow came back, feeling shy all of a sudden, though he had never before been shy on a stage. He had accosted all sorts of men on the stages, and made many dear friends that way. But now, as the fellow sat down across from him, Walt stared out the window, down at the ground where the shadows of masts and rigging were everywhere. As the new passenger had come closer, Walt had peeked and seen that he was young, or at least he looked very young, despite the big brown beard on his face.

"Hello," he said. Walt did not reply, and that was when Hank offered his first posthumous demand. *Say hello, Walt.* But Walt remained silent.

The young fellow began to sing a tune, "Woodman, Spare That Tree," falling into a hum sometimes when he forgot the words. When they had been up the East Side, and along the lower margin of Central Park, the fellow spoke again. "You are on for the ride, just like me." Walt said nothing, and Hank chided him. *I've never known you to be rude.* Walt put his head down and pretended to sleep. His palms were burning and his heart felt as if it were riding just under his chin. *Just look at him,* Hank said. *Take a good long look. Then you'll know.*

"Bostonians are supercilious towards everybody," the fellow said.

Walt let out a little counterfeit snore.

"Are you from Boston?"

Walt opened his eyes, but did not look up. "I am not from Boston," he said. "It's only that I would prefer not to have a conversation."

"Well, you might have said so." The young man muttered to himself for a while, and when they had passed down to the oyster boats at Tenth Street, he stood up and exited the stage. Walt's shyness and fear evaporated immediately, and then he wished he had not been so rude, and he was inclined to chase the man down just to apologize to him.

But he was only gone for a minute. Before the car could leave him behind, he returned with a bucket of oysters and sat down again in his spot. Very soon Walt could hear him slurping them and throwing the shells down on the floor among the straw and dried mud. "Oh damn," he said suddenly. Walt looked up to see that he had cut his thumb trying to shuck an oyster. There were only four fingers on the hand he'd injured; he was missing the littlest finger of his left hand. He brought his thumb to his mouth, staining his lips with blood. He looked away from the door and met Walt's gaze, and Walt saw that his eyes could not have been more like Hank's if he had stolen them and set them in his own head. Walt got a feeling, then, which crowded into his heart with the shyness and the fear, but did not displace them. This fellow, this boy, was intensely familiar—he felt sure he'd met him before, or seen his face, though he knew he had not. *Give him a kiss, Walt*, said Hank. *Embrace him. He is for you, and you for him, a great true comrade and a great soul. He is a builder.*

"Are you well, sir?" Walt asked him, because the thumb, out of the young man's mouth now, was bleeding profusely. Walt thought back to an instance in Armory Square when his own thumb had been cut by a scalpel covered with gangrenous filth. His thumb had swelled up like a plum, then, and taken months to heal.

"It's a scratch," said the boy. Now Walt thought he was definitely a boy, not even twenty years old, though deep lines of care were writ on his brow. Walt leaned over, very slowly, to inspect the wound.

"It's deep. It should be bandaged."

"It's not so deep," he said. "See? Now it's drying up." He gave it a few shakes, and the trickling blood slowed and stopped.

"But it was deep," said Walt, who thought he'd seen a flash of white bone between the lips of the cut.

"No," said the fellow. "I think it wasn't. And I am a doctor. A connoisseur, if you will, of wounds." He put out his bloody hand for Walt to shake. "Dr. George Washington Woodhull," he said, "but you may please call me Gob."

Walt stared and stared at him, but did not take his hand. Though Armory Square was so fresh in his mind that he sometimes thought he could still smell blood and ether in his beard and his skin, it took him a moment to place the name Woodhull.

"Well, you are Walt Whitman. You don't need to tell me. I knew it the very moment I entered this car. Who else, I ask you, looks like Walt Whitman? And see here, the whole city has been notified of your visit." He moved over, sat down next to Walt, and took a copy of the *Times* from his coat. " 'With the advent of autumn,' " he read, " 'Walt Whitman once again makes his appearance on the sidewalks of Broadway. His large, massive personality; his grave and prophetic, yet free and manly appearance; his insouciance of manner and movement; his easy and negligent but clean and wholesome dress—all go to make up a figure and an individuality that attracted the attention and interest of every passer-by.' " Walt stared, remembering Dr. Woodhull of Armory Square, barely listening to the personal notice in the paper, though he was very pleased with it. He'd written the outline himself and submitted it to a friend at the *Times*.

"Mr. Whitman," said the boy. "I am so glad to meet you." He put his hand out again, and this time Walt took it. It was a small hand, but strong, and the boy squeezed so hard Walt thought he might whimper. He pumped Walt's arm and with every shake Walt got a feeling, a happy feeling, as if this young fellow were pumping him up with joy. *See?* Hank said. *Do you see him, Walt? Do you see him?*

The next day Walt went planting in the park. While he waited for his new friend, he searched out places where he thought people might settle down for a picnic. Kneeling in a good spot on the meadow, near the lake, he tore up some grass and made a little bed of it on which to rest his book. He'd inscribed it earlier in a neat but carefree hand: For *you*.

It was his conviction that he was most successful with the reader in the open air, and so he planted, certain that a person who encountered his poems among the natural splendors of this park would be charmed and changed by them. He sat down on a bench some hundreds of feet away from where he'd left his book, and watched. Opening a paper and pretending to read it, he thought not about his prospective reader, but of Dr. Woodhull—of Gob.

Gob had invited Walt to walk with him, and walk they did, all over the city for hours and hours, so today even Walt, a perennially enthusiastic and untiring perambulator, had sore feet. Walt confessed that he already knew a Dr. Woodhull, and Gob confessed that Canning Woodhull was indeed his father, though he had not seen him since he was five years old. They talked about poems because Gob insisted that he was a great admirer of Walt's *Leaves,* and they talked about politics because as night fell there began a grand Democratic meeting and torchlight procession. Democrats poured out into the street by the thousands, and the whole city was lit up with torches. On Second Avenue, Walt and Gob climbed up on a stalled omnibus to watch the procession go by. There were models of ships some sixty feet long, fully manned, and liberty cars overflowing with women in robes of red, white, and blue. Every member of the parade carried a torch. Gob laughed at a lady who wore a hat made of Roman candles, which shot tiny fireballs into the crowd along the sidewalks. The two of them had parted after the last straggler in the procession, a child wearing a placard proclaiming for Seymour, had passed by. They arranged to meet the next day in the park, and then Walt went home, thinking of his new friend, wondering that he had ever been afraid of him. Hank was silent, except to make an occasional exclamation. *O joy*, he said. *O happiness.*

In the park, Walt kept watch over his book, but though a few people passed by it, no one stooped to pick it up. His spirits were beginning to droop when he heard Gob's voice behind him saying, "Hello, Walt!" Gob was proceeding rapidly down the carriage path, accompanied by a laughing redheaded female in liberated dress. Only their upper portions were visible above a hedge that ran along the road, and these seemed quite impossibly to be floating. Walt figured they must be on bicycles, but when they came around the hedge he saw that they had contraptions on their feet, big rubber wheels the size of a person's head, two for each foot, attached to iron braces that fit under their shoes.

"Look, Mr. Whitman," said the lady, who was pretty and fat,

with eyes like her companion's, blue and Hankish and beautiful. "We are velocipedestrians!" She waved her arms, catching her balance as she stopped her rolling.

"This is my aunt," Gob said, "Miss Tennie C. Claflin. When I told her I was to meet you today, she could not stay away."

"It is my great pleasure, sir," she said, taking his hand and shaking it vigorously. "My very intense pleasure." She was dressed in a dark blue tunic and skirt of blue wool, with a pair of yellow bloomers on her legs that demanded even more attention than the wheels on her feet. All over the park, as far as Walt's eyes could see, people were pointing at her, but she seemed not to notice.

"Do you like my land skates?" Gob asked Walt. He'd told Walt the night before that tinkering and inventing were his avocations, that he had been educated as an engineer as well as a physician, and Walt had talked about his engineer brothers, George and Jeff.

"They are very particular," Walt said, because he did not quite know what to make of the skates. Tennie insisted on surrendering hers so that Walt could try them out. They held his arms and pulled him to and fro over the grass by the lake, until he got some skill with the things.

"It's just like ice-skating!" Walt said, very pleased with how he was flying down the road at what must have been a full ten miles an hour. He imagined a notice in the papers: *Walt Whitman was in the Central Park yesterday, riding on the wheels of the future*. Gob put his fingers on Walt's wrist to steady him, then took his hand. They skated full around the lake, returning to find Tennie seated by the water. She rose and ran to them, a confusion of blue and yellow fabric, flashing her legs at the whole wide world, waving in her hand the book she'd found.

"A dark place," said Tennie, "but I like it." Walt had taken them to Pfaff's, because he thought Tennie would liven the place up considerably. It had become rather staid since the days before the war when Henry Clapp and Ada Clare held court there. "We are in my neighborhood, you know," she said. "I live with my family in Great Jones Street, Number Seventeen. You are welcome to visit, Mr. Whitman. My sister would be delighted to meet you. Of course, don't come by thinking to see little Gob, here. Great Jones Street is not great enough for him. He lives in Fifth Avenue, and doesn't care for visitors."

"The house where I live is gloomy," Gob said. "It was my teacher's. When he passed on he left it to me."

"Did you hear of the horrible murder in France?" asked Tennie. Walt said he had not. "A man named Gaucher went for a stroll in the Tuilleries and noticed a fine handkerchief abandoned on the wet ground. Now, he is a man of limited means, this Gaucher. He has never been a fortunate person, but he blesses his good fortune that he has found this truly exquisite piece of material, which he is already planning to sell before he picks it up. But no sooner does he take it than he discovers that in doing so he has uncovered a horrible staring eye. A hideous, staring green eye. It belonged to the youngest child, the only member of a family of five not buried completely by the fiend who killed them."

"I hadn't heard!" Walt said.

"No," said Tennie. "Of course you hadn't. It's a year off yet. Sometimes I am confused. But worry you not, Mr. Whitman. Those poor babies will be sheltered in the Summerland."

"I think they'd rather shelter on earth," said Gob. "But what say have we got in it, eh Walt?"

"Pfaff's used to be a lively place," said Walt, feeling bewildered. "Back in its day."

"Gob, fetch us some frankfurters," said Tennie. "I am hungry for a frankfurter and thirsty for a beer." As soon as Gob left, Tennie leaned over to Walt and whispered to him. "Mr. Whitman," she said very slowly. "Listen to me. I am beautiful and I love you. I think you have got a child for me, a noble and perfect man child. Our boy . . . do you not already love him? He must be gotten on a mountaintop, in the open air. Not in lust, not in mere gratification of sexual passion, but in ennobling pure strong deep passionate broad universal love!"

As she spoke, Walt had shrunk back from her, so far that his chair was leaning away from the table and he might have fallen over if Gob hadn't come up behind him and steadied the chair with his hip. Tennie had been charming, previously, and now she was just another alarming female.

"Walt," said Gob, "I think my aunt has played a joke on you."

"A joke!" said Tennie. "Mr. Whitman, I only sought to amuse you!"

"Of course," said Walt. "Of course." He took his frankfurter from Gob, who was scolding his aunt.

"It's a cause with me, Mr. Whitman," Tennie said in her own defense. "The manufacture of liveliness is my cause."

Among the men and women the multitude, Hank said, *I perceive one picking me out by secret and divine signs*. Walt was at his desk in the Attorney General's office. It was one o'clock on a snowy afternoon in early December of '68. To the casual observer, he appeared to be very hard at work, bent over a sheet of paper with his broad-brimmed hat on the desk beside his arm. He looked to be copying some official document, writing a bit and then glancing again at the original, but in fact he was copying a letter of his own, making it prettier to look at and more pleasing to the reader's ear.

Dear Gob,

I send you a few lines, though there is nothing new or special with me. I am still working in the same place, and expect to be here all winter (yet there is such a thing as a man's slipping up in his calculations, you know). My health keeps good, and work easy. I often think of you, my boy, and think whether you are all right and in good health, and riding yet on the Belt Line when the mood takes you.

I suppose you received the letter I sent you. I got yours November 15 and sent you a letter about the twentieth or twenty-first, I believe. I have not heard from you since.

Congress began here last Monday. I have been up to see them in session. The halls they meet in are magnificent. The light comes all from the great roof. The new part of the Capitol is very fine indeed. It is a great curiosity to any one that likes fine workmanship both in wood and stone. But I hope that you will come here and see me, as you talked of—Whether we are indeed to have the chance in future to be much together and enjoy each other's love and friendship—or whether worldly affairs are to separate us—I don't know. But somehow I feel (if I am not dreaming) that the good square love is in our hearts, for each other, while life lasts.

As I told you in my previous letter, this city is quite small potatoes after living in New York. The public buildings are large and grand. Most of them are made of white marble, and on a far grander scale than the N.Y. City Hall; but the oceans of life and people, such as in N.Y. and the shipping etc. are lacking here. Still, a young man ought to see Washington once in his life, any how. Then I please myself with thinking it will be a pleasure to you to be with me, Gob, I want you to write me as often as you can.

Walt folded up the letter in the envelope and took a break to post it. Outside, he leaned for a moment against a streetlamp, because he was momentarily overcome with a feeling like the one he'd had in Central Park—there were magical wheels on his feet and he was flying along hand in hand with his comrade. This feeling kept returning to him, the same way a tossing sea feeling would return to him as he fell asleep after a day playing in the surf. *Acknowledging none else*, Hank said. *Not parent, wife, husband, brother, child, any nearer than I am. Some are baffled, but not that one—that one knows me.*

Walt got no reply to his December letter. Christmas came and went, and though he was among good friends, he felt lonely. He and Hank welcomed in the New Year sitting by his window. Walt made a punch of lemon, scotch whiskey, sugar, and snow from the windowsill. "To the year!" Walt called out to the black sky. *Year all mottled with good and evil!* shouted Hank. Another week passed, and another and another, with still no word from Gob. Walt gave up hope of hearing from him again, and cursed his own extreme nature. How stupid, after all, to feel such a ridiculous attachment! "We will leave omniphily to M. Fourier and his moony-eyed compatriots," Walt said to Hank. "It is not for Walt Whitman." Hank said, *Not in any or all of them O adhesiveness! O pulse of my life! Need I that you exist and show yourself any more than in these songs.*

But on the evening of January 20, as Walt sat in his favorite (and only) chair, watching the snow fall outside his window, there came a knock at his door. He listened at it a moment and heard voices. A woman was saying, "Are you certain this is the address?" Walt opened the door and saw a regal-looking lady dressed all in blue, with a white tea rose at her throat, with yet another pair of Hankish eyes set in her head. Gob, obscured by her tall chapeau, stepped around her and clasped Walt to his chest.

"Hello, Walt!" he said. "Hello, my friend! Here I am, just as I promised. And here's my mother, too. Victoria C. Woodhull, but you may call her Empress Eugenie."

"Really, Gob," said the lady. She put out her hand and waited patiently for Walt to take it. She stepped into his room, making it seem somehow as if Walt had drawn her in, though it was not his intention to do that.

"Walt," said Gob. "Get your coat on and don't be pokey. We're late for the female convention." Walt put his coat on, and his shoes, while Victoria Woodhull said various things, none of which he heard very well because of his agitated state. She complimented him on his room, looking around at the dingy walls, the socks drying on the bedpost, and the curtains nailed up on the wall, where they wouldn't block his light or his view. The thing that ought to have been under the bed was out in full view, and it was brimming. Her glance fell on it and moved on.

"An honest room, Mr. Whitman," she said. "Simple and austere. Yet when I close my eyes I can feel how it is a palace of wisdom."

"Considerably less than that," said Walt. "A lean-to of good sense, perhaps. Or a thatched hut of affability. I don't often have visitors."

"Well," said Mrs. Woodhull. "Come along, then." She offered Walt her arm—and yet when he took it he got the feeling somehow that he had offered her his—and they were off. It did not occur to Walt to ask where they were going until they were situated in the fine carriage that was waiting outside.

"Where else but the female convention?" said Gob. It became clear that he thought Walt had received a letter detailing the plans for this evening. When he realized Walt had received none such, both he and his mother were embarrassed and apologetic. Mrs. Woodhull offered to return him to his room, but Walt declined. "I like nothing better than a surprise," he said, which was not entirely true. But this particular surprise—that Gob should appear unexpectedly at his door and pluck him from out of a still pool of sadness—was altogether fine and good.

The three of them proceeded to the National Woman Suffrage Convention, the first ever to be held in the capital. At Carrol Hall, they sat together among a very heterogeneous congregation. There were men and women, whites and Negros, people with a look of wealth about them and people whose clothes declared their poverty. With a rolled-up program, Mrs. Woodhull pointed out those on the stage.

"There's Mrs. Mott, in the Quaker bonnet. She looks sweet and grannyish, doesn't she? Well, she is no ordinary granny, though I hear she is sweet-tempered. There is Mrs. Stanton, next to her. Don't you think, Mr. Whitman, that she looks like a queen?"

"Certainly," said Walt. Mrs. Stanton did look queenly, with her hair all in white ringlets, and with her nose, the fineness and nobility of which Walt could appreciate even at a distance. And she possessed an enormous, immensely solid-looking bosom, which seemed to him sturdy enough to be the foundation upon which a queendom might be raised. "And there," he said, "on the end of the platform, with the Eve-like disarrangement of hair, that is Dr. Mary Walker. I knew her during the war, when she was your husband's colleague."

"My former husband," Mrs. Woodhull corrected. "And speaking of men, is that Senator Julian on the right? I understand he is friendly to the cause. That preacher I do not recognize. He is not a Beecher."

The preacher was finishing up his opening prayer with an ill-considered reference to Eve: he called her Adam's spare rib. This started a stir which continued through two more speakers. The crowd only quieted when it came Mrs. Stanton's turn to address them.

"A great idea of progress is near its consummation," Mrs. Stanton began, "when statesmen in the councils of the nation propose to frame it into statutes and constitutions; when Reverend Fathers recognize it by a new interpretation of their creeds and canons; when the Bar and Bench at its command set aside the legislation of centuries, and girls of twenty put their heels on the Cokes and Blackstones of the past."

Walt got quite wrapped up in Mrs. Stanton and her speech. He liked her anger and her eloquence and her bosom. She inspired him to get lost in his own fancy, and he pictured her a giantess, one hundred feet high, who waded into the Potomac and launched ship after ship from her rampart breast, a thousand ships each filled with a thousand angry women. These women were about to fire great broadsides of explosive discontent at the capital when Walt was distracted by a pressure on his shoulder. Gob had lobbed his head there and was sleeping soundly.

"My brother died at Chickamauga," said Gob. "That's where he died." He and Walt had adjourned to a saloon after just a few hours of conventioneering. Mrs. Woodhull had stayed on, though she was already belittling the proceedings as a series of teacup hurricanes. "They talk and talk and talk," she had said, "when they ought to be *doing*."

"My brother died in Brooklyn," said Walt, speaking of Andrew. "With his throat rotted out." After a bottle of whiskey between them, their conversation had taken a maudlin turn.

"Tomo ran off when we were eleven. Walt, I ought to have been with him. We ought to have been together, there at the end."

Walt wasn't much of a drinker, but he tried to keep up with Gob, who seemed to take after his papa, the elder Dr. Woodhull, with respect to liquor. The whiskey had made Walt's emotions labile and monstrous. He stared at Gob's sad face, turning over in his mind the idea of him dying, arm in arm, with his twin brother, the two of them riddled identically with bullets, whispering goodbye, goodbye to each other as they drifted off the earth. What a scene—it was enormously horrible and enormously beautiful. It caused him to cry. Hank, drunk too, said, *O adhesiveness! O pulse of my life!*

"Yes, yes," said Gob. "My sentiments exactly. I used to cry for it, until it occurred to me that tears do nothing. They comfort the living, but do they appease the dead? Do they want our tears? Is it useful to them that we mourn? Life might spend all its days grieving for lost life. You'd think something could be done with it."

"All the blood," said Walt. "All the precious blood. A great work ought to be coming, oughtn't it?" He was sobbing, uttering a choking call like a hairy animal. It attracted the attention of the other patrons of the saloon, horsecar drivers and conductors all, and many of them Walt's friends. A few came over to comfort him and glare at Gob. "Walt, is this fellow causing you some upset?" they asked. Walt shook his head, but all the boys kept casting angry looks at Gob, so he and Walt left the place, taking a walk up to the Capitol. As they walked, Walt apologized for the inhospitality of the boys in the saloon. "Everywhere I go I have friends," he said. "But nobody like *you*."

They sat on the steps of the Capitol passing back and forth another bottle.

"Drunker and drunker and drunker and drunker," said Walt.

"Do you know what I am thinking, Walt?" Gob asked.

"You are thinking of Mrs. Surrat," said Walt, "because she was hanged over yonder." He pointed across the snowy grounds, across the street to where the old prison used to stand. "You are thinking, 'Poor dear, I bet she was just somebody's dupe.' And you are thinking how it would upset your mama and all those other sufferables that a woman can hang but she cannot vote. I saw John Surrat's trial this summer. He is very young. I sat near him. It was hot in the courtroom, and he kept me cool with his big palm-leaf fan."

"I was thinking," said Gob, "that we ought to take shelter from the snow." Even as he spoke, Walt noticed that the snow was falling again, thicker and faster than earlier. Gob stood up, gathering his enormous black coat about him—it seemed to Walt that there must be room for two of him in it, or one of him and one of Walt. He ran up the Capitol steps, taking them two and three at a time. "Come along, Walt!" he said. "I see a little cottage where we can shelter!"

It was close to two in the morning, so there was no one about on the grounds, and there could be nobody inside the Capitol but a stray guard or two. Yet Gob was knocking as if he expected some bleary-eyed innkeeper to rise from his bed and open the door. "Hello!" he called out. "Open up for two travelers weary with the cold!" Walt laughed, but the door popped open with a great loud click, throwing cheery yellow light onto Gob's shoes.

It was at just that point that the evening began to seem dreamlike and strange to Walt, but not frightening. Somewhere a little voice—not Hank's, though—was urging him to flee over the snow and throw himself in George Washington's arms, to cling to the General till dawn. But the voice was whispering through smothering pillows of booze and contentment. Walt could barely hear it. It was easy to ignore. He followed Gob into the grand building, and walked after him down the gorgeous painted corridors.

"They say this place is haunted," Gob said. "They say you can see the ghost of a workman who fell from the scaffolding while they were building the new rotunda. They say his neck is at a horrible angle and he moans in a most frightening manner."

"I'm not afraid of spirits," Walt said.

"There's also a demon cat. A great big one, black as soot, with red coals for eyes. It always appears before somebody important dies. And they say these statues come alive on New Year's Eve and dance with one another to celebrate another year of survival for this delicate, sickly Union."

They had come to Statuary Hall. Walt paused by a statue of Mr. Adams and tried to imagine him stepping down from his pedestal to click his marble heels around the room. "Come along," Gob shouted as he ran away. "To the House Floor. We shall legislate!"

When Walt came into the House Chamber, Gob was already down at the bottom. Walt called to him: "John Quincy Adams died right there. In the middle of a passionate speech he suffered an apoplectic fit and fell down dead. In times of trouble, he reappears and finishes his speech. If you listen to the whole thing you will find that at the very end, he reveals the solution to whatever national crisis is pending. A very convenient arrangement, I think. It's said that Mr. Lincoln came here during the war, in hope of a consultation, but Mr. Adams did not show."

"Spirits are notoriously fickle," Gob said.

"I make a habit of coming to watch the proceedings here. But I think I will give it up. I am sick of the shrewd, gabby little manikins, all dressed in black, all supremely lacking in ability." Walt paused a moment and looked around the room, feeling bold and drunk and powerful. "From right here they might do it," Walt said. "They might do a great work with the blood, might have done, but I begin to think it will turn out to have been all for nothing."

"Shall we make it better, Walt? Shall we legislate?" Gob bounded up to the Speaker's desk and, picking up a gavel, banged it on the wood. "I hereby declare," he shouted, "that brothers are nevermore to be separated! Let it be so written into the laws, natural and unnatural, the laws of this Union and the laws of every state!" He let go with the gavel again. "Mr. Whitman," he shouted, "what say you, sir?"

Walt raised his hands in a grand gesture. "Let it be so!" he shouted. "And furthermore make it forbidden that true friends and comrades should ever be separated!"

"Not by distance!" said Gob. "And not by death! Let it be so!" He banged again with the gavel, pounding away with it, relentless and furious, until it broke in half in his hand.

Walt kept wondering, Where were the guards? They were not drawn out by the racket he and Gob made in the Capitol. Now, in the Model Room of the Patent Office, there was no sign of them as Gob's boots made sharp, loud noises. Gob stomped up and down the aisles, peering into the glass cases by the light of a match. Walt walked behind him, looking at Ben Franklin's printing press, at the models of fire extinguishers and ice cutters, guns and rattraps. Gob was deeply excited. He said he was looking for something, and he wanted Walt to be there when he found it. There was a whole series of cases containing treaties between the United States and various foreign powers. Gob lingered over Bonaparte's sprawling, nervous-looking signature on the treaty of 1803. Nearby were various Oriental articles. Walt pointed at an Eastern saber, at a Persian carpet presented to President Van Buren by the Iman of Muscat. "Is that it? Is this what you seek?" Gob shook his head and moved on.

"Not that," Gob said. "Not this either, but maybe . . . this." He shone a new match on another model, very plain and roughly made, representing a steamboat. A ticket on it read, *Model of sinking and raising boats by bellows below. A. Lincoln, May 30, 1849*. Hank spoke up, his voice very loud this time in the immense quiet of the Model Room. *He was a builder, too.*

"Is that it?" Walt said. "Is that what you require?"

"No," Gob said. "But it is related to the thing I require. Ah, there it is." With very little ado—he only cranked his arm back a little—he put his elbow through the case next to the one containing Mr. Lincoln's boat. He reached in and removed a hat, which he immediately set on his head.

"It's a crime!" Walt said. "It's a crime what you did!" But he didn't say it very loud, and in fact he found the vandalism somehow exciting. He had the old thrill back—the buzzing in his soul like Olivia's frantic wings, and he did not know if it was the crime, or proximity to Gob, or the drunkenness that caused it. He lit another match and held it near the tag that dangled from the brim of the hat. *Hat worn by Abraham Lincoln,* it read, *on the night of his assassination.*

"There," said Gob. "Now my thinking is much improved." He put his hands on his face and was silent awhile. Walt closed his eyes too, and saw sick and wounded boys laid out on cots between the glass cases, saw blood gleaming by gaslight on the polished marble floor. When Walt opened his eyes again, Gob had turned back to the broken case.

"Look!" Gob said. "I need that, too!" He reached in, to another shelf, and removed a length of cable. He pushed it in Walt's face and rubbed it against his cheek, asking, "Do you know what this is? It's the Atlantic Cable. The thing itself!"

"A crime," Walt said. As if at his call, a guard came at last, and found them. He called out, "Hey there!" Gob took Walt's hand and ran, pulling him along, dragging him and lifting him painfully by one arm, so fast and smooth Walt wasn't quite sure if their feet were touching the ground. They ran toward the guard and knocked into him, sending him sprawling as a train might send an unlucky cow sailing over a pasture. Walt heard him land with an oof and a curse, and then they were flying down the stairs, Walt stumbling at every step and Gob bearing him up.

Did they go after that to Ford's Theatre? Walt was never sure, and later when he asked Gob, he'd only get a shrug for an answer. It was like remembering something through a great space of water. Walt was thinking they would go into the theater and embrace in the spot where Lincoln had died. Their marvelous passion would go out from them in waves, transforming time, history, and destiny, unmurdering Lincoln, unfighting the war, unkilling all those six hundred thousand, who would be drawn from death into the theater, where they would add their strong arms to the world-changing embrace, until at last a great historic love-pile was gathered in Washington City, a gigantic pearl with Gob and Walt the sand at its center.

But the box was gone. The whole theater had been gutted and refitted as a medical museum. Gob led Walt up a spiral staircase from the first floor, which was cluttered with clerks' desks, past the second floor, a library, to the top of the building.

The third floor was filled with hideous curiosities, testaments to the ways in which human flesh is heir to misery. At the top of the stairs, Walt was greeted by a row of jars containing heads that looked, because they were near a window, to be suspended in moonlight. Three Maori heads from New Zealand grinned at him as he walked towards them. He bent down to look at their empty eye sockets, their cheeks striped with betel-juice tattoos, their glowing white teeth. Nearby, there were tumors piled like candy in a jar. Walt had a perverse notion that he and Gob would go bobbing for them like apples. He turned away from the tumors and considered all the bones—they hung from the ceiling in complete or partial skeletons. There were skulls lined up on shelves, trephined or saber-whacked or bullet-ridden. Gob began plucking booty from the ceiling and shelves, putting into a sack he'd pulled from his coat the arm bones and leg bones, the finger bones and toe bones and ribs and pelvises. "I need them, Walt," he said. "I need the bones." When his sack was full he made as if to leave, but then his head swung around, as if pulled by Mr. Lincoln's hat, to a place where three human vertebrae were mounted on a stand. Walt lit a match to read the ticket:

> No. 4,086—The third, fourth, and fifth cervical vertebrae. A conoidal carbine ball entered the right side, comminuting the base of the right lamina of the fourth vertebrae, fracturing it longitudinally and separating it from the spinous process. From a case where death occurred a few hours after injury. April 26, 1865.

A separate ticket indicated that the bones belonged to Mr. Booth. They looked to Walt to be stained, as if people had spit on them. Gob put them, too, in his sack. He leaned over and whispered in Walt's ear, his voice sounding almost like Hank's. "I need the bones," he said. "I need them for my engine. You see, I'm building an engine to bring them back, my brother and all the rest. A machine to abolish death, to lick it like a cowardly Reb. I need the bones, I need the hat, and I need you, Walt. I need you especially." Walt tried and failed to imagine the machine that would require such matériel.

That was the last Walt remembered of this very peculiar evening. He did not remember the walk home from Ford's. He did not remember taking off his coat and shirt, his pants and boots. He woke once before dawn with Gob's sleeping head on his chest, and then woke again in the morning with his head on Gob's chest.

Walt sat up in bed. Gob said his brother's name, "Tomo," but didn't wake. Walt looked around the room and saw no bag of bones, but there was a hat placed neatly on the table by the bed. It was an ordinary-looking hat. There wasn't any tag on it. But it was black, and tall, and made to fit a big head. Walt took it up and put it on his own aching head. *Listen, Walt,* Hank said. *Do you hear it?* Walt listened dutifully, and he heard a noise. At first he thought it was Gob's breathing, low and steady and deep, but then he understood that it was something different, a deeper, mightier sound, like a giant breathing, a noise of distant waves crashing, a noise like the sea.

3

"LOOK THERE, WALT," GOB SAID. "HOW DO YOU LIKE THAT boat?" It was July of 1870. Walt and Gob were in New York. They'd gone down to the water to watch the Queen's Cup race, part of a crowd of one hundred thousand spectators gathered on the shores and hills all around the harbor. Walt followed Gob's pointing finger to a boat called the *America*.

"It's the handsomest little craft I ever laid eyes upon," Walt said, but really he was in love with all the boats, and they all seemed very beautiful to him. Walt watched the white sails flapping in the breeze, and the boats tearing along in the green water, trailing flags and streamers and throwing white spray from their bows. He leaned against Gob and tried to think of nothing, to let the lovely darting shapes command his vision and his mind. But thoughts of Gob began to crowd out the boats—first he imagined sailing with Gob in the *America*, how it would delight them both to move so fast. And then Walt imagined them moving over the water without need of a boat. Hand in hand, he and Gob ran over the bay, and leapt howling off the tall tops of the waves. It was always this way; it wasn't enough merely to be with him, being with him inspired thoughts of him even as they were together. *Your Camerado*, said Hank, and indeed it seemed sometimes that Gob was that, a friend above all friends. Yet sometimes he seemed a stranger, even after a year and more of companionship. Or better to say instead that he was strange, but never a stranger. For he *was* strange, infinitely strange. He had strange knowledge, and strange obsessions. His profession was medicine, but he dedicated his life to his wondrous, tyrannical engine—wondrous because he truly meant it to abolish death, tyrannical because he was enslaved to its creation. "I give it everything," he said to Walt, on one occasion, "and it gives me nothing."

He is a builder, Hank said, but Walt often feared that Gob was a little mad, that his dry, obsessive imagination had been set on fire by the death of his brother. Gob kept the engine at his house, a five-story mansion on Fifth Avenue in the neighborhood of the ever-growing Catholic cathedral. Madame Restell, the infamous abortionist, lived not three houses down. Gob knew her. He called her Auntie.

Walt had disliked the house from the instant he saw it, when he got a grand tour the first time he came to New York to visit Gob. It was a lightless place, and it looked not to have been cleaned in years. Every wall, even in the kitchen, was lined with books. Walt squinted to read their titles as he passed them. There was *Orthographic and Spherical Projections, Determinative Mineralogy, Design of Hydraulic Motors, On the Vanity of Arts and Sciences,* but there was not a line of poetry to be found. Everywhere Gob's building stuff was scattered—giant gears and metal beams piled in the dining room, magnets heaped on the parlor sofas. "The servants left when my teacher died," Gob said. Walt asked about that teacher, about how it was that Gob lived apart from his mother, and why he had been living in New York for longer than his mother had—he'd been there, Walt gathered, since the autumn of 1863, but Victoria Woodhull had not arrived until '68. To all his questions, Gob simply replied, "It doesn't matter. It's all past." Walt came to imagine this teacher as a sort of anti-Camerado, an unfriend who was both wise and cruel, the sort of beast who likes to destroy friendships from the comfort of his grave.

"What's behind there?" Walt had asked, at the end of the tour, when they'd come to Gob's bedroom at the top of the house, the place where servants were usually quartered. Walt pointed at a giant iron door a few feet from the bed.

"My workshop," Gob said softly. He had become quiet and nervous as they ascended into the high parts of the house. On the fifth floor, Walt stuck his head into an abandoned and neglected conservatory. The room was full of dead plants, and carpeted with dead leaves. "There's nothing in there," Gob said, pulling him through the only other door off the long hall.

Walt looked around. This was the one clean room Walt had seen in the house, a bedroom furnished in a simple style, except for the bed, which was huge and ornate, hung with white curtains that shivered and undulated in the breeze from a window open despite the cold. A blue skylight let tinted sunshine into the room. There was a wardrobe, and a pine desk covered with mathematical doodles. The floor was wooden, piled with rugs, except in one corner, which was paved with a little circle of stone. While Walt was looking around the room, Gob had gone to this corner, undone his pants, and dropped them. He fell to his knees and bent his head to the ground. Walt looked away too late—he saw the horrible thing like a fleshy eye winking at him obscenely.

"I'm ready," Gob said softly, but Walt had fled, out the door and down the stairs. He kept running all the way down Fifth Avenue, and hurried to Brooklyn, hurried even to Washington, taking the first available train after bidding a very hasty goodbye to his mother. Back in his room in Washington, he felt he could catch his breath at last. He wept because he thought his beautiful friendship had been ruined. Gob sent him a package with a simple note. *Forgive me*, he wrote. *I thought for a moment that you were my master*. He enclosed a present, a copy of *Leaves*, the only gift, he said later, that he was absolutely sure Walt would like. Gob inscribed it with a line modified from Emerson: *True friendship, like the immortality of the soul, is too good to be believed*.

Walt wrote back: *Dear Gob, you must forgive me for being so cold the last day. I was unspeakably shocked and repelled from you by that proposition of yours—you know what. It seemed indeed to me (for I will talk plain to you, dearest comrade) that the one I loved, and who had always been so manly and so sensible, was gone, and a fool and intentional murderer stood in his place. But I will say no more of this—for I know such thoughts must have come when you were not yourself, but in a moment of derangement—and passed away like a bad dream.*

Indeed, they said no more of that incident, and for all that it was terrible Walt came to be glad it had occurred, because it revealed the gigantic nature of their friendship—it seemed to him that only the best and purest sort of friendship could conquer such a horror. So if Gob invoked horror once or a hundred times, so if he was a little mad or a lot, so if he was a boy of seventeen who often acted like an old man of seventy-seven—so what? Walt had taken the measure of his feeling for Gob, and discovered that as wide and deep as his own soul.

The day after the Queen's Cup race, Walt and Gob went out to Paumanok, because Walt had been promising for months to take Gob to the ocean. "Two hundred and twenty pounds avoirdupois!" Walt said, striking his naked chest and belly, then running off into the surf, into the terrific breathing noise of the sea. He liked to hurl himself around in the water, throwing his body against the breaking waves, or swimming along with them until they bore him up and carried him, flipping and spinning, towards the shore. Gob was more reserved in his play. He entered the surf slowly and purposefully, walking until the water was halfway up his chest, then swimming with powerful, even strokes, ducking under the waves like a dolphin till he was beyond them, then heading straight out into deep water. "Where are you going?" Walt shouted after him, but got no answer. Because Gob was in a poor mood—the outbreak of the new war on the Rhine had had an extraordinarily depressive effect on him—Walt feared, for a moment, that he meant to swim towards the east until he tired and drowned. Hank said, *I hate the swift-running eddies that would dash him head-foremost on the rocks!*

But very soon after he had disappeared against the horizon, Walt saw him again, heading back, his bobbing head growing from a speck to a blob as he came nearer. He swam as even and serene as when he had gone out. A wave picked him up, sent him tumbling forward to land on his feet. He walked out of the ocean, up the hot sand to the shadows under a dune, where they'd left their clothes. Walt waded ashore, then ran to him.

"What a display!" he said. "I feared you'd be drowned."

"I like to swim," Gob said. "It's the first thing I remember in my whole life, swimming with my brother."

"Do you feel better, then?" Walt sat down, put his arm around Gob's shoulder, and gave him a squeeze. He wished he hadn't asked. As soon as he did, Gob seemed to remember how sad he was.

"I don't," he said. Walt tried to cheer him with a dinner of cold roast chicken, and with talk about the beach. He told Gob how he'd come to this same stretch of sand when he was a boy, spearing eels in the winter and gathering seagull eggs in the summer. Somehow this pleasant reminiscence brought to Gob's mind the latest murder to delight sensation-loving New Yorkers. Mr. Nathan, a distinguished Jew, had been bludgeoned in his beautiful house.

"My mama says she spoke with that dead man," Gob said. "It was the son who did it, she says."

Walt said he thought it was terrible that a boy should beat his father to death with a lead pipe, that it reflected a failure to cast aside irritating thoughts. "I am not mastered by my gloomy impulses," he said. "That is the main part of getting through the battle and toil of life, dear Gob—keeping a cheerful mind."

"Don't you think of them, Walt?" Gob asked. "Those Frenchmen dying as they move on Saarbruck? Mr. Nathan crying out for mercy from his furious son? Your brother calling out in the madhouse, dying among strangers?" Walt had lost another brother that winter, Jesse. He'd been mad for years, since taking a hard fall from off a ship's mast. Walt had had him committed to the King's County Lunatic Asylum, and had visited him just once. Jesse had sat very quietly while Walt put a gift in his lap—fresh bread and jam from their mother—and while Walt told him news from home. But then without warning Jesse had leapt from his chair and wrestled Walt to the ground. He bit his nose and licked his eyes and called him a despicable hater of cabbages. Now he was dead, and Walt found that, having already put his brother out of his mind after madness claimed him, he did not in death seem so much farther away. How to explain? Jesse's and Andrew's deaths seemed small, and yet the thought that Gob might die was incapacitating to him. Indeed, it *had* incapacitated him. If he thought on it too long he would work himself into a terrible state, getting woozy with sadness and fear. His hands would burn, a lump would swell in his throat, and he'd have a terrible attack of diarrhea. If Gob had been out of his sight for much longer during that long swim, Walt might have fainted away into the water and drowned himself.

"Of course I do," Walt said. "Of course I am sad. If I let it, it might consume me. His heart tore, and I wonder if it was not the accumulated burden of madness and woe that tore his heart apart as hands might tear a paper bag. Sometimes I think I can hear him, raving and crying and dying. I can think on his life—what it might have been if madness hadn't claimed him, and I can love that lost life as I can love Andrew's lost life, and grieve for him. A person could live his whole life like that, in service to grief. You've said as much yourself. What does it do? It will not bring them back, to hollow yourself out, to crush your own heart from loneliness and spite. My friend, it will not bring them back."

Walt liked these words less and less as he spoke them, because they seemed conventional and cowardly and stupid, and at odds with his own experience. Hadn't Hank come back to him, in a sense?

Surely, said Hank. *Surely I did*. And Gob said, "It might, too."

"Mr. Whitman," said Tennie. "You are fatter and saucier than ever." Walt was at Victoria Woodhull's house, invited with Gob to a party on a warm September evening in honor of Stephen Pearl Andrews, an ultimately learned and ultimately radical man, and a very frequent contributor to the paper Mrs. Woodhull had started with Tennie in May of 1870, *Woodhull and Claflin's Weekly*. They were a very special pair of sisters. In the winter they'd opened up their own brokerage house. Walt had visited their offices a few days after they'd opened, when the rooms on Broad Street were still packed with reporters and curiosity-seekers. The lady brokers had received Walt and Gob in their private office. Walt kept a huge walnut desk between himself and Tennie, but offered sincere compliments to both ladies. "You are a prophecy of the future," he told them.

"New York agrees with me," Walt said to Tennie at the party, looking around for Gob but failing to find him. Mrs. Woodhull's house was not so large as her son's, but it was much prettier. The guests were gathered in two large parlors, the walls of which were hung with purple velvet and white silk. White roses were everywhere, in vases and in pots, strung along banisters, and even hanging from the ceiling in flower-chandeliers. "This is a fine house. I think it must be roomier than your house in Great Jones Street."

"Great Jones Street?" said Tennie. "Did we ever live in that dismal alley?" A man came up to them, a great big tall well-gristled fellow in a black suit. He took Tennie's hand and kissed it, then looked at Walt coolly.

"Dr. Fie," Tennie asked, "have you met Mr. Whitman? He's Gob's dear friend, you know. And mine too. Mr. Whitman, Dr. Fie is also a friend of our Gob." Walt put his hand out for the doctor to shake. Dr. Fie considered it a moment before he took it.

"I'm a physician," Dr. Fie said, shaking Walt's hand hard and slow. "What's your profession, Mr. Whitman?"

"I write poems," Walt said.

"Mr. Whitman took care of our sick boys during the war," said Tennie. "Didn't you, Mr. Whitman?"

"Did you?" asked Dr. Fie. His smile was not friendly. "No doubt you healed them with verse."

"I gave them the medicine of daily affection and personal magnetism," Walt said.

"Very efficacious, I'm sure," said Dr. Fie.

"Dr. Fie," said Tennie, "do you doubt that magnetism is strong medicine?" She put out her finger and poked Dr. Fie in his broad chest and he leapt up, as if shocked. Tennie threw her head back and laughed very loud. This attracted her sister, who stepped gracefully across the room, nodding and smiling at her guests, until she came to where Walt was standing.

Mrs. Woodhull nodded at her sister and Dr. Fie, then asked Walt to walk with her. Walt was afraid she might ask him again to endorse her bid for the Presidency of the United States in 1872: She had declared herself a candidate back in April, in a letter to the *Herald*.

"Isn't Tennie a delight?" she asked, but before Walt could answer she started talking about the late war between the French and the Germans. She said Louis Napoleon fully deserved his defeat.

"Yes," said Walt. "Even with all his smartness, I consider him by far the meanest scoundrel that ever sat upon a throne."

"It's cheered Gob," said Mrs. Woodhull. "To have all the killing done with." She leaned over and whispered in his ear. "Yet he seems a little gloomy, this evening. Would you investigate the cause?" They rounded a giant fern, whose drooping branches were hung with roses. Gob was sitting alone on a deacon's bench. "Well, Mr. Whitman. I hope I will be in Washington this winter. You may expect me to call on you." Mrs. Woodhull gave him a little push towards Gob, who did indeed look gloomy, though earlier in the day he'd been very happy. He and Walt had had one of their customary walks along the river, and the sight of all the German steamers covered with bright flags had made Gob caper.

"Hello!" Walt said as he sat down. "I thought I'd lost you."

"I'm just having a rest."

"You've been mighty cruel to that flower." Gob had taken a rose from the fern and plucked out all its petals. They were scattered on his lap.

"Yes," said Gob. He took the petals up and began to manipulate them, rolling them into tiny cigar shapes and tying them together end to end. "How do you like the party?"

"It is more subdued than I expected. I thought there would be more emancipated dress. More Free Love. More people hanging upside down from the ceiling shouting out revolutionary slogans. I thought Dr. Graham would be here, peddling his sawdust muffins. Did you know your Aunt Tennie is the author of a pamphlet? She gave me a copy." Walt took it out of his pocket—*The Non-Participatory Female, and Other Natural Abominations.*

Gob laughed. He took the pamphlet and put it in the fern pot. Then he went back to weaving the petals. Walt watched silently. For five minutes, Gob's nine fingers made a quiet frenzy of obsessive, repetitive motion. When he was finished, he took Walt's hand and tied the bracelet around it. "There, my friend," he said. "A present for you." Walt held his hand up, pulled at the bracelet. It was as strong as any good yarn. Hank spoke: *Camerado, I give you my hand! I give you love more precious than money, I give you myself before preaching or law; Will you give me yourself? Will you come travel with me? Shall we stick by each other as long as we live?*

"Thank you," Walt said.

"It's just a trinket," said Gob. "Don't get all sobby-eyed. Look here, I need your opinion." He leaned across Walt and spread the branches of the fern, revealing a scene from the party: a young lady in conversation with a hideous man. Walt knew the man. It was ugly Benjamin Butler, the congressman who had wanted so badly to evict Mr. Johnson from his fancy house. Walt didn't know the young lady. She looked to be about twenty-five years old, and was very small and dark.

"Do you see her?" Gob asked. "Do you think that girl is pretty?"

"My boy," said Walt. "Princess Ugly of Ugly sur Ugly could stand next to Ben Butler and seem beautiful merely by comparison. She'll have to stand away from him before I can make a proper judgment."

Just then the doorbell rang, and from the guests a little cry went up proclaiming that Steven Pearl Andrews had arrived. Walt and Gob joined the crowd that gathered around the door to the parlor to greet him. A welcoming round of applause went up, louder and louder until a servant came into the room accompanied not by Mr. Andrews but by a small, skinny figure with a broken hat on his head and a dirty bag in his hand. The applause wavered. Perhaps because the man did not know what else to do, or perhaps because he was drunk, he took off his broken hat and bowed deeply. Tennie said, "Doc!" but didn't go forward to greet him. It was Walt who did that.

"Dr. Woodhull," Walt cried. "It is a great pleasure to see you again!" There was a stir among the guests, but nobody called for him to be thrown out, though he looked like a sandwich-board man and smelled like decay. He was desperate and drunk and charming, come back to his wife because he had heard of her fame from far away, and because he had nowhere else to go. Mrs. Woodhull received him graciously. So did her second husband, Colonel Blood, who took him upstairs to bathe and change, and gave him a too-big suit to wear until he could get some good clothes of his own.

Dr. Woodhull turned out to be the star of the party, telling hospital stories to Dr. Fie, talking about Armory Square with Walt, and scolding Mr. Butler for insulting the honor of the women of New Orleans. Everyone was kind to him save Gob, who wouldn't speak to him, and barely would look at him. Gob went back to his seat by the fern, and Walt stayed with him while he glowered at the floor.

"Who cares about that ridiculous drunk?" he said. "*I* am Dr. Woodhull."

Walt saw Mrs. Woodhull present her memorial to the combined Judiciary Committee of both houses of Congress in January of 1871. Tennie came with her, as did the young woman Gob and Walt had seen talking to Ben Butler at Mrs. Woodhull's September party. The three women all wore like attire: dark blue skirts and masculine coats, shirts, and ties. From the waist up they seemed to be dressed as men. Walt considered their three identical alpine hats, tipped at identical angles, and thought of Dr. Mary Walker. She would never have worn such a hat.

The three ladies sat together at a mahogany table in a little conference room in the Capitol—a faulty stove had poisoned the air in the much grander room where Mrs. Woodhull was supposed to make her speech. Various fat, red-nosed politicos sat across the table from her and her two supporters, waiting patiently for her to begin. Walt leaned against a bookshelf at the side of the room, feeling a bit dizzy. He had just recovered, in late November, from an attack of a recurring illness he was sure he'd contracted during his time at Armory Square, a weary, feverish malaise that Gob had skillfully lifted from him.

Besides congressmen and senators and reporters, the room was packed with famous radical females—Mrs. Woodhull had audaciously scheduled her presentation on the very day the Woman's Righters were opening their winter convention in the capital. Her plan was for them to cancel and come observe as Congress granted her the unprecedented honor of a formal and respectful interview. They did come to observe, and they whispered among themselves in shock. They thought Mrs. Woodhull and her sister—especially her sister—were scandalous. Everyone had heard how Mrs. Woodhull was a Free Lover, how she was divorced, how she had declared in her paper that marriage was the grave of love, and prostitution a profession that ought to be regulated into respectability.

Gob was there, too. He stood next to Walt, hand in hand with a pale child of five or six years, whom he called Pickie and who was, he said, his new ward. "I found him two weeks ago in a drift of snow in Madison Square," he told Walt. "Could I leave him there? Could I leave him to the weary mercy of an orphanage?" Pickie was a friendly child, but a strange one. Walt decided three minutes after meeting him that he had been driven mad by whatever cruelties he'd suffered before Gob found him.

"There you are!" Pickie said to Walt, when Gob had introduced them. "There you are at last!" He rushed over and gave Walt a hug around the leg. "Pick me up!" he cried. "Pick me up, Uncle Walt!" Walt took him up, and when he gave him an affectionate squeeze the boy made a curious noise, a deep, resonant burp, and the air around him suddenly reeked of blood. Walt put him down. The boy was stroking his face like a fly. Later, Walt noticed that there was a big hole in his beard, as if someone had taken a bite out of it. *Wonderful child!* Hank said. *Wonderful wonderful child!*

A very strange boy, but Gob seemed to love him, so Walt was kind to him, and never harped on the boy's obviously defective nature. Gob petted him and hugged him and fed him hard red candies from out of his pocket. Walt found his attention drawn to the two during the speech. They chattered and whispered like schoolboys, even when Walt shushed them. Gob and the boy were dressed alike in fine gray wool suits with blue waistcoats and neckties that matched the uniforms worn by Mrs. Woodhull, her sister, and the young lady, who, Walt had discovered, was called Maci Trufant. She was employed by Mrs. Woodhull as an editor at *Woodhull and Claflin's Weekly*. Walt had decided that she was pretty, after all.

Mrs. Woodhull started out nervous and pale, looking as if she might soon faint under all that powerful attention, but she soon bucked up. Spots of color appeared in her cheeks, and her voice grew strong and mellifluous. Her hand rose to her throat to stroke the petals of the tea rose fastened there. She was speaking from memory, so her other hand was free to wave and undulate, as if conducting the mood and attention of her audience.

It was a pretty speech, and a powerful one. Gob told Walt it had been dictated by Demosthenes, Mrs. Woodhull's spirit guide, that it had poured out of his mother's mouth as she lay on her own dining-room table, and that Colonel Blood was only able to keep up with her dictation because Stephen Pearl Andrews had taught him his newfangled method of shorthand. She pleaded for a declaratory act to the effect that women were already entitled to vote by the Fourteenth Amendment. "The sovereign will of the people," she said, "is expressed in our written Constitution, which is the supreme law of the land. The Constitution makes no distinction of sex. The Constitution defines a woman born or naturalized in the United States, and subject to the jurisdiction thereof, to be a citizen. And it recognizes the right of citizens to vote."

It was simple and glorious. Walt was sure that he ought to have paid better attention, because it seemed to him that something very important was transpiring in his presence. But he was distracted by little Pickie's serene pale face, and his candy-red mouth, and his chattering whisper. And being in the Capitol brought to mind the strange night Walt had spent with Gob here, so when he wasn't contemplating the boy he was contemplating that night. He was still afraid to go back to the Patent Office, lest someone recognize him as a thief or the accomplice to a thief.

After Mrs. Woodhull had finished, after she was applauded at length by every person in the room and whisked away in the arms of the now-adoring suffragists, Walt and Gob went out for a walk with Pickie on the Capitol grounds. They had a little time before they had to attend a party at the Willard Hotel in celebration of the great day. Walt and Pickie went out onto the snow, leaving Gob to stand on the great porch, where shortly Miss Trufant accosted him. He turned away from her after a few moments and came to Walt, packing snow in his hands as he walked.

Walt threw snowballs at Pickie as he climbed on the statue of Washington. Gob threw his own snowball, perfectly aimed, but Walt batted it aside before it could strike his head. Gob clapped his hands. All his autumn gloom was gone. Walt laughed just to see him laugh.

"How does your work go?" Walt asked him. Little Pickie jumped from Washington's arms and did somersaults in the snow. He sat up, lowered his chin, and snotted in his muffler.

"Excellently!" Gob said, smiling very wide and clapping Walt on the back. "So very well!"

The boy ran over and put his cold hands against Walt's cheeks, put his red lips to his ear and whispered to him. "My name is Pickie Beecher!" he said. "I come before."

"He aspires to greatness," said Gob. "Today he is a Beecher, tomorrow he'll be an Astor or a Vanderbilt." He leaned down and looked at the boy, who was dancing in place, but stopped as if Gob had stilled him with his gaze. "Woodhull," Gob said. "Now you are a Woodhull." The boy laughed and threw himself down in the snow to roll like a dog in filth. Walt was thinking, Woodhull, I like the sound of it, and Hank said, *Walt Woodhull, I like it too.* Walt looked away from Gob, who had lifted little Pickie up in his arms. He closed his eyes and imagined Gob, an angel of charity, reaching out to him instead of Pickie, as Walt lay abandoned and forgotten in the snow of Madison Square Park. He opened his eyes again, and saw Miss Trufant standing alone on the porch. When she noticed Walt looking, she turned and walked away.

"I have come to New York to die," said Canning Woodhull. He and Walt were in a saloon that catered specifically to veterans. There were old regimental flags on the walls, and groups of men—now amputated or perpetually despairing or with ruined health—still loyal to those flags, who sat under them and drank. "My beautiful wife has visions of the future. She sees a paradise coming—crystal cities and sunshiny days. I have told her, Mr. Whitman, that everybody is prescient, everyone can see the future. You can do it now. Close your eyes, calm your mind, extend your extraordinary vision through the mist of time. Do you see? There you are in your coffin. I wanted to be near my wife when I died."

"I like this place," Walt said. He had gone to Mrs. Woodhull's hoping to find Gob when there was no answer at the house on Fifth Avenue, but instead had found Dr. Woodhull. "The boys are still good," he said, looking about him at the devastated men, some not so very much older than Gob, who leaned against each other and sang "Jeff Davis's Dream."

"War wraiths," said Dr. Woodhull, and poured out his own story of ruin. He'd gone south after Armory Square was closed, and worked in a hospital in Charleston. Dr. Mary Walker went north to continue a career of professional female radicalism. Poor Canning Woodhull deteriorated without her, and without the war. "It made me something better than I am," he confessed to Walt. "I used to dream of illness, and how it might be conquered. Ah, I talked with Aesclepius in my dreams, and he told me secrets. Now I cannot even talk to his dog, and I dream only of my own death. There I am in my coffin. Do you see me?"

"No," said Walt. He tried to change the subject. "I am a good friend of your son. An exceptional young man. I think you must be very proud of him."

"He hates me!" Woodhull moaned. "Oh, Gob hates me with good reason. I only came up here to die. I would have been content just to crawl under her bed and slowly expire, but she was kind to me. She feted me and made her friends my friends, and now I have caused her the most immense trouble." It was May of 1871, convention time, and Mrs. Woodhull had charmed the National Woman Suffrage Association meeting in New York. But the very next day the papers had published an account of a lawsuit brought by her mother against Colonel Blood. The public eye looked closer at Mrs. Woodhull's family and discovered that there were other Claflins besides her sister, and they were a grappling, squabbling bunch. The family disharmony was aired in court, and it became public knowledge that Victoria Woodhull had two husbands living in her house. "I am a bother to everyone I meet!" Dr. Woodhull said. Walt patted his hand.

"Not to me, sir," he said.

"Oh Mr. Whitman," Woodhull said dismissively. "You are *everybody's* friend."

* * *

There were other strange nights, besides the one at the Patent Office and Ford's Theatre. Sometimes Gob would put on the hat, and Walt knew something curious would be presented to him as he walked with his friend in the city. They never had another session of naughty vandalism, but they wandered in naughty places, up Front Street and Water Street, where thugs stepped out of the river fog on cold evenings, only to be thrust aside by Gob's strong arm. Once they leaned over the water and Gob shone a light on the river. Walt saw a baby, dead from a smashed head, floating a foot or two beneath the surface, one hand in its mouth and the other reaching towards him as if to tug at Walt's fascinating beard. "The river is full of them," Gob said softly. "Any day of the week you can come down and see them floating." He took Walt farther up South Street, to a slip where a French steamer was docked, where they waited in the darkness, Walt asking repeatedly what they were waiting for, and Gob only saying, "Patience." Suddenly, white light came blasting out of the sky, so bright Walt thought they must be in the midst of some impossibly silent explosion. But then there was noise, the spit and hum of an electric arc light burning high on the ship. "Isn't it beautiful?" Gob asked him, luxuriating in the light as if it were warm sunshine. Walt held up his hand in front of his face, thinking it looked in that light like the hand of a corpse.

Another night they headed for Greenwood Cemetery in Brooklyn. Walt paused under the entrance, a massive sandstone edifice that looked like a little cathedral. Moonlit statues stared down at them while Gob picked the lock on the gates: a group representing the raising of the widow's son, another representing Faith, Hope, Memory, and Love. "It should be your motto," Walt said of the phrase carved into the stone above them. They passed inside, pausing, before they had walked very far, by the monuments of Charlotte Canda and De Witt Clinton. Little Pickie was with them on this graveyard outing. He leapfrogged over headstones, ran down into the empty moonshade beneath a willow. The three of them wandered over acres of cemetery, Gob offering comments every now and then: "There are one hundred and fifty thousand buried here," or "Walt, we are gliding into eternity."

Walt visited the grave of McDonald Clarke. "What a fellow!" he said to Gob. It made him glad, to think of the man, but Gob started to cry. "The heavens ought to open up!" he shouted. "They ought to weep!" Gob pounded his fist on the headstone, and the heavens did open up: a heavy summer rain began to fall, dark and thick and warm.

Each strange evening would end with a trip to Gob's house, to the fifth floor. They'd walk into Gob's room, passing by the stone circle (not even casting a glance at it), and pause before the iron door. Gob would throw it open, revealing his enormous workshop and his engine, a great nonsensical conglomeration of mechanical parts that sat under an enormous telescopic gaselier whose fittings were cast in the shape of birds that shot flame out of their beaks. Glass tubes and iron gears, steel ribs, yards and yards of twisting, wrist-thick bundles of copper wire, here and there a bone, after all, from the theater—it was bigger every time Walt saw it. *It's for you*, Hank would say. *You are a kosmos*. Gob would say, "Won't you help me, Walt? Won't you help me win?" as he started a steam engine or activated a battery. "It's not ready yet," Gob would say, "but it will be, and then it will require your help to be complete. Will you give it to me, Walt?"

"Yes," was always his answer. Walt would reach his hand out and touch a copper pipe, cold despite the June heat in the house. Pickie would dance around in a circle, saying, "Little brother!"

Sometimes they'd drink on these nights, but even when they didn't, Walt would have a drunk feeling by this time. "You are the most important, Walt," Gob would say to him as they lay in bed together. "There are others who will help me, but no one is as important as you are." He'd sleep as dawn came, and wake with Gob's head heavy as a chunk of wood on his shoulder. He'd look over and see the iron door, closed again and locked, and he'd have something in his belly, a question turned into a feeling—did it all happen? Every time Walt woke up he made a decision; he didn't care to know the answer, he didn't care about the answer. Gob was real, their beautiful, mountain-high, sea-deep affinity was real, squeezing him was real, his snort and his sleepy smile were real and natural and perfect.

Walt was invited to read a poem at the fortieth annual exhibition of the American Institute, a festival of industry. On September 7 he went with Gob, Tennie, and Miss Trufant to the Cooper Institute.

"I think you'll be a most welcome change from Mr. Greeley," Miss Trufant said to him before he mounted the dais to begin. It was usually Horace Greeley who gave the address every year. "He blathers."

"Thank you, my dear," Walt said.

The displays were still being assembled when Walt, dressed in a gray suit and white vest—gifts from Gob—climbed a stand to open the exhibition with his poem. On the fringes of the crowd, men in their shirtsleeves worked with hammers and saws and wrenches to put in order the displays of goods and machinery. They put down their tools as Walt read, so by the time he was half done the racket of assembly had quieted. He was thinking as he read of Gob, who stood holding Walt's Panama hat at the foot of the stage. Tennie and Miss Trufant stood next to him. The iron door swung open in Walt's mind, in the same way that the doors of Armory Square sometimes swung open to release memories of sickness and dying and death. The door opened and Walt saw gears and batteries, smelled acid and coal and fresh white steam. He heard Hank's voice reading with him as he spoke: *Earth's modern wonder, history's seven outstripping, high rising tier on tier with glass and iron facades.*

When the poem was done, after Walt had retired to enthusiastic applause, Gob took him around to look at the displays. Gob was keen on all of them, a sewing machine or a buttonhole maker put the same light in his eyes as a screw propeller or shiny electric engine, and he seemed to know all the intimate details of every machine's operation. They examined a harvester that could clear a field of oats in twenty-two minutes, a furniture suite made entirely of india rubber—here they lost Tennie, who sat down in an intricately carved chair and held court for the workmen.

"I think science is his religion," Maci Trufant said. Walt talked with her some, as Gob stared, open-mouthed, at a copper vat the size of a cottage.

Mrs. Woodhull held a reception for Walt at her home. All that night, Gob was in an ebullient, bouncy mood, the result, Walt figured, of his spending the day at a celebration of machines. Tennie, inspired by Walt's poem, was playing "find the muse." "Not here!" she'd say, peeking under a chair cushion. She looked behind curtains and said, "Not here either! No, she is installed among the kitchenware!" Walt couldn't tell if she was mocking him or not.

This night, it was Walt who retreated to the bench behind the fern, peeking out occasionally to watch Gob circulating among the elegant radicals, laughing with Tennie, putting his hand on Maci Trufant's arm. Eventually Mrs. Woodhull came and sat down next to Walt, and invited him to a Spiritualist convention up in Troy, for which she would depart late in the evening. Walt politely declined.

"Well," she said. "I think your poem would be well received there. I am sorry I missed it earlier. You see, my duty to the workers kept me busy all day." She'd taken on new responsibilities recently, besides those of publisher and broker and presidential candidate. Now she was the head of Section Twelve of the International Workingmen's Association. Walt said she must be fearless, to associate with Communists. "Yes," she said. "Demosthenes tells me, 'Be radical, be radical, but not too damned radical.' Still, I go where I must in Heaven and on the earth. If I worried what people said of me, then I would stay home all day in bed, prostrate with nervousness. But I think you know as well as I do what it is to be maligned by distempered, ignorant maleficos." She thrust out her wrists, showing him how she'd sewn the 120th psalm into the sleeves of her dress.

" 'I am for peace,' " Walt said, " 'but when I speak, they are for war.' "

"It's not easy, is it, Mr. Whitman, trying to improve the world?"

Maci Trufant and Gob were married in April of 1872, in Plymouth Church. How they came to be married in the church of glorious, greasy-headed Henry Beecher, Walt didn't know. He had been under the impression that Beecher and Mrs. Woodhull were enemies for all that Theodore Tilton, Beecher's chippish adjulant, had been a near constant presence at Mrs. Woodhull's house the previous summer. Walt's misery was compounded by the seating arrangements—he was put next to Tennie and the other Claflins. "Mr. Whitman," Tennie said to him as they were waiting for the ceremony to begin, "you've cut your hair and beard all away!"

"Yes," said Walt. "All my acquaintances are in anger and despair and go about wringing their hands. 'Who are you?' they ask me."

"I like it," Tennie said. "It's taken ten years off you. Why do you deliberately cultivate the aspect of old age?" She looked like she wanted to say more, but she was hushed by music.

Walt put his hand to his greatly shortened beard. He'd cut it all away in anguish when he'd gotten the telegram from Gob announcing his engagement. The news had come as a total surprise. Walt had just returned to Washington from New York, where he'd taken a fat leave of two months spent almost entirely with Gob, during which time there had been no mention of the pending marriage. When Walt got the news, he had sat up all night in his favorite chair, with a glass of whiskey punch in one hand and a letter, recently received from Tennyson, in the other. "He says I have a large and lovable nature," Walt had said to Hank, who all that bad night would only say one thing over and over, *You are a kosmos.*

The wedding was a simple and beautiful ceremony, marred only by Tennie's constant whispering that her nephew and Miss Trufant were making a terrible mistake. Any other church besides Plymouth would have been bursting with the guests—Gob had joked to Walt that his wedding was a campaign event. Mrs. Woodhull's star was taking crazy dips and turns. It seemed to Walt that she could not appreciate how different species of radicalism were immiscible, how a Woman's Righter could hate her for being a Communist, how a Communist could hate her for being a Spiritualist, how a Spiritualist could think her a fool for putting too much faith in Graham Crackers.

There was no one Mrs. Woodhull could not alienate, but it seemed there were always people who loved her. The wedding and its association with respectable Mr. Beecher brought out all her old supporters. She sat looking prim and regal as her son was married to her protégé. A moon-faced reverend, not much less dramatic than Mr. Beecher, invoked for the couple the perpetual tropical luxuriance of blessed love. *But when I hear*, Hank said, *of the brotherhood of lovers, how it was with them, how together through life, through dangers, odium, unchanging, long and long, through youth and through middle and old age, how unfaltering, how affectionate and faithful they were. Then I am pensive—I hastily walk away filled with the bitterest envy*.

The guests filled up a whole ferry getting back to Manhattan for the celebration at Mrs. Woodhull's house. Walt tried to hide away in the bow, but little Pickie followed him there.

"Well, Pickie," Walt said, "now you have a mama." Pickie shrugged and showed him two uncut emeralds, which he pulled from his pocket as Walt talked. "They are for my brother but you may have one, since you are for my brother also." When Walt didn't take either jewel, he put them away and said, "My brother is absent. Your brother is absent. They are absent from this boat, absent from there and there." Pickie pointed with either hand at Brooklyn and Manhattan, and then up over his head. "They are absent from the sky. The whole world is made up of the absence of brothers." He took Walt's hand, and stood with him in the bow, under swarms of gulls flying in circles above the boat, looking back at the milling radicals swarming like the gulls around Gob and his bride. Walt had been the very first to congratulate them—he had made sure of that, that his congratulations were first and heartiest. He'd kissed Gob and said, "My dear boy, I am so very happy for you." Now Walt looked away from Gob and the new Mrs. Woodhull and stared out across the water at the place where the tower for the great bridge rose high on the Brooklyn shore. Had he gone there one strange night with Gob? Had Gob borne him up to the top of the Brooklyn tower and showed him the impossible vista? It all seemed unreal—every year of perfect loving comradeship seemed unreal and impossible, a ridiculous dream inspired by loneliness. *I too knotted the old knot of contrariety, blabb'd, blushed, resented, lied, stole, grudg'd.*

"Oh, be quiet, Hank," Walt said, for the first time ever. Hank was quiet, but another voice spoke next to him.

"Mr. Whitman," said big Dr. Fie. "You look pensive."

Little Pickie took his hand out of Walt's, pointed at the Brooklyn tower, and said, "It comes before and makes the way. It is like me."

"Yes," said Dr. Fie. "Run along, Pickie." The boy ran a few steps and stopped, and started to grab at gulls when they swooped close to the deck. Dr. Fie nodded at the tower. "Can you imagine the bridge?"

Walt said, "I think it will be glorious." Dr. Fie smiled, and then he leaned close to Walt's face.

"I'm sure you do. I'm sure you can see it in all its glory. You are so precious and able, Mr. Whitman. You with your swaggering walk and your great soul and your distinctive absence of necktie. But I know you, sir. I know you well, and you are not very much at all. You think you are special, and yet really you are not. Really, sir, you are nobody at all. Really you are the least important person in all the world." Dr. Fie went away, then, not elaborating on his attack, or explaining it. Instead he took Pickie into his big arms and walked back to the crowd. Walt hung on the rail and looked down at the rushing water. Usually he was sensitive to cruel words, but it meant nothing to him, today, to be attacked by a stranger.

Canning Woodhull died two weeks after his son's wedding. Walt went up to see him buried at Greenwood Cemetery, though he had planned not to return to New York for a long time. He'd encouraged his mother to move to Camden with George, so he could visit her but not have to look at all the places in Brooklyn and Manhattan—every last place, everywhere, it seemed—where he and Gob had wandered.

It was a pretty, white funeral, filled with joyous songs—a Spiritualist funeral. Mrs. Woodhull and Tennie and Maci Trufant and all the Claflin ladies wore matching white dresses of white silk, with lace at their throats, and white skirts that became stained green at the hems by cemetery grass. Gob and Dr. Fie wore white suits, with white silk ties and diamond stickpins. Pickie Beecher was dressed to match them precisely, except he had a ruby pin in his small tie, that glinted there like a spot of fresh wet blood.

The joyous white mourners were gathered next to a coffin draped like an Easter altar with white linen and lilies. It was lowered down into the ground while everybody sang a very happy song. Mrs. Woodhull herself officiated—Mr. Beecher was nowhere to be seen. She spoke elegantly and harshly for the dead man, saying her husband was a genius, selfish and inconsolable in his need for drink, and that death had translated him into a happy spirit who worked with all the other spirits to hurry the day when Earth and Heaven would be married into a single perfect place. Walt stood with his arm around Gob, who'd sidled up to him as his mother spoke, and listened. Walt was dressed in a respectable black suit, and felt he must look like a penguin in a wilderness of ice.

Gob stayed on after his mother and her family had left. Even after the new Mrs. Woodhull went wandering off among the tombstones with Dr. Fie, he stayed, looking down into the grave. Because Gob had asked him to, Walt stayed with him. Gob began to cry. Not, Walt was sure, because he loved his father, but simply because he loved all the dead. Walt gave him a long squeeze and sang a song for him, one as joyous as those sung by the white mourners. He leaned over, singing loud and sweet into the grave:

"My days are swiftly gliding by, and I a pilgrim stranger,
Would not detain them as they fly, those hours of toil and danger;
For O we stand, on Jordan's strand, our friends are passing over."

At the end of June, Walt took a trip to New England, to read a poem at Dartmouth College for its commencement. It was a pleasant journey, but it did nothing to distract him from his unhappiness. Maci Trufant came from this country.

He did not wish to hate her. He was not jealous, no matter what Hank said. He felt sad, and he felt a fool, and his stomach hurt when he thought of them together, so close and so happy. A person could not have two Camerados—such intimacies of the soul could only be shared with one other—and Gob had chosen the girl to be his. *Does the tide hurry, seeking something, and never give up? O I the same*, Hank said. But Walt did intend to give up. He was steaming down the Hudson on the Fourth of July, dozing as the boat passed through a series of thunderstorms punctuated by bright skies, when he made his decision. As he slept, he dreamed he was a little spider, throwing out silk from his belly, delicate tendrils that drifted into a void in search of a nonexistent other. When he woke he took out his latest daybook from his pocket and made an entry: *To GIVE UP ABSOLUTELY and for good, from this present hour, this FEVERISH, FLUCTUATING, useless undignified pursuit of GW—too long (much too long) persevered in, so humiliating. It must come at last and had better come now—LET THERE FROM THIS HOUR BE NO FALTERING at all henceforth (NOT ONCE, under any cir-*

cumstances)—avoid seeing him—OR ANY MEETING WHATEVER, FROM THIS HOUR FORTH, FOR LIFE.

Oh Walt, said Hank. *You can't mean it.*

Walt and Gob wrote letters back and forth, through the rest of the summer and the fall of 1872. *Work keeps me here,* Walt wrote. And *Mother has gone to Camden, so now really I have little reason to return to Brooklyn.* And *I am very sorry for your mother's declining fortunes. I think it was a mistake for her to clobber Mr. Beecher—he and his friends will clobber her back hard and long.* Mrs. Woodhull's fortunes had indeed taken a precipitous dive after seeming to peak in May, when she gathered a faction of Woman's Righters to herself and formed the People's Party, who nominated her as their candidate for President, with Frederick Douglass as her unwitting running mate. After her nomination, people began most vigorously to persecute her for her beliefs. She was turned out of her fancy house, and business dried up at her brokerage. Beecher was her enemy again. Indeed, she perceived him and his sisters Catharine and Harriet to be the chief architects of her misery. She retaliated by publishing an account of Henry Beecher's affair with one of his parishioners, the wife of Theodore Tilton. Mr. Beecher practiced as Mrs. Woodhull preached—why was he not denigrated as she was? A man named Comstock had her and Tennie and Colonel Blood arrested for sending obscene materials through the mail. They spent election day in jail, and remained there intermittently, from October on.

I miss you, Walt, Gob wrote. But his life seemed to be proceeding very smoothly and happily without Walt in it. His work went very well—*You should see how our little friend has grown,* Gob wrote, meaning his engine. He reported that his wife got more beautiful every day, and every time he put pen to paper the weather in New York was balmy or crisp or the beautiful snow was falling like a blessing. (In Washington, meanwhile, it was sweltering or bitter stinging cold or ice fell from the sky and slew horses by the dozen.) Little Pickie was contented and fat, but he missed his Uncle Walt. *A very happy family, the three of you*, Walt wrote. *How nice for you, my boy.*

Eventually, Walt stopped answering letters. For a while he sent only tiny notes. *So busy! Will write soon!* Once, in a little fit of loneliness and spite, he sent just an empty envelope, and then he sent nothing. Gob's letters he placed unopened in a cigar box, which he hid in his wardrobe. Hank scolded him endlessly, becoming increasingly shrill—*You are a kosmos. He is a builder. You must be together. You must help him. How can we come back if you don't help him?* Walt ignored him, or scolded back, and at last drove Hank to silence. Then his winter was truly silent and dark and lonely. Walt trudged back and forth to work, looking like an old man again with his beard and hair grown long, and now walking like an old man, too. He slept more and more, though he wished not to, because Hank and Gob waited in his dreams to plead with him.

"You are not he," Walt would say to them both. He dreamed of the reviewing stand in winter, without Mr. Lincoln and without the parade. Only the sign remained, but now it spelled *How are you, Walt?* Hank and Gob were with him on the stand. "You are not the Camerado, and you are not the Camerado," Walt said. Because they were not. One had abandoned him for death, the other for marriage, and neither, he understood finally, had reciprocated his affection and his friendship—their love was never as pure and strong as his love. In the dream, Hank and Gob would crowd around him, enfolding him in their arms. "We do love you," they'd say. "Brother, father, son, we love you—you are our love and our hope. Come back to us. Come back to New York." Then Gob would put his earnest beautiful face in Walt's and say, "Help me win, Walt, please help me win." They would squeeze him and squeeze him until he woke, shouting, "I won't, I won't! Leave me be!"

* * *

Walt went back to New York in the second week of January of 1873 because he wanted to sleep without Gob and Hank pestering him all night long, and also because he thought that seeing Gob again would help rid him of the weighty feeling—the deep grief that he could feel in his belly, as if he'd eaten stones. This feeling was on him like the old feeling he'd had before he went down to Washington looking for his brother. Walt felt tired and hopeless, as if all his days had been lived for nothing, and all his work was nothing more than whispering into his own hands—no one had heard, and no one cared. On the train he slept a dreamless, squeezeless sleep, the first in months. When he woke he felt no less weary.

When Gob opened his door and found Walt standing there, he said, "You're just in time." Beyond the foyer, Walt could see that the house was transformed. Walls had been knocked down, ceilings removed through all five floors, so what was formerly many rooms on many floors was now a huge barnlike edifice spanned by immense arches like the ribs of some leviathan. Gob put on his coat and pushed Walt out the door. "We'd better hurry."

"Where are we going?" Walt asked.

"To hear a speech," Gob said. "Didn't you get my letter? You were expressly invited, and now here you are."

"I got it," Walt said. "I've been dreaming. . . ." He tried to tell Gob that he'd been haunted by him in dream after dream, but for the first time since he was an infant Walt found himself at a total loss for words.

"Ah," said Gob. "We can talk later." Dr. Fie was waiting in the stable with a carriage all ready. He tipped his hat to Walt. "Mr. Whitman," he said. When Walt and Gob were settled in their seats, he took off, driving the horses like a fiend. "Will's a brave driver," Gob said. "He used to drive an ambulance. We'll make it in time."

"Is your mother speaking from jail?" Walt asked.

"Jail?" said Gob. "No, she's escaped! She's escaped to New Jersey."

"My mama, too," Walt said. Gob had his arm around him and was squeezing, but it was not oppressive, as in the dreams. Walt wanted more of it.

Federal marshals were guarding all the entrances to the Cooper Institute, waiting, Gob said, to snatch up his mama if she dared show her face. Walt asked if she would really come.

"Of course she will," said Gob. Walt looked around the rooms for Mrs. Woodhull, but found Gob's wife instead. She was standing amid the crowd, all by herself, looking very tired. She returned his stare for a few moments, then shifted her attention to the stage, where a lady had come forward and begun to talk.

"The enemies of free speech," she said, "have ringed this place round with marshals and police. Though our friends are free from Ludlow Street Jail, the custodians of the law guard the doors of the institute, and neither Mrs. Woodhull nor Miss Claflin can, no matter how much they may desire it, appear upon this platform tonight." This announcement was greeted with howls and hisses.

The lady was trying to shout over the noise of the crowd that she had been deputized to read the speech, and that she would do so if they would only quiet down. As she shouted, an old Quakeress, dressed in a long gray cloak, a coal-scuttle bonnet, and heavy veils, joined the lady on the stage. The old woman walked half bent over, and held her hands before her as if blind. People laughed at her, thinking she was just a confused old biddy who had somehow managed to wander up on the stage, until suddenly she pushed the cloak back so it fell off her shoulders, and tore off her bonnet and veils. Victoria Woodhull stood revealed before the audience.

"Well," said Gob. "There she is." Her hair was all in disarray and her dress rumpled, but she looked proud and mighty. Her commanding presence precipitated a hush over the whole hall. The lady who had begun the speech smiled exultantly and said, "Ladies and gentlemen, I give you Victoria C. Woodhull!"

Cheers and applause filled the hall, but Mrs. Woodhull held up her hands for silence and got it immediately. "My friends and fellow citizens!" she began. "I come into your presence from the American Bastille, to which I was consigned by the cowardly servility of the age. I am still held under heavy bonds to return to that cell, upon a scandalous charge trumped up by the ignorant or the corrupt officers of the law, conspiring with others to deprive me, under the falsest and shallowest pretenses, of my inherited privileges as an American citizen. In my person, the freedom of the press is assailed, and stricken down, and such has been the adverse concurrence of circumstances that the press itself has tacitly consented, almost with unanimity, to this sacrilegious invasion of one of the most sacred of civil rights!"

She detailed all the particulars of the conspiracy against her. She told how Anthony Comstock was Beecher's tool, how his agents had ransacked the offices of the *Weekly,* how Mr. Comstock had sworn to destroy her utterly if he had to spend all the energies of his life upon the job. But she didn't look as if anybody could destroy her, that night. She was vibrant and magnetic and fascinating—even the marshals stared at her in wonder, and listened raptly. They seemed to forget that they were obligated to arrest her. Walt forgot some of his sadness, watching her.

At last, Mrs. Woodhull made her concluding exclamation. "Sexual freedom, the last right to be claimed for man in the long struggle for universal emancipation, the least understood and the most feared of all the freedoms, but destined to be the most beneficial of any—will burst upon the world!" There were roars of approval. She tore the rose from her throat and hurled it like a bomb into the crowd, then ran off the stage and up the aisle, through the reaching arms of people who tried to touch her as she passed, all the way to the back door, where two marshals were standing. She stopped, crossed her hands at the wrists, and surrendered.

"That was that," said Gob.

* * *

Walt and Gob went to Pfaff's after the speech. Gob seemed uninterested in visiting his mother in jail. "She won't be there for long," he said confidently, "and I have a more pressing concern, tonight."

"What's that?" Walt asked.

"You, of course," said Gob. "You've come back to me, just as I hoped you would and knew you would." They sat together for a while in silence, Gob's hand on Walt's hand, not touching their beer. Every so often, Gob would reach out to lift Walt's chin so he could look into his eyes. "Yes," he'd say, with deep satisfaction. "Yes, there you are."

They went for a walk, after Pfaff's, a long walk arm in arm, through the late-night crowds on Broadway, up even into the park, where they sat by the lake, holding hands in the same place where Tennie had found Walt's planted book years before. Ghostly-looking sheep were out on the meadow.

They still had not said very much to each other. Walt wanted to protest, to say it could not be as it was before, to say, "You are not he." But it was easier not to speak, and Walt had a fear that if he made a noise, Gob would take his hand away from him and never give it back again.

"My work is done," Gob said at last, after an hour of sitting. "It's complete. It only lacks you, Walt."

"Me," Walt said softly. Gob did not take away his hand.

"Did you think I was lying when I said I needed you? When I begged you to help me win, did you think it was a jest? They want to come back. Can't you hear them begging to come back?"

"Not anymore," Walt said. Though he'd spoken to Gob of Hank, he'd never mentioned the boy's posthumous chattiness.

Gob stood and pulled Walt up after him. "Come home with me," Gob said. "I'll show you something wonderful."

"Your wife is there," Walt said, but Gob ignored him. Now, Walt wished Gob would let go his hand. He felt afraid again, as he had been on the stage when he met Gob for the first time. Gob pulled him along, all the way down to the house on Fifth Avenue, where little Pickie opened the door just as they approached it and said, "Welcome Master, welcome Kosmos."

Inside the house, Walt got a better look at the transformations it had undergone. "My little brother," Pickie said, waving his arms around at everything. The engine was everywhere. It had grown down from its fifth-floor room, through the ceilings and the walls until, it seemed, it had become the house itself. Here was a big red dude of a fire engine, there was an electromagnet as big as a man. But one part stood out because it was larger than any other, and because it was located in what might as well have been the center of a thing that was otherwise mischievously asymmetric. That part looked like the gate to Greenwood Cemetery, complete with a gatehouse, and the whole thing sheltered under a pair of wings. The gatehouse was lovely, a little church of glass and bone and steel. It was full of gears—visibly turning through the glass—which ranged in size from one story high to as small as the nail of Pickie's thumb, and they spilled out of the gatehouse to spin all over the room. The gears turned all sorts of contrivances, most of which seemed to be doing no useful work at all. The very biggest gears conspired to turn the wings—Walt squinted at them a few moments before he realized that they were glass wings, made of photographic negative plates.

Dr. Fie and the new Mrs. Woodhull were both there, looking grave and serious. "Are you here?" Dr. Fie asked him, sounding cordial for once. He put his big finger out in front of him and poked Walt in the belly. Walt did not bother to answer the question. Dr. Fie looked to be drunk or confused or in pain. Maci Trufant Woodhull said, "God bless you, Mr. Whitman."

"There it is," said Gob, sweeping his hand out to indicate the whole house. "The engine. It's complete, except for you. There's a place for you in it, Walt. I need you to go in it, and then it will bring them back, all the six hundred thousand, my brother and Will's brother and Maci's brother and your Hank, too. All the dead of the war, all the dead of all the wars, all the dead of the past. We'll lick death tonight, Walt, if you'll help us. I'm ready. Will's ready, and Maci is ready. Pickie is ready and the engine is ready. Are you ready?"

Walt opened his mouth to answer, paused a moment without saying anything, and then he ran away. He fled past Will Fie, pushing him aside when he tried to stand in his way, and knocked down Maci Trufant. He ran, jumping over wires and dodging under steel struts and copper pipes, until he was in the foyer, and then out the door. He ran down the marble steps and then down the street, not slowing till he had passed Madame Restell's house and the Catholic cathedral. He stopped, looked back for pursuit, and saw there was none. He sat on the steps of the still-unfinished cathedral and put his head in his hands. He tried to quiet his fear but found that he could not. Once, as a child, he'd almost drowned at the beach. A powerful wave had picked him up and thrown him down against the sea bottom, and held him there as if it were trying to murder him. He'd got a lungful of water and was quite sure he was going to die. Even back then, when he never gave a thought to death, when he did not even know yet what it was, it still frightened him. Now he was frightened again in just that same way, blind panic filled him up. When he heard the voice, he thought at first that it was Gob calling after him, but it was Hank, long silent but shouting now: *Walt! Walt Walt Walt!*

"No," Walt said.

Walt. Please help. I want to come back. We all want so bad to come back. No one can do it but you. Nobody loves us like you. Please go back you have to go back you have to nobody loves us like you.

"I'm afraid," Walt said.

Don't be afraid it's a good thing you're going to do. The best ever.

"I can't," Walt said. But Hank said *you can* and *you must*, and so Walt did. He went slowly back up the street to Gob's house. The door was still open. Gob, his wife, little Pickie, and Dr. Fie were all waiting patiently, as if they knew he wouldn't be long in returning. They put him in the gatehouse, bundling him with wires into an iron and glass chair. Young Mrs. Woodhull settled Mr. Lincoln's hat on his head. Now it was decorated with a corona of silver spikes, each of which plugged into a hole in the crystal wall of the gatehouse.

"Bless you, Mr. Whitman," said Maci Woodhull, again as she put the hat on him, and she kissed him on the forehead as a mother might do. Walt thought then of his mother, thought he saw her bustle by outside with a stack of pancakes on a plate, thought he caught the wholesome odor that fell off her.

"We're ready," said Dr. Fie, and closed the crystal door of the gatehouse.

Gob put his face up against it and called through. "Don't be afraid, Walt," he said. "It's all for the best."

Hank said it too. *It's for me. It's for us. Thank you, Walt.*

Walt watched through the door while Pickie ran speedily up and down ladders, flipping switches, closing connections, activating batteries, while Dr. Fie stoked up engines all over the room, while Gob's wife went around spinning up cranks and adjusting knobs. Gob held up his own hand before his face and stared into it. Walt tried to imagine the aftermath of this night. Not, he was sure, the abolition of death. For all that Gob was strange and wonderful, despite all the extraordinary things he'd shown Walt during their strange evenings, he knew no one could make that happen. Sparks might light up the Manhattan sky like fireworks, the whole house might fall down and leave them miraculously untouched, a whale might be driven to swim through the Narrows and throw itself on the shore of the Battery, but when dawn came the next day, the dead would still be dead. Hank might finally be silent, and Walt would leave this place and not think of Gob ever again. Maybe that would be the great miracle, that Walt would be true to his nonexistent Camerado but finally not suffer for his faith.

"Now!" said Gob, and Hank said, *Goodbye, Walt.* Unnatural light flooded the gatehouse, and a great noise started up in the air all around him—a cranking, grinding, coughing machine noise that settled into a giant breathing noise like that noise of the sea. Magic images danced all around Walt—the faces of boys and men cast on the floor, and dead bodies, torn by bullets and shells, shimmering on the glass walls. He looked down at his chest and saw a picture there—a row of bodies laid out along a fence.

Goodbye, Hank said again, very sad, and Walt thought of how he'd sat with him as he died. Hank's eyes had darted fearfully in his head, and he had clutched Walt's arm with great strength despite the morphine Dr. Woodhull had given him to soothe his last hours. He'd not said goodbye, then, just "No," over and over again until he couldn't get the breath out to make the word, but still his mouth formed it silently, "No." "Goodbye, my dear," Walt had said, giving him a rich, desperate kiss on his lips.

Walt stiffened in his iron-and-glass chair because a terrible pain filled his head, as if the hat spikes had suddenly been thrust into his troubled brain. The pain moved out down his neck, through his chest and arms, his belly and loins and legs. He let out a hoarse scream, and wished he had run harder and farther from this place, wished he'd run right off the island and kept on going south till he reached the very tip of Florida, because it seemed he would have to run very far away to be safe from this immense agony. He screamed again and again, then called out to Gob, who was standing just beyond the crystal door with light in his hand. Walt cried out to him, but the pain only got worse. Walt spoke again, much softer, and then again, so soft he wasn't even sure if he made a noise.

"Help me," Walt said.

IT WAS TIME TO RUN OFF TO THE WAR: THEY'D BEEN MARKING off their growth against a crooked doorjamb, and very recently had reached a notch representing a height Tomo figured suitable for soldier boys. Tomo thought they could pass for fifteen, and if they couldn't fight they could at least be company musicians. They both had bugles, though Gob was not so fine a bugler as Tomo. Gob knew the calls, but they came out like the bleating of an anxious sheep. It would do, Tomo said of Gob's playing. It was Tomo's firm belief that the whole army was desperate for musicians.

Tomo dragged Gob from their bed, a square of ticking stuffed with dried corn husks. They slept on it with one blanket and no pillow but each other's back. Gob said, "Don't get rough. I'm rising." But he lay there a few moments more.

"I'll kick you," said Tomo. Gob rose to his knees, then to his feet. He'd gone to sleep in his clothes; he had only to put on his shoes to be ready. Tomo had procured new Jefferson bootees for them the previous summer and put them aside for this night.

Gob stood on the bed. "Goodbye room," he said, taking in one last look at the place he and Tomo had lived almost all their life. It was a small room, not more than three times larger than their bed. The rough pine floor yielded splinters endlessly. The ceiling was stained with candle smoke. "Goodbye bed," said Gob. "Goodbye books." They did not have many books, but Gob loved them all. He ran from the bed, knelt by a little stack of books that leaned against the far wall, near the wardrobe, and picked one up.

"We got no room for books," said Tomo, standing by the open window, though Gob knew he had *Hardee's Tactics* crammed in his own bag in the orchard.

"Just one more," said Gob, but he only touched the books, and did not pick one up. He already had a complete works of Shakespeare in his knapsack, the gift of the town schoolmarm, who usually threw fruit at them when they put their heads in her window and looked in on the schoolroom where they were not welcome, but sometimes, if they made her angry enough, threw books. Some of their library came to them by way of Miss Maggs's furious hand; most came from their mama.

"Goodbye house," said Tomo in the birch tree that grew close up against their window, stepping carefully down from branch to branch. Gob followed him slowly, not less nimble but more fearful. "Goodbye mill. Goodbye barn. Goodbye Mr. Splitfoot." Mr. Splitfoot was their grandpa Buck's Appaloosa. Tomo waved to the barn as they passed it.

"Goodbye orchard," Gob said softly as they walked among apple and pear trees that yielded abundant fruit every autumn.

They walked to a clearing that industrious Tomo had made himself, hacking away to make a little round place among the trees. Their knapsacks were hidden in the clearing, behind a wall they'd built of mud and broken bricks. Scarecrow Confederates—props for games—looked real where they crouched behind the wall. Gob half expected one to issue a dry wooden challenge at them as he approached. Gob helped his brother into his knapsack, then shrugged into his own while Tomo lifted it onto his back.

"It's burdensome," Gob said, not precisely complaining, just noting the fact. In his sack he carried the book; three candles; an extra shirt; two pairs of drawers; wool socks stolen from Buck (their grandma made them with hexes against wetness and cold knitted into the fabric); a pocketknife; a tin plate; a little fork and a big spoon; and a wedge of fatback half the size of his head, wrapped in a piece of waxed paper. A canteen slung from a strap on the sack banged against his chest as he walked. His bugle swung from a strap on the other side.

"Like it ought to be," said Tomo. Gob knew his brother's pack was just as heavy. Tomo was outfitted just like Gob, except he had two pair of their grandma's magic socks, and a knife upon whose bone handle were carved scenes from the life of Andrew Jackson. He also carried all their money, ten dollars held back last summer from their humbug earnings.

"Goodbye Anna," said Tomo. They paused in front of the house. "Goodbye Aunt Tennie. Goodbye Uncle Malden. Goodbye Aunt Utica. Goodbye Mama. And goodbye Buck, God damn you straight to hell."

Gob looked at the silent house. Darkness made it look less like a shack, and hid the flaking paint and the sagging rails on the porch. The house sat on a hill above the town. Another hill rose behind the orchard, and beyond that hill rose wooded hills where lived a mad hedge wizard called the Urfeist. It was rumored that he was incredibly ancient and withered, that he was a contemporary of General Washington, that he was an Indian half-breed, or the spawn of an animal. It was known for a fact that he had an appetite for children; those foolish enough to wander into his domain returned with their voices stilled by horror and the littlest fingers of their left hands missing. And it was known that people sometimes went to bargain with him, and received power great or small depending on what they offered up to him, and on the quality of their ambition. Grandma Anna had been to see him. She lacked a finger and had small witch's power in accord with her petty desire; she wanted one day to ride around in her very own carriage.

The boys turned away from the house and walked down the

east side of the lower hill. They would catch the train where it ran down from Brandon, the next-nearest town. "Goodbye, Mama," Gob whispered. They had not taken twelve steps when he saw a flash of white darting among a copse of hemlocks at the foot of the hill. He ran off immediately to investigate.

"Where are you going?" Tomo called after him. "We got to hurry. We'll miss the train."

Gob stopped and turned around. "I saw a boogly!" he said, and ran again down the hill, tripping in his haste but rolling immediately to his feet and back into his run. Soon he'd entered the deeper dark under the trees. He thought that darting white shape was a spirit. It was his fondest wish to see one. The family business was fortune-telling; every summer they went out in a garish wagon to comfort and fleece those bereaved by the war. Gob and Tomo were frauds. In dim rented rooms they spun out sweet stories for grieving wives, mothers, fathers, brothers, sisters, and lovers. Whatever the loss, they would deny it, whether by claiming it had not happened at all (He is alive!) or else by claiming that the loss was meaningless (The dead are not dead—your beloved is smiling on you from his spirit abode!). But Gob and Tomo had never seen a spirit, or heard spirit music, or moved a planchette except with their mundane fingers.

Their mama, who did see spirits, said that they would see as she did, one day. "When you are men," she said. "When you are grown up." Tomo was a doubter—the dead, to his mind, were dead. He would believe in spirits when he saw one for himself, and that would be never. Gob was more inclined to believe. He would hold his mama's hand and will her power into him when she was in a trance. Always he saw nothing. She'd come back to her senses and kiss him on the head. "Ah, be patient, my little man," she'd say. But he would rather talk to famous dead personages than be patient. His mama talked with Josephine, with Bonaparte, with an ancient Greek who would not reveal his name. Gob's imagination was always filling empty air with shining spirit bodies—his three dead aunts, Augustus Caesar, Marie Antoinette bouncing her head like a ball. He knew they were not real, but hoped with a full heart that one day they would be. As he ran past the tree trunks he imagined the spirit he was chasing to be General Jackson, still quite upset after his recent death at Chancellorsville. A hideous warbling noise assaulted Gob's ears. Restless spirit! he thought. Miserable spirit, to complain so horribly!

But it wasn't a spirit. It was a girl, wrapped in a white sheet, with her long blond hair let down so it dragged behind her as she ran among the trees, emitting the peculiar warbling sound. Her name was Alanis Bell. She was their neighbor. She lived at the bottom of the hill, and practiced a forbidden affection for the two boys. If her mama ever caught her talking to them, she got a beating with a splintered ruler.

"There you are," she said, running over to Gob. The way her sheet covered her feet, it looked like she was floating. "Where are you going?" Tomo ran up beside Gob, panting and scowling.

"To the war," said Tomo. He pulled at Gob to get him going, but Gob pushed his hand away. He thought Alanis Bell was fascinating, though Tomo hated her.

"To the war?" said Alanis Bell. She put her head back and made the warbling noise again.

"Hush up!" Tomo said to her. "You'll get us caught!" But she kept warbling, until Tomo threw a stick at her. It struck her head, and stopped her warbling but did not make her quiet.

"I was mourning you!" she cried, rubbing her head. "I was mourning you like I mourn for Walter, but now you'll get no mourning from me!" Walter was her brother, whose death at Shiloh had set her to running in the woods. "Now, I'll be glad when you die! Go on! Get out of here. Go on and die! Two less Claflins in the world. Every good person will celebrate!"

"We're Woodhulls, you goddamned idiot *girl,*" said Tomo. "Come along, Gob." They left Alanis Bell cursing them in the hemlocks. They hadn't walked for five more minutes, though, when Gob stopped.

"It's a bad night to go to the war," he said. "A person shouldn't start a trip on a full moon."

"The light's best then," said Tomo. "We better hurry."

"It's a bad thing," said Gob, "to be cursed at the start of your trip. Let's go tomorrow."

Tomo stopped and turned around to face his brother. "Let's go tonight," he said. They had already stayed home on three other nights on account of Gob's fretting. "Let's go tonight or let's not go at all."

"Well," said Gob. But he didn't move as he was supposed to. The train whistle sounded in the distance.

"We got to go," said Tomo.

"Well," Gob said again. "We could not go, too." It was brave of him, to make the suggestion. It was Tomo, five minutes older than he, who had always directed their lives.

"Not go?" said Tomo, immediately furious. "How could we not go? There's not a reason in the world not to go."

"I don't want to go," Gob said for the first time. He'd never said it before, not in so many words, because during all the daydreaming and planning, it had always seemed to him that they would not ever actually do it, and also because he was sure that whatever his brother wanted, he must come to want too. And yet he wanted not to go. He wanted nothing less than to go to the war.

"Well, why the hell not?" Tomo asked, very quietly, but his voice was full of anger.

"I just don't want to," Gob said simply. Tomo took him by the shoulders and gave him a shake. Gob said, "I'm afraid," and Tomo shook him again.

"What's to be scared of?" Tomo asked him. Did he think that Rebs were to be scared of? Rebs were to kill like a hole was to dig. And didn't he know that Tomo would kill any Reb that dared bother his brother? While the train got closer, Tomo went on and on. He scolded and cajoled. He called Gob a bad brother and a false friend, he called him a yellow-bellied girl.

"You'll run for that train before it's too late," Tomo said.

Gob said, "I'm afraid to die." He closed his eyes and tried to screw his feet into the ground. "I'll go tomorrow."

"Will not, either," said Tomo. He took a few steps away and said, "God damn you, then," and he ran off. He ran towards the train, and Gob ran away from it. Gob ran past Alanis Bell's white form, still darting and ululating among the hemlocks. He ran back home, to the birch tree that grew close up against the house. Only when he had climbed the tree to the height of their bedroom did he turn and look for his brother. He could see the smoke from the train hanging like a low cloud against the clear sky, but he couldn't see the train, and he couldn't see Tomo. While he was running he had been too afraid to feel regretful, but now he did feel that way. He pounded his fist against his head and cried, but though he felt very bad indeed, there was a strange elation in him. He felt a selfish happiness, a greedy appreciation of safety, there in the tree, and he could not reconcile that feeling with the noise of the train, with Tomo's receding from him.

"Wait!" Gob said, thinking he would climb down the tree and run after Tomo. But haste made him clumsy. He fell from the tree, knocked his head against the ground, and bit his tongue. Then he was asleep for a while. Alanis Bell came up the hill to watch him, and she might have stroked his head or said a comforting word to him, but she was disgusted by the way his leg was twisted up at a terrible, unnatural angle, and she left him there. She went back to the little hemlock wood, where she ran and danced under the moon, and sang for her brother.

For a week Gob was senseless from the blow to his head, and when he woke he was transformed into a creature of regret. Every time he heard the train whistle blowing in the distance he thought how he had abandoned his brother, and been abandoned by his brother, how if he had not been afraid they would still be together. The brotherless days ran miserably one into the next, until Gob woke one night absolutely certain that Tomo had been killed. He tried not to believe it, for fear that his belief might make it so, but though he struggled against the knowledge, it was confirmed at the end of the summer, when Tomo's body returned to Homer.

Gob was not supposed to be one of the pathetic, maudlin bereaved. Tears were appropriate for ordinary people, but Claflins were special; the lie of death was undone by their magic senses. His mama scolded him when he cried for his brother.

"The dead are not dead," she said. "Would you cry if Tomo moved to Wyoming? The Summerland is closer than Wyoming." This did nothing to comfort Gob. Wyoming seemed to him a place incredibly far away. In fact, he was not even sure where it was, and he knew it must be a place peopled exclusively by savages and bears. It was no place he wanted his brother to be. He said so, and his mother put her soft white hand over his mouth and told him again that the dead were not dead, but more alive even than the living. They dwelt happily in the Summerland.

Gob had cottoned to that notion when he was a child, but Tomo had always hated it. Now Gob hated it too. Now he suspected that the dead were dead, that death was like sleep without dreams, or like being locked in a dark wardrobe where you did not hear or smell or feel or touch, where you did not sleep or wake, where you did not even contemplate the darkness, but you were one with it, and it was a big, horrible nothing.

He asked his mama if she couldn't bring Tomo back to visit. Couldn't she talk to him? She said that she could. They put out all the lights in his room except for a single candle. She grew still and quiet, and then began to sway lightly from side to side. "Mama?" she said. "Is that you walking in the light? Is that you? Is that my brother Gob? How come you look so sad, Gob? Don't you know I'm a living spirit? Don't you know I'm walking by your side, and one day you'll see me just like Mama does, when you're a man? Don't you know how it's true, Gob?"

Gob thought he would float away from joy and relief, and grabbed at the mattress for purchase. He talked for a little while with Tomo, asking what it was like in the Summerland, if there were other children there, if he was treated nice. But his mama's answers began to make him suspicious. He was an experienced humbugger, and something seemed to him not right. Was there a message for Alanis Bell? "Yes," replied his mother, who knew nothing of Tomo's hatred for the girl. "Tell her I miss my sweet friend." Gob began to cry then, because he knew his mama was lying to him, because he felt certain in that moment that there was nothing beyond death but the filthy, silent grave. He fell back on the bed and imagined he was falling into a grave himself—he was falling, and he might have fallen forever if a furious rage had not come welling up in him. He opened his eyes and saw his mother peering down at him with concern. "Gob?" she said. "What's wrong, brother?" He shouted at her, not words, just a howl, and he struck at her face with his fist. He chased her from his room, and when she was gone he pounded on the door he'd slammed behind her, and he howled and howled.

Gob was lonely for the first time in his life, and hoped being near Tomo's body would rid him of this new feeling. He sat on a wooden chair near the flat rock in the orchard where they had sometimes laid out their dinner, and that now was Tomo's headstone. Gob felt no less lonely for sitting there, but though it made him sad to sit and consider how his brother's body lay beneath the ground suffering the abuse of worms, there was no place else he felt comfortable. He held in his fist the letter Tomo had written but not mailed out of Secessia, which he'd read and reread, torn up and reassembled with paste and thread, buried and retrieved.

The family was kind to him, each in their own way, after Tomo's body came back from the war, escorted by a pair of soldiers who told that a generous Rebel general had arranged for the body to return to Homer. Anna fussed over Gob's wound; it was she who saved him from death. Children died from such terrible bone breaks. She set the leg and bound it up with all sorts of sweet-smelling herbs. Gob, drunk on her medicines, had a sudden fear she was making him delicious for cooking. "Mama," he cried out, "is she going to eat me up?"

Tennie came out to the grave, bearing a sunflower, which she laid against the stone. She told him Tomo was not in the Summerland. None of her spirit friends there knew him. But that did not mean he wouldn't go there eventually, and pass from there to the living earth with great ease. "My dear child," she said, "there is no death." Gob said nothing. He did not believe her.

"What are you doing here?" Utica wanted to know when she came out to visit him. It was night. Gob had been all day in the orchard. "Do you think he'll come out of the grave if you sit here and stare? Do you think he'll come down from Heaven? Well, he won't." Utica was a doubter when she was sober. Drunk, she was susceptible to rage against such opinions as were held by most of her family. "A body don't return from where he's gone, my little friend." She'd had a beau, a cooper in Brandon, where Claflins were less infamous, but cholera had killed him, and he had not returned to her when she pleaded, alone or with her sisters. "You are a dreary, moping thing," she said. "They die. What do you want to do? Spend all the rest of your days here? Do you want to crawl into the grave with him? You make me nervous. Do you realize how you make me nervous?" Utica nudged Gob from his chair and said, "A gentleman always makes room for a lady." Without complaint Gob sat on a nearby stump. Utica passed him her glass of whiskey.

The glass was chipped, so Gob cut his lip as he drank, but found the taste of blood and whiskey pleasant. Utica pulled a bottle out of her dress and drank with him. "How your mama would shriek if she saw you with whiskey!" she said, and then tittered. She got up and walked away, but soon returned with a veil. She stood on the chair with the veil over her head, waving her bottle and reciting all the female lines from *A Midsummer Night's Dream*. She stepped down and twirled around the grave, looking ghostly and magical. Gob watched his aunt spin and shout, but said nothing, and when she finished and bowed, he did not applaud. Her swirling white veil reminded him of Alanis Bell, who never came to visit him at Tomo's grave.

"Dreary boy," Utica said, but not without some affection, and she refilled his glass before she walked off into the trees, idly waving the veil behind her. Gob drank his whiskey and then cupped his hand before his mouth to smell it on his breath, thinking of his father.

The whiskey put into his head the seemingly excellent idea of kneeling on his brother's grave and digging in the dirt. He was not sure if he was digging to rescue Tomo from the grave or to make a home in it for himself. He grabbed fistfuls of dirt with his left hand and threw them over his shoulder. With his right he dug with the glass. He had only made a shallow Gob-shaped depression when he grew tired, but he lay down in that and pressed his eyes against the fresh earth. It smelled of old apples. Something that might have been a piece of turkey bone pressed against his cheek. Something else brushed against his neck, crawled along his skin for a few inches, and then turned away. All he saw was darkness. When he sat by the grave and closed his eyes, he sometimes got the feeling that Tomo was standing behind him, reaching out a hand to touch his shoulder, but every time Gob turned around there was only empty space. Now as he nestled atop the grave there was not even that feeling, but he pleaded anyway for Tomo to step out of the darkness before his eyes. Darkness could hide anything. Why wouldn't it hide his brother? Doors could conceal anything. He had opened and closed his bedroom door at the house, hoping each time to find Tomo on the other side. Once it had revealed his mama, who had creeped upstairs to try and reconcile with him. He shut the door in her face.

He imagined Tomo staring up at him now with his one good dead eye. It was dried and rheumy when Gob peeped under the coffin lid at the funeral, shriveled like a very old grape. Gob stared back, conjuring Tomo's supine dead image, coloring him with an additional two weeks of decay. If he kept digging, he would eventually be able to reach out his hand to touch the dead flesh. It was just the few feet of earth and a few inches of wood separating them. Or it was just a few feet of earth and whatever walls God might throw up between the living and the dead. But if the earth would yield to a human hand, why not those other walls? "I will bring you back," Gob swore to his brother, speaking into the dirt so he soiled his tongue and his teeth. And not just as a spirit like their lying mama said she saw. He would somehow bring his brother back into living flesh. He would find a way to do that, because his brother would do the same for him, and because he was to blame for Tomo's death—he felt sure Tomo would not have been killed if he'd gone with him. This was Gob's conviction: that he had killed his brother with his fear as surely as the Rebel had with his bullet. The prospect of living a life without Tomo was no less impossible than the prospect of somehow turning him from a rotten horror to a warm living boy, and if fate had determined that he must do one or the other, he would much prefer to do the latter. "I will bring you back," he said again, and the words were a great comfort to him, because he could only reconcile himself to his brother's death by thinking it temporary. Feeling at peace, Gob snuggled deeper into the dirt, and listened as a gust of wind came into the orchard, shaking the trees and knocking fruit to the ground. There was another noise—he could hear it if he listened very, very hard, a noise like a giant softly breathing, or like the ocean, which he remembered from his distant childhood in San Francisco. The noise rose and fell, lulling him to sleep.

Gob's ignorance necessitated a teacher, but who could teach him how to defeat death? He thought of Miss Maggs, simply because she was a teacher, but he was sure she could only teach him how to be bitter and ugly and how to be a bad shot with a book. His mama might have been a candidate if she hadn't been such a shameless liar. He did not trust her any longer, and if she could not even bring Tomo's spirit to talk to him how could she put life back in his flesh? For the same reason, Aunt Tennie was not suitable. Utica had no knowledge he needed. Grandpa Buck was not stupid, but Gob needed no instruction on how to cheat people. Uncle Malden was as dumb as he was smelly. Grandma Anna had only small power, and anything he might learn from her he could learn from her teacher. So Gob turned on his heel, away from Homer town, and he walked through the orchard and up the high hill, then into the woods beyond that, up into the highest hills where the Urfeist lived. It was a simple decision; there was only one person in his whole world from whom he had any hope of even beginning to learn what he must. But, though it seemed simple and right to take the trip into the highest hills, he felt dizzy and weak and cowardly as he shuffled along under the dark trees. He knew very well what the Urfeist took from the children he captured. Weighed against his brother's life, it seemed a small thing. And it made great sense to him that he should have to do something fearful to undo the consequences of his fear.

Alanis Bell found him as he was passing over the high hill.

"Gob Woodhull," she said. "Where are you going?"

"Get away from me," Gob said. She danced around him, skipping and throwing her hands out. Her prancing seemed an offense against his sadness.

"It is a beautiful night," she said. "Where are you going in such a hurry?"

"To see the Urfeist," he said. That put an end to her prancing. She grabbed his arm.

"Hush! You know better than to say that name. You'll call him down on us!" He pulled his arm away.

"Leave me alone," he said, but she kept clutching at him.

"He'll bite your finger! He'll eat you up! He'll break your bones!"

"I'll break yours!" he said, pushing her away from him. "I'll lift you up and break you in half, you girl!" He had pushed her down and now he was standing over her, ready to step on her or kick her. "Go away," he said quietly. He turned away and walked on.

"Go on!" Alanis Bell called out behind him. "I don't care!" But the warbling noise came drifting after him as he walked. He stopped up his ears with his fingers.

Gob did not know where he was going. He simply wandered. It was common knowledge that the Urfeist could smell a child from miles away. Gob closed his eyes and pretended to be asleep, because it was also said that the Urfeist drew sleeping children to him with a call that only they could hear and follow. More than one child slept with a leash that ran from ankle to bedpost, to prevent just that sort of wandering. Gob got quite lost.

The wind had picked up, and a bit of slivered moon was in the sky. It peeped out occasionally from between racing blue clouds, and lit the spinning fall of oak leaves when the wind nudged them off the trees. Gob happened upon a hawthorn bush. Resting next to it, he saw that a shrike had left a tiny shrew impaled on a long thorn. If that is not an omen, he thought, then my name is Mary Lincoln and I own many fine gowns. It was just then, when cowardice very nearly overwhelmed him, that he caught sight of a cheery yellow light beckoning through the bush.

He picked his way through with care. He hid his hands in his coat and hunched his face down against his chest, but still he got a scratch high on his forehead. He wondered if the odor of blood would draw the Urfeist from his cave. Gob stood watching the entrance for a long time. There was a space cleared before it, where roses were planted in orderly rows, and when he moved a little closer he saw that taller rosebushes flanked the cave mouth, which opened into what must surely be the highest hill in the woods. The entrance turned as soon as it opened. All he saw was yellow light flickering on gray rock.

"I'm here," Gob said, speaking so low he could hardly hear himself above the wind.

"I know it," said a voice beside him. The Urfeist looked just how people made him out to look. There was the scraggly iron-colored hair, the jaunty red cap. He wore a chemise of some animal's skin, and the kilt of fingers was pulled up high on his hairy belly. His feet were wound with bark. "You are welcome here, child," he said. "I've been waiting for you." He was always waiting for a child to come to him. The Urfeist smiled, showing strong white teeth that would have been the envy of a horse.

"I want something," said Gob. "I'll pay for it. I want my brother back. He's dead but I want to bring him here again, into the world. It's got to be so he's a living boy." He kept babbling because the Urfeist said nothing. He only moved one long finger slowly towards Gob's face. Gob did not try to back away, but he did not think he could have, had he tried. The Urfeist put his finger gently against Gob's lips.

"Hush," he said. He left his finger there for a long moment. Gob was dashed with horror, as if someone had filled a bucket with pure liquid horror and dumped it over his head. Now he found he could move, so he turned and ran, faster than he thought he'd be able to, with his bad leg. He burst through the hawthorn, hardly aware of the scratches he got, and went running through the woods towards home. He felt borne up by fear, lifted and pushed by a great, blowing terror. His mama chased him, sometimes, when she was drunk on her visions of personal glory. She always wanted Gob then, not Tomo. It was Gob she wanted to catch up in a crushing embrace, and it was into his ear she wanted to pour her rushing sibyl's monologue—she'd go on and on about all the fantastic things that lay in store for her and her sons, how she would be the leader of her people and deliver all the world from misery, how a golden age would be born in her and through her. Gob came to fear these attacks of hers. He'd run from her when she had the particular look in her eyes, when he knew what was coming. Tomo would exhort him, saying, "Run, Gob, run!" He'd flee through the orchard with his mama close behind, her arms held out in front of her and her hands grasping for him like the jaws of some small, famished animal. She always caught him, always spoke her glory into his ear, telling him how her sons were part of her, how they were connected by mystic cords, so no matter how far away he or Tomo went they would all three still be one.

Gob never looked back, but he thought he could feel the Urfeist pursuing him, drawing closer and closer. He was certain, then, that the monster would kill him. He was certain that it would tear off his head and kick it all the way back to Homer, or that it would sip blood from his wrists until he swooned away into death. He knew that he should stop running and face it, anyhow, that he must do this for Tomo's sake, and yet he did not. He ran all the harder, but he couldn't run fast enough to escape it. Gob knew when the Urfeist was just behind him, and closed his eyes just before the thing knocked into his back and sent him sprawling among dry leaves.

"Hush," the Urfeist said again. He undressed trembling Gob with great tenderness, which was horrible because it was not expected, and though he looked thin and weak as Anna, his grip on Gob's neck was strong, and the weight of him on Gob's back felt heavy as the world. He worked to a chanted, unintelligible cadence. When he was finished, he lifted Gob up, took his limp hand into his own and put Gob's left littlest finger in his mouth.

He bit it clean through. Gob could not watch it happen, but he imagined the Urfeist's mouth opening wide and moonlight racing between the clouds to strike his white teeth. Gob thought then how the bite was a mercy because it distracted you from the other thing, and he made a noise, though he'd sworn to himself he would make none. It was a pitiful sound, a single plaintive, dwindling *O* like a girl might make if you stole away her dolly. He heard the sound as if somebody else was making it, and then he fell back on the ground, what remained of his finger pulling from the Urfeist's sucking mouth with a wet pop.

When he woke, Gob was inside the Urfeist's cave, a distinguished dwelling. There were rugs laid three deep on the stone floor, and the furniture was elegant and expensive-looking. Dressed again, Gob was draped over a blue damask divan. Another cave opened up onto the one he lay in, and another opened up beyond that. Gob's hand was bandaged neatly; there was just a little spot of pale pink fluid at the place his finger had been. The Urfeist was smoking in a matching blue chair directly across from him.

"I know who you are," he said. "Did your grandmama send you to me?"

"No," Gob said, and then he asked again, "Will you teach me?" It occurred to him how he had extracted no promises from this creature before he submitted to him.

"What would you like to know?" said the thing. He still wore his bark shoes and red hat, his skin shirt and the horrific finger-kilt, over which Gob's eyes darted in search of his own lost digit. But the Urfeist seemed the very picture of urbanity, and spoke with an air of refinement that reminded Gob of the way his mama talked when she was trying to make people think she wasn't a Claflin.

"Everything," said Gob, figuring only that would be enough to sustain his oath. The Urfeist laughed. He was rolling something between the thumb and forefinger of his right hand. When

Gob saw that it was his finger he went over and tried to pluck it away from him, not afraid anymore, just full of anger at the thing and at himself for coming up here. "Give it back!" he said. The Urfeist stood on his chair and dangled the finger just out of Gob's reach. Gob spit on him. This only cheered him further, so Gob bit him on his tough shin, thinking back to the tough leathery black skin of a turkey he and Tomo had once cooked whole over a fire in the orchard clearing. The Urfeist howled and with his great strength tore Gob away from his leg. The Urfeist raised Gob by his shirt until he looked directly into his eyes.

The Claflin gaze was formidable. Gob and Tomo had played a game of staring over the hedge at Alanis Bell's mama as she lay taking the sun with her Bible, until she'd get up and flee inside her house, saying, "Those eyes! Those eyes!" But the Urfeist did not flinch. He had one blue eye and one brown, the latter set crazy in his head as if he'd stuck it in there only just lately, a replacement, harvested from some brown-eyed child, for the lost original. Gob did not flinch either. He imagined himself a soldier and thought bullets and bayonet stabs at the thing. Slowly, the Urfeist put him down and then considered him at length. They stood there with their eyes locked together for many minutes before the Urfeist said, "I will teach you," and then beat Gob savagely with a hickory paddle he had been keeping special against the day when he finally took an apprentice.

Gob took to wearing an old black coat of Malden's. The family thought he'd put it on in mourning, but in fact he was using the too-long sleeves to hide his hand and his bruises. He thought for sure that his mama or Tennie, with their ostensibly preternatural senses, would detect some change in him. But when he came down out of the hills at dawn, and put on Malden's coat and waited at the kitchen table until the house began to stir around him, no one remarked that he seemed different. They were busy getting ready to go out on another humbugging junket, the last of the season, which ran in time with the war season. There were supplies to be loaded: a tent under which a person could tell fortunes al fresco; salt pork and hardtack diverted from the Army of the Cumberland; bottles and bottles of their own patent medicine—Miss Tennessee's Magnetio Elixir. Gob watched the bustle but did nothing to help, and no one scolded him for it. Except for his mother, they were all still indulging him on account of Tomo's death.

Regardless of the indulgence they afforded him, Gob was beginning to think that his family had already forgotten that Tomo was dead. How they went on with their lives! Not as if nothing had happened, but as if nothing had changed. To Gob his brother's death was as gross and certain a change in the world as an extra moon hanging in the sky. But the Claflins settled back into their old routine as if death had no power to touch them.

That night in October of 1863, there was a celebration in the yard. All day, Anna had brewed the elixir in a cauldron over an open fire. Tennie ladled it into blue bottles, to which Malden glued labels covered with Tennie's picture. The elixir was mostly whiskey, added after the mixture had cooked, with a hefty dash of laudanum, and spices to make it less palatable—if it was too delicious nobody would believe it medicinal. When it was bottled, and when they were all drunk (except Gob and his mama), the Claflins celebrated the end of their little labor, and the dawn of their journey, the last before winter came and made the business of slaughter impractical, and the business of humbugging unprofitable.

Buck had his banjo out. He plucked while Tennie and Victoria and Utica and Anna danced round the fire, and when they were tired of dancing they lingered outside. Utica reclined in the dirt, muttering Shakespeare to the embers. Buck sat in the darkness beyond the fire smoking and sipping whiskey while Anna leaned against him and mumbled into his beard. Victoria and

Tennie sat in dilapidated rockers on the porch, whispering to each other. They ignored Gob, who stood for a while and watched them, then retreated into the orchard. His mama had become acutely intolerant of his grief, and his unbelief offended her. She had abandoned her attempts at reconciliation, and she was cool to him, lording over him her certain knowledge of life beyond life. Tomo was alive and well in the Summerland; Gob's mama said it did not behoove a son of hers to lack faith in that certainty. Gob hated her for saying this, and hating her, with the pure, furious hatred of a child, made it much easier to take leave of her and the others. Watching them from the orchard, he was whispering goodbyes again. Goodbye mill pond, goodbye mill, goodbye house. The Urfeist had made departure from Homer a condition of his tutelage. Homer was only his summer retreat—he had stayed too long already. If Gob wanted to learn from him, he would have to accompany him to his winter quarters. They would leave not just because the Urfeist found Ohio intolerable in the winter, but because it was no place for him to teach what Gob needed to learn.

Gob was about to go to the grave again and say his last goodbye to Tomo when he heard laughter at the house. It was just one person laughing, at first—it sounded like Tennie—but then the others joined in, and he could hear his mama's high, clear laugh floating above the rest. Before Tomo died, Gob hadn't got mad over every little thing. He did not have Tomo's temper. But he suffered a flare of temper, that night, as bright and hot as the one that had burned against his mama when she afflicted him with her hideous lie, and against the Urfeist when he taunted him with his own finger. Gob ran back through the orchard, towards the remains of the fire and the dark shapes around it. They were still laughing when he got there. His mama and Tennie had come down from the porch. They were standing with the others near the fire, laughing and holding their bellies. Gob stood before them and raised his arms. In his coat, and in the darkness, he looked like some baleful spirit, but they laughed harder when they saw him. It was likely that they were laughing at some remark of Tennie's, or some crude joke of Buck's. It seemed to Gob, though, that they were laughing at him, or worse, at Tomo, or worst of all, at Tomo's death. He ran towards his mama, stopped just before her, and shoved his wounded hand in front of her face.

"Have you forgotten?" he asked them all. "Have you forgotten already?" His mama stopped laughing and reached out to gather him into her arms, but he ducked away. Before he ran off, he made her a promise. "I am dead," he told her quietly. "I am dead, and you will never see me again. I'm going to the war."

It was dramatic and delicious, that pronouncement. It made him feel better as nothing else had. It put an excellent feeling in him, how her proud face fell at his words, how it suddenly filled with hurt, as it ought to have for Tomo.

She followed, but the black coat made him difficult to see. Even with his leg, he escaped her. He ran up to the high hills of the Urfeist, thinking, Goodbye, I hate you! at all of them.

His new teacher was waiting outside the cave. "You're late," the Urfeist said, and though he had the paddle in his hand, he did not use it. He sat on a rude cart, among a collection of trunks and crates.

"Have you nothing to bring?" the Urfeist asked. Gob said that he didn't, but he had filled his pockets with dirt from Tomo's grave. The Urfeist put out his hand and helped Gob up onto the cart. "Away, Paymon," he said to his horse. They started off down a path that Gob had not noticed on his previous visit, and he half expected it to close up behind them. Gob looked back at the dark cave mouth until they made a turn and it was lost among the trees. "Your happiness is irrelevant, and may even work against your cause," the Urfeist said, putting his arm around Gob's neck. "But I think you will like your new home."

PART TWO

The Glass House

In what census of living creatures, the dead of mankind are included; why it is that a universal proverb says of them, that they tell no tales, though containing more secrets than the Goodwin Sands! how it is that to his name who yesterday departed for the other world, we prefix so significant and infidel a word, and yet do not thus entitle him, if he but embarks for the remotest Indies of this living earth; why the Life Insurance Companies pay death-forfeitures upon immortals; in what eternal, unstirring paralysis, and deadly, hopeless trance, yet lies antique Adam who died sixty round centuries ago; how it is that we still refuse to be comforted for those who we nevertheless maintain are dwelling in unspeakable bliss; why all the living so strive to hush all the dead; wherefore but the rumor of a knocking in a tomb will terrify a whole city. All these things are not without their meanings.

HERMAN MELVILLE
Moby-Dick

1

"YOU ARE YOUR BROTHER'S IMAGE," SAID CAPTAIN BROWER. This wasn't exactly true. Will and Sam Fie looked alike in the face, but Will was a much bigger boy. He stood six foot three in his socks, weighed two hundred and fifty pounds, and he wasn't the least bit fat. Sam was three years older, but had had to leave off beating on his little brother by the time Will was twelve. Will would catch the punches easily, and Sam's fist was like a crab apple in his big hand. "If you're half as brave as him, we're lucky to have you."

"I'm not," said Will. Captain Brower thought he was joking. Will was strong, and stubborn, and often obedient, but if bravery had been one of his qualities, he would not have been frightened to stay at home. He would not have been afraid to open the door to his bedroom when his mother brought the news of his brother's death upstairs. The door had shaken as if assaulted by a strong wind, and Will had not wanted to open it because he thought, just for a moment, that a door could bar such news from your life.

Captain Brower was in Syracuse to help recruit replacements for those who had fallen, like Sam, at Bull Run. He had written a letter, saying that he would like to venerate in person the parents who had raised such a boy as Sam Fie. But before Brower could visit, Will had proceeded to Syracuse with a forged letter, in which his mother expressed her love for Sam's captain. Here was her other son, whom she could not dissuade from going to the war. She vouched for Will's age, and asked Captain Brower to take good care of him.

In fact, she had spit on the Captain's name and his offer to visit, calling him a murderer, and saying, "How dare he show his face here?" Over meals that for Will were at first a hard chore and then a deep misery, she'd accuse Captain Brower of having sent Sam to his death. Then she would pound her fist against her heart, and put down her head to cry while Will and his father stared at their cooling meat. They would remain that way for so long that Will imagined they might sit like that forever, a miserable tableau vivant. Some enterprising fellow might come along and cut away a wall of their house, so curious people could pay a dime to file by and peep in on them. There would be a sign: *Toll of War in Onondaga County, New York—September 1862.*

Will had departed from his parents' house late at night. His mother lay asleep on the green sofa upon which she had made it her custom to grieve until exhausted. He looked at her breathing noisily through her open mouth, and debated whether he ought to kiss her goodbye. As he leaned down he thought better of it—she might wake, after all, and inaugurate some sort of hideous, tear-soaked scene. He turned away from her and imagined, as he walked through the door, that Sam's ghost went past him, taking his place in the house as surely as he was taking Sam's place in the war.

Captain Brower shook his hand, and then embraced him. Will was mustered into the 122nd New York Volunteers, called the Third Onondaga by its local-minded members. He sent his bounty money home to his parents, along with a short note. "Now I am one of Father Abraham's three hundred thousand. Goodbye."

Six dead men without shoes—their feet are swollen and their swollen chests have burst the buttons on their shirts. Behind them is a broken wagon, hooked to a dead horse. In the distance stands a church where pacifists once gathered to worship.

* * *

In Maryland, on the way to Harpers Ferry, where the Third had been called to help put an end to General Lee's frolicking, Will saw his first Reb, a dead one who lay where he'd been killed outside a church at Burkittsville. Wounded were moaning inside the church. "What a hymn!" said Jolly Forbes, a long-faced boy who was one of the few who would associate with Will.

Company D had welcomed Will initially. A cry of "Sam's brother!" had followed him wherever he went, and total strangers embraced him and wet his thick neck with tears. "It is good to see you, my friend," was a common refrain. "I am not your friend," was Will's unvarying reply. So great was their love and respect for Sam's memory—there were at least a dozen men who claimed he'd saved their lives—the men of Company D might have let this rude behavior slide, and loved Will for all that he was sullen and he wanted no friends. But he was actively boorish, and proved himself in no time to be a great ruiner of fun. He would knock a man down for cursing in front of him, and if he came upon a bottle of whiskey he would break it. While they were encamped outside of Washington, some man's cousin had attempted to sneak in a barrel of whiskey. She had dressed it up in a little white frock, put a white bonnet on it, and heaped it with soft blankets. Soldiers in the know cooed over it, reached into the perambulator, and pretended to stroke its chin. Jolly Forbes came by and looked in. "Madame," he said, "that is the *handsomest* baby I have ever seen." Will was behind Jolly, and when he saw what it was, he reached in, grabbed it out, and dashed that baby to the ground.

Where Sam had saved men by the dozen, Will put them by the dozen into the guardhouse with his tattling. Begging Sam's forgiveness, they cursed loudly against the Devil-sent prig. Will was thrown out of the Tiger Mess, where Sam had been a member. The other members wrote out a dishonorable discharge on a gigantic piece of hardtack. *Expelled for crimes against good-naturedness*, it said. In the end, he had only Jolly and assorted other rejects to mess with.

At the church, two men were busy around the dead boy. A photographer was yelling at his assistant in French. Will knew enough French to understand that the fat little photographer—he was only about five feet tall, and shaped just like an egg—was very displeased. He wanted the assistant to turn the dead boy's head into the sun, but the boy was ripe and the assistant was sure that to touch him would be bad for his own health. The photographer stomped over, reached up to grab his assistant by the neck, and threw him down into the dead boy, whose arm flopped over in a friendly embrace. The assistant scampered away, howling as if the corpse had bitten him. The round photographer bent down and began very carefully to compose the Reb's limbs. He stretched out the boy's arm above his shoulder in the grass, and opened his hand. The photographer looked up and scowled at Will. "Your goggling eyes!" he said. "What are you looking at?" Just then, Captain Brower came up alongside in the passing column.

"Walk on, Private," he said to Will. "There's no time for dilly-dallying." Will looked a little longer at the dead boy. He was wondering how Sam had fallen, if he had looked the same as this swollen, flyblown boy. He turned and gave the Captain a stiff salute, then continued walking.

Not fifteen minutes from the church, they passed the battlefield of South Mountain. Dead Rebels were stacked shoulder high along the road. Will wondered if this construction was the work of the round Frenchman. He looked down at the ground as he passed the corpses, afraid to meet their staring eyes. He thought of Sam's body again. There would have been a funeral, back in Onondaga County, which Will had missed. Later, Will would have a dream in which he climbed a wall of bodies as high as the moon. Every body was Sam's, and every mouth as he passed it whispered, "Aim low, Brother!"

Jolly dropped back in line to walk with him again. He held up his canteen to the orderly dead before he took a drink of water. "To your health, boys," Jolly said.

They are swollen in this picture, too. It almost makes them look healthy, such big barrel chests, such thick legs—their clothes can barely contain them. They lie along a fence in various positions. This one has got his hands thrown over his shoulders. That one has got his hand on his belly. Where are their shoes?

The Third Onondaga was ordered away from Harpers Ferry just as they reached it, drawn down off the mountain by General McClellan's sucking, gluttonous need for reinforcements. But they arrived too late to participate at Antietam. Will spent the night of September 17 helping carry in wounded. If they were not too fragile, he could carry them one under each arm. The darkness was a mercy—it was easier to venture among the dead when you could not see them. At dawn, he was squatting by a small fire, drinking coffee with Jolly. The sun came up and seemed to shine specifically on a house near a line of battered woods. The walls were laced with cannonball holes, but a merry white column of smoke was still rising from the broken chimney.

"Sometimes," said Jolly, rolling his tin cup between his hands, "I worry that there is no purpose to anything. It would be the very worst news, I think."

"God has abandoned that field, at least," Will said, hooking his thumb over his shoulder to point at the heaped dead of the Irish Brigade. It was his shame that he lacked faith. But it made a sort of wicked sense to him that the universe should be an orphan, its own only parent, raised on a diet of self-taught, ignorant cruelty. He worried that there was nothing beyond the tangible world, that there was nothing beyond death but oblivion. On the way to Harpers Ferry, he had imagined his own death, trying to decide if he wanted to linger or go in a flash. These thoughts were his dispiriting occupation since he had become a soldier. He feared God, even though he was secretly certain there was no such fellow, and worried that some punishment greater than a joyless life might be in store for him.

"I think I shall be melancholy for a while," said Jolly, putting his elbow on his knee, and his chin in his hand. He looked very much like Will's brooding mother, in that posture. Will was just about to leave when a spindly corporal came to fetch him and bring him to Captain Brower's tent. Will found the little French photographer there with the Captain. They had filled up the tent with cigar smoke.

"Here's the boy I had in mind for you!" said Captain Brower. He introduced Will to the photographer, who was called Carnot, but Will privately dubbed him Frenchy.

"I know him," said M. Carnot. "I know his goggling eyes." He barked a few questions at Will in French. The Captain said Will knew French—was this true? Could he read? Was he a disciplined worker? Were his hands steady? Was he a Catholic boy?

Will answered slowly, once in French, and then again in English. He knew his French from a distant neighbor lady back in Onondaga County, to whom his mother had sent him for lessons because she was sure it would civilize him, though his father said it would sissify him. Of course he could read; he liked to think he was as disciplined as anybody; his hands were steady and he was not clumsy. "I am not a Catholic," he added belatedly.

"Excellent," said M. Carnot. "I am through with superstitious idolaters. You'll do."

Captain Brower clapped Will on the back.

"Pardon me, sir," said Will. "Has some business been transacted?"

Some had. Will had just changed hands. M. Frenchy needed a new assistant, his last one having been bayoneted on the previous day by a wounded Reb when he approached, hesitantly, to rearrange the seemingly dead boy's limbs into a more dramatic pose. Will would make an ideal assistant, the Captain was sure, because of his French, and because he was industrious and smart. Will had the same feeling as when he'd been kicked out of the Tiger Mess. He got no certificate this time, but he had the distinct impression he was being thrown out of Company D.

This wasn't precisely the case. Will would still eat and sleep and fight with his company, but he was also to serve as assistant and bodyguard to the extremely well-connected M. Frenchy, who had letters from on high, through Sedgwick and McClellan all the way up to Stanton, giving him permission to put himself in the way, taking pictures of the field. Frenchy called himself an artist and a scientist; his aim, he said, was to quantify and qualify the brutality of war.

Packed bodies in a sunken road. Try as he might, Will could not resolve them into separate boys. They lay in a dead tangle, arms and legs thrown over each other. It struck him that they would embrace each other forever. Will put this picture high on the north wall of the house.

Will carried photographic equipment and helped arrange the dead, always looking away from their faces as he moved them. Some were stiff. Frenchy had screamed at him when he balked at forcing a fallen cavalryman's arm into a more pleasing position. Will broke the poor man's shoulder, crossing his arm over his chest, and he wondered that the whole Rebel army did not come pouring down on him, for so abusing their dead. When he was not posing the bodies, he was helping to bury them. Will put the cavalryman by himself in a deep grave lined with hay. Frenchy cursed the burying, because his precious dead were vanishing into the ground.

The Third joined the lazy pursuit that toddled after the fleeing Rebels. As they traveled, Frenchy taught Will the photographic process, screeching at him when he wasted a plate. He spent hours in Frenchy's cramped wagon mixing collodion from guncotton and sulfuric ether and alcohol, then coating the mixture onto glass plates. Frenchy scolded like a harpy, and whenever Will did something that displeased him especially, he would emit a furious, resonant honk, like the noise of a calliope. But he also spoke generous praise—his assistant was learning quickly. Pressed for time, he brought a plate back to Will in the wagon, and let him develop it while he took another wet plate and went to make another picture. Will removed the plate from its holder. He held it over a pan and poured developer over the glass. The developer reeked like a cocktail of vinegar and blood, and he almost dropped the negative when a violent sneeze shook him. Leaning down, and squinting in the dim yellow light of the lantern, he could see the image, rising out of the glass as if up through water.

A boy with his legs all twisted up impossibly: someone has stolen his hips and replaced them with a little stretch of earth. His hand is cupped behind his ear, as if he is straining to hear some news. Will put this one on the east wall, where it would catch the light of the rising sun.

At Fredericksburg, Frenchy was made busy by the carnage below Marye's Heights. It was December, and bitter cold. Frenchy was lost in a wilderness of borrowed coat—his own was still wet from a fall off a pontoon bridge into the Rappahannock. He swam like an otter, and had looked like one, with his wet brown hair and shiny black eyes.

With his head in his camera, Frenchy was blind to danger. It was Will's job to keep an eye out for sneaking Rebels. A truce had been called, to gather the dead and wounded, but Will did not trust them to keep it. A profusion of boys was strewn on the ground, none of them closer than a hundred yards to the stone wall against which Burnside had thrown them.

"Did you ever think you'd be a *photographer?*" Frenchy asked from under the camera hood, saying the word with great reverence.

"No," said Will. When he was a boy, he had wanted to become a sailor, because he and Sam had been great admirers of *Typee,* and had imagined a scummy pond behind their house to be the wide green bay of Nukuheva. Later, Will thought he would be a doctor, for no good reason except that to doctor was not to farm like his father. Now, he thought he might have been growing up all this time merely to be a brick in a wall of corpses.

Frenchy pulled his head from the camera and made a confession to Will, to whom he was beginning to show something like affection. It was his hope, he said, to take a picture of a soldier at the precise moment of his death, because he believed the departing soul, invisible to a human eye, could be seen by the camera. Soon after his confession, Frenchy found a squirmer on the cold field, but by the time he'd moved the camera and made it ready, the boy was dead.

Will was much in demand that whole day through. In the late afternoon, when the light had grown too bad for taking pictures, he took up a pick to open the frozen ground for graves, and worked at it till his arms and shoulders burned. He wanted to weep from exhaustion, but there were always more dead to bury, some of them naked because ill-clad Rebs had crept forth from the lines to steal their clothes in the night. When he stopped working, he could barely raise his arms to feed himself. He found Frenchy in a hospital tent, with his camera set up by the bedside of a blond-headed boy who looked for sure to be a goner. Will's hands were a mess of blisters. Frenchy gave him a plate to develop, but he dropped it, which earned him a cursing so thorough Will had to resist an urge to knock the little man down. Frenchy nearly got ejected from the tent, for all that he brought out his omnipresent letters and waved them like a little set of battle colors. He took up his vigil again, and sent his assistant away.

Will went back to Company D. They'd been held in reserve for most of the previous day, having seen just a smidgen of action when they were called up in support of a battery below Fredericksburg. Despite the shells bursting over their heads, their only casualty was a boy who had been overcome with excitement and accidentally shot himself in the knee. Jolly was having his dinner with a few other members of the Leper Mess. A tall thin fellow named Lewy Greeley, who was unpopular on account of his incessant proselytizing, was lamenting his fate. "This is the worst regiment ever," Lewy said, stabbing beans with a spoon. "We see no good action and are overrun with godlessness. I think I will go off and join the 110th." He meant the 110th Illinois, a regiment composed entirely of Methodist ministers. He nattered on about them incessantly, about their somber uniforms and pious behavior: they sang booming hymns as they loaded, primed, and fired. God was with them in precisely the way he was not with this here assembly of lawyers and farmers.

"I'll cut you a new mouth to whine with, if you don't shut up," said Jolly, who was not known for making idle threats. Will sat back on his heels, picked out hot beans with his fingers, and raised them slowly to his mouth. "Did you see the sky last night, Tiny?" Jolly asked him.

"I did," Will said. There had been a fantastic display, the night after the battle. The northern lights had come south to blaze in the sky above the Union right. Will had lain on his back to watch, holding to his eye a cracked lens pilfered from the wagon, thinking it would be fine to take a picture of such a thing as that festive sky.

"Do you suppose it was a sign? Do you suppose it was God waving his hanky for the Rebs? Perhaps it is our purpose to lose."

"We were good Christians today, then," said Will.

"No," said Lewy Greeley. "Not ever."

A catalogue of expressions—fear, sadness, rage, surprise, tenderness, even what appears to be a broad smile, this last on a head connected only by strings to the neck it once rode upon. A catalogue of parts—arms and legs, trunks and bellies, ears and noses, a flat section of skull. The hair is still attached, but the rest of the body is nowhere to be seen. It might be a muskrat, crouched in the grass. The whole west wall is a catalogue of parts and faces.

In May of '63, Will drifted across the Rappahannock with a few other members of Company D. Lewy Greeley was there, and so was Jolly. It was just before dawn. They were going over to clear out some intractable sharpshooters who were making it impossible to lay down pontoons for a bridge. Lewy was twitching with excitement. Months of idleness in winter camp had made him a nervous creature. A few times, at night on picket duty, he had fired blindly at the enemy lines. That morning, he could barely contain himself. Inhospitable Rebs were firing at them already, though their visit was supposed to be a surprise. Lewy kept trying to stand up in the boat. A wag in a neighboring boat had stood up and shaken his ass at the Rebs, then crouched down again without taking a hit. "Let go, you big ape!" Lewy said to Will, tearing his sleeve free of Will's fingers.

"Stay down, Lewy," said Jolly. "It's positively unhealthy up there."

Lewy paid him no mind. He stood up in the boat and said, "Look at me! I am a *marine!*" A bullet took him in the head. He fell down and was still, and made no noise, but his blood rushed out from him, and pooled around their knees.

"Ah, Lewy," said Jolly. "You were too much of a bother for this world."

The Rebs offered up a few more volleys, but left the bank with hardly any fight at all. Will sat by a fire, ostensibly guarding the engineers as they worked, but really he was looking at Lewy's body, wrapped up in a coat upon the riverbank. He wished he had a picture of him, because he had discovered he could better empathize with a picture of a dead boy than with the dead boy himself. Looking at the pictures he could wonder, What did the boy see as he died, where were his thoughts? If he had a picture of Lewy's body he might have wondered if Lewy, in the half-second during which he took his bullet, thought of his Methodist regiment, and hoped to join them in Heaven though he could not join them on earth. If he could have chosen a word and spoken it as he died, what would it have been? Did a color fill his mind as he expired? With a picture, Will might have tried to imagine how it felt to be wounded like Lewy, he might have held a hand up to touch his own pulse beating in his temple. As it was, he was filled with a stony, gray feeling, and found he was already forgetting what Lewy looked like.

Lewy Greeley, carefully arranged. He looks noble in a way he never did in life. He lies with his arms folded over his chest, his little face serene and pretty in a patch of morning sunlight. He might be dreaming. Will put him on the north wall, with all the other boys from Company D.

"I've failed!" Frenchy said, sitting by his wagon a few days after Lewy's death, after Company D and the rest of the Army of the Potomac had scurried back over the Rappahannock in the wake of the great disaster at Chancellorsville. Frenchy had been cross because the wounded, dying, and dead were left on the other side of the river where he could not photograph them. He had retreated to a hospital tent and taken up a post next to a boy who was clinging to life despite the amputation of both his legs, and repeated assaults by the bloody flux. In his delirium, the boy thought Frenchy was his mother. Previously, Frenchy had wandered away for food or drink, or fallen asleep, at the critical moment, but this boy wailed piteously if he left his side, so he was there for the death. "Miserable, hideous failure!" Frenchy said.

It was a very pleasant night, with the moon shining out full. He'd come stomping and cursing through the moonlight to where Will was sitting by the wagon, thinking back to the other side of the river. There'd been plenty of fighting, even at night when Will was free to join it. The beautiful moonlight had settled over everything, though it seemed to Will that it should recoil from boys whose heads decided to go every which way at once, from open bellies and naked bones.

Frenchy cast the plates on the ground at Will's feet, breaking a plate in half. Will took the pieces up and held them to the moon: there was the boy from the hospital tent, his terrible wounds preserved forever. Will found himself wondering if it was not the opposite of mercy to have preserved them so. The boy in these pictures would always be in pain. His face was a blur—he seemed to have a multiplicity of mouths, all of them calling for his mother. But in the last picture, the broken one, he was still. "It was just as he went," said Frenchy. "I know that it was, but there is no exhalation, there is nothing but air about him."

Will left Frenchy to his misery, and walked off with the broken pieces of the last plate in his two hands. He wandered aimlessly through the camp and out of it, thinking that he held in his hands proof of the nonexistence of souls. He thought of Sam, how he had been friendly when they were small, aside from the occasional beating, and how he had been distant when they were older, how they had fallen out with each other over something unspoken and unknown, and how there was no hope of reconciliation between the living and the dead. He sat down on the ground and hung his head. There was a burning behind his eyes, and his belly contracted violently, as if it were trying to retch. He felt his mouth turning down, very slowly, at the corners. He remembered how ugly his mother always was in her weeping, and he tried hard not to cry. Nonetheless, he wept, and as only a boy of his size and strength could, great sobs, his chest heaving with the strength of three lesser chests. It made him afraid to think that everything he was could vanish into an abyss when he took, as he felt he must, his mortal wound. And it made him unbearably sad to think how everything that Sam was had simply ended.

Will had wandered into a graveyard full of Union dead. He'd buried some of them himself the previous winter. After he'd quieted down from his sobbing, he sat there a while, and thought he must have fallen asleep, because he was sure he was dreaming when gaily dressed women drifted into the graveyard. There were seven of them. Four carried lanterns, which they set down in a great square pattern. They put their heads together and whispered, and seemed to be waiting for something. Soon, a little man came tiptoeing into the graveyard. He bowed to them and took out a fiddle from a case, then started to play a jig. The ladies began a sprightly dance upon the graves of the Union dead.

They did not see Will in his dark uniform, did not see how, with their dancing, they turned his sadness to rage. The piece of plate, when it came flying out of the darkness, must have seemed like a judgment from whatever god guards the dignity of the dead. It struck a woman in the hip—in her petticoats or her flesh, Will could not be sure. She shrieked and the ladies dispersed, leaving their lanterns behind.

A boy with a hole where his chest ought to be. He is arranged on his side. His big serious eyes look directly at the camera. His left hand is stretched out, his hand is open as if in supplication, as if to say, *Give it back*. He is the fourth image from the right, in the second row from the bottom, on the south wall.

"My mama says I should remember that I am fighting to preserve the best government on earth," Jolly said. It was dinnertime on the evening of the second day at Gettysburg. The Third Onondaga had taken up position too late, again, to have seen action. Other regiments made fun of them, saying their ugly faces scared away the elephant. Will thought it must be his mother's doing, this safety. Her towering grief would not allow him to be hurt—it was of such a nature that even fate must be afraid of it. "But my father, he says we must help the slaves even if the Union goes all to smash." Jolly held up two letters, one from his mother and one from his father, in either hand. "What do you think?" he asked Will.

"I don't know," Will replied. He took the letters from Jolly's hand and put them behind his back, passing them from hand to hand a few times before he told Jolly to pick one. Jolly chose the left hand, and Will handed him back the letter. Jolly opened it and looked at it, rubbing his eyes wearily.

"Well?" said Will.

"Well, I am fighting for the slaves," said Jolly. They sat alone for a while, before they started making their dinner, a coffee beef stew. Jolly had taken off his shirt and rolled up the sleeves of his long johns, because of the heat. They were the only two members of the Leper Mess left, the others having died or deserted or been absorbed into more respectable associations. They spent a little while crushing hardtack for their stew. "God save me from this cracker," Jolly said, struggling to break it. Will crushed his easily into a fine powder, and made dumplings with water from his canteen. These he set gingerly into the stew, amid pieces of beef and vegetables. Jolly leaned over the pot to pour in a cup of coffee, and then they took turns sprinkling in crushed cracker to thicken the stew. "Oh, it will be delicious!" said Jolly, but when it came time to eat he said he was not hungry, and gave his portion to Will.

After their meal, they lay down in their dog tent, not sleeping though both were exhausted from their recent march—they'd gone twenty miles a day for three days. "I think sometimes it might not be real," said Jolly. Will's guts were making a racket, complaining about the stew. "When I was a boy my mother told me the whole world was just the dream of a sleeping bear, and that we had to be careful not to be too horrible in our behavior towards one another, because we might shock the bear into wakefulness, and he would go about his day, and we would be no more. That was blasphemy, I know. But couldn't a war be God's conscience fretting with itself? Maybe he has put himself down for a nap, but his digestion is poor, and it has troubled his dream. All our history might be no longer than such a nap, don't you think? His troubled conscience has dreamed a war. I worry, anyhow, that we will wake him. Do you think we will wake him?"

Will had no answer. In the silence, Jolly took his hand and put it over his chest. Jolly's heart was fluttering. "Is it beating?" Jolly asked him. "Am I alive?"

"Yes," said Will, and took away his hand.

"Sometimes I wonder."

The images look like portraits of ghosts. They are pale where living people are dark, dark where the living are pale. When the sun passes through the glass negatives, it is like a visitation from beyond, the way they shimmer and glow. At night, when he goes into the unfinished house with a lantern, the backing darkness makes ambrotypes of the images, and the dead take on the tones and shades of the living. It makes sense to him that it should be so, that the dead should be more solid, should look more real at night, and that the day should make ghosts of them.

Frenchy had new hope, which stemmed from a new plan and a new technique. He had determined that he'd failed to capture the boy's departing soul because his medium was insensitive. He needed a better collodion—hadn't Fox-Talbot's calotype process been similarly insensitive, hadn't it also been defective? He was gone for two weeks in June, consulting with a learned gentleman in New York. When he returned, he had a new collodion formula. It was the same as the old one, except he added three drops of a liquid from a mysterious-looking blue bottle. The liquid looked and smelled like whiskey, and Will was tempted to smash the bottle.

Will and Jolly got separated in the last day's fighting at Gettysburg, of which the Third had more than its fair share. Will got called away by Frenchy, whose mule had died in the quartermaster-seeking overshots of the Rebel artillery. Will himself pulled the wagon while Frenchy screeched at him to hurry. Ambulances and sutler's tents were meeting their ends all around him. Will and Frenchy fled down the Baltimore Pike until they came to a place of comparative safety, where they waited amid a crowd of other fugitives. Frenchy's powerful letters of recommendation helped him to appropriate a new mule. By the time Will got back to the Third's position on Culp's Hill, it was almost night. He spent the evening looking fruitlessly for Jolly.

On the Fourth of July, Will ventured out into the rain with Frenchy. For the first time, they saw many boys from the Third dead on the field. There was a boy, one of the first Will had met, who as they waited in the train to leave Syracuse had asked Will to do him a favor. "Hey, Goliath," he'd said. "Give me a boost." Will had hoisted him through the window, thinking for a moment he'd had a last-minute change of heart and was going to desert prematurely. There were women clustered around the train, come to bid good-bye to the boys of Onondaga County, and all the boy had wanted was kisses. Will held the fellow by his boots as he puckered his lips up obscenely and meshed them wetly with the wanton lips of three, five, and then ten different women. In the end, Will had dropped him on his head, and so lost his first friend in the regiment. He was a little fellow, whose lips were wide and thick. On reflection, Will understood how he might feel pressed to kiss excessively with them. Now they were gone, torn away by a bullet or a fragment of shell. Each time Will stepped in wet, soft places on the field, he worried that he'd trodden upon those sensuous lips.

Frenchy had just scolded Will for moving a pile of dead into convincing "as they fell" positions—he was supposed to be looking for the dying, not playing with the dead—when Will uncovered a living Reb. The Reb opened his gray eyes and began to squall when Will grabbed his arm. "Don't bury me!" he said. "I ain't dead, you son of a bitch!" It was a marvel, though, that he was alive. His belly had been opened, and his guts were spilling promiscuously from the wound. "Go away," he said to Will, once it became clear to him that Will was not going to bury him. "Ain't it enough that you killed me? Why don't you leave me in peace? My granny is coming up to get me. She'll be here soon. She doesn't care for greasy Yanks, and one who shines and stinks like you would offend her."

"I'll take you to the doctors," Will said.

"No," said the Reb. Frenchy came waddling up excitedly.

"You beautiful boy!" he said to the Reb.

"Leave me be," he said. But they wouldn't. Will cleared away the bodies from around the boy and Frenchy gave him sips of whiskey from a flask. As Frenchy set up his camera, the boy put down his head and seemed to sleep, so while Frenchy wasn't looking Will picked him up and carried him back to a hospital tent. The boy woke and began to scream horribly, and Frenchy screamed horribly, too, honking and honking as Will hurried away with the prize. Will held the Reb tight, lest something vital spill out further and drag along the ground. By the time he had reached the hospital, the boy was silent and dead. Will put him down on a door set on two sawhorses, which had lately served as a surgery table. Had Will felt anything leave as he walked? Had a spirit passed through him? It would have felt like a chill, he was sure. But he had felt nothing. He sat there for a long while, not wanting, anymore, to assist Frenchy in an enterprise that now seemed stupid and vile and immensely rude.

No matter, though. Frenchy was dead, when Will went back to him, shot through the chest as he was taking a picture. Jolly had been his subject, dead now, too—though Will was certain that he had been mostly alive for his portrait. Jolly had no obvious wound on him. Will thought he must have died of sadness and uncertainty, but when he looked closer he could see that Jolly had been shot in the thigh. He'd crossed his legs demurely, as if to hide the wound. His brow, when Will laid his hand on it, was still warm, but even as he knelt there it grew cold. For a little while he knelt with his hand on Jolly's head, thinking of his friend dying all night long. Will's eyes were closed. He was waiting for someone to shoot him. He wanted to say something but seemed to have forgotten, for the moment, every word he ever knew. His mother intruded into his mind, then. She dragged her green sofa onto the battlefield and reclined upon it. She gathered Jolly into her lap and cried out, "Where is it written that a woman has got to bear such a load of heartache?"

Frenchy's camera had fallen over, but the plate inside was safe and whole. With the plate closed up in a box, Will walked to where the new mule had taken the wagon, a few hundred yards away. Under the yellow light, he poured the developer over the plate and waited for the image.

There is Jolly's long face, his lips turned down in a frown. His eyes are open. His head is resting on his arm. He is pointing at nothing. He has wrapped his mouth around a piece of grass. Something is rising from him. It looks like a bit of dark mist in the shape of a wing.

In the Wilderness, and at Spotsylvania, at Cold Harbor and Petersburg, the Third saw the elephant abundantly, and it trampled them. Frenchy would have had many opportunities to take his world-changing picture. Brave or foolish behavior got Will back into the Tiger Mess—he saved some lives and became better liked. He wanted friends, all of a sudden, as immediately and as intensely as he had not wanted them before. He would still smash your whiskey, but that became something they could overlook in the dwindling fraternity of Company D. The boys all got in the habit of writing their names and the addresses of their families on slips of paper, which they pinned to their shirts before they went into battle. Will had a slip pinned to his shirt, but it was not his parents' address—he didn't want even his dead body to go back home. Instead he'd written, *Sam, here I come.*

Will had many near misses. It seemed that bullets wanted to touch him. He got grazed on his arms and legs, along his scalp. He lost an earlobe. But he never got a serious wound, though he felt at last that he was ready for one. Jolly's picture, which he kept in his knapsack by day and under his head at night, cheered him. Such a spirit-shape might rise from him, when his bullet finally found him. Such a spirit-shape as rose from Jolly might have risen from Sam, might abide in some place free from the heavy cares of the war and the world.

Generous Frenchy had made up a sort of will, which he would have changed, no doubt, had he lived after his assistant betrayed him at Gettysburg. He'd left instructions with Captain Brower. In the event of his death, Will was to have his cart and all it contained, as well as a big brass key, with an address at which one could find its lock. Will sold the cart. The new mule went back to its former owner, from whom Frenchy had bullied it. Will kept only the key and Jolly's negative.

After the war, Will went to Brooklyn, where his key opened up a musty photography studio on the fourth floor of a building in Fulton Street. The rent, he discovered, was paid through the next two years. He walked among the props—marble columns, rich draperies, painted backgrounds depicting mountains or the sea. He stood for a while under a massive skylight, looking up at the gray sky. In a dark corner, beneath a gigantic rubber blanket, he found neat tall stacks of negatives, hundreds and hundreds of them, all taken during the war, some of which he'd developed himself. Frenchy had been sending them back to this place.

Will built the glass house on the roof. There was a derelict greenhouse up there, whose clear panels he tore out and replaced with the boys by the church, the boy with no hips, the catalogues. All the hundreds of negatives became four walls and a roof. Finally, there was Jolly's picture—it went over the door in what Will thought must be the position of honor. Will put it in place, the last panel, and the house was finished.

It still lacked an hour till dawn. He went inside without a light and sat in the middle of the house. It was likely and certain and necessary that something would happen when the sun came to shine down on him. But what? Would the white ghosts assault him? Would he hear Jolly's voice whispering a question? Would the mist that might be Jolly's spirit depart from the plate and settle over Will like manna? Maybe ghosts would crowd the house, and maybe Sam would be among them. Maybe Will would fall asleep under their images and dream their vanished lives.

Maybe nothing would happen. Dawn was in the sky, now. The sun was just starting to peep over a neighboring building. Will closed his eyes and he waited.

2

IN SEPTEMBER OF 1867, WILL SAT IN THE AMPHITHEATER OF the Bellevue Medical College with his head clutched between his hands, staring fixedly at Dr. Gouley, a lecturer in morbid anatomy. Dr. Gouley was a sweet-looking man whose gentle voice belied the gruesome content of his lecture. "The skin of the child," he said, "was dry and hard and seemed to be cracked in many places, somewhat resembling the scales of a fish. The mouth was large and round and wide open. It had no external nose but two holes where the nose should have been."

"Are you all right, Will?" asked his neighbor, a small young man named Gob Woodhull. As there were no proper seats left in the crowded amphitheater, they sat next to each other on the steps. "Are you going to have a fit? The way your eyes bulge, it worries me."

They had met a month before, after Will had collapsed in the hospital hallway. When he came back to his senses, Will was in a bed in Ward 10, surrounded by noisy consumptives. Little Gob, for all that he looked like a fifteen-year-old in store-bought whiskers, had picked him up in the hallway like a child and carried him to bed. "It's a divine affliction, what you have," he said.

"It's not," said Will. He could barely see, and he felt cold, though it was hot in the ward. No, it wasn't divine, what he had. They were from the glass house, these attacks of sympathy that culminated in shaking, foaming fits. Medical school was the last place he should be, in his condition, because the sad natural histories of disease became personal to him. His mind would come loose from its moorings and drift on tides of turbulent fancy, so he found himself becoming the sufferer, or someone who loved the sufferer, and he would contemplate their troubled, failing lives until the fit came along, inevitably, and put an end to it. He'd collapsed in the hall on account of a young German mother, recently delivered and now afflicted with a debilitating fistula that made her smell so horrible her family had turned her out of the house. He hadn't cared so much for other people's trouble in the past. Even his own mother's agony had occurred at a distance remote from his heart, but the house had changed that.

In the amphitheater, Will told Gob, "I'm very well, thank you." But he was not very well. Dr. Gouley was lecturing on Harlequin Fetus, a rare but especially awful congenital deformity, and Will feared that he would soon be overwhelmed.

"The eyes appeared to be lumps of coagulated blood, about the bigness of a plum, ghastly to behold. It had no external ears, only holes where the ears should be. The hands and feet appeared to be swollen, were crumped up, and felt hard. The back part of the head was very much open. It made a strange kind of noise, very low, which I will now attempt to imitate." Dr. Gouley cleared his throat, lowered his head, and emitted a rumbling bass cry like the complaint of a sickly cow.

"Fascinating," said Gob. "I should have liked to examine it." Another student shushed him. Will closed his eyes and saw a hideous, bark-skinned Harlequin Fetus toddling out of the blackness in his mind. It held out its crumped-up hands at him and from the shocked O of its mouth came a word: "Papa."

"You're about to blow, aren't you?" said Gob. "Should I take you out of here?"

"No," Will whispered. He imagined the poor mother who gave birth to such a child, how her bliss would become horror when she saw the thing that had emerged from her. He did not want to hear any more.

"It defeats the purpose of a lecture," said Gob, "if you plug up your ears." This time, he was assailed by a whole chorus of shushings.

"It lived about eight and forty hours," said Dr. Gouley, "and was alive when I saw it."

Debilitating sympathy, fits, spirits—these were the gifts of the house. Something must have happened as Will sat there, with the sun shining bright but not warm through the picture panels, though in fact it had seemed at first that nothing happened. He had looked around at the confusion of images on the floor and on himself, but he felt no different. Ghosts did not detach themselves from the picture, Jolly's soul did not come sifting down upon him. He fell asleep and had a perfectly ordinary nap.

He spent the whole first day after he'd finished the house at mundane tasks, cleaning, eating, writing up an advertisement for people to come get their portraits taken by him—he'd started a little business and was doing pretty well at it—and he went to bed feeling disappointed and relieved that nothing had happened. But he woke in the early morning to the sound of artillery, great crashing booms that sounded as if they were being fired from just below his window on Fulton Street. When they were small, Sam had tried to teach him how to wake within sleep, to know he was dreaming while he was dreaming. "Then you are the master of your whole world," Sam confided. Then you could fly, or squeeze ice cream from a stone, or turn animals to chocolate with your touch. Will could never learn to do this. But when he woke that night surrounded by people staring down at him, he figured he must at last have woken up inside a dream.

He reached to touch Jolly, hoping to turn him to chocolate. Jolly was moving his mouth but Will couldn't hear him—he thought he must have been deafened by the cannon. Jolly was solid and very cold. He would not turn to chocolate, or stop moving his lips. The others were talking, too. Frenchy and Lewy Greeley and even Sam, who stood away from the bed and looked at Will like a stranger. There were many boys from the Third Onondaga, some of whom he'd barely known, and there were boys Will had never seen before. All of them were chattering at him silently, except for one, a boy who looked like a tatterdemalion Gabriel, because he was dressed in shabby clothes and had only one wing where a more affluent angel would surely have two. The boy did not move his mouth, but only stared and put a bugle—it was bright and pretty, not shabby at all—to his mouth to blow it noiselessly. Will closed his eyes as the artillery sounded again, trying to wake up. But he was already awake, and when he opened his eyes all his guests were still with him.

"I mean to make a pilgrimage," Will said to Gob, "to the valley of Aesclepius, where I will tie the carotids of a rooster and make a sacrifice of him. Will you go along with me?" Sometimes, Will thought that if he left the country the silent ghosts would not be able to follow. Wasn't it said that they could not cross water? Yet they followed him easily enough across the river from Brooklyn.

"I have work in this city," said Gob, passing his finger back and forth through the single candle at their table. "I think I will be retained by it for years." They were in a filthy saloon in Hester Street, sitting with a bottle of whiskey between them. It was November 5, 1867, Will's birthday. He was twenty-three years old. Gob, who Will had figured as immensely rich, had taken him to stuff at Delmonico's, and then Will had brought Gob to this saloon, one of his haunts since the house had changed him into a rank sensualist. Sympathy and spirits and fits—sometimes these seemed easy to abide compared to the last gift of the house, the other, which was a package of lustfulness and wantonness and drinking whiskey, which Will hated almost as much as ever but now had need of, though it never seemed to make him drunk.

Jolly and the angel boy had come along to the saloon, too. Jolly kept pointing at Gob, the same way he had led Will to Bellevue a year before and pointed at it, and led him inside, still pointing, to the office of the secretary, Dr. Macready. Since his appearance, Jolly had been silently guiding him through his life, pointing out the path he must take. Will went where Jolly pointed, because it was the only way to soothe him, and because it felt right to do it. Will had never organized his life by faith or ambition until he built the house—that work had seemed right and true and necessary. He had built it, hoping when it was finished it would practice some magic to make him serene. Now it was building him into a sad, discontented creature, and yet this also seemed right and true and necessary.

"Years and years," Gob said unhappily.

"You mean doctoring?"

"Partly," said Gob. He was a brilliant student, not liked at the school except by the faculty, who doted on him. He was haughty, and tended to correct his peers at every chance, wielding his immense knowledge like a blunt stick. In the army, they would have stuck him in a leper mess. Will had had no friends at Bellevue before Gob arrived, though he'd been there already for two terms. He hadn't wanted any friends—his wartime sociability had departed when peace came—and had not wanted either to be friends with Gob, but the boy had pursued him relentlessly since their encounter in the hall, and soon they were pretty fast.

"What else, then?" Will asked.

"Ah, I think I just might tell you, but not tonight. It's not birthday talk, and I'm sleepy, anyhow. And you have got to go cut up your capers." A lady in red boots had come up behind Will and leaned over to pat him on his chest.

"Shall we dance?" she asked him.

"I'm off, then," said Gob. "Happy birthday, Will."

"Is it your birthday, Mr. President?" asked the lady.

"Maybe," Will said to her, and asked Gob if he wouldn't stay this time for the private can-can dance. Gob shook his head and took up his coat. The tatterdemalion Gabriel cast a final glance at the saloon musicians, three drunks on the stage who made a cacophony on piano, fiddle, and cornet. Then he followed Gob, both of them barely visible in the dark between tables. The angel boy looked back before they left the saloon and waved goodbye. Jolly waved back.

"Come along, Mr. President," said the lady. Will had forgotten her name, though she'd danced for him before. He followed her towards the stairway, a whiskey bottle in one hand, her hand in the other. Jolly followed after them.

"You know I am not the president of anything."

"Not even the League of Large Gentlemen?"

"No," said Will. She took him up the stairs and onto a creaking wooden gallery, along which the private theaters were set. Will's dancer held a curtain open for him, and he passed in, Jolly right behind him. The room was directly over the trio, so the music was very loud.

The dancer pushed Will towards the far wall, where a photograph hung, two ladies dressed only in hats, their four breasts pressed together. Will sat down in a dirty yellow chair while the dancer closed the curtain, and Jolly flattened himself against the wall. The woman started to dance, kicking up her legs in that confined space. A few times she almost kicked Will in the head with her boots, but after a few near misses he became adroit at dodging her, even as he watched her take her skirt in her hand and toss it around. There were tiny bells sewn into the hem that made a small music which was sweet compared to the din below. She was not wearing any underclothes. She turned around, leaned forward, threw her skirt up over her head, then shook her dimpled ass in Will's face.

"Why don't you give it a slap?" she asked, but he did not do that. She had a few bruises back there already, one of them very much in the shape of Italy's kicking boot. She turned around again, holding her skirt up so it obscured her face but left her crotch in plain sight. It wasn't young anymore, what she had. It looked old and broken down, but still he thought it was fascinating. She inched towards him in tiny steps. It seemed to Will that it took forever for her to cover the scant distance from the curtain to the chair, and when at last she arrived to press herself into his face he thought that he would die, or at the very least fall away in a fit. The smell of her turned his stomach yet delighted all his base instincts. Jolly watched her too, though he tried to give the appearance of not watching her.

She stepped back from Will, reaching down with one hand to stroke his face, his neck, his shoulder. Still holding her skirt up, she undid her blouse and freed one of her breasts. Pendulous and covered with scars, it was utterly unbeautiful. It reminded Will of the breast of Mrs. Hanbury, a patient in Ward 23 at Bellevue. She was an ancient Negro woman, somnolent to the point that she would have seemed dead if she had not been hot to the touch. Once, Will was obliged to move her breast so he could listen to her weak heart. The breast seemed four feet long to him. It was unwieldy, a sock filled with sand, and it sought to thwart him; its wrinkled nipple was a mocking eye. The dancer's breast was unpleasant like that, but still it demanded his attention. She pushed it towards his mouth, but he only stared at the thing. She took the bottle from his hand, did something unspeakable with it, then put it to Will's lips. He drank greedily, not minding how the liquor ran down his chin. "Oh Jolly," Will said. "What am I doing?"

"Jolly indeed," said the lady, her hand on his pants now. "You're doing well enough."

Occasionally Jolly and Sam and Lewy Greeley and Frenchy and a dozen others would gather around a luxurious divan—the rudest ladies always preferred to drape themselves on it for their portrait—upon which the angel boy would sit with his legs crossed under him, his one wing waving lazily in the breeze from an open window. Will would demand of them, "What are you looking at? What?" Scolding them never did any good. He'd swum with Sam in a clear spring when they were boys. He'd looked down and seen fish through the clear water, floating and moving their mouths just like these spirits, open and closed and open, but never a sound came out. "Stop looking at me!" he'd say, but they wouldn't, and the only way he could escape them was by covering up his own eyes.

Being friendly with Gob was good for Will's education. Though technically his junior, Gob was farther along than Will; he'd been apprenticed to a respected German physician, Dr. Oetker, for three years before he came to Bellevue. His performance on the entrance exam had so impressed Macready that the secretary had made Gob a junior assistant in the second surgical division.

Under Gob's aegis, Will was allowed to assist on a surgery with the great Dr. Wood himself. It was a daring procedure, an exhilarating bowel repair. The fattest man Will had ever seen lay on the table. He'd been set on by would-be murderers after a feast, and their stabbing knives had poked three holes in his vast belly. Will and Gob hooked out loops of bowel and held them steady while Dr. Wood, a neat man who sported a boutonniere of violets on his black coat, sewed up the wounds. Will thought of the boy he'd carried over the field at Gettysburg, and how his guts had been similarly exposed.

"So you see, Mr. Woodhull," Dr. Wood was saying, "how you must put your stitches through the fibrous tunic of the intestine." He was finished with his suturing, and now he inspected his work from various angles. He took a decanter from another assistant and began to pour oil liberally over the wound. He smiled and said, "A little olive oil will facilitate the return of the bowel to the peritoneal cavity."

Surgery made Will partial to ether. Assisting Dr. Wood, he was often assigned the role of anesthetist. He'd apply Squibb's ether to the patient with a cone made of newspaper, a towel, and a wad of cotton. He filched small quantities and brought them home to Fulton Street for use in making collodion, and for sniffing. He liked to sit with all the lights out but the curtains open, and take little whiffs of ether until he passed into a dreamless black sleep.

It was better than hooking arteries or bowel, this ether-duty. Will never got sleepy administering the ether, but he sometimes developed a carefree attitude during the course of an operation. It made him bold.

"Doctor," he said to a senior assistant during a multiple amputation, "please stay away from the patient's head. You will cause her to combust." The assistant had a lit cigar wedged between his teeth.

"She says her mother was frightened by an elephant when she was pregnant," said Dr. Wood. The blond-headed girl on the table had been born with an extra finger and seven extra toes. Dr. Wood was pruning the girl to a better life. Whenever anyone noticed her finger she had suffered fits of hysterical blindness and St. Vitus's dance. "What do you think of that, Mr. Woodhull?"

"I think elephants are formidable creatures, sir," said Gob. "I think it is sensible to fear them." Dr. Wood laughed too long and too loud. Gob's hands, dexterous despite the congenital absence of one finger, were educated while Will looked on, wondering if his friend couldn't take the girl's extra finger as a replacement for his own. It didn't seem beyond him. Under Dr. Wood's tutelage, Gob tied off arteries and sewed up wounds, and once even opened up a skull with a Hey's saw. Will would have liked to do some cutting of his own, but Dr. Wood seemed unlikely ever to let him. He often looked scornfully at Will's big mashers and said, "*Those* are not the hands of a surgeon."

Many nights, Gob and Will would sit up with fresh amputees, watching over their wounds for signs of secondary hemorrhage. The patients would be arranged in their beds in a circle around the two students, with their stumps facing inward. Gob and Will would sit back to back, observing the stumps.

"I think blood is beautiful," Gob said during one such vigil.

"You wouldn't," said Will, "if you'd ever been covered in it for days. It loses its charm."

"I like it because it is perfect, because it does its work perfectly. A perfect fuel for a perfect machine." Jolly was walking up and down the ward, not waving or speaking, just turning his head this way and that, regarding everything with sadness and longing. Will looked away from him, his attention drawn to a stump that twitched briefly, and when he looked back Jolly was gone. The spirits came and went like that.

"I hate the smell," Will said. "And anyhow if I were less tired and more articulate I would argue that we are not perfect, body or soul." The stump that had twitched began to bleed again, so Will leaned forward to tighten a band of elastic around it, but this was not sufficient. He had to plunge his fingers through the stitches and feel blindly under the flap, seeking to catch the leaking artery between his fingers. The patient was screaming and the sheets were soaking through.

Gob put his little hand in, too, and in a moment he'd caught the vessel and pinched it. "Ah," he said, over the patient's screaming. "Feel that!" Will put his finger along Gob's and felt the blood beating. The strength and the rhythm of it did seem like a miracle, just then. "Perfect," said Gob. "Oh, I wish I could build like *this*."

Sometimes he'd feel the pressure of eyes on him as he walked, and looking back he would see them. Jolly was always out in front, taking measured, even steps. Will would keep walking, thinking they might go away if only he ignored them, but he never could. He'd look back again and again, and each time there'd be another, until there was a long train of them following him down Broadway or the Bowery or Fulton Street. They stepped fluidly among the living, never touching them even on the busiest streets, while Will, always looking over his shoulder, knocked packages from the arms of ladies, and got tangled in their parasols. "Stop following me!" he shouted, but he knew this would do nothing to deter them, and it did not.

* * *

In the lying-in ward, the women waiting to deliver kept busy making shrouds. Will wondered, as he walked among them, how many would lie buried in their work. Bellevue had a reputation as a nest of puerperal fever. Gob had switched to the second medical division after the end of the first term. Dr. Wood offered to make him a senior assistant, but Gob said he felt drawn to the medical wards, to the cholera and consumption and pneumonia. Will shadowed him there, and saw how his patients did better than others. Gob eschewed calomel and tartar emetic in all cases. He dosed the weak of heart with foxglove. He gave calcined magnesia for excessive flatulence, carbonate of soda for dyspepsia, a mixture of turpentine and gin for worms. Patients with intractable dry coughs who got no relief from syrup of squills were healed by a weird elixir. "Moss squeezings, bat's blood, and death angel," Gob said, and Will thought he must be joking.

They liked to go around the wards at night. The nurses were untrained and incompetent, sentenced to Bellevue to serve out ten-day terms for public drunkenness. They would find them snoring in a corner, the remains of Friday's fish dinner smeared on their frocks, while patients called out for assistance or mercy or death. Gob and Will might turn a patient on his side so he could urinate, a veteran with a bullet in his bladder that acted as a ball valve, or sit at the bedsides of cholera patients, measuring out grains of morphine into a cup of hot water. The cholera patients had shriveled fingers. Their lips were blue, and their clammy faces were shrunken.

By January of '68, Will had become an assistant in the first medical division. He spent most of his time in the basement, among the alcoholics and the insane. "They are all very unreasonable down there," he complained, when he came upstairs at night to visit Gob. "You are living the life here on the second floor, let me tell you." He would sit on a bed and throw wadded-up gauze at a passed-out nurse, saying, "Wake up, Sairey Gamp!" or else assist Gob in taking pulses and listening to hearts and lungs. When the patients were all asleep they would sit in a window, staring at the East River and talking quietly. They both belonged to a not very exclusive club of surviving brothers.

"Sam was the companion of my youth," Will said one night. "But then we grew distant."

"I failed him," said Gob, raising his hand as if to touch the full moon framed in the window. A cold wind was whipping up blue foam on the river.

"How does that happen? He was the only other person in the world, and then he was no one."

"If I had been with him he would yet be alive," Gob said quietly.

"He was a stranger to me, when he died," Will said. "Do you think that's a crime?" He looked around the room for Sam, thinking that talk of him might summon him. He wasn't there, but Jolly was pacing up and down the ward, looking at his feet as they walked.

"Help me!" said a cholera patient, sitting up suddenly in his bed. Will was too late with the bucket.

In the morning, they would go for a walk on the hospital grounds, which used to be filled with orchards of peach and apple and plum trees, but now were covered with small and large buildings of gneiss rock and brick. They would wander for a while in the cold, both of them exhausted but neither in a mood for sleep. Gob, Will discovered, had a morbid imagination. It seemed to Will that Gob was becoming a doctor for the wrong reason, not because he loved life, but because he was obsessed with death. Not that it was the right reason, either, to become a doctor at the direction of a spirit.

After their walk they might seek out Dr. Gouley, to assist him with an autopsy, Gob weighing livers or kidneys or brains while Will measured the thickness of a heart. Dr. Gouley, a lonely man, was happy for their company. "You work well together," he said to them on more than one occasion. Sometimes he invited them to put on loupes and do a detailed dissection. Gob liked to pull on the tendons of a flayed hand and make it beckon invitingly to the other corpses. When the organs were all removed, and there was nothing left in the late person but watery blood pooling in the gutters alongside the spine, Dr. Gouley would stare lovingly into the body and put his hands into the pink fluid, lifting it and holding it in his palms until it ran through his fingers. "My boys," he would say. "Do you see how we are vessels?"

The spirits followed Will to a place called the Pearl, a saloon run by a woman of the same name. It was a hideous dive. A white-painted glass ball as big as a head hung over the door. Inside, it looked at first glance like any other saloon—dim and smoky, with sawdust on the floor. But there was a door in the back, and if you went through it you found yourself, not outside in the alley, but at the top of a staircase, and if you took those stairs down you entered a bagnio, a maze, in whose secret recesses prostitutes reclined expectantly.

Will went downstairs without looking back to see how many followed. At the bottom of the stairs, he opened the door to the maze. Down there it was musty, and it stank of fish. What might once have been stored there he never knew, but it seemed like a place that must once have held bones. Along the twisting, turning way there were recesses, hidden by thin curtains, where couches sat. Some of the curtains were drawn, and if there were lights inside they threw copulating silhouettes onto the hanging fabric. Grunting cries rang off the low ceiling.

There was something he liked about these seedy, curtained places. He had enough money from portrait-taking that he could visit a nice house, someplace on West Twenty-fifth Street, where the girls were pretty and all the fornication was done amid the trappings of purity. He might visit every one of the Seven Sisters' houses, or dress up in his finest clothes for a visit to Josie Woods's. He'd heard about those places—white sheets and soft beds, girls with clean hair and shining faces who dressed up in old-fashioned hoop skirts and spoke with great refinement—but he had never visited one. The glass house had made him honest in his debauchery; when he wallowed he wallowed like a pig.

He went in through the first open curtain he found. There was a girl sitting on a green couch piled with blankets. She was reading a book by the light of a lantern hung on the wall. A pair of cracked spectacles were balanced on the end of her nose.

"Close the curtain, darling," she said, without looking up. "I never like to put on a show." Already, a cloud of witnesses was crowding inside, jostling him with their cool flesh. Jolly's and Sam's were the only familiar faces, though there were a dozen or more with him. He couldn't meet Sam's eyes, but he couldn't leave the place, either, couldn't go home and read, couldn't even content himself with rubbing up against some pretty, unsuspecting lady on a Second Avenue stage, as a more restrained fiend might do.

He had whiskey with him, and she asked to sip it from his mouth, so he took some and he kissed her. She would not take off her glasses and they bumped against his face. She lifted her dress, really just an old and stained shift of silk, put her book down gently on the couch, and lay back, putting one arm behind her head. Pushing her glasses up high on her nose, she told Will to take down his pants. He opened up his jacket and his shirt so he could press his skin against hers. She was clammy and cold, and her breasts were pimply, but he kissed them as if he loved them.

After a while, the girl gave a little titter. Will thought it was because his work was unsatisfying and ridiculous, but in fact she was laughing at some bit of humor in her book, which she had picked up again, and was reading over his shoulder. He propped himself up on his elbows and looked down at her.

"What, darling?" she asked. "What? It's Mr. Dickens. I can hardly put it down. Not for anything. So go on. Just go right on with it." The spirits, crowded close, were nodding avidly, and their mouths were moving as if to say, *Yes, do.*

* * *

"Hold still," Will said, because Gob would not stop fidgeting. "You'll ruin the photograph."

"Sorry," said Gob, but he kept moving his eyes and his head to look at the pictures around the studio. Will had brought him to Brooklyn for a complimentary portrait, motivated by friendship and by Jolly. Will was thrilled to be able to teach Gob the photographic process, because he'd learned as much about medicine from Gob as he had from their professors. And as they walked on South Street one day, Jolly had pointed repeatedly at Gob and then at Brooklyn, making it very obvious that he wanted Will to take him there.

"I'll bind your head to the stand," Will said.

"What's that one?" Gob asked, moving his arm, too, to point at a plate negative taken at Bull Run. It was not one of Frenchy's. Will had been collecting them from other photographers.

"Now it's ruined," Will said, taking his head out of the camera and scowling.

"Is that one from Chickamauga?" Gob asked, walking over to examine the plate.

"No," said Will. "I have none from that battle. That's three plates you've wasted. Why can't you hold still?"

"Where are the pictures from Chickamauga?" Gob asked. He went rooting among the mounds of pictures and plates on tables around the room. Will finally made him understand that there were no pictures from Chickamauga, but Gob was fascinated by any picture. He held the negative plates up to the light and closed his eyes and said, "Oh!" With their sleeves rolled up and their collars loosened, they looked at every picture Will owned. Gob delighted especially in the stereoscopic images. He sat cross-legged on the floor, looking at Mr. Gardner's gruesome photographs, reaching out his hand repeatedly to try and touch the carnage that floated before him.

When there were no more pictures to look at, Will taught Gob how to take and develop a photograph. He mastered the process immediately. There were people who did not have to be shown a thing twice to learn it, but with Gob you almost didn't have to show him even once. When Will asked how he knew to make the negative for an ambrotype thin and light, Gob only said, "Well, it makes sense, doesn't it?" He insisted on taking Will's picture, and Will obliged him, though he didn't like it. He stood in a formal pose, next to a broken plaster column and an urn. He was surrounded by spirits, Jolly and Lewy Greeley and even Sam, who stood away from him, but still within the picture. Gob developed the picture himself, mounted it as an ambrotype, and then presented it to Will.

"Ah, you're a professional," Will said. It was a good picture. He looked like a big hulking fool, with his sleepy, stupid gaze and his slack idiot's mouth: Gob had captured him. There were no spirits in the picture, but they clustered around Will to look at it, as if expecting to find themselves in the glass.

Just as the day ended, they went up to the roof. Will had never shown the glass house to anyone, because he had no friends with which to share any secrets, least of all a peculiar monument to death, a greenhouse fit for the cultivation of fat white tombflowers. But he thought it would interest Gob, because pictures fascinated him, and because death fascinated him. And Jolly pointed urgently at Gob, at the stairs, at Gob again, and made sweeping motions with his hands, as if to shoo the both of them up to the roof.

"You're a builder, too," Gob said when he saw it. It was a warm Sunday in February. The last night's snow had been melting all day off the glass house, so it looked clean and fresh and wet. Gob reached out with his hand, running his finger from plate to plate. A crowd of spirits gathered, between eyeblinks, to watch him. "May I go in?" Gob asked.

"Certainly," Will said. Then he thought how it might change Gob as it had changed him, and he said, "Wait, it could hurt you."

"I'm sure it won't," Gob said, and he went into the house. Will put it down to a trick of the setting sun, how yellow light flashed inside. Spirits were all around them. They joined hands to circle the house, and then they danced around it, first one way, and then the other. Will had never seen them all so happy. Even ever-angry Frenchy was happy, even Sam was smiling and dancing. Only the angel boy didn't dance. He perched on the top of the house, blowing his bugle at the sun.

Did it follow, Will wondered, that if you could see them you ought to be able to hear them, too? What logic governed such interaction? He could hear the cannon still sounding, still deafening, still waking him every so often from sleep. Often it was just Frenchy standing watch over his bed. Sometimes he had a plate with him, one upon which pictures flashed like the images from a magic lantern. Will saw the faces of strangers, night landscapes, scenes of the war, a shack on a hill with a decaying orchard behind it, a dark thick wood at twilight. Frenchy would point at the images and talk, wearing the same expression as when he'd been Will's living instructor, an angry, impatient look that very often got screwed up into a raging scowl as he yelled and yelled.

"I can't hear you," Will would say, when Frenchy worked himself into a fury. "But it suits you, sir, this quietness. I think it has made you likable, dear Frenchy." This made him angrier, but Will, grumpy anyhow at being woken, felt compelled to tease him. "Dear, meek Frenchy. Quiet as a mouse!"

Will stood on Fifth Avenue, looking up at Number 1 East Fifty-third Street, wondering if his friend could really live in this enormous house. Gob had invited him for supper, reciprocating, Will supposed, the invitation to Brooklyn. "We'll eat," Gob said, "and then I'll show you something."

It was only a day since Gob had stumbled weeping out of the glass house. Will had caught him by the shoulders and said, "I knew it! It's hurt you to go in there." But Gob said he was crying tears of joy, and then he hurried off, saying only that he had work to do.

Gob opened the door, looking exhausted but very happy. "My friend!" he said. "There you are!" He clapped Will on the back and drew him inside. It was the finest house that Will had ever seen, though very dirty. There were three reception rooms and two drawing rooms, with what must have been five hundred mirrors hanging on all their high walls. In the dining room there was a table four times as long as Will was himself. There was a meal already set up: soup, corn, green peas, cabbage, beets, puddings and pies, a salad of dandelion greens, pork with stewed apples, steak with peaches, salt fish with onions, coffee and wine and cold root beer. Gob played with his food, arranging it in patterns on his plate, but not eating much. "I'm never hungry when I've been working," he explained. Will waited for Gob to speak of the glass house, to tell him what had happened inside, but he said nothing of it. Will had been ready, when Gob came out, to make a confession to him: *I see spirits* or *I fear I'm insane*, and he had hoped, he knew now, that Gob would say, *Oh yes, those pesky spirits. They're everywhere!* It would be so pleasant, so unburdening, to share the affliction. But Gob gave no sign of seeing the spirits. As Will had approached Manhattan on the ferry, they'd run like children, leaning dangerously over the rails, pointing excitedly at the churning water. When Gob opened the door, they'd swarmed into his house like yokels bustling to get into Barnum's. Now, they sported everywhere in the room. Sam stood by the table, looking sadly at a pudding, not a foot from Gob's elbow.

Will sighed. Since Gob was not forthcoming, he would be rude. Gob was talking about how long ago, with Dr. Wood looking on, he'd removed a tumor from the jaw of Emily McNee, the Sozodont dentifrice heiress. He was praising her teeth when Will interrupted.

"What did you see, there in my little house?"

"Ah," Gob said, smiling and passing a hand over his eyes. "What did I see?"

"Yes," said Will. "That's what I asked."

"What did *you* see?"

"I saw nothing," Will said, "but now I see . . . spirits. There. I've said it. Sir, I think it cost me my sanity to go into that place."

"Spirits!" Gob said, and Will thought at first that he was angry. He put his face in his hands, and his voice was plaintive. "I wish I saw them! I wish I did. But that comfort is denied me."

"Comfort? You don't think," Will said, "that such visions are manufactured by a sick mind?"

Gob raised his head and gave Will a scornful look. "You insult my mother," he said. Will did not know whether or not to apologize, because now Gob was laughing, louder and louder, and pounding his fist on the table so forcefully that plates danced and glasses tipped.

"Come along," Gob said, when he had calmed some. "Let's have the rest of the tour." He took Will's arm and walked with him. In the parlors, there were marble-topped tables, armchairs and sofas of black lacquered wood inlaid with mother-of-pearl. There were rugs two and three deep on the floor, stained in the corners but otherwise bright and beautiful. And there were books everywhere, stacked on tables or furniture, or against the walls. Will picked one up at random. It was dusty and smelled of mold, but the binding was rich leather, and the title stood out in gold on the spine: *The Dove of Archytas*.

"Of course," said Gob. "You'd like to see the library, wouldn't you?"

That room took up most of the second and third floors. They climbed a spiral staircase to the iron mezzanine and looked down at the floor, where a score of grandfather clocks, all run down and silent, were set randomly around the room, among golden armillary spheres and dusty overstuffed chairs.

"My master liked clocks," Gob said.

"You mean your late uncle?" Will asked. "Dr. Oetker?" At Bellevue, Dr. Oetker had had a reputation for brilliance. Will had heard that he had made a fortune catering to the ills of fashionable and unfashionable society.

"He was not my uncle. But he admired a good clock. He'd ask me sometimes, 'Who is the god of the future?' "

"Professor Morse?" said Will. Gob laughed.

"That answer would have gotten you a slap."

"What was the answer, then?"

Gob was silent for a moment, and then he said, "I don't like clocks. It used to be my job to care for them, but since he died I've been, as you can see, on holiday. Onward and upward."

He took Will out of the library, and they went down halls that were increasingly, in the upper levels of the house, littered with little pieces of machinery. Gears and struts and cranks and cylinders, they lay in the halls, or they were piled in the guest bedrooms and parlors. In one room, empty of furniture except for a magnificent bed whose mahogany posts were carved with laurel and acanthus leaves, Gob was reunited with a friend. "My aeolipile!" he said, speaking of a tall bronze globe, decorated with a figure of the wind—a gleeful face with pursed lips and puffed cheeks. It was obviously broken, cracked at the bottom and looking as if it were missing parts. "I made this when I was a child," he said to Will, putting his arms around it and hugging it to him. "I haven't seen it for years."

Gob's bedroom was on the fifth floor. "Lots of stairs," Will said, "to climb every night."

Gob shrugged. There were two doors off the hall at the top of the house. One was made of wood, the other iron. The iron door was open, rusted on its hinges so when Will stumbled against it it moaned horribly. He peered inside and saw the gray shapes of dead trees, lit up by weak moonlight falling through a dirty glass roof. "Not in there," Gob said, pulling Will away and opening the wooden door. This was the neatest place in the house. There was a blue skylight in the ceiling, and a second iron door in the wall on the far side of the room.

"Don't stand there," Gob said. Will had stepped into a circle of stone, set incongruously in the wood floor.

"Sorry," Will said, because a look of extreme displeasure had passed over his friend's face. He walked out of the circle, and Gob smiled again.

"Now I will show you my house," he said.

"I think you just did," Will said, misunderstanding. Gob opened the second iron door in the far side of the room and they entered a place crowded with spirits and machinery. It looked like the pack-hole of some industrious squirrel, one that robbed factories instead of trees. There were gears of all sizes, great tangles of cable, stacks of lumber and steel plates, and underneath an ornate gaselier an assemblage that Will knew must be a machine of some sort, though he had never seen anything like it. Some spirits were caressing it, others milled happily about the room, gazing at pieces of matériel like fascinated gallery-goers.

"What is it?" Will asked, pointing to the machine.

"A combination," Gob said, "of resistant bodies so arranged that by their means the mechanical forces of nature can be compelled to do work accompanied by certain determinate motions. It's an engine. *My* house, you see, like *your* house."

Will looked at it, his hands in fists at his sides. It seemed familiar and wonderful, and horrible, too, in the same way his glass house was horrible. "Are you compelled to build it?" Will asked. Gob grabbed him roughly by the shoulders, and Will thought he would eject him from the room, but instead he embraced him, crushing him with his little arms, crying happy tears again and saying, "Oh Will, oh my good friend, you understand me. You are a builder, too."

There was another spirit, initially as furtive as the others were bold, and the only female. She flitted outside Will's window, or she hid in the shadow of an alley at night, and he'd only catch a glimpse of her as he passed by. She was different because she was shy, and because she looked to be a complete angel. He'd groaned when he saw her. Somehow it was bearable to see a half angel. It did not bode the same ill for one's mind or one's equanimity. But she was entire. There was no missing her strange wings, her great height and fine green robes that looked to be hewn out of malachite, or the spots of green light that floated around her head like a crown of emeralds. She had strange wings and strange eyes. They were the darkest eyes Will had ever seen, flat and black as if someone had gouged them out and filled up the sockets with ink. Her wings were white and not made of feathers but tiny things like fingers or the beard of a cuttlefish.

One night he woke, not at the sound of the cannon, but because a cat was screaming on his roof. He lay with his eyes closed, thinking the animal might have become trapped in the glass house. When he opened his eyes the spirit was there, kneeling by his bed and leaning over him, so close he thought she might kiss him. She opened her mouth, and then she fled. Not a moment later, the little angel boy arrived, looking furious, stomping silently around the room. He turned to Will and shook his finger at him.

It was the last question Will would have asked, what the machine would do. He might not ever have known, if Gob hadn't volunteered the answer. He had never known what the glass house would do—he'd just built it. He assumed that Gob, too, was building in ignorance of ultimate function. But Gob told him, standing in his workshop, the purpose he meant for his machine to accomplish, and it did not seem so terribly insane. Or it seemed properly insane, to build a machine to abolish death. Only the most reasonable of lunatics could devote his life to something so sensible and worthwhile, to put aside all other work and devote himself to this ultimate concern. "Will you help me, Will?" Gob had asked. "I mean to lick death, but I can't do it alone. Will you help me win?" Jolly and Sam were standing on either side of Will, and their lips seemed to be moving in the same manner as Gob's, asking the same question.

"What can I do?" Will had asked, because it seemed to him that he could do nothing. He confessed that he had built the glass house from blind, ignorant compulsion. He wasn't an engineer or a mechanic. He did not understand steam power or aeolipiles or how steel was different from iron. But Jolly was jumping up and down, pointing to himself and at Sam, as if to suggest that they would help him.

Will waved his hand at all the parts and pieces around the room, at the machine under the gaselier. "I don't understand any of this. I don't know how to use such things, or how to make them."

When Will said this, Gob only smiled wider. "I'll teach you, my friend," he said. "And then we'll build together."

"Sam," Will said, "why don't you come over here and sit with me?" Every so often he'd set two chairs by the big window over Fulton Street, sit down in one, and pat the other invitingly. "It's nice on a cold day," he said to his brother, "to sit in the sun and look out on the snow and the people bundled in their coats and think how you're warm. Come and sit for a while. We'll just be quiet together." He patted again, gestured with both his hands, but Sam only stood on the far side of the room and eyed him warily. He shook his head as if to remind Will that he was a spirit, that he couldn't feel such pleasures as warm sunlight, couldn't touch the glass to marvel at how cold it was. Or else he shook his head just to say I will not sit with you, to say I do not know you, to say you are not any more my friend now than you were when I lived.

"I used to hate liquor," said Will, taking a sip from the big flask of brandy he and Gob carried with them in the ambulance. On a cold spring day in 1868, Gob drove them hurriedly through a light snow to Number 344 East Thirty-second Street, where a lady had been shot by her deranged sister. Gob had finished his two terms of lectures. Those and his long apprenticeship with Dr. Oetker were enough to earn him his diploma from Bellevue. He might have become a house physician, but chose instead to enter the newly established ambulance service. Will, though he hadn't yet earned his diploma, and wouldn't until he'd completed another term, joined Gob in the ambulance, which had lamps placed on the sides and a reflector attached to the roof. The word "ambulance" was emblazoned on all sides, but this did not stop Gob from yelling at anyone who blocked their way, "Can't you see this is an ambulance?"

The calls came in by telegraph from the police headquarters. The job was always exciting, especially at night. When they were working, Gob and Will slept in a room over the ambulance stables, a bell above their bed. When it rang it also caused a weight to fall which lit the gas. They would stumble around, blinking in the light, grabbing for their coats, and then rush to the ambulance. The harness, saddle, and collar were suspended from the ceiling, and dropped into place automatically at the sound of the alarm. Not more than two minutes ever passed between the time the bell sounded and the time they rushed out of the stable.

Will handed the flask at Gob, who declined it, saying they would not have enough when they got to their patient. In a box beneath the seat were blankets and splints, tourniquets and bandages. They had a straitjacket and a stomach pump and a copy of Gross's *Hints on the Emergencies of Field, Camp, and Hospital Practice.* They had a medicine chest with emetics and antidotes and morphine. They never failed to lack something, however, when they arrived at the scene of misfortune.

Will put his hand out to catch the swirling snow as they sped along down Broadway. This was their third call of the day. Earlier, a junk dealer had been crushed by her own cart when it tipped and fell on her at the foot of Roosevelt Street. Before that, a woman getting off the rear platform of a Third Avenue horsecar had been run over by a sleigh. Both those patients had lived.

The gunshot woman died cursing her sister, though they cared for her wound as best they were able, covering it with lint saturated in balsam of Peru, and enlarging the exit wound so it could drain properly. Back at Bellevue, they saw her set up in a bed in Ward 26, and made her comfortable with brandy and morphine. Will wrote down her last words, *Damn you Sally*. He had a collection of those. He wrote them in inch-high letters on fine creamy white paper: *Is it over?; Do you hear the pretty music?; I would rather live; No; What help are you?; Tell my horse I love her.*

When they were not at the ambulance house, they were at Gob's house. So far, Will had made what seemed to him to be merely decorative contributions to the construction. He tied last words to strings and hung them from the body of the machine, or he fixed death masks to it, and Gob made a fuss over Will's efforts, like a doting, overpraising parent. Will felt ignorant and useless, but his education had begun in earnest. He had thought Gob had a masterful knowledge of medicine, but now he was coming to believe that he had a masterful knowledge of everything.

One day in April, he had Will follow him through the house with a wheelbarrow. Gob took books from where they lay and threw them in. "Oh yes," he'd say, picking up a volume, "you had better be familiar with this, if we are going to make any progress." Each title was more dismaying to Will than the last: *Optics, Acoustics, Thermotics, Stability of Structures, Intellectual and Ethical Philosophy, Higher Geodesy, Analytical Geometry of Three Dimensions, Calculus of Variations*. Then there was all the Aristotle: eight books on physics, four on meteors, thirteen on metaphysics, two on generation and destruction. "What am I forgetting?" Gob asked as they stood in the library, the wheelbarrow already overflowing. He looked thoughtful for a moment, then said, "Of course, the Renaissance Magi!" He scurried around the room, plucking books from the shelves. Will looked at the authors' names, men of whom he had never heard, books that looked to be a hundred years old or more. Paracelsus and Nettesheim and Della Porta, Albertus Magnus and Mirandola and Dr. Dee, Gob tossed them about without a care for their ancient bindings and brittle pages.

"You will learn!" Gob kept saying, but days spent reading about

Determinative Mineralogy or the Seven Names of God made Will suspect that Gob's faith was misplaced. He would put his face between his knees and have a spell of worry. "It's too hard, Jolly," he'd say, because Jolly was always leaning over his shoulder when he read. Jolly would shake his head and smile and wag his finger, as if to scold him for his despair. Will took to reading in the glass house. Inside, it was pleasant and warm in the spring, but he went in even after summer came, and sweat ran off his nose to drum on the pages of Della Porta's *Celestial Physiognomy*, because it seemed to him that his brain was more agile in there, and it restored some of his faith in himself, since it was proof that he could, after all, build something.

It was in the glass house that Will got what he considered to be his first good idea. He was struggling with a simple book of algebra, wearing nothing but his pants because it was so hot. Sometimes when he got frustrated he would abuse Gob's precious books. Usually he would imagine a face for them, a mocking face embossed on the leather cover, with a snide mouth that he would punch and punch until his fist ached. He did that for a while, staining the leather with his sweaty hand, and finally threw it against a wall of the house, where it knocked out a plate that fell on the rooftop but miraculously did not break. He took up the book gently (he was always kind and loving to them after he abused them) and went outside. He picked up the plate and considered it, and holding the book in one hand and the plate in the other, he had his idea. Jolly stepped up from behind him, shivering with excitement. He seemed to know what Will was thinking. Will closed his eyes and imagined a great shield of negative plates that could be placed over the engine, with a bright light positioned above them, so that they rained down images on it, filling it with lost lives.

Will thought it was a bug hurrying across his cheek. They came out of his walls in the summer, fat black moist-looking things that he doused with acid to kill them. Sometimes they crawled on him while he was sleeping, but when he woke he saw that the tickling pressure on his face was not from little feet but from a wing. She moved them just like fingers, the not-feathers. The angel looked earnestly into his face, closed her eyes, and trembled as if with a sob. Her wings made a noise like broken glass shaken in a bag. She opened her mouth again, and to Will's great surprise, words came out of it.

"Creature," she said, "why do you participate in abomination?"

In August, Will got another invitation to dinner, this one from Gob's mother, Mrs. Woodhull, who was recently arrived in New York. She'd set up her house in Great Jones Street, not with her son. "I wouldn't let her live with me," Gob said, when Will asked why she didn't stay in Fifth Avenue. "Not in ten thousand years."

"Is she a difficult person?" Will asked, thinking of his own difficult mama.

"Yes. And she is always surrounded by difficult people. But you can judge her for yourself tonight. Oh, yes. I like that. My friend, you are a genius of building!" They were installing the images over the engine. Gob had jumped up and down and hugged himself when Will showed up at his friend's house with a rented cart full of plates.

"I like it too," Will said. They were hot and filthy from their work. Now the machine would shelter under a giant flower of picture negatives. It was late in the day, but the sky was still bright outside, and the plates they'd installed were gently lit.

"We need a brighter light," Gob said. "Maybe the brightest light ever."

They kept working until it was almost time for dinner. Will might have kept going and going with it—he was filled with the same feeling as when he'd built the glass house, a mixture of trepidation and certainty, because he knew he must build but feared what he was building—but he noticed the time and excused himself to go home and change his clothes. He was an hour late when he arrived at Number 17 Great Jones Street. A man fully as big as Will, but fatter and hairier, opened the door.

"What do you want?" he asked.

"I've been invited to dinner," Will said, thinking the man must be a servant because he smelled like a stable.

"Not by me," the man said. He made to shut the door in Will's face, but before he could do that, a lovely red-haired woman came up behind him, scolding and pinching him. He yelped just like a dog and stood aside.

"I know you are Dr. Fie," said the lady. "Please come in, and do not mind my rude brother."

"Not a doctor yet, ma'am. Are you Mrs. Woodhull?" Will asked, though this lady looked too young to be Gob's mother.

"Her sister." She said her name was Tennie C. Claflin, spelling it for him. She took for herself the flowers he'd brought for the hostess, a summer bouquet of daisies and violets. She put one of each in her hair and kissed Will on the cheek. This made him blush and veer towards a fit, though what she excited was not his sympathy.

"Push her off now or she'll slobber on you all night long," the brother said, then shuffled away down the hall.

"Come along," Miss Claflin said. "Everyone is waiting to meet Gob's good friend. Our Gob! Lost to us for so long, but now we are together again. He tells me you see spirits."

Will opened his mouth but did not speak. He felt more faint, and hotter. He stumbled over a man's boot left carelessly in the hall. Miss Claflin kept him from falling.

"Was it a secret? Forgive him for telling it. There are no secrets in this family. And don't worry that we'll think less of you. I see them too, you know, as does my sister. You are like us, sir. Hello! Here we are, everybody! Here is Dr. Fie!"

They'd come to the dining room, where a crowd of people was gathered around a worn oak table. Gob was sitting with another beautiful lady who Will guessed must be his mama. She had dark hair, and wore a fine purple dress, and Gob was her very image. There was another aunt, less friendly than Miss Tennie C. Claflin, this one called Utica. Her eyes—they all had the same eyes, a shade of blue so dark it almost seemed purple—were hooded, Will could tell, from too much laudanum. There was a shriveled-up old woman who looked as if she might be some clever making of Gob's, an effigy of nutshells and bark, but with those same voracious blue eyes. She was his grandmother, and like Gob she lacked the smallest finger of her left hand. There were three men—an old one-eyed fellow who looked like the Devil, the big hairy one who'd answered the door, and finally another man with elaborate whiskers and brown eyes. They were introduced as Buck Claflin, Uncle Malden, and Colonel Blood, Gob's stepfather.

Colonel Blood shook Will's hand, but the other men ignored him. Miss Claflin sat him down between herself and drunken Utica. Then the family proceeded to feast. Grandma Anna brought out bowls full of peas and potatoes, and plates heaped with lamb chops. There was a diversity of manners among them. Miss Claflin and Mrs. Woodhull and Gob and Colonel Blood ate primly and talked in low voices, but the others ate with hand and knife, and shouted. Buck and Malden fought over a chop.

"We have been all through the western states," Miss Claflin said to him, turning the conversation to herself and her family after asking many prying questions about Will. "We gathered gold and golden opinions wherever we went. And we gathered up the Colonel, too. He comes from St. Louis, where he consulted with Vicky for the sake of his wife, who suffers terribly with a condition I am not at liberty to discuss. Vicky is a clairvoyant healer, you see. And in that regard I am not myself without power. But when she saw the Colonel, Vicky fell into a trance, and the spirits of the air spoke through her, betrothing them on the spot. Then he came along with us."

"A rash man," said Will.

"He's a hero. He has got six bullets in his body. And do you think it rash when one magnet comes together with another, as nature has decreed that they must? Is a river rash because it flows from a high place to a low one? Is it rash of the sea to yearn towards the moon? He only did what he must. Now, do you really think he is rash?"

Before Will could speak, Gob's mother raised her voice above all the others. She had been talking excitedly at Gob, pausing every now and then to embrace him. He suffered her hugs with an expression of perfect neutrality.

"All these years of wandering and wondering. The beautiful Greek has at last revealed his name to me. It is Demosthenes. Do you know what that means?"

"That's Vicky's spirit guide," Miss Claflin whispered. "He is her mentor and her constant companion."

"I don't," said Gob.

"It means that all my waiting is over!" Mrs. Woodhull said. "Now, now it can begin! Close your eyes, darling." Mrs. Woodhull sat in her son's lap and put her hands over his eyes. "There, don't you see them? Don't you see the great things that are coming?" Will closed his eyes, because everyone else was doing it, and saw the angel in his mind, and thought how her hair was red like Miss Claflin's, and how, even as she had asked him again why he participated in abomination, he cherished lascivious thoughts of her.

"It's another sign," said Mrs. Woodhull, "that you've returned to your family. Isn't it so good to be together again, all of us? Now we'll all be together forever. Come, everybody! Come and embrace our sweet lost sheep!" Miss Claflin hurried down to the other end of the table and threw her arms around Gob. "I could squeeze you till you pop!" she declared. Blood put his hero's arms around him, and Anna slipped her withered stick-limbs around his belly. Utica knelt down and clutched his leg, overcome suddenly with emotion and drunkenness. She wept against his pants. Big Malden put his long arms around them all and squeezed. Buck sauntered down and made as if to walk by the affectionate heap. He stopped and considered it for a moment. Then Will thought he would join the embrace, but instead Buck turned and backed his ass into the great lump of bodies.

Gob had disappeared entirely, and Will did not know if he should join them or quietly slip away. They chattered and squeezed and writhed and cried, and began to quarrel among themselves, saying, "You are squeezing too hard," or "Let me have a grab at him, hog!" Buck was cruel to Utica, calling her a whore and saying that the only thing worth a damn in her had been her virginity, and wasn't it a shame how she had ruined that herself with a carrot when she was eleven? Then Mrs. Woodhull's clear strong voice rose up, saying would you blame a vegetable for your own hungry sin?

"Come along, Will," said Gob, who was suddenly next to him. How he had escaped from his family, Will could not tell. They slipped away from the pile as it degenerated into individual quarrels. The grandmother called Colonel Blood a corrupter and a schweinehund, and attacked him with a potato.

"I'm sorry," Gob said, when they were outside in the twilight on Great Jones Street. "They're a rough bunch."

There was a spirit, a young fellow dressed up in the fetching uniform of a Zouave, who made a habit of staring at Will, then scribbling on a pad of paper the same size as the plate which Frenchy always carried with him. Will thought the soldier must be taking notes on his behavior, in order to tattle to whatever otherworldly ministry exists to register such transgressions. Will only discovered that the spirit was not taking notes, but drawing a picture, when he was finally shown the finished piece. "Who are you, anyhow?" Will demanded, because he did not like the portrait, in which he was naked, and possessed of an embarrassment of stiff, dripping organs of procreation. They stuck out from him like quills on a porcupine. In twenty arms he held a variety of bottles, each one containing, he was sure, some foul liquor. "Did I commission this insult?" Will asked and looked away from the picture. He would have liked never to look at it again, but the spirit would put it in his way, so he'd have no choice but to see it where it hung on a stage, or in the hospital wards, or on a Broadway streetlamp where thousands of people passed it in a day, but did not know it was there.

"It's very warm in here," said Miss Claflin. "Is it always so warm?" She had arrived unexpectedly, and now was in Will's studio sitting for a carte de visite. He'd answered the door in his shirtsleeves because he'd thought she was Gob, come over for another load of negative plates. "I'm here for my portrait," she'd said, as if he had invited her. He'd hurried to dress himself properly while she poked about the studio, choosing a setting for her portrait, just a plain chair in which she sat sideways.

"You mustn't talk, Miss Claflin."

"Call me Tennie," she said. "I insist upon it, and I won't tell you again." She was wearing a heavy-looking yellow dress, with a dark red wrap of silk thrown over her shoulders, hiding her arms and her hands, and her hair was coiffed up formidably on her head like a great pair of ram's horns. Her oval face was aglow with perspiration.

"Hold still your head, Miss Tennie, or else your face will be all a blur." Will thought of Frenchy's blond hospital boy, with his blurred, cursing mouth. Tennie held still, and stared unblinking at Will, so he felt not at all hidden behind the lens and under the hood. But she was oblivious to the spirits around her. So much for her claim that she too, saw them, Will thought. Sam and Lewy Greely and Jolly walked around her, all of them peering and gawking as if they'd never seen a pretty lady before. Frenchy stood close by the camera, scolding. Will exposed the negative, counting out fifteen seconds, then put the cap back on. "I'll return," he said, and left to develop the plate. He found he was breathless, waiting just the few moments as he poured the developer down the plate. Then her image was there, ghostly and reversed. He went up to the roof to make the print in the sun, then came back to the darkroom to tone and fix it. A half hour passed before she was represented to his satisfaction, as pretty and bold in the picture as she was in real life.

"I think you'll be pleased," he said as he came out of the darkroom. "I think," he continued, but then he quite forgot what he was going to say. Tennie C. Claflin had taken off her clothes and sat dressed only in her hairdo, in the very same pose as before, with her head still stuck quite securely in the stand. Her clothes seemed to have melted off her like spun sugar in a hot rain. All the spirits had fled, except Jolly, who had retreated against a wall, where he turned his face towards the ceiling but his eyes towards the lady.

"It's warm, Dr. Fie," Ms. Claflin said. "It's so terribly warm."

"Do you remember your first time?" she asked him.

"No," Will said, turning in the bed so she could not see his face. "Not really." But he remembered it clearly. It was not three days after he'd finished the glass house. He'd been walking on Broadway, followed by spirits. It was early in the night, but the prostitutes were already swarming. It had always been his habit, when they gestured at him, or when they called out something rude about his size, to ignore them. But this time, when one waved him after her down Grand Street, he followed. "Are you lost?" she asked when he approached. She stood just beyond the reach of a streetlamp, so a little light fell on her dress and her neck and her hair, but none on her face.

"Probably," Will said. His stomach was all knotted up, the way it had always been during a hot fight, and just like then he felt quite certain that he had no say in his actions. His feet were walking after this bad woman like his eye and his hand had conspired to shoot his enemy, and when he had her against a damp wall in an alley, it was as terrible and inevitable as having the life of a Reb. He raised her dress up over her head, and the delicate but filthy material caught on her snaggly teeth as she smiled at him.

"I was seven years old," Tennie said excitedly.

"An early start," Will said, glad she could not see the dismay on his face.

"Vicky started even earlier. I was in Pennsylvania. Mama and Papa had sent me off to live with relatives, because we were so poor. Aunt Sally's fruit spoke to me from the cupboard. 'We are for you!' they said. 'Come in and have us!' There were some wormy apples on the table, so I asked, 'Aunt, where have you hid all the good fruit?' She called me her darling and said the apples were the best she had, but I walked to the cupboard and I showed her. It was my sister Thankful, still a little girl as she was when she died, who spoke in the voice of a peach and called to me from the cupboard. After that, I heard her and saw her always. Wasn't it that way with you? Some spirit you loved sought you out, and then you saw others?"

"No," said Will. "I saw them all at once."

"Well," she said. "Why should it be the same for everybody? Oh, there she is now! There's my Thankful!"

"I don't see her," Will said.

"You wouldn't. She is only for me and Vicky to see."

"Does she speak?"

"Faintly. She is saying, 'I heard you talking of me.' "

Tennie began to have a one-sided conversation, talking of a place called Homer and agreeing that the orchard there had the sweetest apples ever. As she spoke, she seemed to forget Will, though she had him clasped firmly in her arms. Her conversation became a sleepy mumble, until finally she fell quiet. Will felt her twitch a few times. He lay awake as spirits came to visit, a procession of them like shepherds and animals passing by the sacred crib, gazing down on him and his lady acquaintance and smiling. He thought the angel would come again to scold him. She never did arrive, but long after all the other spirits had gone, the boy with the trumpet remained, hunched up in a corner of the ceiling.

"Avaunt," Will said, to no effect.

The boy shook his head and blinked slowly, and Will fell asleep with him still up there, staring down.

3

"ONE THOUSAND OF THE BEST MEN IN THE CITY," SAID GOB, "and two thousand of the worst women." He and Will were about to go into the Bal d'Opéra at the Academy of Music, an annual affair notorious for its licentiousness. It was January of 1870, a warm night in what had so far been a very mild winter. Will feared that Gob's machine was changing the weather, making it inappropriate to the season. Weather-making would suit the thing—that was something as dramatic and as large as the machine itself. It seemed, certainly, that it ought to do *something*. And yet it was plain to Will that the machine did nothing.

"Prepare to enjoy yourself," Gob told him as they walked across Fourteenth Street and joined the crowd at the entrance to the Academy of Music. There were people in costume waiting to get in, and a crowd who had gathered to gawk at them. Will and Gob were accosted by an old man, a filthy preacher. "Going to see the delightful whores!" the man shrieked. Will could not tell if he and Gob were being condemned or congratulated.

Gob shook his wand in the man's face and said, "Indeed." He and Will were dressed alike in jester's costumes, with bells on their caps, wands, and shoes, and with half-masks that sported obscene long noses.

Inside the Academy there was every sort of costume, some of which strayed considerably from the French theme. Will and Gob were not the only jesters, though only they had obscene noses. Will could not count all the Sun Kings and Marie Antoinettes, one of whom carried her head under her arm. A high-collared cloak gave her the illusion of headlessness. When she approached, he could see her eyes peeking out from where a neck ought to have been.

"Go and tell that woman that her morals have come loose," Will said, pointing randomly at a woman sitting in a man's lap near a mammoth champagne fountain on the stage. She was dressed as a seminude ballerina, in a tutu that left the whole of her legs exposed. Jolly, the only ghost present, was staring at her.

"You can tell her yourself," said Gob, and they walked down to the fountain. It was made in the shape of Notre Dame. Will marveled at it, at how the champagne ran down off the high towers to trickle into a very abbreviated Seine.

"To loose morals," toasted Gob, as he and Will took their first glass of champagne.

"To Parisian carousing," said Will. "Wasn't it Mr. Jefferson who said a little debauchery every now and then is a good thing?"

"Actually, I think that was my aunt," Gob said. He turned his head to point his long nose at a box over the stage, where a woman dressed as a shepherdess was standing with two more naked-legged ballet girls and two men in plain evening dress. "There is my mother," he said, smiling. Usually he scowled at her, but tonight, Will knew, he was in a very happy mood. He thought the building was going very well, and did not seem to mind that the machine did no apparent work.

Up in the box, Mrs. Woodhull waved her crook at them. Gob bowed. Will raised his glass to her. "Shall we go up?" Gob asked. Will said he would follow in a moment. He looked around for Tennie, worrying, briefly and irrationally, that she might grow angry at him for ogling all the loose women. But she was not a jealous person. The idea that they might be true to one another was ridiculous to her. Will would have liked for them to be married in spirit or practice, if not in name, but she would have none of it, and anyhow whenever he tried to be faithful to her he failed. Gob's view of the situation was simple. "She is too much, my friend," he'd say. "You should give her up."

Will approached the ballerina, who had been abandoned by her lover of the minute and was staring forlornly at Notre Dame.

"Mademoiselle," he said. "Aren't you an actress? Didn't I see you in *Mazeppa*?"

"No," she said, hurrying away from him. "I think you did not." Will dipped his glass again and sat on the edge of the pool. He looked down at the bubbles clinging to the side of his glass, and it seemed to him that the way they let go and rushed up to burst at the surface must be like the motion of souls flying off of the earth. Jolly sat next to him, his head jerking this way and that.

"Not everyone has the good sense to appreciate a fool." Will looked up and saw Tennie struggling under a gargantuan wig, fully four feet high, studded with boats and dolphins and, high above all, an angry golden sun face. "Do you like my coiffure?" she asked him.

"It's large," said Will. She smiled, cracking her pancake makeup. She wore a black silk mask over her eyes. She lifted it up briefly to wink at him and whisper, "It's me, Tennie C."

"I thought you were Mrs. Astor."

"This wig will snap my neck, soon, and then my good time at the ball will be ruined. Well, I did not come here anyway to enjoy myself."

"Didn't you?"

"No," she said. "I came tonight to observe. Vicky is going to write an article for Mr. Bennett and I am going to help. We will expose all these panting dignitaries who think a mask is shelter for hypocrisy."

"Are there famous people here?"

"Oh yes." She put her hands up a moment to adjust her wig. "But come with me, I need to steady my coif." She walked over to a wall and leaned her head back against it. "There," she said, taking the glass that Will offered. "Thank you. See over there? That Cardinal

Richelieu is Mr. Bowen, of Brooklyn. And there, the musketeer who licks his lips so often, that is Mr. Fisk."

"Is Mr. Whitman here?" Will asked.

Whitman was Gob's friend. Gob had a plan for him. He'd use him as a battery in his machine, a horrifying notion, at first, to Will, though Gob was unperturbed by it. When Will suggested that it might be wrong to use Mr. Whitman so, Gob looked confused for the first time since Will had known him. "I don't understand," he'd said.

"Mr. Whitman certainly is not here," she said. It was clear to Will that she admired the poet. "He would not come to a place like this. Are you an admirer or a detractor?"

"A detractor, I think. He is a fool who goes about in a costume and pollutes our literature with ceaseless exclamations." It gave Will pleasure to insult the man, because he disliked the very notion of him. How could someone so thoroughly silly be so vital to the machine? Will had come to know that he was not himself a genius—not someone like Gob who could intuit all the possibilities of matter—but merely a hard worker, and he resented people like Mr. Whitman who claimed to approximate the divine function of creation when all they really did was take notes on the fevered wanderings of their undisciplined minds.

"I suppose there is no solidarity among fools," Tennie said tartly. She nodded at a headless Marie Antoinette, who walked by just then and waved at them. "That was my friend Mrs. Wabash. And there is Madame Restell. The ball is made officially wicked by her presence." Will looked at the pudgy little queen she indicated, wondering if it really was Madame Restell, the abortionist of Fifth Avenue. She raised an eyebrow at him as she passed.

"Anyhow," Tennie said, "I must return to my work. You are charming but not famous, and I am already familiar with your vices. There's Mr. Challis, the broker—I'll follow him." She stepped away from the wall, swaying under her wig. "Those antique French ladies, what necks they must have had!" She handed him her glass and went in pursuit of Mr. Challis, who was watering himself at the fountain. Will watched her strike up a conversation with him. She touched his arm and leaned on him. She spoke something directly into his ear that made him burst out laughing, so loud Will could hear it even at a distance.

On the floor, people were dancing, throwing themselves around with wild abandon. Jolly was among them, his eyes closed and his head thrown back rapturously, dancing unpartnered, unseen and untouched by the living. Sam had joined him. He beckoned to Will, smiling—he had become more friendly as work on the machine progressed. Now they were close, or at least he stood close sometimes, often just inches away. Will figured it a reward for his untiring work on the machine. He watched them for a little while. Their beckoning was more seductive than the flashing legs of the ballerinas. "They command you, don't they?" Gob had asked once. Will hadn't answered right away, but he had thought, Shouldn't they? He was still a physician and a photographer, but though he still labored at these professions, they were no longer his work.

Days later, he'd answered Gob's question. They sat close together at his long table, both of them eating directly from the same roast chicken. Gob said, "What will we eat, after we are successful? If cutting off the chicken's head only makes it uncomfortable, then what are you left with for dinner? Cabbages?" Will put down his fork and knife and drew patterns on the table with his greasy finger.

"I think they command us all," he said after a while.

Wheel, lever, pulley, wedge, screw—all through winter, Will mastered simple machines. Gob would present him with one and then demand that he describe its properties mathematically, and after a few months of Gob's persistent tutelage, Will was able to build a machine of his own. Nothing like Gob's engine, it was just a humble plumping mill.

One evening Will arrived in the workshop to find a gift of

lumber stacked on the stone floor. From the pile he chose a pole, a slim birch trunk with the bark still on it. To one end of the pole he attached an ironwood mallet, to the other an oak water box. He then drilled a hole in the middle of the pole, and slipped a heavy dowel through. Will's machine was a peculiar-looking thing—it might have been the weapon of some giant hairy god who lived in the woods, worshiped by animals and trees.

Back in Onondaga County, Will would have set his plumping mill up where it could catch the spray off the waterwheel that turned his father's gristmill. As this was New York City, he set it up on Gob's roof between two blocks of wood, and poured the water himself from a pitcher so big even he had to lift it with both hands.

Will filled the box. The weight of the water lifted the hammer higher and higher, until the angle was such that the water ran out of the open-backed box. Now the hammer fell with a dull thud against the snow-covered roof. It was hardly a glorious sound, but Will felt a glorious sort of joy when it worked. He filled it repeatedly, watching it rise and fall for hours, till the eastern sky began to lighten and he could better appreciate the handiwork of his little mill. He'd neglected to put a pestle under it. It pounded no grain into flour. Instead it had broken a hole in the snow. Will considered the black hole and imagined Sam or Jolly climbing out of it, and no sooner had he done so but there they were, smiling at him and silently praising his little contrivance. It seemed barbaric compared to the complex and mysterious thing in the room below him, yet they bowed to it all the same. Will kept filling the box, so the plumping mill, with its up-and-down motion, seemed to return their courtesy.

Sam came and stood next him, and leaned his head closer and closer to Will's until they were touching, and when they touched Will became lost in the pleasant memory of standing with Sam when they were little boys, gazing down into the well behind their house. The sun shone full down to the water that particular noon, and they could see the snakes there at the bottom, twisting and curling over each other. "Ain't it grand, Will?" his brother had asked, and they'd stood watching until the shadows returned to cover the water once again.

In March of 1870, Will and Gob watched as the first caisson for the great bridge was launched into the East River from a Brooklyn shipyard. Gob was fascinated by the bridge. The late Mr. Roebling had been one of his heroes—he had a little picture of his bridge over the Ohio, which he sighed over sometimes as if it were the portrait of a pretty girl—and he had exchanged letters with the junior Roebling, who'd taken over the work of building the bridge after his father died. Gob would go on about the principal of the caissons and how it related to their own work. The caisson was a giant house that sank down as men dug out its floor, falling slowly through silt and mud and bedrock until it rested beneath the earth, an empty coffin upon which the great bridge would stand its foot. Gob spoke of a caisson of the spirit, built of discipline and grief and despair, in which he and Will would sink down until they rested in the lightless depths of their own souls. Inspiration and success would proceed from that deep place, Gob said. To Will, this made a vague sort of sense, and he nodded, the way he always did whenever Gob made such pronouncements. Will could understand, certainly, that their work was not the work of contented or happy men.

The caisson was fascinating, regardless of whatever philosophy Gob attached to it. It was so very large. Will knew its dimensions because Gob had repeated them endlessly—one hundred and sixty-eight feet long by one hundred and twenty feet wide, twenty feet high and three thousand tons heavy. Yet it seemed much larger, and the sloping walls gave it an Egyptian feel, as if it might be the base of a pyramid or a pedestal for a sphinx. The roof was covered with air pumps and tackle and various other pieces of machinery which Will could not recognize. "Isn't it beautiful?" Gob asked. There was something childish in the way he hopped restlessly from foot to foot, waiting among the crowd of thousands for the launch, which went off without a hitch. The thing fell gracefully down to the water.

"There it goes," Will said, holding his belly because he felt a lurch when the last block was knocked away and, when the thing started to fall, he had a feeling in his belly as if he, not the caisson, were falling, urged along by his fantastic mass into the gray river. Gob cheered with the rest of the crowd, shouting himself hoarse. Will cheered, too, very awkwardly at first, because he could not even remember the last time he had raised his voice this way. He emitted a few cracked, coughing yawps, and these seemed to clear the way in him for something smoother and more musical, a high, enthusiastic yodel that brought to mind the terrific hollering that the Rebs used to do. Will yelled louder and louder, until it was just he and Gob screaming in the now quiet crowd, until, like Gob, he'd used up his voice.

Will wrote in his casebook: *He has had twenty-five to thirty discharges from his bowels in the past twenty-four hours*. He was sitting at the bedside of a cholera patient, a fifteen-year-old boy whose fat cheeks made him look even younger than he was. Will put down his pencil and reached out to push the sleeping boy's sweat-matted hair away from his eyes. He was sure that the boy would die.

That spring, Will had among others under his care a consumptive longshoreman, a cigar maker with intermittent fever, a clerk with pneumonia, a syphilitic sailor, a washerwoman with pleurisy, a shopgirl with plumbism from her makeup, a decayed actor who'd attempted suicide by hammering a nail into his head. All these patients died, despite Will's sincere good intentions, his knowledge, his skill, and his careful watching. He'd sit with those who had no family to attend their death, thinking that in watching them take their last breaths some deeper knowledge would be revealed to him, something that might help in the construction of Gob's machine.

He learned the pattern: the limbs would cool, and the underside of the body would darken; patients would become sleepy and confused, often mistaking Will for someone they loved, reaching out their weakening hands to caress his face; their breathing would become shallow, and thick spit would pool in the back of their throat, so each breath, when it came, rasped and rattled; at the very end the breathing would cease and the heart would stop, and they would void their bladder and their bowels, a final gesture of disrespect for the world that they were leaving. He learned the pattern, but not the secret. He learned nothing exceptional, except how it was impossible that a person should live and breathe and be one moment the repository of an undying soul, and the next be just a body, just cooling flesh.

Will had gone to the second medical division at Bellevue. Gob had grown bored with the ambulance service, and quit at the end of '69. He had a gaggle of patients that he had inherited from Dr. Oetker, and, when he was not at work on the machine, he kept himself occupied with them. These wealthy men and women were never really sick, just obsessed with their bowels or the dimming luster of their hair. Will didn't understand why Gob bothered with them.

The cholera boy died like the others, alone but for Will. Gob's machine was already a success in one respect—working on it staved off Will's fits. It blunted his empathy, as if work on the salvation of the sick and the dying made it easier for him to shake off their suffering. But when the work went poorly, as it had lately, the fits returned. He had one on account of the cholera boy. As he sank into oblivion, rattling and crying out with fear despite Will's attempts to soothe him, Will sank down, too. His guts cramped up and he let out a moan, and as the boy died Will shook and drooled and bit his own cheek.

He woke with his head in the lap of a drunken nurse. He looked to where the boy lay in his bed, his mouth and eyes both slightly open.

"Have a little sip, sir," the nurse said, bringing a flask to his lips.

"It will help you to recover." He sat up and stood away from her, scowling, taking the flask and telling her to get to work cleaning the boy's body. Will looked around the room for his spirit, but it wasn't there. To be haunted immediately would have been unprecedented. Will never saw them so fresh, but always a period of weeks would pass before they appeared to him, former patients who accused him with expressions of betrayal, as if they were furious he had not saved them. "It takes a little while," Tennie told him, "for them to learn to come back. It is not easy for them."

When Will left Bellevue that evening it was to go to Number 15 East Thirty-eighth Street, Tennie's new address since earlier in the year. Mrs. Woodhull had rented a mansion with some of the new fortune she'd gathered in the stock market. As he walked he checked intermittently over his shoulder, still afraid the cholera boy might appear. The boy was never there when he looked, but other spirits followed, Jolly and Sam and the rest, stretched out behind him in a line. He went twice about a streetlamp, hopped over garbage on the sidewalk, crouched low to duck under a horse who blocked his way as he crossed the street, and every spirit walked, hopped, and ducked precisely as he did, as if he blazed the only trail they could take in the world.

As he turned off of Fifth Avenue he could see Tennie, sitting in her window as if she were still living in Great Jones Street. "Darling!" she called out as the spirits filed up behind him, "I've been waiting for you!"

Will's machines were always loosely adjusted and ill-controlled. He fixed Gob's aeolipile, but when he fired it up it wobbled as it spun, and instead of making a clean whistling hiss it screamed like a lovelorn cat. Still, he continued to learn and to build. Gob mostly praised his efforts, though he could be harsh: of an arc lamp that Will assembled from two pieces of charcoal and a powerful voltaic battery, Gob said dismissively, "It makes more heat than light."

Gob's machine, meanwhile, was looking more and more like a person. They'd undone the thing it was before, removing the concretions of years until they uncovered something that looked like an iron-and-glass lamb, and then they undid that, too, because Gob declared it simply wrong, an immature form suited to a lesser task than abolishing death. Now it had glass ribs and a pair of round copper hips. It stood on legs as skinny as a bird's, made of steel and wrapped around tightly with copper and gold wire. All the bones Gob had brought from a trip to Washington were carved into gears, or fused into struts. Inside the glass ribs was a second set of bone ribs, made from leg bones and neck bones and pieces of shattered pelvis. When they worked, Gob wore a black hat, fetched on the same Washington trip. He claimed it had belonged once to Abraham Lincoln, and said that he felt inspired when he put it on.

The variety of surfaces, the little glass boxes filled with tiny gears of gold and platinum and iron and steel, the looping wires and cables that spread out like wings behind it, the umbrella of picture negatives that sheltered it from the glare of the gaselier—these all made the machine fascinating to look at, but they did not make it functional. "It's not finished," Gob said once as they worked, when Will raised the issue of failure. "But it will be finished. My friend, you are impatient like the dead. I am never glad I cannot see them or hear them, but I know they must carp like fishwives, clamoring for the work to be done, and for the walls to fall. But we go as we must, and no other way. You are with me, and Walt is with me, and we will not fail."

"The Kosmos," Will said, looking at the machine and wondering what Mr. Whitman's place in it might possibly be. Would he hold a cable in his hand and pass his vital energy along to waken the thing? Would he read his ridiculous poetry at it, and rouse it into a fury at the corruption of verse? He imagined the machine raising its arms to smash the man.

"Yes," Gob said, with a dreamy look on his face. "The Kosmos." Will turned his attention to the splicing of wire. It was something he enjoyed, weaving together the metal, strand to strand. Of the Washington booty, he liked best the piece from the Atlantic Cable. He thought it both pretty and perfect: the seven copper wires that formed the actual conductor, the insulating wrappings of thread soaked in pitch and tallow, the layers of gutta-percha, and finally the surrounding, protective coat of hard mail made from twisted steel wire. Once, before they'd worked it into the machine, he had held one end while Sam put his hand around the other, but Will had felt nothing and heard nothing.

"You'll fail," was what the angel said, during her rare and brief visits. And she repeated her question: "Why do you participate in abomination?" He had gathered, eventually, that by "abomination" she did not mean his dalliances on Greene Street. She meant the machine. "Do you think God is against our work?" he'd asked Gob after one of her visits. "He is indifferent," was the reply. When Will told about the angel, he thought Gob might laugh at him and say that though spirits walked all around us on the earth, there was never any such thing as an angel. But Gob had only nodded and said, as if it were the most ordinary and sensible of statements, "Oh yes. The angels—*they're* very much against us."

"What do you know of angels?" Will asked Tennie. They were in her room on a hot night in July, nestled in what she called her Turkish corner. She had a bed fit for a princess, but sometimes she preferred to sleep here, where she'd hung a silk tent from the ceiling. Inside, she spread soft carpets and brocade pillows on the floor. She set two scimitars on the wall, bejungled the interior with rubber plants and ferns, and flanked the entrance to the tent with two squat plaster pillars, upon which two oil lamps burned and smoked.

"I saw them when I was small," Tennie said, "but never since." She'd reached her hand into a fern and was lazily waving its leaves back and forth, generating a little breeze. "Vicky saw one, once. I was just a year old, and almost died from diphtheria. Vicky saw an angel come down and wrap me in its wings."

"Trying to smother you? Were they horrible wings?"

"Certainly not. It was a healing touch. I was restored by it. Everyone but Vicky had given me up for dead." She reached for a glass of water and took a drink. "I saw Mr. Nathan," she said. "Have you seen him? He doesn't look happy. I think he wants justice for his murder. You know, I don't think I'd care much what happened to my killer, after the fact. I think my concerns would be less mundane." She took another drink of water. Will put his hand high on her belly, just under her ribs, imagining, as he sometimes did, that he could see through her skin to watch the functioning of her organs, and see her stomach writhing in appreciation at the cool drink. She talked about her day. He wasn't ever sure what exactly she did with her time, but he knew she was always busy with brokerage business or paper business. In her room she had a little desk where she composed articles for the paper she and her sister had launched in May. Once, when she was writing, he asked her, somewhat peevishly, if she was exposing Mr. Challis. "Mr. Who?" she replied.

He put his hands all over her, feeling her liver as it slipped past his hand when she breathed in deeply, and calling out, as he touched them, "Lungs, kidneys, spleen."

Tennie laughed, saying her spleen was *here* and not *there,* moving his hand. She claimed to be intimately familiar with her inner workings. It was part of her talent as a medical clairvoyant and a magnetic healer, to know her own body so well. "Yes, yes," she said, "put your hands on me, and I will put mine on you." She reached up to his chest and his back, as if trying to capture his heart between her hands.

"The telegraph, too, has a body and a soul," Gob said. Will was making Daniell batteries, pouring an acidulated solution of copper sulfate into a copper cell and putting a porous cup inside it. Inside the cup went a cylinder of zinc, surrounded by a weak acid. The whole thing was enclosed within a glass jar. The assembly was delicate and laborious, and he'd burned holes through half his shirts, being careless with the acid. But Will liked the work. He thought the batteries were elegant, with their cups within cups within cups. He could spend whole days making them, and he often did, so they had hundreds by the end of summer.

"You cannot see the vital principle that animates it," Gob said, staring at a stock ticker that had been set in his machine before they'd remade it. He'd taken the ticker all apart and half-reassembled it. He was in a mood, mourning the fact that he could not see spirits in general and his brother in particular, when he devoted his life to them, and when a person like his mother could see them, and hear them, even, it seemed, have tea with them. Will thought of his own mother's lamenting.

"It won't bring them back," Will said, "to merely complain."

"But it will," Gob said. "Don't you understand? What's grief if not a profound complaint? It's what the engine will do; it will complain. It will grieve with mechanical efficiency and mechanical strength. It will grieve for my brother and for your brother and for the six hundred thousand dead of the war. It will grieve for all the dead of history, and all the dead of the future. Man's grief does nothing to bring them back, but just as man's hands cannot move mountains, but man's machines can, our machine will grieve away the boundaries between this world and the next. And then, sure as the rails run to California, the way will be open."

Will kept working, kept his eyes on the battery and his attention on the task of filling the little porous cup with acid. But though he didn't look at Gob, he knew how his face must be animated with pride and anger and sadness—it was the look he got when he made grand statements about their work. It was a difference between them, that Gob liked to talk so much where Will preferred simply to work. And that talkiness was part of the reason, Will figured, for Gob's cleaving to Mr. Whitman.

Later, Gob put the ticker back together completely and then worked it again into the machine—it sat in the place where a navel would on a person. Then he went downstairs to read. Will was still patiently assembling batteries fifteen hours after he began. It was then the angel paid him another visit. She stayed awhile this time, a full five minutes. Will ignored her, as had become his custom. But before she left, Will had looked up to see her pointing with fingers and wings at the engine. "God hath not wrought *this,*" she said.

Will considered a fresco on Mrs. Woodhull's parlor ceiling: it depicted Aphrodite surrounded by her mortal and immortal loves. They were clothed, but the goddess had exposed herself fully, and any guest who cared to stretch back his neck could gaze on her nakedness. Tennie was going on about Mr. Whitman. She got overexcited on his behalf whenever he was nearby. Gob had brought him to a party given in September of 1870 by Mrs. Woodhull in honor of Steven Pearl Andrews and his massive brain. Mr. Whitman was walking around the room with his hostess, having just left, thank goodness, Will's company and Tennie's, and still she went on about him.

"I had a vision," she said, "in which he grew out of the ground like some wholesome weed. He was a green man, with daisies and bluebirds in his hair. Little animals came out of the forest to play about his feet."

Will rubbed his chest where Tennie had given him a little shock. It hadn't hurt, but it was always a surprise, when she did it. He wanted her to do it again.

"Let's go upstairs," he said. "I'm tired of this party."

"Already? Mr. Andrews hasn't even arrived."

"Let's go away," he said. "Let's go away tonight on a journey. Have you been to Canada? It's a foreign country, you know."

"I'd heard," she said, and gave him a look that he knew too well. It said, *I'm bored with you.*

"Do you see how he walks?" she asked, staring after Whitman. "Like a bear, heavy and shambling and careless."

"He is a magnificent creature," Will said hollowly. "He is a kosmos." He thought of Gob. They'd argued, earlier, because Will had made disparaging remarks about Whitman. Will had said this whole kosmos business seemed to him a senseless honor and an unearned distinction. "Who named him Kosmos, anyhow?" Will had asked. "Was it his cat? Is he also the Marquis of Carrabas?" Now, Gob was nowhere to be seen.

"I know you hate Mr. Whitman," Tennie said, and went away in search of punch. He watched her go, leaning to speak a word or two into the ears of various men as she passed them. Mr. Challis, the licentious broker, was not at that party, yet Will found his thoughts drawn towards the man and colored with jealousy. When he was with her, when he came half awake in the night and she was wrapped all around him, when her hair lay heavy on his face and the very air he breathed was flavored by her, then he got a feeling that she surrounded him utterly, and this was a notion that comforted him and agitated him. He would think of her as a beautiful house, one entirely unlike Gob's house, a place without secret basements where bones hung in chains from the ceiling and swayed and clanked in sourceless breezes. In his mind, he would go from room to room, each one stuffed with bright trinkets, and find way up top a machine whose purpose was the manufacture of delight. It was good to wander there, to look at her machine and listen to its noise, which was the noise of her snoring, chortling breath. Yet inevitably he encountered other men as he wandered in the rooms, always there were others who tended her machine, men who were strangers to him, who, when he opened a door and surprised them where they lounged in the supremely comfortable furniture, peered at him and asked, "Who are you?"

"Are you sleeping, Dr. Fie?" asked a lady who had come up and stood silently next to him. Will thought it was Mrs. Woodhull, but when he opened his eyes he saw that it was Miss Trufant, a girl who was her secretary and aide-de-camp in her war of reform. She was dressed up like her mistress in a skirt and a masculine coat.

"No, I'm quite awake," he said.

"Mr. Andrews will stimulate you, if you are sleepy. I think he must be the most intelligent man in the world."

"I think that person is Dr. Woodhull," said Will, because he'd promised Gob he'd say flattering things about him in her presence. Gob had a giggly, schoolgirlish affection for this small, dark person. "What do you think of her?" Gob would ask over and over. "Do you think she is pretty?"

"I think you are besotted with that fellow," she said. "Tell me, Dr. Fie, does Dr. Woodhull keep the stars in his pocket? Can he bring down the moon to give you as a good-evening present?" She smiled.

"Don't you admire him, too?"

"Oh, I am indifferent to him. But I think two persons as devoted as you two should marry at the earliest convenience." She folded her hands in front of her. Will looked down at them, noticing how they had a particular quality of loveliness—he thought how it must be difficult to make two things so perfect and small. She put them behind her back. "I said that in jest, Dr. Fie. But now I think I have offended you."

"Not at all," he said, but she was blushing, and she turned the conversation to the subject of the Fourteenth Amendment and its bearing on woman suffrage, something about which Will knew nothing at all. Very soon, she excused herself, saying she had to seek out Mr. Butler. "Yes," he'd tell Gob later, as he always did, "she's very pretty."

Mr. Whitman got ill standing in the rain watching the funeral procession of Admiral Farragut. Will, when Gob brought him in to consult, diagnosed pneumonia, because Whitman's lungs were wet as sponges. The patient insisted it was an old sickness contracted during his time in the Washington hospitals, and that the rain had weakened him and made him susceptible. He asked to be bled, because that always improved him when this illness was on him. Gob gave him an elixir and put him in one of the huge beds at Number 1 East Fifty-third Street, in a room that hadn't been opened in years. Whitman got sicker under their care, feverish and delirious, calling out in lament for David Farragut, and then for a variety of persons. He mumbled names: John, Stephen, Elijah, Hank, Hank, Hank. "Dr. Woodhull," he moaned. "How is my fever-boy?" Even Will tried to comfort him, putting his big hand on Whitman's hot sweating head and saying, "Hush, sir."

Gob bled him over Will's objections. It was a surprise to Will, because Gob had always protested that bleeding a patient was only ever as helpful as biting him. "It's what he wants," Gob said, another surprise, because it was a fundamental rule of doctoring that the patient's wishes were generally irrelevant to his care. Gob wielded a scarificator like a practiced leech, and bled his patient into a white porcelain bowl. Will half expected the man to bleed light or perfumed air, but it was ordinary red blood that seeped out of his veins. When he was done, Gob let Will do the bandaging while he transferred the blood to a green glass flask, and added a powder which he claimed would keep it from clotting up. "Yes," he said, swirling the blood in the flask, "this will certainly be useful."

As winter came, Gob kept saying they were nearly done building, but Will never believed him. It didn't seem grand enough, the thing they'd made over these two years. It wasn't much bigger than Will himself, and though it was complex and strange-looking beyond description, still it did not seem strange or complex enough. So he kept protesting, "It's not enough."

"Enough of what?" Gob would say.

"Of . . . what it is."

Gob would laugh, and go back to his tinkering. It looked like a fashionable angel now, because the masses of cable looked like wings, and because the body of the thing flared out in the back like a bustle. Its arms held aloft a great empty silver bowl, just under the canopy of negative plates. Gob had adjusted his gaselier to burn acetylene. The gas, which they made themselves from water and calcium carbide, gave off an acrid, garlicky odor. When lit, the gaselier threw off painfully bright light that fell through the plates, and the images were caught up and focused into the bowl by means of lenses hung on wire so thin they seemed to float like bubbles below the picture negatives. "What goes in the bowl?" Will asked repeatedly, but Gob said he didn't yet know. He said he'd dreamed the bowl, but not its contents.

Gob found the answer in December. Though there were hundreds of batteries already scattered around the room, Will made more, and he had been making them all night when Gob burst into the workroom at dawn, his face still puffy and creased from sleeping, to declare that he had at long last learned what went into the bowl.

That night they went to dinner at Madame Restell's. "She's been asking me to dinner for years," Gob said, just before they walked the two blocks down Fifth Avenue to his neighbor's house, "but I have always declined. She was my master's good friend, and like an aunt to me, you know, yet I have neglected her. I don't regret it—I have aunts enough as it is, and they cause me sufficient distress, thank you. Anyhow, I sent her a message this morning, and the reply came immediately. So perhaps I am forgiven."

Madame Restell was delighted to see Gob. "How you've grown!" she said. At dinner she ignored Will to ask Gob about his life. He told her about his work at Bellevue, but failed to mention his mother, or, of course, the machine. He said he and his friend Dr. Fie were writing a textbook of anatomy, that their specimens had been destroyed in an unfortunate fire, that they had a publishing deadline and only blank pages where they should have drawings of fetal anatomy. A delicate favor, he admitted, but could she possibly accommodate him?

"Such a young man," she said, "and already at work on a book! Oh, you will be distinguished just like your uncle. How he would be proud!" Of course she would help, she said. She partook heavily of the sweet wine she kept at her table, and grew tearful when she talked of Gob's old teacher. "Sometimes I pass by the house, and I find myself climbing the steps, and only when I am standing at the door, about to ring, do I remember that he is gone. Oh, he was taken in his prime!"

"But Auntie," said Gob. "You should ring the bell. You certainly should." When she embraced him, he looked at Will over her shoulder and rolled his eyes.

After dinner, she took them downstairs into her basement office. They did not loiter in the finely appointed rooms where she received clients or performed procedures, but quickly passed into an unfinished back room, and went past rack after rack of dusty wine bottles to a group of barrels set aside in a little corral. A single gas jet was burning low on the damp wall.

"Here we are," she said. "How many do you require?"

"Just one," said Gob. She had pushed back the sleeves of her dress and taken a pair of tongs from where they hung on the wall. She lifted the top off a barrel marked *Pork*—that was to fool the postal authorities when she shipped out specimens to medical schools all over the country, charging, as she did, outrageous prices.

"Just one? I have them to spare. Let me give you two or three. Or let me give you four. It is no imposition, my dear."

"Only one, thank you. Just whichever is freshest."

"Ah, that would be young Mr. Tilton. Or rather, little Mr. Beecher." She replaced the barrel's lid and went to another, and as she fished out the abortus from the brine she gave its history. It was not her habit to betray confidences, but she was drunk now, and overcome with nostalgia for her old friend and his ward, so she talked freely of how she had helped Mrs. Tilton and Mr. Beecher eject from the world the consequence of their love. Will caught a glimpse of glistening pink flesh as she put the boy into a plain gray hatbox. She looked in for a moment before she put the top on. "A beautiful specimen," she said. "Almost whole. And I know you will draw him beautifully. He will live on in that way, at least. Come upstairs. I'll wrap him for you."

Walking home with the hatbox wrapped up neatly in white paper like a purchase from Stewart's, Gob told Will how in his dream his mother had summoned him to her house on Thirty-eighth Street. She received him in the conservatory, where she sat under a little tree that still had its autumn colors, though it was winter in the dream as it was winter in the world. She sat for a while, not speaking, and Gob sat next to her silently while the little tree dropped its brilliant leaves between them.

"This is a dream," she said, suddenly and matter-of-factly. Then she reached under the bench and brought up what Gob thought at first was a jar of his grandmother's marmalade—it was red and yellow, the very same shades as the settling leaves of the tree, and it was in just the kind of jar Anna used for her preserves. But when he looked closer at it he saw that it was a little fetus, and he knew it had been canned fresh out of his mother's womb. "Here," she said, "is your brother. This is your brother, come back to us at last." He'd reached to take the jar from her, because he was overwhelmed with the feeling that he must take it and cherish it always, but in his haste he dropped it. It cracked on the bench, and the unfinished child fell out in a burst of orange-and-red liquid. It rolled among the fallen leaves, where it kicked and squalled.

From out of that dream, Gob woke understanding what they had been missing all these months. The machine required flesh and it required blood. Blood would catalyze the return, and Gob knew that it was the purpose of the machine to harness the energies of loss and grief and bring them to bear on the silver bowl, to call back a spirit—his brother's—and see it installed in flesh. And he knew that once this was accomplished, the walls between the dead and the living would become weak and soft, because the law that declared there was no return from death would be broken, and this law was the foundation of the walls that kept the dead out of the world. The machine would reach through the weakened wall and pluck them, one by one, back into life.

"It's so simple," he said. "Don't you think?"

Will said nothing. He only held the box and kept walking, trying to ignore the reek of blood and pickles that rose from it.

Gob pored every day over heavy books out of the library—books that looked hundreds of years old and were not in any language that Will could recognize, let alone read. Gob would exclaim every now and then as he read, while Will played with the engine, testing the light or making adjustments to the picture negatives, rearranging them by theme—belly wound, amputation, advanced decay. He put the fetus, as Gob directed him, in a glass jar full of brine, and sometimes he would sit and watch it, expecting it to move an arm, or swing its head to look at him.

They began one evening in late December, a few weeks after their visit to Madame Restell. Gob put on Mr. Lincoln's hat and surrounded the engine with symbols and words drawn with colored sand on the stone floor between the batteries. Some he copied from the old masters he'd studied, some were his own creations. At midnight, he emptied the child from the jar to the bowl. Then he walked around the machine, stepping over the wires and glass string that led in from the outlying elements—boxes and batteries and pieces of mirror. He walked around once for every year of his brother's life on earth, then walked back the other way once for every year that he had been dead. He poured out the blood from the green bottle into the bowl, and immediately it began to spin and sing. When Gob signaled to him, Will threw a switch to activate an arc lamp—they'd given up on acetylene, too, as not sufficiently bright, so now, beneath the ornate gas chandelier, they'd installed an electric light. It sparked up and glared above the negatives, throwing images into the bowl and down onto Gob.

Will ran all over the room, ducking under wires and jumping over batteries, stoking boilers, opening valves, and pulling levers. A steam engine roared and puffed and moved its pistons, and motion was fed along from gear to gear. Will had thought he understood at least the physical workings of the thing, how the steam became motion, how each gear turned another, how the force of movement was amplified or changed in direction. But, having thrown all the switches and opened all the valves, he stood panting against the wall near the door, feeling that he understood nothing. It had never shivered and hummed like this before, though they'd fed it with the batteries and the steam engine. It had never made the house shake, or made him dizzy with all its stationary whirling. Every part of it seemed to be in motion. The glass gears and the bone gears and the iron gears were spinning, the glass and copper ribs were twisting in their sockets, the cable wings seemed to be undulating slowly. He didn't know how it made the bowl sing and spin, or how it summoned spirits. They crowded into the room, coming in by tens and twenties whenever Will blinked against the glare from the lamp. The light was so bright he thought it must shine through the spirits, but in fact it made them look more real, heavier and paler. It made them look more real, but not more alive. They looked waxy, like exquisitely preserved corpses. Yet they smiled like living people. Their mouths were moving and their faces were animated with what could only be ecstasy or great pain. All Will's dead were there, joined by dozens of strangers, and by the little tatterdemalion angel, who floated in a corner and watched with a serious expression on his face.

Gob fell to his knees before the engine, threw out his arms, and gazed into the light, crying out what seemed to Will to be the only appropriate magic words. "Come back!" he shouted, again and again, till he was hoarse from it. "Come back, Tomo. Come back and be alive." Will thought he saw something rising from the bowl, a shadow that grew in the middle of the light. It got bigger and bigger—it was definitely the shape of a boy, who raised his hands up to press against a negative, and in doing so, cracked it. The light went out suddenly, shattering like a rocket's burst into tiny sparks that dwindled and were gone. Cables fell out from their sockets and wove like cobras, throwing sparks and hissing before they fell dead to the floor. Then it was utterly dark in the room.

The noise of the bowl hung a moment longer in the air and then it, too, was gone. Finally, the bowl fell from the top of the machine, and something landed in front of Gob with a huff. The bowl rolled away in the darkness and rang once when it hit a battery. Will held his breath and heard the noise of another person—it was certainly not Gob—breathing in the dark. He groped in front of him, but felt nothing except the glass battery jars. They were so cold they burned his skin.

"Hello?" Will said tentatively.

"Happy birthday," came the voice, lilting and lisping, the voice of a child.

Will scrambled back to the wall and turned up the gaselier. There was a boy on the floor before Gob. He looked to be about five years old, had long curly brown hair and shining black eyes, and he was covered in blood, great smears of it against very pale flesh that striped him like a barber's pole. The boy stood up, shading his eyes from the light, and stared defiantly at Gob, who stared back incredulously and said, "You are not my brother."

"My name is Pickie Beecher," the boy said. "I come before."

It fell to Will to clothe and feed the boy. Gob, in the first few days after the birth, had retreated to his room, where he sat on his haunches in the stone circle and rocked back and forth, humming. He wouldn't speak to Will, or to the boy. Spirits clustered around him, looking concerned, and around the boy, on whom they doted silently. Pickie Beecher mostly ignored them, though sometimes he might seem to follow one in particular with his eyes.

Will wasn't sure what to do with the boy, who ran around the workshop, naked and bloody, looking at the machine and aping Gob's words. "It is not my brother," he said over and over. Will took him to the kitchen, because it seemed sensible to feed him. Pickie Beecher was not interested in vegetables, or even in cakes or pies. He liked red meat. Gob kept his larder very well stocked, though he generally did not eat very much or very often. There were steaks in the icebox. When Pickie Beecher saw them, he grabbed them up and rubbed them like kittens against his cheek. Then he ran under a table and ate them up in gobbling bites. "Do you like that?" Will said.

"My name is Pickie Beecher," was the reply. "I come before."

Pickie wanted jewels. "For my brother," he said. Will brought him to Stewart's to get outfitted for clothes. The pear-shaped clerk tried to be helpful, but seemed to have difficulty remembering that Pickie Beecher was there. "I wish to purchase clothing for the boy," Will told him.

"Very well," said the clerk. "For which boy?"

"This one," Will said, pointing squarely at Pickie Beecher.

"Of course!" The clerk took a little step back, and quivered a little, as if suppressing an urge to flee. Will developed a theory: people sensed in Pickie Beecher something so unnatural and abominable that they were inclined to pretend he was not there at all, and once, reluctantly, they did notice him, he activated an instinct to run away. Will learned that Pickie Beecher could veil that horrible quality, but he let it shine forth when he was irritated.

The clerk was very gracious. He apologized profusely whenever he could not find the boy who was standing directly next to him, and he brought out all sorts of adorable costumes—Zouave jackets and Garibaldis and knickerbockers—each one more heavily bedecked with pom-pom or froufrou than the last, as if he thought the innocence of the outfit could smother the unease generated by its wearer.

Pickie Beecher was patient. He did not squirm while he was being measured, or cry with boredom, as another child might have. He only repeated his calm request for jewels, for his brother.

"You haven't got a brother," Will told him. "You are unique."

"I come before," said Pickie Beecher. "My brother comes after. But he must have jewels for his person." He spoke very softly, and watched intently the omnipresent cash boys ferrying money from the clerks to the cashiers.

"Would you like to play with those boys?" Will asked.

"No," said Pickie Beecher. The clerk returned with another silly ready-made outfit, a pilot's suit with a matching cap.

"That'll do," Will said, because he was desperate to find something for the boy to wear besides the suit of Gob's he'd cut down very crudely to fit him. The pilot's suit was of dark blue wool, with shining black buttons that looked very much like Pickie Beecher's eyes. Will told him he looked handsome. Pickie Beecher held his cap upside down in his hands and stared into it, but said nothing. Will turned away from him to order a wardrobe from the clerk, a dozen suits of the sort he and Gob wore, sack coats and pants of black wool, with gray vests, stiff white cotton shirts, and three dozen shirt collars, because he was certain that the neck of any boy, even one born out of a silver bowl, would be perpetually filthy. He would go through collars like water. Except Pickie Beecher did not care for water. When Will had tried to bathe him, Pickie Beecher leaped out of the tub and sat down on the floor, where he cleaned himself with his own tongue. When Will tried to cut his hair, the boy had leaped away with a shriek, and blood had oozed from the cut strands.

Socks and underthings, three pairs of black shoes, fifteen undersized handkerchiefs, and a series of hats of varying heights, from stovepipe to porkpie, completed his order. They were all very good quality, better than Will's clothes. It was Gob's money he was spending. The clerk swore to have it all delivered to the house within the week.

"Do you hear, Pickie?" Will said. "You won't have to wear that for too long." He turned back to where he had left the boy staring into his cap, but he wasn't there. "Pickie?" he said. It occurred to him then that he could flee from the store, and possibly escape forever from the boy. It was useless to deny that he felt revulsion towards the little fellow, that he did not understand him, that he was frightened by him. But he also felt, already, a peculiar affection for him.

Stewart's was a very large store. Will searched for a half hour, asking people if they had seen a pale boy in a pilot suit. No one had seen him, of course. In the end, it was Pickie Beecher who found Will. Will had paused under the little white rotunda, and was gazing up at it, imagining an apotheosis of A. T. Stewart for its blank white surface, when Pickie Beecher tugged at his sleeve and said, "I am ready to go now."

"You mustn't run off like that!" said Will. "Where did you go? Why did you run away? I have been looking for you all over this place."

"It was necessary," was the boy's reply.

Outside, it was bitterly cold. Will put the boy in his new overcoat—another ready-made article—and held on to his hot little hand as they went down the sidewalk. Will thought he should be cold, this boy, like a corpse. But he was hot all over, and he got even hotter after a meal of red meat. Pickie Beecher paused to look at the pictures in Gronpil's window.

"Would you like to have a painting? Something pretty to look at?" Will asked.

"No," said Pickie Beecher. "A painting is not necessary."

Back at the house on Fifth Avenue, Pickie Beecher hurried upstairs and pounded on the door to Gob's room, demanding to be let in.

"I have them!" he said. "I have the jewels!" He had pulled a double handful of them from his pocket, rubies and diamonds and pearls in rings and on necklaces.

"Pickie Beecher!" said Will, coming up behind him. The boy looked up, no expression at all on his pale face, or in his dark eyes. He turned his attention to his booty, and his nimble little fingers tricked the jewels off their strings. "It's wrong to steal things," Will said.

"It's not wrong. Not if it's for my brother."

Gob opened his door. "There you are!" he said, looking exhausted but rational. He was still wearing Lincoln's hat, but now he removed it and put it on Pickie Beecher's head. It rested on the boy's ears, covering his eyes. "Here he is!" Gob said to Will. "Our little helper."

Will came to divide his friendship with Gob into two portions—there was the time before the advent of Pickie Beecher, and there was the time after. Ante Pickie became as remote to him as the time before Christ, an era of antiquity, when people built ingeniously but never powerfully, when geniuses like the engineers of Alexandria made clever toys or cold, functionless monuments. The engine that had hatched Pickie Beecher was a thing of the most ancient past, and it came to seem as simple, in its way, as an aeolipile.

The advent of Pickie Beecher heralded a new age of building. He was their little helper, but he did work that was far out of proportion to his size. He fetched things, always saying they were for his brother, and Will came to understand what he meant by that. His brother was the engine, a perfect version of it that they had yet to build. In February of 1871, Will read in the *Tribune* an account of the disappearance of the gears that ran the pneumatic railway under Broadway. They had been stolen. The *Tribune* wondered if it was the work of the horsecart companies, but it was Pickie Beecher who had done it. Will did not know how. Will had no idea how Pickie Beecher executed his fantastic tasks.

Not the work, not the silent, electric motions of the machine, nor the glaring arc lamp that made Will's bones feel warm when he stood beneath it, none of this had seemed unreal, before the boy. But Pickie Beecher made everything palpably strange, and the notion pressed on Will's mind that he might be dreaming, or that he might be part of someone else's dream—Gob's, or Jolly's bear's, or even Pickie Beecher's. He thought sometimes as he worked on the engine, or as he watched Pickie Beecher cut wires with his teeth, that the dreamer must wake under this burden of strangeness.

Pickie Beecher's first work was disassembly. Gob was angry, at first, but then he joined in the careful destruction. "This form, too, has served its purpose," Gob said to Will.

"You let the child rule you," Will said, because he was so fond of his batteries, and Pickie Beecher had absolutely no respect for them.

"But I understand now," Gob said. This was his refrain in the first weeks and months of the new age. "He'll help us, don't you see? He is a guide and a helper. He is a tool, a little engine in service to a bigger."

Maybe, Will thought to himself, he is a clever urchin, fiendish but entirely of this world. Maybe he watched us through the skylight and thought, Now I will drop down and fool them, and then I will have hot food and a cool bed forever. But he could not look three minutes at the boy before this thought seemed ridiculous. This was the transformation their engine had effected, to make the ridiculous sensible and the sensible ridiculous.

The negative plates came out of their frames, the batteries came away from their cables, and the machine fell apart into its constituent copper and glass and iron and bone. Pickie Beecher arranged the pieces to his liking, and then he began to fetch heavier ones. Will would come to the house and find the giant gears leaned up against the walls in the workroom, their teeth almost scraping the ceiling.

The workroom filled up with a haphazard array of stuff, all crammed together until there was no place left to store anything.

"My brother," said Pickie Beecher, "he wants a bigger room."

"Hello?" said Tennie. "Can you hear me?" Will took the tin can from his ear and spoke into it.

"Yes," he said. They were talking over a lovers' telegraph, two cans connected by a string. Tennie was in her Turkish corner, where she'd closed up her silk tent against him, insisting they play with her toy, something Gob had put together in the kitchen downstairs.

"Can you hear them?" she asked. "All those Irish innocents?"

"No," he said. It was July, just after the great slaughter on Eighth Avenue. Angry Catholics had disturbed the gloating parade of the Orangemen and been punished with bullets by the police. Forty-five people had died. Will had seen a few of the wounded at Bellevue, which was also where all the bodies of the dead had been taken. He had stood that afternoon at a window on the second floor and looked down where twenty thousand mourners gathered outside the morgue.

"They are still angry," she said. Then she stuck her head out of the tent and called out, "You may come in, if you bring me fruit." He went in search of it. As he passed a window in the hall, he heard laughter coming down from the roof. Mrs. Woodhull was up there with her new friend, Mr. Tilton. He'd come to see her for the first time in May. Pickie Beecher seemed to hate him. Whenever they happened to be in the same room, Pickie Beecher would confront him, saying, "You are not my father." Mr. Tilton always laughed at him and agreed that he was not.

Tilton was in love. He'd come to the house as Henry Beecher's agent when Gob's mother made a veiled threat to expose Beecher's affair with Mrs. Tilton. He was supposed to soothe her, but she soothed him better. They were devoted companions.

Gob's father was in the kitchen, sitting alone in the dark. "My boy," he said to Will. "I am on the ceiling. Could you help me get down?" He had his pharmacopoeia, a dark wooden box, in front of him. Most doctors stocked theirs with a variety of medicines, but Canning Woodhull kept only morphine in his. "I find it cures everything but constipation," he'd said of it. Will turned up the light to better examine the fruit and pick out the best pieces. Canning Woodhull's eyes were eerie—wide, round, and almost all blue, with pupils closed down to the size of a dot of ink. He reached out to Will and said, "Give me your hand, my friend, before I float away." Will put out his hand. Woodhull took it, shaking it as if in greeting, but also pulling on it, slow and steady. "There," he said. "That's better. How are you feeling this evening."

"Very well," said Will.

"I am not! My friend Colonel Blood says a person ought not to pluck the wings from his butterfly, but it seems to me that he is a man who doesn't know if his grapes are sweet or sour. Colonel Blood is *in* the blood, you see. We are in it, but sometimes I float above. It ought to be contained in bodies. Do you know Sydenham? I used to worship him. But who cares about the mysteries of the circulation when the blood will come out, anyhow? We will put it on the ground until it drowns us. Vicky! Now there's a woman possessed of a natural and indefatigable buoyancy. Tell me, do you think she will love me again?"

"Let go my hand," Will said.

"If you let me go, you'll drown. My floating is all that's holding you up." Will pulled his hand away roughly.

"Good evening," Will said, after he'd grabbed up some fruit.

"I tried," said Canning Woodhull. "I tried to save you."

Gob and Pickie Beecher consulted at a speed Will could not follow, and in a language he often failed to comprehend. Pickie Beecher talked rapidly of how his brother had fifty toes or a caterpillar in his throat, and every revelation sent Gob into an ecstasy of drawing and calculation. The machine was taking shape again, not as a person anymore, but as an edifice, growing into the walls and through the floor. Will had gone into the workshop one morning to find holes bored into the floor—they were all over the room, at least a hundred of them, rough around their edges as if something had gnawed them in the stone and the wood. Gob and Pickie Beecher were busy threading cables through the holes. They dangled in the bedrooms beneath the workshop, connected to nothing. "Little brother is growing," said Pickie Beecher.

Will studied dynamos, because Pickie Beecher had obtained three and deposited them in a parlor. All the furniture had been pushed to the wall to make room for them. They were arranged in a circle, so they seemed to be in silent conversation with each other, each of them chaperoned by the engine that powered it. Will was fond of their principle, of how the current produced in the revolving armature was sent back through the field coils of the electromagnet, increasing its power, which in turn increased the current. It was a building-up process of mutual and reciprocal excitation, and it reminded him of Tennie, because kissing her brought this principle to his mind. While Gob and Pickie Beecher consulted upstairs, Will made an accidental discovery: when he connected one dynamo to another already in operation, the second began to revolve in a direction opposite from the first.

"You are a genius!" Gob proclaimed, when Will showed him.

Pickie Beecher scampered around the two linked dynamos and said, "My brother, he has two hearts!" He stretched his little hand towards the brushes of one dynamo. Will rushed to stop him but was too late. He was sure the little fellow would be cooked alive, but the fat spark and the shock only made him giggle. "It's my brother," he said, when Will scolded him. "He wouldn't hurt me. Not ever."

Sometimes Pickie Beecher acted like an ordinary child. Sometimes he eschewed blood on his ice cream, and sometimes he clamored for a bedtime story or a stick of plain candy. He liked animals. He liked to go to the menagerie in Central Park and visit a hippopotamus with whom he had formed an attachment. Will took him down there one day in the middle of August.

Pickie knew just where his hippo's cage was. He ran to it and grabbed the bars. "Murphy!" he said. "Hello, sir." Will came up behind him and looked into the cage. Murphy looked fat and sleepy, and not entirely well, but better than most of his peers. Pickie rolled a piece of chocolate towards him. He snapped it up without even looking to see what it was.

They strolled among the other cages. Pickie paused before a skinny tiger.

"He would eat me up, if he could break his cage," he said.

"I think he would try," said Will. "He has that reputation. But I would protect you." Yet it seemed unlikely that the boy would need his protection.

They visited a balding lion, and cage after cage of hissing, spitting monkeys. Pickie said he wanted one for a pet. Will said they were dirty, mean animals, and that he'd be happier with his hippo.

"I would make them serve me," said Pickie. "They would be useful."

Will sat down while Pickie ran from cage to cage, gibbering at the monkeys, roaring at the monstrous cats, and reaching his small hands through a cage to pinch the noses of deer.

All his running made Pickie hungry, so Will took him east to the Dairy, where they shared a bowl of ice cream. Pickie took no interest in the nearby playground, or in the children playing there. All he wanted was a ride in a goat cart. Will gave him ten cents and he ran off to clamber into a little buggy, pulled by two goats and captained by a black-haired gypsy boy. Not long after it began, the ride ended in an argument: the gypsy boy accused Pickie of biting his goat.

Will took Pickie up to the lake, because he had the idea that they could both take off their shoes and dip their feet in the water, but Pickie would have none of that. So they sat watching the lazy motion of the pleasure boats, and the boy said many times how he would like to have a swan to love and to pet and to eat. Will ignored him, because his attention was captured by a young couple in one of the boats, whom he mistook for Gob and Miss Trufant, but when they drifted closer he saw that it was not they. Will had seen them here before, though, chaperoning Mrs. Woodhull as she floated conspicuously with her paramour, Mr. Tilton. Gob had begun to follow Miss Trufant that summer, going wherever she went, and when Will had asked him why he did it, he'd only say, "I must." Now Gob was done with his secret pursuit, and he and Miss Trufant walked openly all over the city, keeping an eye on Mrs. Woodhull and, Will supposed, talking about the Fourteenth Amendment.

"Aren't you coming in?" Pickie asked, after Will had brought him to the door of Gob's house. "Don't you want to play with my brother?"

"I'll come later," Will said. He walked down to the Woodhull residence on East Thirty-eighth Street, looking at the ground as he went, because there were never any spirits there. After he passed the unfinished cathedral, he sensed that there was someone walking too close alongside him. He kept his head down even after she spoke.

"Creature," the angel said. "You must destroy that abominable child."

Will said nothing.

"You'll fail," she said. "You must fail."

"I think you must have been the angel who brought the *bad* news to Mary," Will said, finally looking up, but the angel was gone. She had visited more and more as work progressed on the machine, and every time she had told him that he and Gob would fail in their endeavor. She had a special hatred for Pickie Beecher, and never missed an opportunity to urge his destruction. Will was learning to ignore her.

He heard the music a few blocks before he got to the house—tooting, oomping, German brass. There were Germans gathered in a little crowd below Tennie's window, out of which she leaned attractively, smiling and throwing down flowers from a wreath beside her on the sill. She was emulating her sister, running for election in the state congress from the largely German eighth district. Will had seen Tennie make a speech to a crowd of hundreds at Irving Hall. She'd promised them everything Mrs. Woodhull promised in her speeches—freedom and progress and equality—but Tennie had added that she would campaign for their right to drink lager beer on Sundays.

Will stood among the musicians and the serenaders, looking up at Tennie, and the thought came into his head that she was very beautiful, and that what he felt towards her was the highest, best, and most genuine love. She saw Will among the crowd and nodded at him. She was gone for a few moments from the window, and when she returned she threw him a note, casting it down very precisely so it landed just at his feet. She liked to pass notes, and seemed to take the same joy and pride in writing them as a five-year-old brand new to letters. Sometimes she'd hand Will one as they lay in bed, something she'd written hours before and saved to give him after they had wrestled and gasped. Sometimes they stated the obvious, *You are a big fellow* or *We are together, you and I.* Sometimes they boasted of her prescience. Once, after he tripped over his own feet in the dark and knocked a teapot from a table by her bed, she handed him a note sealed and dated the day before, telling him he would do just that. "I can't see very far ahead," she told him whenever he asked her if he and Gob would succeed in their work, if her sister would in fact become the President of the United States, "but I always see true."

He unfolded the note, looking up at her and kissing it before he read it: *Even a blind man could see how I am busy. Go away and come back later.*

The very hottest day of the summer of 1871 came in August. Will went to the house on Fifth Avenue thinking to take refuge in the cool dark library. Letting himself in, he fell over something in the foyer. On the floor, he examined the thing that had tripped him—a bright new copper pipe, stamped with the name of the manufacturer, *Advent Pipeworks*. The pipes ran all over the first floor in neat rows. Will stepped over them, wondering at how they'd sprung up so quickly. At his last visit, three days previous, there had been no sign of them. He found Gob laying pipe in the dining room.

"What is their purpose?" he asked Gob. Could the machine grow so big it would fill up the house from first floor to fifth? It made Will flushed and hot again, thinking about that.

"To make ice," Gob said. He explained how he would boil aqua ammonia in a still, and drive the pure gas through a condenser to liquefy it, then pass it through the pipes, where it would expand and evaporate, stealing heat from the water around the pipes and freezing it.

"But your house," Will said. "You'll get it all wet."

"Help me," Gob said. "It's necessary for the machine."

"Very well," Will said, and put his hands to laying pipe, thinking as he worked of Pickie Beecher saying, "My brother, he likes the cold."

"Do you think she'll like it?" Gob asked, after they'd flooded the place to a depth of five inches and turned the whole first floor to a mess of ice.

"Who?"

"You know," Gob said. *"Her."* Will understood him to mean Miss Trufant.

"Does it matter of she likes it or doesn't?"

"It matters very much." Gob gave Will a puzzled look. "Very, very much," he said.

Gob had been saying lately that Miss Trufant was necessary to the machine. This was something Will did not understand. She was, after all, a girl, and not even one inclined to science. Gob insisted that she mattered to the building, but Will figured this to be a symptom of his ever-waxing infatuation with her.

"All this is for her?" Will asked. He had been thinking, as they worked, of rarefied chemical processes that could only take place at very low temperatures, of the precipitation of a gaseous soul, the opposite of sublimation, where an airy, unexisting thing would be made solid and real. "You said it was necessary for the machine."

"Immediately it is for her, but ultimately it is for the machine. Can't you see how very important she is, Will?" Gob got down on his knees and started to polish the ice with a wire brush. Will thought, as he turned away, What does he feel for her that it's not sufficient to make her a miracle, but he must polish it, too?

"You fellow," Will said quietly. "You must have her." He walked away slowly and carefully out of the dining room, out through the foyer. When he opened the door the night air was so hot and wet he choked on it.

Gob startled him when he pounded on his back—Will didn't hear him come gliding up on the ice. He knocked a few more times on the space between Will's shoulders, then patted it, then pulled Will back to embrace him. "Oh, my friend," Gob said, kicking the door shut with his foot. "I think she makes you green. But don't you know that no one can help me like you? Others are necessary to the building, but none is necessary like you. You are the most vital, the bravest and the smartest of my collaborators. It's you, not her or anyone else, who's most important."

"Now we are all together," Gob announced. He'd brought Maci Trufant into the workshop one night in December of 1871. Will, who was at work on the machine, had scrambled around nervously, trying to cover things up—batteries, bones, a pile of uncut gemstones gathered by Pickie Beecher. He felt as if he'd been walked in on in the bath, but the fact was that she'd been visiting the house since the end of the summer, and had even begun to contribute to the construction. Will had noticed her little touches—blue paint on a copper pipe, pieces of glass twisted into patterns like bows—and he cared very little for them.

Pickie Beecher rushed out from under a table to clutch Miss Trufant around her legs and say, "Welcome!"

She patted him on the back and said, "Little child." He took her hand and led her to the middle of the room, where a number of the holes in the floor had been consolidated into one great hole, which led now through three floors of the house, so standing there she could look down all the way to the library.

"Dr. Fie," she said, nodding at him. "I've been meaning to tell you how your work is most ridiculous." Then she *laughed* at him. She was dressed all in black, with a red sash that cut across her chest and her belly, and a red carnation in her hat. She'd been marching that day in a parade organized by Mrs. Woodhull to honor the martyrs of the Paris Commune.

"Perhaps your eye is jaundiced," Will said. "Perhaps you do not see clearly."

She stared and stared. "You two," she said. "My father was a weekend tinkerer, compared to you."

Gob came forward and joined their hands, left to right, and then he took their free hands up in his own. Pickie ducked under their arms, so he stood in the middle of their circle, and Gob said it: "Now we are all together."

Will broke apart from them. Gob took Miss Trufant's arm and escorted her around the room. They'd lean down together, bending in unison as if connected by a bar from hip to hip, to examine some fascinating piece of machinery. Will went downstairs to the library, where he sat in a chair away from the hole in the ceiling, with a text on steam engines open in his lap to a chapter on the Giffard injector. Pickie had followed him downstairs, and was rooting in a box of stereographs near Will's chair.

"He didn't ask, did he? May she come in? Don't you think he ought to have asked?"

"She is very beautiful," said Pickie. "She is the mother of my brother."

"She just walked right in."

Pickie came over and climbed into Will's lap, sitting on the book Will wasn't reading. He had a stereopticon clutched in his little hands. "See?" he said, putting it to Will's eyes. "It's my brother."

Will didn't like to look at stereographs—they gave him a headache. But Pickie held the viewer hard against his face, so he had no choice. The image slowly gained depth and detail. It was a boy who had been ruined by a shell. He was in two pieces, and bits of grass grew up straight and strong between the halves of his body. Will could see little clumps of dirt stuck to the trailing intestines. "Yes, yes," he said. "I've seen it, Pickie."

"He is my brother," said Pickie Beecher. He sat in Will's lap and put in picture after picture, and said the same thing to each one: "Hello, brother."

"I saw it coming, you know," Tennie said, "this day. And you may ask, How can a person live that way, knowing how all the terrible things are going to happen? It always seemed a thousand years in the future, and that was a consolation. But now here it is, come today. Don't try to fight it, dear. It's something I have learned, that I can always see it coming but never can stop it." She had just given him bad news: she did not love him any longer, and wouldn't see him anymore. She had taken him into her Turkish corner, as if for love, but had instead made this devastating announcement. He fell into a fit as soon as he understood what she was saying. When he came back to himself he saw how he'd made a mess of her corner. She held his head in her lap. Was it not evidence of continuing love, he wondered, how she dabbed at his bitten lip with the hem of her sleeve, without care for bloodstains? She put her finger on his lips when he tried to plead with her. Didn't he feel it? she asked. Didn't he feel how there was no joy in it anymore, not for either of them?

"But there is still, for me," he said weakly, around her finger.

"Yes," she said. "I knew you would agree with me. See how easy we make it, because we are friends?" He brought up his hands to touch her breasts, but she stopped him. "I could," she said. "I could touch you, and not love you. But I know you wouldn't want that."

"You think you are special," Will told Mr. Whitman on the way back from Gob's wedding, "and yet really you are not. Really, sir, you are nobody at all. Really you are the least important person in all the world." It made him feel better, to say this. Seeing Whitman at the bow of the ferry, looking so carefree and happy in his solitude, Will had felt a pressure in his throat that he thought was vomit, but was actually just a set of hard words that wanted so badly to come out. He left Whitman there and took Pickie Beecher to the back of the boat, where people had gathered around Gob and his new wife. Will stood far away and watched Tennie talking and laughing, pretending he was admiring the traffic on the river—the hay barges and sand barges, the giant sailer-steamers. For her part, she did not even glance at him. Will found he loved her better every day since she cast him off, and during the ceremony he only had thoughts of marrying her. It was stupid, he knew, to think that another person could abolish your unhappiness, but what cure was there for want of Tennie except Tennie herself?

Gob was solicitous, yet he never seemed to understand how a person could be sad just because his aunt refused him her company. Canning Woodhull, however, was very sympathetic. He and Will became friends in the days after the wedding. They caroused together in low and high places, in Water Street dives and the bar at the Hoffman House. Will took him to the Pearl, and he took Will to the Seven Sisters', where they visited five of seven houses in as many evenings.

But every night they would return to Mrs. Woodhull's house on Thirty-eighth Street, where they'd sit in the kitchen and drink until it was almost dawn. The senior Dr. Woodhull was a very good listener, and it was a relief to Will how he never tried to offer hope, how he never tried to convince Will that his situation would improve. "It will get worse," he said. "You will love her and want her more and more. Every day something else will drop away, until there is nothing left but her. And you will come to know that every good thing in life was her, and every bad thing was lack of her."

"Why?" Will asked. "Why did she go away from me?" He didn't mind, just then, how he was like his mother, complaining in a darkened room.

Canning Woodhull usually had no answer to this question. He would shrug, or else answer with another question—"Why did she go away from *me?*"

One night, when they had been drinking for a good long while, Dr. Woodhull looked up and met Will's eyes—something he rarely did; usually when they talked he looked only at his glass. He said, "Don't you see that it's the same answer to all the questions? Why did she leave me? Why did he die? Why is the world the place that it is, full of dirty pain?"

"But what is the answer?" Will asked. He grabbed Canning Woodhull's bony wrist across the table.

"My boy, I will tell you. Wait here for me, and prepare yourself to receive the information."

Dr. Woodhull pulled away his wrist, and went out of the room. Will sat alone, staring at a dwindling candle. He was anxious, at first. He wanted the answer to his question, and imagined that Dr. Woodhull must have gone upstairs to consult an enormous book. But he'd had so much to drink that he fell asleep with his chin in his hands, though not for very long. It was still dark when he woke to screaming. He went upstairs and discovered its source. In the hall he saw Mrs. Woodhull, not very much dressed, her hair wet with blood. She was being comforted by her Colonel, who was drenched just like her. Will went into their room, where he could see Dr. Woodhull, and how he had crawled into his wife's bed to cut his own throat while she and her husband slept. It was a mighty stroke that he had dealt himself. He'd cut all the way down to the bones of his neck. He must have crept into their bed ever so carefully, not to have woken them with the intrusion of his body, but only with the flooding warmth of his blood. Pickie Beecher was there, jumping on the sodden mattress, and Tennie was kneeling by the bed next to her mother, who had rested her cheek on Canning Woodhull's chest.

"Oh, Doc," said Tennie.

Spirits scolded him, shaking their cold, pale fingers, and screwing up their faces at him. Even Jolly frowned at Will, whenever he sat alone drinking. Neither was the angel very friendly. She got more shrill with every visit. "Doctoring is a bust," Will told her a few nights after Canning Woodhull's funeral. He hadn't been to Bellevue in weeks because he couldn't go near the patients without having a fit. He'd taken a leave of absence, but really he didn't plan on going back until the machine was finished, but by then he hoped he'd have no more work there anyway.

"Do you think, creature, that it will all go away, when the abomination is complete?" the angel asked.

"You're pretty," he told her.

"Do you think it will be for free? Do you think you can ruin the natural order for no price at all? The Kosmos will die, and worse. His soul will be abolished utterly. There will be nothing left of him, not even a memory. From such murder you hope your joy will be born."

Spirits came and chased her off, and then they gathered around him—Jolly, Sam, Lewy, Frenchy, all of them equally furious. He could tell what they were saying: "Get to work!"

Will would have liked to do just that, but lately the building was going badly. Gob seemed not to understand anymore what to do with the confusion of parts they had created, and the dreams which formerly had guided him now only confused him. Even Will, looking at the machine, could tell there was something wrong with it, that its elements did not blend together into any sort of harmony. For the first time, it looked like nothing to him, not an angel, not a person, not a lamb. It was merely a random association of components. Pickie Beecher scolded them both for their failure, but could not seem to help them, either. He could only offer more parts.

Nonetheless, Will went to Gob's house that night in July to apply himself to the machine, and spend the hours till dawn engaged in a nostalgic practice—making batteries. Their manufacture brought to mind happier days, when Tennie was still with him, and when the machine seemed almost to build itself. He had thought the house on Fifth Avenue would be quiet and dark, and that Gob and his bride would be in bed in the Fifth Avenue Hotel, where they had taken rooms because the new Mrs. Woodhull refused to live under the same roof as what she called the "pathetic contraption." But, though it was two o'clock in the morning when Will arrived there, the house was brightly lit.

"There you are!" Gob said when Will came inside. "Come and see this!" He took Will's arm and dragged him up all the stairs to the workshop. Gob was so excited, Will thought something truly spectacular must be waiting on top of the house. Perhaps the machine had spit out another strange child, a wiser boy than Pickie Beecher, who could be a better guide to them. But it was just the junior Mrs. Woodhull on the other side of the iron door, seated at a little desk on a peninsula of floor. A crowd of spirits surrounded her, as they had at Canning Woodhull's funeral, when she and Will had walked together and talked in the shade of a tree that grew over new graves. She had declared against the machine even as the spirits fawned over her and looked at Will with expressions that were somehow both angry and pleading.

Gob, still dragging Will, rushed to the desk and grabbed up the drawing that the lady was working on.

"Look, Will," Gob said. "Do you see?" He held the paper scant inches from Will's face, and Will saw a giant pair of wings made entirely of glass negative plates. "Our dry time is over, my friend. Dear Maci will show us the way."

"Don't you believe it, Dr. Fie," said young Mrs. Woodhull, whose hand was already at work sketching another part of the machine. "Not for an instant!"

"What will happen to him?" Will asked Gob. "Might Mr. Whitman be . . . injured?" Will hoped that he would be. He hoped there would be just a little bit of pain, enough to crack the poet's happy exterior. When he was in a very bad mood, Will thought that he would like to see Mr. Whitman cry.

"Of course not!" Gob said, but the angel insisted that he was lying.

One night as Will was leaving the Pearl, she fell on him out of the sky. She knocked him to the ground and wrapped him up in her grotesque wings. "Look now, creature," she said, "and see the truth." Will felt pain, bright and white, like a moment when he'd been struck in the face with a gun many years before. It had been an accident. A fellow member of Company D had turned in the darkness with his gun held out, and the barrel had taken Will just above the eye and knocked him senseless. Now, Will was stuck in the moment when he had first realized that he hurt, and the moment went on and on. Through the glare, he saw Mr. Whitman screaming like a woman, high and frightened and hysterical, piteous wailing shrieks, and he understood absolutely that something that truly was abominable would happen to that man.

This vision seemed to go on forever, but in fact it was just moments before the spirits came and chased away the angel. She ran from them, flying up to perch on a lamppost. They jumped at her like dogs, but she batted them away with her fists.

"Do you see now?" she asked him.

"Never trust an angel," Gob said, when Will told him of the visit. "They are the most notorious liars."

They finished in the winter of 1872. Gob declared that their creation was precisely the machine he had been dreaming since his brother died. It had been quite reshaped by Maci Woodhull's prolific hand. Since the summertime Will had taken to sleeping in the house at Fifth Avenue, and had given up entirely on doctoring, or even photography, except to take pictures of the machine as they put it into its final shape. Will's days and nights ran together, until he was no longer sure what day it was. All he knew was that it was winter, and that history was continuing to unfold outside of the house. Indeed, there was some sort of excitement happening with Gob's mother, but Will was not sure what exactly. Whatever it was, Will felt safe from it in the house, where he was often alone with Pickie Beecher during the day.

Then Will would have a rapture of building, and he would imagine that the machine was his alone—his life's idea and his life's work. He'd imagine that skibbling Pickie Beecher was his own unnatural child, and sometimes he'd imagine that Tennie had died tragically and the machine was meant to bring back her alone. "She died *tragically*," he said one night to Pickie Beecher. "Eaten by bees. And why do we specify tragically, anyhow? Is there any other sort of death?"

"It's all very bad," the boy agreed. In the last months he was Will's constant companion. He was another good listener, if a poor conversationalist, and of course he was the very best helper one could ask for. Will had only to want a tool before Pickie Beecher ran up with it clutched in his tiny hands.

"I will make an adjustment," Will said, "to ensure that the machine will also bring back dead love. So Canning Woodhull, when he walks again among the living, will have his wife again to hold him. Unless, of course, she never loved him at all, in which case I am powerless to help him." He worked and he slept, and sometimes he ate, when Pickie Beecher brought him food.

As the weeks went on he came to be unsure, sometimes, if he was waking or sleeping, because he built in dreams as constantly as he built while he was awake. His sleep became fractured, so he only took it in spells of an hour or two, and when he'd wake, he'd see Pickie Beecher sitting atop some fantastic new piece of matériel that he'd stolen from only he knew where; he'd see Gob's wife sketching at her desk; he'd see Gob wrestling a strut into some novel position. Will would rise and join the work. In the last weeks, he woke to see Pickie sitting on a little red dude of a fire engine, a locomotive smokestack, and a lens nine feet in diameter. When Will and Gob hauled it into place the nine-thousand-candlepower arc lamp—meant to shine down through the picture negatives—was amplified to ninety thousand candlepower. It would be, Will was sure, the brightest light ever.

"Do you really believe that it will do anything but gurgle and smoke?" the new Mrs. Woodhull would ask Will every so often.

He always had the same answer for her. "Of course I do." Will thought her doubt would have become fatigued, by now, but she still called the machine ridiculous, and mocked it ruthlessly, even as she helped to build it. She claimed to have nothing at all to do with the hand that was guiding them with its drawings, and sniffed derisively when Will pointed out that it was attached to her wrist.

The spirits got happier as the machine got bigger. When it had grown to maturity—so it filled up the house and there was nowhere left for Will to sleep but cradled among its omnipresent arms and legs, its hundred thousand pieces, its crystal and iron gate and gatehouse—then they never walked but they danced, and they never opened their mouths but they seemed to be singing.

"Am I awake?" he'd ask Pickie Beecher, thinking back to the night when Jolly had asked him a similar question. Pickie Beecher usually pinched him in answer, but often it wasn't enough to convince. What if Will dreamed the whole thing through to its glorious conclusion? What if the machine did its work, and death was abolished, and Will got to see all the dead rise and stretch their stiff limbs, and smile? What if he got to embrace Sam and Jolly, only to wake a moment later in a world where his work was still undone, where people still died? He doubted the angel, when she arrived every now and then to call him *creature* and say he must destroy the abomination, before it was too late. He doubted that Mr. Whitman would come to them, meek as a lamb to be their battery.

But Walt Whitman did come. "Are you here?" Will asked him, poking the man in his heroic belly. It seemed unreal, all of it: all the house-sized gears turning; the wings beating; Mr. Whitman reclining in the gatehouse; a light flaring in Gob's hands, and an answering light from the arc lamp, amplified and expounded through the lens to shine down so strong through the glass Will thought it must burn the images into the poet's skin. Even that light seemed unreal, and though Will had grown accustomed to spirits, the ones that flooded the house, lining up for their turn to pass through the gates of the machine, all seemed strange and fake. "Now I will wake," he said to Pickie Beecher, "and we'll have to do it all again!"

"It's my brother!" Pickie Beecher shouted above the noise. "He is here!" Mr. Whitman began to scream, and the spirits, with the little one-winged angel at their head, surged forward towards the gate. Then it finally did seem real, and only then did Will wish it were not. He would have done it all again, learned of Sam's death, gone off to the war, suffered his apprenticeship under Frenchy. He would have gladly suffered all the debilitating fits of medical school. He would have loved Tennie again, even with the knowledge that he would lose her. He would have lost himself in all the seasons of dreamtime building. He would have done these things twice or three times. He would have done them over and over forever, if only he could wake away from the horrible screaming, so much worse than what the angel had him taste, if only he could have that, just that, be not real.

"WHO IS THE GOD OF THE FUTURE?" THE URFEIST ASKED Gob. It was one of two questions he posed repeatedly during their trip to New York. Gob's first answer was, "Time." That was wrong, and warranted a savage beating. On the first night in the house on Fifth Avenue, as they stood in a library full of clocks, the Urfeist asked the question again. This time Gob said, "Death."

"Yes," said the Urfeist, "death waits at the end of every future." He looked sad or afraid or dyspeptic whenever he asked that question. He had lived a gluttonous portion of years, and he still did not want to die. There was almost kindness in his voice when he would say that if Gob worked hard enough, the god of the future might fall by his hand.

They went to New York by horse cart, stage, steamer, and railroad, and each new conveyance was fancier than the last, so by the time they approached Manhattan, they were traveling in a luxurious Pullman car. All during the trip, the Urfeist spoke of machines, and how he would teach Gob to build them. "It's the only certain means to bring back your brother, my ugly one," he said. "Mechanically."

Every morning as they'd traveled, the Urfeist had woken Gob by breathing hotly into his ear, and sometimes the rushing noise invaded his dreams, so he heard the ocean sound as he dreamed of his brother. The noise would issue from Tomo's mouth when he tried to speak, and before he woke Gob would catch glimpses of copper and iron and glass as Tomo pointed to them. "It is the noise," the Urfeist said, "of your machine. The one you must learn to build, if you want to save your brother from death."

The Urfeist was an expert builder. Gob discovered that his first day in the thing's beautiful house. Evidence of his new master's skill was everywhere, devices large and small, locked away behind doors or placed in special alcoves in the long halls: a windmaker, rattraps big enough to catch children, singing candles, skittering iron insects, and books that turned their own pages as you read them. Gob wandered among the little machines, feeling admiration and envy as he beheld them. They would inspire him to hurry to the library and pick a book at random from the shelves, then sit in a chair among the clocks, or sprawl on the floor beneath a great golden armillary sphere. He'd read until the Urfeist came and found him and asked another question. "What is a machine?"

"A machine," Gob would reply, his voice seeming to him mechanical itself as he recited the definition taught him on the journey from Homer, "is a combination of resistant bodies so arranged that by their means the mechanical forces of nature can be compelled to do work accompanied by certain determinate motions."

"Precisely," the Urfeist would say.

"Do you see how your mind is small?" the Urfeist asked Gob. "Do you see how you are clumsy and powerless? Do you want your brother back? You will not have him by flailing. Hurl blind rage at the walls, they will not break. Such machines as you would build—death would laugh at them! Death would laugh at you! Death is laughing at you now, saying, 'Think of everything your brother was, everything he wanted, all he might have seen or heard or felt. Every morning he might have woken to, every night he might have put down his head on his pillow, every dream he might have dreamed as he slept—these things are mine now. I have stowed thousands of days away in my pocket where he will never live them, but I give them to you—you may imagine them, you may consider him planting his bare foot in the cool mud under the mill pond (on a hot day, is that cool mud not a joy?) and then you may consider how he resides in my dark pocket never to escape. You are a small piece of work, boy, lazy and coarse and no threat to me because your machine is here in my pocket, too, where it will never be born because you are too lazy and stupid to bring it out. You will accomplish nothing, and then I will have you, too. I will wait for you here at the end of your span of joyless pointless days.' "

Gob sat on his vast bed and studied a book the Urfeist had given him, one picked as suitable for inspiring the fancy of an ignoramus. In the library, he had passed it to Gob and then rummaged in another stack. Two minutes later he'd changed his mind, saying Gob wasn't ready for that book: it was too fine for him, he could not be trusted to care for it. But Gob was already running up to his room.

It was one of the notebooks of Leonardo. "Do you want to be like him?" the Urfeist asked Gob the next day, after Gob had spent the whole night poring over the fantastic drawings. Gob nodded and got beaten for it with the hickory paddle. "Do not!" said the Urfeist. "He dreamed everything and built *nothing*. Do you want to be a silly dreamer, or do you want to bring your brother back?" Gob wanted to bring back his brother, yet he lost none of his affection for the notebook. His eyes lingered for hours over pictures of gears and wheels and wings. He thought it would be most satisfying if he could garner such skill and draw the machine he dreamed about, but when he tried he only made a line that rose and fell as the noise of the machine rose and fell, a neaping ebbing line that fell back on itself, and was lost eventually in a tangle of similar lines.

Though he couldn't draw his own machine, Gob found he had no difficulty copying the notebook drawings. He drew on the workroom floor with a piece of charcoal, copying pictures of finned missiles and vertical drilling machines, chain drives and sprocket wheels, Archimedean screws and waterwheels and well pumps. He did not know what he was drawing, but the shapes were lovely and familiar to him. He saw them in his dreams, amid spinning gears and puffing steam. In the center of the room the Urfeist had designated as his workshop, Gob copied a picture of an ornithopter. There was room enough to make it about as big as it was meant to be in life. He turned down the gas, and lay atop the thing, imagining that he rode it through the sky in search of his brother.

In New York, the Urfeist did not live the solitary life he lived in Homer. He had many friends, who called him Dr. Oetker, and thought he was a German radical who had fled with his fortune from the upheavals of '48. The accent that the Urfeist affected around his friends reminded Gob of his grandmother, and made him think of home. He wondered if his mother was missing him, and if she thought he was dead. When he tried to picture her face he could only envisage a white tea rose, the sort she wore at her throat when she wanted to make herself look distinguished.

The Urfeist's friends came to dinner, and clustered by the score around his table, where servants waited on them dressed in fancy livery, with ridiculous white wigs on their heads. Gob helped them set the table, taking as his job the setting of place cards above the plates: Mr. and Mrs. Lohman; Mr. Vanderbilt; Mr. Burns. Gob was not invited to dinner, but he would watch from just within the kitchen, and listen to the conversation.

Gob might have been lonely, except he had his studies to keep him occupied—there was always another book to read. And occasionally there were other children in the house. They would pass through, when the Urfeist began to feel old and melancholy. He told Gob he brought them to cheer his soul, but Gob felt certain he was eating them and hanging their bones to dry in the basement. They arrived, fetched from one of the charitable institutions of the city, and most of them were very happy to have stepped from the sad orphanage into a mansion. For a few days they stuffed at the Urfeist's big table, and rolled hoops with Gob down the long halls of the house. Gob would show them his workroom, his books and his drawings, but these rarely provoked any interest. "What's behind there?" they would ask, pointing at the iron door outside Gob's room.

"The green room," Gob said, and would not say any more about it, because it was into that room that the Urfeist retired when he wanted to put on his kilt and his hat and his skin chemise. It was filled with plants and carpeted with grass. The ceiling was all glass. At night the moon shone down on the skillfully potted ferns and roses and palms, and it did not take much imagining to think yourself lost in the wilderness. There was even a small cave built into a wall, where the Urfeist slept sometimes on a pile of leaves. Gob said nothing of the room, but the Urfeist told the children of it, saying he would take them in if they were good and show them that beautiful place, where birds sang under the glass roof, and where candy trees flourished, aching for children's hands to pick their heavy fruit. The children all went in there, after a few days of feasting and playing, of sleeping in crisp white sheets in big beds. They passed through the iron door, hand in hand with the Urfeist, and Gob did not see them again, but after they were gone the Urfeist would declare himself filled with a youthful energy, and for a time all his melancholy would be departed from him.

* * *

"Unhappiness is the lot of spirits. They are denied bodily delight, but they are creatures of desire. Desire is all that's left to them. They want to live again! They want to be with you, all you desolate millions. How will you live without them? How will they continue without you? What sort of heaven can there be when brothers are apart? My dumb one, my little boy, my ugly poodle, just poke a hole in the wall and the desire of spirits might pour through and tear the wall apart. Do you see how your work is small? Just a tiny hole through which you might drag your brother. A tiny hole, but it may as well be big as the whole earth, if you stay lazy and stupid, if I cannot reform your base, contrary soul. You may as well bring down the moon to touch the seas, smash the crystalline firmament and let down a rain of stars. Why did you come to bother me? Why, now, do you even try?"

"When I beat you I make you smarter," the Urfeist told Gob. "When I love you I make you more tender."

Gob felt no more tender than when he had first visited the Urfeist. He was not even sure what his teacher meant with that word, and he was not inclined to ask. He associated tenderness with girlishness. Girls were tender towards their dolls and their mamas. Girls had tender white flesh that gave when you poked it with your finger. If anything, Gob felt heavier and denser than before. Back in Homer, when his grandmother fell to reminiscing about her "terrible master," she'd say, "Ach he put the *worm* in me!" She'd say how the worm was still in her, and run a hand down her front and declare, "He is there, in a coil around my backbone. Oh, he never leaves me alone!" Gob could never tell if she thought that was a good thing, or a bad. He considered his heaviness and wondered if what he was feeling was not the extra weight of Anna's worm.

Gob did feel smarter, though. He felt very much smarter than before. The hickory paddle was decorated on one side with multiplication tables and on the other with the alphabet. He already knew his multiplication tables, of course, but now the Urfeist was teaching him better math, powerful geometry. For months Gob saw triangles everywhere. Houses were roofed in triangles. Pine trees in the park were simple triangle shapes. Staring at the faces of strangers on the street, he could make their features dissolve into a grand association of triangles.

Gob began to measure time by the books he read. The winter of 1864 was all Latin and Greek primers. The spring was Aristotle. The Urfeist knew his Aristotle intimately, and he tested Gob's retention of his reading, paddle in hand. He knew his Aristotle so well that Gob thought sometimes that he *was* Aristotle, soured by the centuries into a finger-kilt-and-blood-cap-wearing madman. Plato and Euclid, Archimedes, Ctesibius, Archytas of Tarentum—sometimes Gob's eyes felt weak, but he loved what he read. He would rather sit with a book than with the Urfeist. His favorite thing was to sit in his room with a giant dusty book in his lap, some whiskey in one hand and a brick of sweet chocolate in the other, partaking of whiskey, knowledge, and chocolate in succession. He stole the whiskey from the pantry, and usually when the Urfeist smelled it on his breath he beat him, but sometimes he rewarded understanding with some sort of powerful liquor.

Often, Gob would get a shock of recognition as he read. A picture of the aeolipile of Hero raised the hair on the back of his neck. Here, surely, was a part or a piece of his own machine. "The aeolipile," said the Urfeist. "Is it a spiritous or self-propelling machine?" It was spiritous, Gob said, and he proceeded to build an aeolipile of his own, working with scraps of metal from a basement room full of such scraps. It was not pretty, when he'd finished, but it functioned. Gob filled it with water, and lit a fire under it. Steam rose through the support tubes, then shot from the engine tubes, and the sphere began to rotate, and kept rotating for as long as there was water and fire to make steam. Such was a spiritous machine, one that moved by the power of air or steam, whereas a self-propelling machine moved by means of wheels and pulleys and weights. When the aeolipile provoked no beatings he copied other machines—the miraculous altar and the magic amphora and the fire pump.

"Toys!" said the Urfeist. Such science as was familiar to the Alexandrian engineers seemed to annoy him. He forbade Gob any more copying of Hero, and said he was ready for stranger and more powerful knowledge. Gob thought that meant he would at last be allowed to put his little hands on the *Principia,* which lay in the library under a glass case the unlocking of which Gob could not figure. But the Urfeist introduced him, instead, to the Renaissance Magi: Paracelsus and Nettesheim and Della Porta, Albertus Magnus and Mirandola and Dr. Dee. Gob wanted to try making a homunculus, but the recipe called for semen, something he could not yet manufacture. "Everything in time," said the Urfeist, in a tone that might have been gentle and avuncular coming from another mouth. He taught Gob herbs. Asafetida has a horrid odor and is useful for exorcisms. Lilies keep away unwelcome visitors. The scent of mandrake will put a person to sleep. Elm protects from lightning. Gob wanted to know, if that was true, why was there a lightning-struck elm not fifty feet from the house? In answer he got a beating.

"But I have been waiting for you. Spirits beg for masters. They want to be dominated, and those spirits who are my slaves have spoken of you, promised that a boy would come one day to learn all I could teach. Are you him? Are you the boy who would become a master of spirits, a magus, an engineer? Such a small mind. Such a yearning towards sloth. I think you must be made from your brother's leftover material—there must have been something extra, but not enough for a whole proper boy. God made you, a half thing, a well-intentioned but poorly executed gesture. Perhaps it was your brother I was meant to teach. But you are sweet in your way. We will have to make do."

Gob was not a prisoner in that house. He could have left, but he never tried to catch a train west to Ohio, back to his mama and his obstreperous relatives. He was there to learn, and he was learning, and the more he learned, the more he realized that he was laboring under a world's weight of ignorance. And anyhow, whenever he remembered his mama, it was mostly to hear her laughing at Tomo's death, and then he would feel fresh rage towards her.

Gob's life was mostly work, but it was not all work. Sometimes the Urfeist took him out to restaurants or oyster bars. They went for rides in Central Park, racing against the sleek equipage of the Urfeist's friend Mr. Vanderbilt. They saw plays. The Urfeist was a great devotee of Edwin Booth and Charlotte Cushman, and did not miss a production that featured one of those actors. The Urfeist was also partial to opera. He had one of those highly coveted boxes at the Academy of Music. During intermissions tastefully dressed people came to visit the Urfeist in his box, and he introduced Gob as his ward, the child of a cousin who'd died of cholera the year before, his last living relative. "What happened to his hand?" they would whisper to the Urfeist.

"A congenital deformity," he'd reply.

"I am dismayed by current developments," said Madame Restell. She sat next to the Urfeist at one of his to-dos. He threw dinner parties whenever news of a great battle reached New York. Ostensibly, he was celebrating the increasingly frequent Union victories that came in the spring of 1865, but Gob suspected his master was just celebrating the carnage. "Dundrearies, sluggers, muttonchops, burnsides, beavers. I think there is too much variety in facial hair—there ought to be a regulation. Some have ventured so far beyond the pale I shiver to think of them. I offer as an example the type of man represented by Mr. Greeley, and those hideous *things* that proceed from out of his collar. It makes me shudder!"

"I don't think Mr. Greeley can be regarded as representing any type but his own, Annie," said the Urfeist. This brought laughs from all around the table. The scandalous, rich friends of the Urfeist were lingering over port and cigars. They flouted convention by staying at the table, and the ladies partook with the men. Gob usually eavesdropped from the kitchen, where one of the servants always gave him a cigar of his own. But tonight Gob was in the dining room, standing just off to the side of the Urfeist, who had called him out to entertain his guests. Gob had been reading aloud from a report of the battle at Spotsylvania. One of the guests had interrupted him to say that General Grant ought to grow a beard, because it would hide his features, which were obviously those of a dipsomaniac. "He flaunts it, with his bare face," said the guest. This prompted Madame Restell to make her comment on the chaos of facial hair threatening to undo society.

"That Grant!" said another guest. "An efficacious general, but he must be cruel. He's who makes me shudder."

"That Grant!" said the Urfeist, standing up and proposing a toast to him. "There is a man who is not afraid of death." His guests all drank to that, but the Urfeist did not. "And what sort of man," he asked them, "is that?"

"A hero," came the reply, and "A leader," and "A ruiner," this last from a man who made his great living selling shoddy wool to the Union army.

"No!" said the Urfeist, with such vehemence that some of his guests flinched. He clutched his glass so hard he broke it, and Madame Restell gave a squeal. "What sort of man?" the Urfeist cried. "What sort!"

"A fool," said Gob, wondering if the Urfeist would beat him in front of his guests, but his teacher laughed, and looked surprised at how he'd broken his glass and cut his hand.

His guests laughed, too, rather nervously, and the Urfeist said, "Forgive me, friends. The war excites me, you see. It excites me."

"Chicago is the mud hole of the prairie. Do not visit there. Cleveland is better. There, elegant villas are surrounded by orchards and gardens. Cincinnati is a porkopolis: a fine place to live, if you are a pig. New York is really the only place to reside, except in summer, when one really must retire to the countryside. Make dumplings from 2 cups of flour, 1 teaspoon of salt, 1 tablespoon of lard, a cup of milk, 4 teaspoons of baking powder, and a pinch of child's blood. These are light, fluffy dumplings—to eat them is to eat air. But stray from the recipe and you'll eat lead. The holy names of God are: Dah, Gian, Soter, Jehovah, Emmanuel, Tetragrammaton, Adonay, Sabtay, Seraphin. A woman has a little piece of chicken between her legs by which you may rule her."

On the Saturday before Easter, Gob walked down Broadway, on his way to Barnum's museum, so completely absorbed in his thoughts that he did not notice the hush on the streets, or how some of the hanging flags had been draped with black, or how the rosettes of red, white, and blue had been replaced with black. It was late in the afternoon. He'd stayed up late, reading Della Porta's *Celestial Physiognomy*. It was almost dawn before he went to bed, where he had uneasy dreams, not of the machine, but of his Aunt Tennie. She was weeping and he could not console her.

He was thinking, as he walked down Broadway, about Mr. Watt's double-acting engine, about how it was such an improvement over previous models, since it introduced the steam from both sides of the piston. This led Gob to consider how everything he himself had built so far seemed to act only from one side. That, he was sure, was inappropriate and a waste, because he knew, suddenly, that his machine must run on such a double-acting principle. But he didn't know what such a principle would be, unless it was that Tomo was dead, and yet he must not be.

Barnum's was closed. Black crepe was strung around the door, and all the posters were edged in black. A large plaster urn was set on a granite pedestal by the door, and bore an inscription: *Dulce est pro patria mori*.

"Poor Mr. Booth," said Madame Restell, many days later, meaning Edwin. "I saw him in *Macbeth*. I think his anguish will inform that role, if he ever plays it again."

"I think I would hide forever, if my brother did such a thing," said another guest. "I could never forgive such atrocity." The Urfeist had a funereal feast, on the eve of the arrival of the late President's body in New York. Gob, trotted out again to amuse the Urfeist's friends, wanted to say that a brother ought to forgive a brother any misdeed, any at all. He wondered if Tomo might still be angry at him.

Gob felt sick. He'd eaten too much, and the guests were making him dizzy with their demands upon his memory. The Urfeist had made him memorize the minutes of Dr. Abbott, the physician attending at Mr. Lincoln's death.

"Eleven thirty-two p.m.," said Madame Restell, continuing the game.

"Pulse forty-eight," said Gob. "Respirations twenty-seven."

"One forty-five a.m.," said another guest.

"Pulse eighty-six. Patient is very quiet. Respirations are irregular. Mrs. Lincoln is present."

"Six o'clock!" said an excitable lady. "Is he dead yet?"

"Pulse falling," said Gob. "Respirations twenty-eight."

"Seven o' clock," said the same lady.

"Symptoms of immediate dissolution," said Gob.

"Will he never die?" the lady asked.

"Patience, my dear," said the Urfeist. "Seven twenty-two."

Gob said, "Death."

"Hate death. It is the only sensible thing to do. What pale thin shields the living hold up against him! Nevermore with anguish laden! Sweet rest! Let us cross over the river and rest beneath the shade of the trees! Let us recline in the dank grave. Let us become wispy hurting creatures. Let us desire flesh, sunlight, a cheek laid against our own, let us even desire the sting of a bee. Spirits will do anything for a taste of flesh—this is the wisdom of the necromancer, who does not love death, but hates it, hates how it lurks under every thing, every root and leaf, every creature's skin. Every dumb child's happy face is a mask by which death hides his own smiling face from the world. Do you know how death mocks us? A world is not fair that says, 'Partake of these days while I ruin them,' for what joy can you have when every last thing exists only so it may one day be taken away from you? Do we not want eternally? Do we not love eternally? Do we not hate eternally? Why then is death a miser? Why does he steal our allotment of forevers? Why does he lick me every day with his wet hungry gaze and say, 'Though you still live and breathe, do you see how you are already dead?' Do you see how you could spend a whole life grieving for your own self? Don't you hate him, my ugly one? If only you weren't so ugly and stupid, if only you could make a determinate motion to wound smug death. If only you were not destined for laziness and failure, for dreams instead of works."

"They say she is a female Wendell Phillips," said the Urfeist, speaking of Mrs. Burleigh of Brooklyn. He'd brought Gob to see her lecture on the condition of children in society. All part of his continuing edification, the Urfeist assured Gob, who felt tricked. He'd been under the impression that he was being taken to see handsome, inspiring Anna Dickinson, not some lesser-light nobody from across the river.

Mrs. Burleigh was lecturing at Association Hall, under the aegis of the Sorosis Club, which sounded to Gob like an association for the diseased. Organ music played as the audience got settled, and Gob watched Mrs. Burleigh, red-faced, vital-looking, and pregnant, sitting quietly at the foot of the stage. Her tapping foot disturbed her skirts in rhythm to the music, until a thin, birdlike woman arose from the audience to introduce her as "the very best friend of our nation's children." This brought a rush of applause from the audience, and a cry of "Huzzah for Ms. Phillips!" from the back.

"My name is Burleigh, thank you sir!" said Mrs. Burleigh. She bowed her head a few moments, as if in prayer, and then spoke: "The general principle acted on in the world is that children have no rights which we are bound to respect!"

She elaborated on this bold statement while Gob shifted in his seat, too restless to care if the Urfeist punished him later for squirming. "What has she got to do with the machine?" he asked.

"Hush," said the Urfeist, and gave him a sharp poke in the side. "You will see."

"Quiet and care are essential to a child's welfare," said Mrs. Burleigh. "Cigar-smoking fathers and gin-drinking nurses are to be avoided. Heavily corseted mothers set a bad example. The groping uncle is anathema in any family not set on the ruination of its children."

The Urfeist frowned and reached into his pocket. He removed a silver box about the size of his palm. When he opened it, Gob saw that it was full of a fine yellow powder, and thought it must be sulfur. He moved his face over to take smell it, but the Urfeist pushed his head away roughly. "It wouldn't do," the Urfeist said, "to have a sniff." He set some on his palm and raised it to his lips, then blew it towards Mrs. Burleigh.

"What is it?" Gob asked.

"Watch," said his teacher. Their neighbor in the hall, a lady in a pink hat and a wine-red velvet dress, hissed at them. The Urfeist brought a handkerchief to his face and breathed through it, and indicated that Gob should do the same. All around, people began to sniff and wipe their eyes as Mrs. Burleigh detailed the plight of American children, depicting them as hapless, abused innocents. People began to weep openly. The lady in the wine-red dress lost her scowl, took a deep breath, and uttered a series of quick little sobs.

"Yes, weep!" said Mrs. Burleigh. "Weep, as the chimney boy cries out 'Weep, weep' for his living and his plight! We are every one of us their tormentors!" She was weeping, too, throwing tears from her face with rough swipes of her hands.

"What did you do?" asked Gob.

"It's your hideous face," the Urfeist said, smiling. "Which brings strangers to tears." The situation was deteriorating. Mrs. Burleigh's chest was heaving, even as she warned against the dangers of too much kissing of children. She decried it as an invasion of bodily privacy.

"They are not your kissing-dolls, Israel. Oh no, they are not!"

Gob was careless with his handkerchief. He breathed the tainted air, and felt overcome by sadness. He began to cry, not in tribute to the woes of childhood, but because it seemed to him in that moment that every last thing in the world was unbearably sad.

"What did you do?" he asked again on the way home. "What is that yellow powder?"

"A simple concoction," said the Urfeist. "I will demonstrate its making."

"It makes people sad?"

"No. It makes nothing. It releases sadness. Every last creature is sad. Do you know why?"

"They miss their dead."

"No!" he said. He looked around him for the paddle, and when he could not find it, gave Gob's head a slap with his naked hand. "No, it is not that they miss their dead. Not that they mourn their beloveds. They mourn themselves. They are sad because they know that they are going to die."

In May of 1865, Gob got an idea from a dream of dead soldiers. A great company of them lay in an open grave and chattered their teeth. How cold they are! Gob said to himself, and he wondered how to warm them. He could not figure that out, but it did occur to him that the noise of their teeth was very much like the noise of a telegraph. He knew the code, and listening very carefully he made out a message—*Bring us back.* Gob woke from the dream, rushed into his workroom, and started work on a spiritual telegraph.

Like most first efforts, it was a failure. But he worked on it for months. The Urfeist chose to escape the city that summer. "It will be a good year for cholera," he said. He packed up his kilt and his hat and his shirt and admonished Gob to read a book a day while he was gone. He had made selections and stacked them in the library.

"Are you going to Homer?" Gob asked him, just before he walked out the door.

"I have never heard of such a place," the Urfeist said. He bent down and kissed Gob lightly on his cheek, saying, "Mind Mrs. Lohmann." Madame Restell had declared that she would be Gob's companion. "We shall have a summer of delight!" she proclaimed.

While his teacher was gone, Gob neglected to read his book a day, neglected plays and Barnum's museum, neglected eating sometimes, enthralled by the workings of the half-dozen stockbroker's tickers he disassembled. He easily mastered the workings of the telegraphs—Professors Henry and Morse were his heroes, in those months. By July he had assembled his own ticker, made of parts looted from the ordinary tickers, and mystical parts he fabricated himself—bits of wire blessed in rituals, tiny golden gears, magnets split with a chisel under the full moon, batteries made from chemicals and herbs. He puzzled for another month over what sort of wire might take a message to the dead. And once he had a proper metal, where would he connect it? Would he have to sneak back to Homer and run the wire down into Tomo's grave? Could he connect it to the many miles of wire that crossed and recrossed Manhattan and hope that the spirits of the dead might hear and speak through that medium? In the end, he decided not to use a wire at all. He devised a means of telegraphing by induction.

Just looking at his spiritual telegraph, Gob should have known that it wouldn't work. It wasn't his machine. Though he did not know what his machine looked like, he knew for a fact that he would recognize it, when he saw it, and he recognized nothing in the dog-sized apparatus on his floor. It stood on four gutta-percha feet, and its silver and glass parts glinted under the light of the gas chandelier. Gob threw all the necessary switches. He had developed a special sense for electricity and other vital forces—he knew the thing was humming with energy. He sat up with it all night long, waiting for it to spit out a message from Tomo—*I am alive, I am coming back to you.*

But it was silent.

When the Urfeist returned in the autumn, Gob was prepared for a beating because he had neglected his studies and squandered his time on a useless machine. So he was surprised when the Urfeist praised his failed effort. "Now we may begin," the Urfeist said, meaning that they could begin to build in earnest. They collaborated on machines. The ectoplasmic arc lamp, the Swedenborgian turbine—these were failures, too.

But these failures cheered the Urfeist. "Of course it will be difficult," he told Gob, with something almost like kindness in his voice. "Perhaps," he said, "you are becoming competent in your science but neglecting your art." He locked the door of Gob's workshop, hid the key, and directed Gob to the library, to the many shelves devoted to the arcane arts. Gob studied dutifully, wishing he could return to his workshop and be a mechanic. But after a few weeks he found a book that intrigued him endlessly, a little primer of necromancy, bound in black leather and written in German. It was full of simple spells that purported to let the living communicate with the dead. Write a message on a piece of slate and bury it in a graveyard; burn your message with peat and the fat of a pregnant hare; the dead will hear you. Gob performed these spells, sent Tomo such messages as *I will bring you back,* and they comforted him, though he did not entirely believe them efficacious.

Gob began to accompany the Urfeist when he called at the houses of sick people. The Urfeist meant to make Gob a physician, to balance Gob's study in necromancy with the study of life. But it seemed to Gob that medicine was an art as thoroughly dedicated to death as was necromancy. What was in a medical book besides loving, intimate descriptions of injury, disease, and, ultimately, death? There was a motto in the little McGuffey's Necromancer that had become dear to him: *My mistress wears a thousand faces*. It was the refrain of the sorcerer, but it seemed to Gob also appropriate to the medical profession. "Yes," said the Urfeist. "It is true. Those root and herb sharks. Those cancer-quacks. Oh, even the distinguished ones, too. Dr. Mott, Dr. Gross, all my esteemed colleagues, they are ministers of hope and despair—and they do not hate death sufficiently."

Every year, in the weeks leading up to Christmas, the Urfeist made a grand orphanage tour. There were a great many to visit. He went, not to make withdrawals of children, but to deposit gifts. He put a sprig of holly in his hat, the servants loaded down a carriage with presents, and the Urfeist proceeded to the Catholic Orphan Asylum, just up the street from them on Fifth Avenue, or the Juvenile Asylum, or Leake and Watt's Orphan House. Gob went with him to the Sheltering Arms, a house up in Manhattanville that accepted the castoffs of other orphanages. The children—some terminally ill, others half-orphaned not by death but by liquor—gathered under a candle-laden Christmas tree and received the largesse of the Urfeist. Gob wondered if the rocking horses wouldn't come alive at night and stomp on some child's tender cranium, if the porcelain faces of the dolls would not at midnight become the glaring white visages of ghouls, if the toy guns would not shoot real bullets and make murderers of innocents. But the gifts were wholesome. The puzzles were just puzzles, the calico cats and gingham dogs lacked teeth and claws. The toys were remarkable only because they were so fine. There were wooden soldiers who marched and presented arms, glass butterflies that, when wound, flapped their wings and waved their antennae, a tiny bear who, when squeezed, growled.

"And what is your name, my dear?" asked the Urfeist. A child had climbed into his lap where he sat by the tree.

"Maude," said the girl.

"What have we for sweet little Maude?" the Urfeist asked of Gob, and Gob rummaged in the bag until he found a doll for her.

"Thank you," she said dutifully, when she had got it. She leaned forward and gave the Urfeist a kiss on his dry cheek, then clambered off his lap and ran away to a corner where she clutched her new doll and rocked slowly back and forth on her knees.

After visiting the Sheltering Arms, they went home. The Urfeist was a great devotee of the holiday. He insisted on having multiple trees throughout the house, each one lit up with candles and strung with gold beads and crystal. The house was swathed so heavily with evergreen cuttings that a person could not pass from one floor to another without getting touched with sap. The Urfeist scattered walnuts in the corners, set puddings and punches on every table, and insisted, in the few days immediately following Christmas, on lengthy sessions of caroling. Candles in hand, he and Gob would proceed through the house side by side, singing "Good King Wenceslaus" or "Adeste Fidelis." Up and down all the stairs, through the parlors and the kitchen, through the dining room and the ballroom, through every room but the green room they walked and sang. On Christmas Eve of 1865, they had a session of caroling, and when they had passed into the upper reaches of the house, and were proceeding through Gob's bedroom, the Urfeist stopped.

"Time for your Christmas present," the Urfeist said to Gob. Gob thought that meant he ought to proceed to the stone corner and get down on his belly. That was what he was doing when the Urfeist said, "Not that. Not now. Come here." He produced the key to Gob's workshop and opened up the big iron door. Inside the spiritual telegraph sat where Gob had left it in the middle of the room. "This is your present," the Urfeist said warmly. "A return to machines. Do you know what time it is?"

"Christmastime," said Gob.

"Yes," said the Urfeist. "But also it is time for you to begin your work, your real work. I think you are ready, now. I think that the abolition of death is at hand."

Gob hung his head down and began to cry, not certain why he should have become tearful. He had, after all, been itching to return to his workshop for months. He looked at the inert, useless telegraph and said, "I will fail."

He got a beating then, a Christmas beating—not very savage at all, just enough to discourage pessimism. When he was done hitting him the Urfeist put away his paddle and took Gob into his arms. "Do not despair, my boy," he said, his mouth against Gob's cheek. It occurred to Gob, as it often did, that the breath of a vulture or a hyena must be very similar to the nidorous exhalations of the Urfeist. "So you are not brilliant. So you are stupid. Did you think I would not help you with your work? Did you think that together we would not succeed? Isn't it the fundamental wisdom of your life, that you will require assistance in this endeavor?"

Gob went out looking for Professor Morse, operating on the very reasonable assumption that laying eyes upon that great man might inspire him to success. Gob would stroll down Broadway, keeping a sharp eye out for a man of some eighty years with a definite look of genius about him. Gob had his engraved likeness from an illustrated weekly, and he would peek at it every now and then as he walked along. He never saw Professor Morse on Broadway, though it was widely known that the man took a daily walk there. So Gob lurked outside Morse's house on Twenty-second Street near Fifth Avenue, and finally saw him come out one rainy afternoon in March of 1866. He was not remarkable-looking, after all. Gob ran across the street and caught him before he stepped up into a cab. "Professor!" he said. "Professor, a word with you, please?"

Professor Morse turned to Gob and peered at him through rain-spattered spectacles. "Yes, sir?" he said. He looked closer and said, "Can I help you?"

Could he? It seemed to Gob that if he could formulate the proper question, then Mr. Morse could indeed help him. But Gob did not know what question to ask. He stood there silently in the rain, blinking at the eminent man. Professor Morse smiled at him and pressed a dime into his hand. "Good day, young fellow!" he said cheerily, and drove off. Gob brought the dime home and affixed it to the telegraph.

As the dime was the first of many accretions, Gob never figured his quest for Professor Morse to have been fruitless. An urge made him put the coin on the telegraph, but once it was there he had a notion of the telegraph as the heart of his machine, and after that notion dawned, there dawned another, as naturally and simply as one day following another—something poorly remembered from his dreams, a conviction that the machine would have a heart, that it would take its shape around a center. The telegraph would be the heart of the machine. The Urfeist manifested a childish excitement when Gob told him of his revelation. Together they became incorrigible affixers. Glass pipes, miniature armillary spheres, copper and silver wire—the telegraph grew until it was a globe of stuff.

The Urfeist insisted that Gob would find his inspiration mostly in dreams. Gob got a beating for merely suggesting that they take a trip to the Smithsonian Institution to consult with Professor Henry. Mornings, the Urfeist hovered around Gob's bed, watching him sleep and waiting for him to wake. It was no way to start a day, waking to the unsavory visage of the Urfeist. "Did you dream?" he would ask. "Did you see?" If Gob shook his head, then the Urfeist would make him sip from a big blue bottle of paregoric, and say, "Continue sleeping. Continue dreaming." He kept a pencil and notebook by Gob's bed, so if Gob woke when he wasn't there Gob could make notes himself on what he saw in his dreams. And he thought that he did see things in his dreams. Every night, he was sure, he saw the whole, fabulous machine. It breathed and worked. But he forgot, when he woke, what it looked like, and how it functioned.

Buttons, bones, string and wire, marbles and pennies and glass straws—Gob made his machine out of anything he could find in the house, and the Urfeist had basements full of every possible thing. "I am a collector," he said sometimes, as if this made him distinguished, and it was true that the Urfeist collected treasures, little figures of wrought gold, paintings rolled up and stuck under beds, sculptures locked away like prisoners in the basement. But mostly the Urfeist collected trash. He had a room stuffed with broken furniture, a room where broken glass was scattered a half foot deep over the floor, and set in the ceiling where it glittered like stars. There was a room full of what Gob was sure must be a disassembled steam engine, and a room next to that one full of stacked rails.

Gob went picking and choosing among the rooms, waiting for things to seem necessary to his work. It would happen—one moment a glass ball was only a glass ball, but the next it would be the eye of his machine, and he would rush it to his workshop and install it. Every so often, the Urfeist would come and inspect his machine and insult it, saying it was loose and ill-planned, the child of an undisciplined and undiscerning mind. He would lift his hand as if to smash it, but then say he couldn't be bothered even with its destruction. "What is it?" he'd ask. "Is it a glass sheep? Is it a pet to guard you from loneliness?"

It was true that it looked like a sheep now. It had a barrel-shaped body and something like a head that hung down between its legs, as if it were grazing off the floor. But where a sheep might have a heart, this thing had the stock ticker, grown with accretions to twice its original size. The machine was electrical and spiritual, with an umbilicus that left its belly to split and run to twenty batteries, and feet that stood in silver cups of a mystical fluid which Gob had mixed according to a recipe in his McGuffey's Necromancer. When he activated it, the ticker vomited up wriggling streams of blank paper: they exited the machine like a growing tail. It was a failure because it did not carry a message from his brother, and this was what he sought to amend. The answer, he was sure, was to keep adding things.

For all that the Urfeist ridiculed the thing, Gob knew he secretly admired it, because he'd looked through the keyhole into his workroom and seen his teacher gazing at it or running his long nails over all its smooth parts. Visiting with it took up more and more of the Urfeist's time, and he began to build on it also. The two of them worked on it in turns, Gob too afraid to say how he resented and admired his master's contributions, the Urfeist too proud to acknowledge how he was now collaborating with his student. But one night, as Gob served up his master's rat pudding, the Urfeist made an observation. "It lacks the crucial element of desire. How can it bring him back, if it cannot want him?" After that they began to work together, and always on that problem—how to make the unfeeling thing feel?

The answer, they decided, was to put a feeling thing in it. "We shall have to bind you up," the Urfeist informed Gob, sounding almost sad. With wire thin as thread he wrapped Gob under the thing, and ran a thicker wire from Gob's heart to the mouth of the sheep. "Of course there has to be a little pain," the Urfeist said, pushing the sharp wire through the skin of Gob's chest. He sank it no more than a half inch, but Gob was sure he felt it pierce his heart. "You are not a kosmos," the Urfeist told him, "yet perhaps you will do. Perhaps you are sufficient for a short message." He opened the current in the batteries, mixed up the mystic fluid with a glass wand, blew a harmonica in the four corners of the room. The telegraph did what it always did, danced and hummed and chittered. "You must sink down," the Urfeist said, pinching the wire delicately between his thumb and finger and twisting it round so it spiraled deeper into his student. "Think of your brother," the Urfeist said, but Gob didn't need to be told. It was easy for him to sink down to a place where there was nothing but absence of Tomo, and need of Tomo, and love of Tomo.

"Yes," the Urfeist said. "Yes! Sink down! There *is* a message!" Gob did not hear the noise of the stock indicator, but he felt it as a ticking in his bones. He felt his vitality go out of him like a single breath. If he hadn't been bound up with wire he would have fallen. He hung his head and moaned because he hurt all over. The Urfeist was moaning too, but in pleasure. The spiritual telegraph had relayed a message. "What does it say?" Gob asked weakly, after the Urfeist tore off the message and looked at it.

"Nothing," the Urfeist said, but Gob could see even from far away how there was ink on the paper. The Urfeist stuck the message away in his vest and said, "Your machine, it was a failure. You yourself are a failure. Why do I waste the time it takes to teach you? I might as well kick you as try to give you knowledge." He did kick Gob, and then he walked away, taking out the slip to read it again.

"What does it say!" Gob shouted, but the Urfeist left him alone without answering. It was a day and a night before Gob wriggled out from the wires, before he went looking, bleeding and furious, for his master. The Urfeist wasn't in the library or the dining room, or even among the tall plants of the green room. Gob walked faster and faster as he searched, and every time he found another room empty of the Urfeist, he quickened his pace. The Urfeist was not in any of the parlors. He was not in the library. Gob was running when at last he found his master, curled in a ball in a bedroom. "Where is it?" he said, and "Liar!" He wasn't afraid to yell and demand, or even to strike his fists against the Urfeist's back. "Give it to me!" he said, but he found that he was able to take the note for himself because his master was cold, still, and dead. A look of angry denial deformed the Urfeist's ugly face. He had torn off his shirt, and Gob could see the livid handprint, the size and shape of his own hand, over his master's heart. The message was very simple: *You are dead.*

Gob dropped the paper as soon as he'd read it, because he thought it must kill him, too, this powerful message from his brother that he was sure must have been meant for him. You are dead, it said, because he ought to be dead with his brother, and he ought to be dead for betraying his brother. "It did too work," he said to the gray face of the Urfeist. Sure that he, too, would die any moment, Gob lay down next to his teacher, lifting one of the cold hands to lay it across his own neck.

PART THREE

THE WONDERFUL INFANT

Towards the close of the visit, for such it really was, I was shown what I now know to have been a panoramic view of the future. The mountains and valleys changed places with the seas, the entire face of the nation underwent a transformation. Cities sank and people fled before appalling disasters in dismay. Then a wondrous calm settled over everything. Confusion, anarchy and destruction were replaced with a scene of beauty and glory which is beyond the power of language to describe. The earth had been changed into the common abode of people of both spheres. The spirits said that all this would be realized during my life and that in making it possible I would bear a prominent part.

VICTORIA C. WOODHULL
From Mr. Tilton's biography

1

BY MAY OF 1862 IT SEEMED TO MACI TRUFANT THAT MADNESS had become the national pastime, and that her parents had only performed a civic duty by losing their minds. Her mother went insane first, slowly and with considerable subtlety in the first months of her decline; she had a growing fascination with beans. Initially, she praised them for being shapely and nutritious—strange comments, but Maci figured her mother had read an article on beans in one of her weeklies. When she insisted the cook serve them up with increasing frequency, Maci assumed her mother was dabbling again in Dr. Graham's tasteless diet. But, little by little, beans came to dominate her mother's life. She celebrated them to the neglect of her husband and children. She sought to make herself pure, eating no food but beans, and so she died.

Maci had flipped desperately through her uncle's medical books, not trusting him when he said he had no remedy for his sister's bean-madness. Now, Maci hated beans. For many months, she had flung them from her plate if some grossly insensitive person served them to her. Lately she had eaten them again. They were ashes in her mouth but they were what she and her father could afford. His own madness had driven them into desperate financial straits, and it did not come delicately.

It fell on him like a swooping bird. Maci imagined it, bird-shaped and screeching, falling down on his head to muss his hair into an ageless madman style. Not long after his wife's funeral, he was in his study writing letters thanking people for their kind sympathies when his hand began suddenly to write of its own accord a letter to him from his dead wife: *My darling, I never was not, nor will I ever cease to be. We travel from ever to ever and time is only a span between eternities. You will be called to do a great work. I am watching you with love.*

One day he was a bereaved Universalist minister admired for his antislavery stance and his charitable work in prisons (people called him "the Prisoner's Friend"); the next he was a fledgling Spiritualist prophet. Within months, he was declaring himself the Apostle of Precision, delegate on earth of an Association of Beneficents who spoke to him from a place that was not quite Heaven. Ben Franklin, Thomas Jefferson, and John Murray all spoke through his hand. With growing discomfort, and finally dread, Maci was introduced to the mortal Apostles of Devotion, Harmony, Freedom, Education, Treasures, and Accumulation. Some were men and some were women. They all had a look in their eyes which Maci could only call deranged.

She watched them milling in the parlor of their house on Mount Vernon Street and felt a seething anger. Several times, Maci threw as many out as she could before her father discovered her and called her rude. She pleaded with him to stop all this, but he would take her in his arms and explain that the very Chairman of the General Assembly of Beneficents had called on him to carry out the greatest work yet attempted by man. He would build a living machine, an engine whose product would be not energy but peace. He would call it the Wonderful Infant.

Her brother, Rob, was gone. He'd fled at the beginning of their father's decline, after many arguments, and a final one when he'd struck their father on the head and knocked him out. "I hoped he'd be sensible when he came to," he told his sister. "But he started jabbering about electritizers and elementizers as soon as he could speak." Rob left to live with their mother's family, and then he went to war. Maci resisted their entreaties to join them.

"Your situation is so peculiar," said her Aunt Amy, a plain woman fond of elaborate dresses.

"I must stay with my father," said Maci. She'd been so certain of that, speaking to Aunt Amy's pale fat face. It had made her serene, somehow, to embrace this obligation. Her father was her first friend, the man who had shaped her mind and her heart. But now she doubted, and her loyalty to him was a source of agitation rather than comfort. He had spent them broke on matériel for his engine and on contributions to the Panfederacy of Apostles. They lost their house in Boston and Maci found herself losing things which were precious to her, not just dresses and jewelry, but dreams. Her father had always talked of launching her off to college when she turned sixteen. But she was called back from Miss Polk's School for Young Ladies to help tend to her mother, her sixteenth birthday came and went, and when Maci left Boston, it wasn't for college. They moved to the wilderness of Rhode Island, where electrical and spiritual forces were favorable to the Infant's construction. Maci hadn't thought there was any wilderness left in Rhode Island. She had thought it must surely be filled with people who had fled, for one reason or another, from Boston. She imagined them, dissenters all, packed cheek by jowl from Providence to the coast. But this place was empty, just their lonely cottage and the shed on the cliff, the nearest neighbor nearly a mile away, across a saltwater pond at the bottom of a hill behind the house. Various Apostles came and visited them, sometimes bringing parts for the machine.

The porch in front of the house leaned precipitously, and the steps were crooked. When Maci walked from one side to the other, she worried it might pitch her headlong over the cliff and onto the rocks below. Standing carefully on the porch, she listened to the noise of the sea and the noise of her father hammering in the shed, which came together to give her a creeping sense of doom. When she covered her ears with her hands, she could hear the beating of her anxious heart, which she sometimes imagined to be the quick footsteps of voracious madness, hurrying to claim her. Her mother and father had gone insane. Rob had rushed to join a regiment of Zouaves with an alacrity and fearlessness that spoke of a weakness of sanity if not an absolute absence thereof. Maci expected to be the next to lose her mind. At least it would happen here, where no one would notice and she would stand out less in company than in Boston, where her family's shame would be completed with the departure of her faculties. Would she eat beans exclusively? By July, they'd eaten themselves out of beans, but Maci had a basket of cranberries in the kitchen, and she had noticed a previously unappreciated beauty in the small forms, nestled together in a mound, very pretty in the morning sun that poured through the drafty window. Would these cranberries dominate her fancy? Or would she build something impossible, perhaps a flying machine to sail over the cliff and into Block Island Sound? A gin that separates emotions in a confused mood? A cloud buster?

Maci walked gingerly down the steps, then went around the house and down the hill to the rotting dock that jutted out into the pond. She got in a little boat and took up the oars. "Poppy!" she called out towards the shed. "I'm going out!" There came a pause in the hammering, but no answer. She began to row out towards the neighbor's house, where she would beg flour. She had plans for her lovely cranberries.

A few days later Maci gnawed on one of her flat, greasy cranberry biscuits as she read a letter from her brother.

> *Our route from Roanoke Island to Norfolk took us through Croatan Sound and the North River, to the Elizabeth River by way of the Great Dismal Swamp. Tugs pulled us in little boats through the swamp canal—I was put in mind of you traveling hither and thither on the pond behind the Hotel de Trufant—did you write that it is called Potter's? It was new and strange*

and silent in there. You ought to see such a forest of cypresses, with their gnarled roots peeking above the water, and whisks and festoons of Spanish moss clinging to the branches. There are curious holes in the roots—they look like round open mouths. I swear I heard one call my name. Sister, ought I to fear for my sanity? It was no ghost that spoke, the root did not declare itself old Uncle Philip with his listening-horn and his green teeth. Cotton-gum and sweet-bay, a curious juniper and holly, huddles of bamboo-cane: you will see that I sketched them for you. I have hidden Uncle Phil somewhere in the drawing—can you find him? Such odd birds in this place! We are all equally strangers here and no one can tell me their names. When we passed a Negro standing mysteriously by the shore I asked him the name of a small, bright thing that darted back and forth over our heads. He said, "That's a Jesus-bird!" Not, I am certain, the proper name for the thing.

You must go back to Boston and Aunt A.

Rob ended all his letters, Cato-like, with that admonition. There was money in the envelope, two months of his second lieutenant's salary, and there was a thick sheaf of illustrations. There were the straight columns of the cypresses, and hidden Uncle Phil, betrayed by his horn, which stuck out from a stand of bamboo. There was the Jesus-bird and the mysterious Negro; there was a boatful of Zouaves entering a patch of mist. She thought for a moment that her brother had included a sketch of himself—there was a picture of a boy with his same heavy brows and square chin—until she saw the caption written along his neck. *Pvt. G. W. Vanderbilt—he is the Commodore's son, and insists on his privatehood!* He had a wide thick neck, not at all like the piece of licorice her brother balanced his head upon. Looking up from the drawings, Maci saw a blue phaeton coming up the road with its top thrown open to the warm July sun. A woman in a yellow dress was at the reins. When the carriage came near, Maci could see that she was pregnant.

"Girl," the woman said, occasioning Maci's instant and intense dislike, "go and fetch your master."

Maci wrote to her brother that night, huddled at a desk wedged between her bed and the open window. A breeze lifted her hair and threatened to put out her candle.

My dear Zu-Zu,

We have got a new guest here at the Hotel Fou-Fou. Her name is Miss Arabella Suter. She rode up this morning in a pretty phaeton, and she might have been out taking a pleasure-ride if she hadn't traveled hundreds of miles to find our sweet mad Poppy. She is unmarried but quite pregnant—six months if a day. This is not a scandal because what fills her womb is not a flesh-and-blood baby but the living principle of Poppy's machine. I think she has got a bladder beneath her shirt, or else she is fleeing dishonor. The former is most likely. An "accidental" poke with a needle will deflate her, and then we will send her back to Philadelphia. I wonder if she is a Quaker. She does not dress like one. She is as colorful as a Jesus-bird. I shall call her the Apostle of Shame, or the Swollen Apostle. Already I detest her, but I think she will save me from becoming the Apostle of Boredom.

I will not go back to Boston but I remain your loving,

Sister.

As she wrote, Maci could hear her father and Miss Suter laughing in the front room of the cottage. He had welcomed the woman literally with open arms when Maci led her into the workshop.

"Here you are at last!" he had said, rushing to embrace her. Maci had never seen him be so familiar with any lady before, except herself and her mother. Strange that such things could still give her a shock, a wrenching feeling all along her spine, even after the many months she'd been witness to her father's madness. "Maci," he said, "here is that wonderful lady I spoke of!"

"Yes, Poppy," Maci said, though he had not spoken of her before. Maci left the shed, keeping her eyes away from the glass and copper lineaments of the Infant, and went back outside to stare over the cliff. On that clear day, she could see all the way to Block Island. She undid her hair and let it blow in the wind, thinking how she must look dramatic and wild, the very picture of an incipient madwoman. She closed her eyes and wondered if it was obvious to a person when her reason departed. With no one sane to tell her she was on the decline, would she know when her madness came down upon her?

After she'd finished the letter to Rob, she got under her quilt and stared at her brother's sketches. They covered the whole wall opposite the foot of her bed, and now they were creeping across the wall to her left. She got out of bed to put the candle on the floor, to better light them. Back under the quilt, she studied the pictures. They were a history of Rob's time with Company A of the Ninth New York Volunteers. On the far left was an ink sketch of the regiment drilling in the Central Park—Rob had colored their coats with blue ink; their pantaloons and fezzes were red. Maci had nightmares about those red hats. When she was small, her father had told her stories of a monster who wore such a hat, who colored it with the blood of his victims. In those dreams, her brother was turned from her gentle companion into a man who sopped up the blood of his enemies with his cap, then wrung it into his mouth.

She'd posted the last picture, the sketch of Private Vanderbilt, about three feet from the corner. She rearranged herself in her bed, moving her head down where her feet usually rested. Now she could look out the window at the stars shining above the dark sea, and when she turned her head Private Vanderbilt was just in front of her. For a while she looked into his eyes, wondering that the son of such a man as crude, rich Cornelius Vanderbilt would not buy himself a captaincy, at least. Her sleepy eyes fell to his thick neck; she imagined how her two hands would not fit around it. She closed her eyes but his image hovered behind her lids. Then she opened her eyes again, and kept looking at him until her candle blew out.

When Maci was a little girl, her father had put her under such severe intellectual discipline it made her mother cry. "You'll ruin the child!" she protested, because John Murray Trufant had declared that he would train his daughter to have a brain bigger than that wielded by Margaret Fuller, a lady who had been his friend before she departed to Italy, never again to set foot in America. "It took a whole ocean to douse her incandescent mind," her father told Maci, "but yours will burn brighter yet." Maci, at the age of nine, wrote a sonnet called "The Wreck of the Elizabeth," in which the Countess Ossoli's shining head threw light in the eyes of fishes as she died, and seagulls lamented around the body of her soggy dead child after he washed ashore.

Maci hated Greek and was bad at Latin, but reading was her passion, and her father encouraged her in it even when her overstimulated brain manufactured nightmares to torture her sleep. He buried her in Smollett, Fielding, Shakespeare, Cervantes, and Molière, among others. He made her recite to him every night before bed, and gave her stern lectures to make it clear that he expected her to grow up to be more than a creature of habit and affection. Yet that was all he expected of her anymore, since his change and his madness. It made Maci bitter enough to spit.

Miss Suter passed the pricking test. She gave a little shriek—it was very much like the cry of a gull—and leaped up in the air, seeming just for a moment to levitate over the threadbare rug of the front room.

"Forgive me!" said Maci. She was listening intently for a noise of hissing air, but there was none. Could it be a pillow? she wondered.

Miss Suter had clenched her hands over her belly. "Not to worry, my dear," she said. She'd become quite civil once she realized Maci was not a servant. She had even offered her a few dresses, but Maci declined. The lady's taste was as defective as her reason.

Maci sat Miss Suter down on the sofa and fetched her some tea. She felt some small regret for the poke, which ballooned into something more formidable while she sat next to her and watched the lady stare into her cup. "I want us to be friends," Miss Suter had said a few days before. "Of course you do," Maci had replied in a frosty tone. Now, Maci almost wished she had been more receptive.

"Are you well, Madame?" she asked.

"Of course!" said Miss Suter. "It was a surprise, more than a pain, though the prick was fairly deep. I am not bleeding. Don't think that I am."

"And the . . . principle?" asked Maci. Very slowly, she placed her hand on the lady's belly. Miss Suter made no move to draw away. There was flesh under Maci's palm; it gave slightly when she pushed against it.

"She is well. She is proof against such little accidents."

"Strange," said Maci. "I think of the Infant sometimes as my little brother. Poppy calls it a boy."

"Yes," said Miss Suter. "The form is masculine, but the living principle which shall animate it is feminine. A wonderful union! We live in fascinating times, my dear."

"Some would call them terrible."

"Oh, she kicks!" Maci felt nothing under her hand, but she smiled anyhow.

She is fleeing her shame, Maci wrote to Rob. *What would Aunt Amy say? A disgraced lady in our pathetic little home. Brother, she shares his bed. I said to Poppy that I thought he was behaving very badly. He called me his sweet moppet and told me that I would lose my doubt when the Infant breathes peace into the world. At night, I go in and look at the thing while they are sleeping. Little Brother has grown considerably over the past months. I think he will outgrow his shed, soon. If he moves into the house, then truly I think I shall go back to Boston and Aunt Amy.*

Rob had sent her another letter, and more sketches. Some detailed a month of camp life at Fort Norfolk (a parade ground pocked with stumps that made drill a chore; a loving portrait of his new Springfield rifle), while others depicted his progress up the James in a steamer called the *C. S. Terry.* There was a portrait of Private Vanderbilt with a view of Fredericksburg behind him; this went next to the other drawing. And there were drawings of which she could not make sense—a whole page filled to within an inch of the top and bottom with charcoal, a stray hand, large as life with hairy knuckles and scars on the fingers. She turned this one over and read on the back, *Pvt. G. W. Vanderbilt, his hand.* Then she realized that Rob was sending her a puzzle, a life-sized Vanderbilt she might put together on her wall. She assembled the pieces as best she could, building him completely down to his waist, except for a missing hand. She wondered if this was Rob's neglect or a hideous wound. *He is by turns coarse and refined, polite and boorish*, Rob wrote. *He says his father's spirit sometimes posseses him. I told him my father is possessed by spirits. I think he is my friend.*

There was one good thing about Miss Suter—she had money. The Infant could have alpaca booties and a silver spoon to put in his mouth after he was born, and there was no more begging for flour from the neighbors while she was there. She took Maci shopping in Kingstown, where people were shocked to see a pregnant woman out in her own carriage buying groceries and dry goods, spools of copper wire and plates of glass. Maci was sure that a mob would come stomping up the road one day soon to burn their house and smash the Infant. At least I will look presentable for them, she thought. Miss Suter was making a dress for her, patterned after one of the dresses Maci had long since sold for necessities. Maci had talked about it wistfully, and Miss Suter had got it into her head to recreate it and make a gift of it to her "dear friend."

While her father worked in the shed, Maci would sit with Miss Suter on the porch, eating the delicious cakes, muffins, and pies that the woman manufactured with a magical lack of effort. Maci had slaved and fretted over her greasy muffins and the tooth-breaking cakes she'd thrown over the cliff in frustration. Sitting thus on the porch, nearly a month after her arrival, Miss Suter ventured a question about Maci's mother. "She was a generous woman," Maci said, wishing that Miss Suter would not ask such questions; she was trying to think of Miss Suter as a spirit-sent servant, figuring that turnabout to be fair play. But Miss Suter's earnest inquiries about her mother made such pretending difficult.

"She liked hymns of all faiths," Maci found herself saying of her mother—she would miscegenate them shamelessly. She was partial to weeklies and monthlies, and followed events in France and England. Once, when Maci was seven years old, her mother had read aloud to her an article on the toilet of Russia. At Maci's insistence she and her mother had dressed up like Russian women. They wrapped white cloths around their head, hung themselves with furs, and pinned jewels on one another. They danced around her mother's room, chanting nonsense and pretending it was Russian. As Maci told this story, Miss Suter laughed so hard she spilled her tea. Maci laughed, too, until she caught herself enjoying Miss Suter's company, whereupon she stopped and looked out over the water with a stony expression on her face.

We arrived in Washington too late to participate in the latest debacle at Bull Run. Now we are camped on Meridian Hill, awaiting orders. Private Vanderbilt is itching to go deal some trouble to Lee. He has taken the invasion of Maryland as a personal affront. I fear I jeopardized our friendship when I insisted Maryland was not Yankeedom, but we are friends again, now. He has offered me his belly band against the cholera. I declined, though we are rained on incessantly, and a goat has eaten much of my overcoat. Washington is not the least bit refined.

Here is the Private's hand for you, clenched in anger against me. Here are his hips. If I sent his legs to Aunt Amy would you go there to fetch them? Go to her, won't you? I think you are withering in that exile.

Maci pinned the ham-fist beneath the empty sleeve. The hips were handsome, she could not help but think so, though she felt hot and embarrassed looking at them. She took them down and put them under the bed, then just as quickly returned them to the wall. She could be a little wanton, here in the privacy of her room on the edge of the world. She sat at her desk and wrote to her brother.

Miss Suter is big as a house (not big as a Boston house, but mind you they build small in these parts) and I cannot think she carries anything but a big baby boy, though she insists it is a female principle swelling in her womb. She requires my help to get up and down the stairs. Some days she is too exhausted by her condition to do anything but lie abed and read novels. Papa spends all his days and most of his nights in the shed. It would be a disaster, he says, if the Infant were not ready when the spirit is born. You may be wondering what sort of doctor will be in at the birth. I wondered that too, until Miss Suter explained to me that good Ben Franklin (the Commissioner of Electritizers, you know) will be there. Of course!

"How I hate to see the summer wane," said Miss Suter, as Maci escorted her down a narrow dirt road, lined on either side with chokecherry and beach roses. It was September. There were still blossoms on the rosebushes, but they were limp now and wilted.

Though it was a warm day, Miss Suter shivered incessantly. She stopped to admire a great congregation of ladybugs swarming over the green leaves. Miss Suter put her hand among them and laughed delightedly when they crawled on her.

"Aren't they lovely?" she asked.

"Poppy always said a girl ought not to play with creeping things."

"But they're delightful. They were the friends of my youth. I would lie in my mother's garden and they would come to me. Sometimes they quite covered me up. If I listened close, I could hear them speaking, telling me what wonderful things were coming. My spirit guide also cares for them. She's a young Indian girl—you put me in mind of her, though of course she is woodcrafty and you are not. I think you hold your head as she does. It is very regal."

Maci had no reply. She often lacked for things to say, on these walks, but Miss Suter did not seem offended by her silence. Indeed, Maci wondered if Miss Suter even noticed her silence. Miss Suter was full of words—they were always leaking from her—and she took every opportunity to instruct Maci in spiritual matters. "This association," she proclaimed down on the beach, poking delicately at the cast-off shell of a horseshoe crab, "this association, the Great Association of Beneficents, will greatly, wisely, and seasonably instruct and bless the diseased, the suffering, and the wretched of the earth."

"Tell me," Maci said, "will they instruct suffrage for women?" Voting was something that Maci wanted very much to do. When she was small she'd imagined that voting was equivalent with wish-getting—she thought a person could go out and vote themselves a fresh peach pie or a new bonnet. It still seemed to her like a great, vast power, an opportunity to execute startling transformations. "How we will change this country," she'd say to scoffing Rob, "when our hand is on the tiller." Before he went insane, woman suffrage had been one of her father's devotions.

"Unfortunately not," said Miss Suter.

I think I envy her, Maci wrote to her brother. *It must be a comfort to believe such things. To believe that Heaven is as comfortable and familiar as your own bed, and that your dog may accompany you there. To believe that the dead have organized themselves for our redemption. To believe that human folly might be dissolved in the exhalations of a good machine. To believe that our own mother might put forth her dead hand to shield you, Brother, from danger. Madness is seductive, pretty, and fat like Miss Suter, but shameful all the same.*

Take care, my Zu-Zu.

In Frederick we were welcomed with the most incredible hospitality. Some good Marylanders took me into their house, where I had an honest-to-goodness real bath. I have stunk of lavender for the past three days and the boys all call me Roberta. These same Marylanders gave me lemonade to drink as I soaked in the tub, and there was no mention of the tyrant's heel. I send you the tub and empty glass as proof of their hospitality, in case you should doubt it. Here, too, are the Private's legs. Not long enough, I think, but I am getting short on paper.

Go to Aunt Amy.

Maci assembled Private Vanderbilt's nether portions. The hips were made somehow more civilized by the addition of legs. He still lacked feet, and consequently seemed to float by her bedside. She put the glass of lemonade in his hand, in case he desired refreshment. The tub she put further along the wall to his left. Rob had drawn himself inside it, his arm hanging down to scrape the floor, his cheek resting on the porcelain edge, an allusion to a picture they'd seen in Paris, one thousand years ago before death and madness had smashed their family. Rob had even wrapped a turban around his head, in the drawing, in case she should be stupid and miss the obvious. It was, she decided, a horrible picture, and the first one she would not give a place on her wall. She took it down and set the edge in the candle flame, then held it by the window as it burned. When the fire was close to her fingers she let it go, and it drifted away into the dark.

M. Zu-Zu,

I did not care for your tub picture. If you send me no more like it I would consider that a kindness. Arabella Suter continues to swell. I think she must be drinking up the oceans, to swell so much. We go down to the ocean sometimes and I watch her to make sure she does not drain the Sound dry with her red mouth.

There is the horn from Block Island blowing now—a mournful sound. I think sometimes it is a lament for lost sailors, a noise that says, "Stay away from these rocks," and "I mourn you." On windy nights, they say, if you stand on the edge of the cliff you can hear the ghostly voices, calling, "God save a drowning man!"

Do you see how you have yellowed my mood with your tub? But for his feet, Private Vanderbilt is complete on my wall. May he guard me from sadness.

Maci's father completed the Infant in the second week of September. "A big boy, Poppy," she said, standing with him in the shed with Miss Suter. The Infant was a great box. The wood that had been in him was gone—that had only been scaffolding, her father said. Now, he was all glass and copper, silver filigree and iron. "Where is his mouth?" she asked. "How will he breathe?" Her father and Miss Suter laughed at her as if she were a five-year old asking why the ocean is blue.

"His true form is on the spiritual plane," said her father. "You see, my dear, I have been constructing in both places. Why do you suppose it has taken so long?"

They had a feast to honor him, ham and baked corn, quahogs

that Maci had dug herself from the mud of Potter's Pond, and a lemon sponge cake. Miss Suter proclaimed it the last warm evening of the year, so they ate on the rickety porch. Maci fidgeted while the two of them said their odd grace: "We believe in the fatherhood of God, the brotherhood of man, a continuous existence, the communion of spirits and the ministrations of angels, compensation and retribution in the hereafter for good or ill done on earth, and we believe in a path of endless progression!" Listening to them, Maci rather wished she could join them in their belief, just as she had wanted to become a slave, when she was a little girl, because she'd been sure, back then, that if only she were a slave, her father would shower her with all the easy, warm enthusiasm he showered on his dear Negro friends, the fugitive strangers who passed through their house in Boston. It had seemed to her jealous little heart that her father had loved them all better than her, because they got presents of effusive affection, while she got more Vergil.

After dinner, Maci and her father pointed out constellations for Miss Suter's edification. Boötes and Draco, Hercules and Cepheus, each was very bright in the sky over the black ocean. "That star is Arcturus," Maci said.

"Where?" asked Miss Suter. "Where?" She waddled over to line up her eye with Maci's pointing finger. "Ah!" she said. The great swell of her belly was nuzzled against Maci's shoulder. Miss Suter gave another cry, and Maci thought this time she did feel something, a little kick.

Maci excused herself and took a walk along the cliff. The moon came up, washing out the stars. Low clouds rushed by, little floating islands that looked about the size of a big wagon. She could not help imagining riding one south to Maryland. If there were just room for one other on the cloud, would she take Rob or Private Vanderbilt flying? She was not sure. She wondered if that was the form her madness would take—fascination with a stranger. She had begun to rearrange Vanderbilt's portrait—switching his hands or arms from side to side, balancing the lemonade on his head, setting his face in the middle of his chest. Rob had kindly sent enough faces to vary his mood—some angry, some sad, but most happy and peaceful-looking. Sometimes she put a peaceful-looking face on her pillow and woke in the morning with smudges on her cheek, and thought that he might have kissed her during the night. Standing by the cliff, she considered a future with him. They would live in Manhattan and manipulate railroad stock.

After a while, she returned to the house and went into the shed to look at the Infant. "Little Brother," she said. "I ought to love you better." She could think of nothing else to add, so she just stared at him for a long while. She could see her own face thrown back at her, twisted up along a silver tube, or shattered by the facets of a crystal panel. Then, she saw her father's reflection. He had entered the shed and was walking towards her, but it looked like his image was rising from the crystalline depths of his machine. He stood next to her and put his arm around her. She closed her eyes, and put her face in his shoulder.

"It's impossible, what you want to do," she said.

"Difficult," her father replied, "but not impossible. And is it any reason not to try a thing, because it is difficult? To the small mind, ending slavery seems as difficult and unlikely as changing the color of the sky. Yet that endeavor proceeds apace."

"I hate him," Maci said vehemently, pressing her face harder into her father's shirt. "I hate all of this so much."

"Oh Maci," he said, stroking her hair. "Don't be envious of him. It will make you ugly, inside and out. And anyhow, don't you know that you are still my favorite?"

I know I risk your displeasure sending you these soldiers. It is not that I wish you to look at them and be saddened, but rather that I must send them away from me. Fold them into squares and sail them over the cliff—maybe they will find peace in the cold water. On the fifteenth, our regiment was ordered down from the westward slope of South Mountain, where we came upon the scene of the previous day's heaviest fighting. The enemy's dead were so numerous that a regiment who passed here before us had to remove them from the road to make way for the troops. They were piled up head high on either side, and made a gauntlet. Private Vanderbilt saw my distress—he is intimate with my moods—and offered to lead me through as I closed my eyes. I declined his kind offer. It seemed a fitting passageway from the land of the living to the land of the dead. I fear it is not the happy place where dwells our mad Poppy's weakened mind. I thought as I walked of living hands grabbing up the bodies of the dead and stacking them like cordwood upon the road. In ten years, the wall might be made of bones, with only a blowing scrap of gray wool still attached to a wrist or a neck.

Sister, this wall is the work of men's hands, and the whole war is the work of men's hands—fingers tear cartridges and pull triggers. I would now that I had not sent you the Private's hands, but here are his feet. I place them just beneath this letter, and the wall beneath that—all the work of my hand. Do not look at the wall.

Go to Boston. Pray for me.

She did look at the picture of the wall. It was an illustration of Hell. There were boys stacked high, their legs and arms intertwined in gross familiarity. Dead staring faces rested against each other, brow to brow. Motes of light danced in eyes that saw nothing, unless it was the moment of their death frozen before them. Try as she might, she could not imagine her brother's face as he walked that gauntlet. But she could see Private Vanderbilt. His face was somehow both tender and stern as he put his hand on Rob's shoulder, and tried to keep his wide back between Rob's eyes and the wall. Maybe later

Private Vanderbilt held him like a brother while he wept, trying to wash out the dead faces from his eyes.

She attached his feet, and at last he stood complete before her. She sat on her bed, watching him and listening to the noise of the surf. "Thank you," she said to him.

I did look at the wall, she wrote. *Such horror! Of course I prefer the Private's feet to such atrocity, but whatever you must send I will gladly receive. How could it be any other way? Are you not my own Zu-Zu? Am I not your sister? You are in my prayers. I think Poppy and Miss Suter pray for you, too, in their way. Two apostles and an incipient spinster are pleading on your behalf—is this not cause for happiness?*

The Infant is complete. Though I am not fond of him, I must admit that he is beautiful. You are not any longer the handsomest Trufant. Nor am I pretty, next to him. He has silver teeth and spun-glass hair and a golden face. He is jewelry, a brooch for a giant. We are waiting now only for Miss Suter to vomit a spirit from her womb. I fear the pall that will settle over this house when their bright hopes are dashed, when only a mundane babe comes into the world. Here is my prediction, I have it from my spirit guide, an Indian girl who inhabits the abandoned shell of a whelk. The baby will come and Miss Suter will flee from it, because it is not a spirit essence, because it reminds her of shame. She will be gone from our lives, and I will have a baby to raise. I shall have to learn to cook properly. We shall sell off the Infant in bits and pieces, and use the money to improve the house, to steady the porch and buy new stoves. Poppy's folly will recede from him when his machine is a failure. We will wait for you here. This war will end. You will come and visit us with the Private in tow. It is a pleasure to dig for quahogs—I will show you. Do you see, then, how happy futures are born from the gray, despairing present? Brother, you have all my love.

* * *

"It's a lazy baby that won't be born," said Miss Suter. She had an urge to go boating, so Maci had taken her out on the pond. Maci worried that the baby would come there in the middle of the water. She had been feeling anxious around Miss Suter because she seemed capable of giving birth quite at any moment. "I so wish it would come. These late battles might not have been, if only she had come last week." She bent her neck forward to stare at her belly. "Why do you wait?" she asked it. It was September 25. News of the battle in Maryland had reached even here. Maci had checked casualty lists in a Providence paper and found Rob's name absent from them.

A raft of yodeling old-squaws suddenly flapped their wings and took off inland. "Running from the storm," said Miss Suter. The wind had been blowing hard for the past three days. Salt-encrusted fisherman types in the village were predicting "a great big blow."

Her father had been into the village, to buy a lightning rod for the roof of the shed. He was installing it when Maci and Miss Suter walked up to the house. He waved to them and said to Maci, "You have a letter, my dear!" Miss Suter toddled over to shout encouragement up at him while Maci went inside. She was sure the letter would be from Rob, but it wasn't. It was from Private Vanderbilt.

There were instances in her life upon which she would later reflect and hate herself. When she was five years old, she had eaten two pounds of chocolate cake, then crawled into a corner and gotten sick like a dog. In the weeks following her mother's death, Maci had considered how she'd broken under no real strain—her children were healthy and she lived a life of privilege—and she had hated her mother for being weak. Later, she would appreciate how anything could break you, how we are all breakable, and she would hate superior, weakness-hating Maci as certainly as she hated five-year-old gluttonous Maci. In this way, she would hate blithe, carefree, stupid Maci, who thought Private Vanderbilt was writing to make love to her. She sat in front of his portrait and read.

Dear Friend,

I know you will have heard by now of your brother Rob's death on the 17th of September, before Antietam Creek. I thought I should write and tell you of his last days. He was my friend, though he was an officer and I am only an enlisted volunteer. It was my great honor to know him. He saved my life on the very day he died. Crossing Antietam Creek, I became mired in the mud and would have drowned had Rob not returned for me under heavy fire, taking a wound in his scalp as he fetched me. He bound it with a strip of cloth and would not go back. From the creek, we were ordered forward, and we lost men at every step. Our color guard was mowed down three times in succession, but at last we drove the Rebs over a stone wall, and they fled towards the town. We were ordered back not long after that, for we had used up all our ammunition and there was no relief for us—no one could support us in our far-flung position. This order did not sit well with the men of the Ninth, and some of them pursued the fleeing enemy. Your gentle brother was among those pursuers. I was with them, too. We ran into their strength. Just two of twenty-five men made it back to our lines. Those two were I and your brother, but his wounds were such that he did not last the night. I was with him when he died. He spoke no words—his wound was in his throat—but I do not doubt that his thoughts were with you at the last. He spoke of you so often, I feel I know you well. I hope you will call on me, after we soldiers bury our guns. I live in Manhattan, at Number 10 Washington Place.

It is a sorrow that men should find it necessary to take one another's lives to establish a principle.

Your friend,
George Washington Vanderbilt.

* * *

Maci kept the news to herself for hours because she could not articulate it. In the end, she walked up to her father and presented the letter to him. He read it with a stern face and said, "My darling. He has passed over into the Summerland. Let us celebrate for him." Maci slapped him, striking his sweet, bewildered face with the strength of her whole arm, then fled to her room, where she would not open the door for him when he came knocking.

The next day, numb habit took her into the village. She stopped before the post office, sat down on the ground, and stared bleakly at the building, a small white house with a roof of cedar shakes. She wanted to weep, but did not. The postmaster saw her sitting there in the street and came out to ask what was the matter. She only said she was tired, and had to rest a little. He brought her inside, where he had mail for her. There was a letter from Rob, and a package that he could have sent up to the house if she wished. Though she ought not to go back up there, he said. Didn't she know there was a storm coming? It seemed to Maci that the big blow was as lazy as Miss Suter's unborn principle. It was waiting politely offshore, as if for an invitation to come in and ravage.

Maci did not read Rob's letter, which had been mailed before Private Vanderbilt's letter, until much later, after two men had pulled up and unloaded Rob's trunk like a coffin from their wagon. At her direction, they put it in her room. Inside, on the very top, were her letters to him. The last one she'd sent was unopened—maybe the Private's dear hand had laid it inside the trunk when it arrived too late for Rob to read it. In the trunk there was an extra uniform, two fezzes, three good wool blankets she'd sent him herself before she'd become poor, and his officer's sword. There were many drawings, including many of her. There she was boating on Potter's Pond. There she was standing by the cliff, hair blowing like a madwoman's. There she was walking down a rose-shrouded path with Miss Suter, who was fatter and prettier in the drawing than in real life.

The trunk reeked of him. She put on his uniform and lay on the bed for a little while with her face in her arm, and then she read the letter.

Sister,

I think I have found my madness. God save me from the noise of breaking bones. Do I worry you? I did not mean to. No pictures for you today—we are in battle. This is just a note to tell you I am alive and well.

Please go to Boston. I think it is the only safe place on the earth.

When Miss Suter heard of Rob's death she said, "Too late!" and struck her fist against her belly. Then she got very pale, and fell back on a sofa, and claimed that she was in labor. For a day and a night, and then again for a day she lay on a bed downstairs and moaned. And all through the night of the storm, she cried out over the creaking of the little house. "Joy!" she screamed. "Love! O, Peace!" Maci watched from the staircase as her father tended to Miss Suter. Occasionally he consulted with the spirits he saw clustered around the sofa. Which one is Mr. Franklin? Maci wondered. Every so often she left her post on the stairs to go and pet Miss Suter's perspiring head, or else to venture to the shed, or else to go upstairs and finish her packing. Early in the morning, after the storm had departed and left a brilliant dawn in its wake, the baby finally came. Maci imagined it twice perfectly: Miss Suter gave a last cry, and an ordinary miracle proceeded from her body, a plain old baby boy who squalled his rage at being deposited in the world. Miss Suter and Maci's father would have stared despondently at each other, wondering what to do with this little baby who was the ruin of their hopes.

Or, Miss Suter gave a last cry—a mixture of exultation and

agony—and her big belly flattened. An odor like pine filled the room, but nothing visible proceeded from her, except hysteria. Then Miss Suter and Maci's father would have made such noises of rejoicing as are made by people who think they have delivered the world from suffering. Her father would have rushed upstairs and pushed open Maci's door to tell her the good news, to take her arm and proceed triumphantly to the shed, where he would show her the Infant, who would be living now, breathing out peace into the formerly troubled world.

But Maci was not in her room. Her drawings were gone. Her clothes were gone. Only Rob's empty trunk remained. Maci was by that time already in Kingstown, waiting for a train to take her away to Boston. She had written a letter, addressed to no one, which was still in her hand when the train came, and when she got on and took her seat. She kept it with her, clenched in her fist, as she watched the landscape rush by. How should a person deliver such a letter? You might burn it, or tie it to the leg of a dove. You might throw it in the sea, or bury it under the earth. In the end, after much consideration, she wrestled the window open, put out her arm, and opened her hand.

The storm shocked Miss Suter into labor. While she cried out in the house, I capered in the shed, smashing the Infant to pieces with a wrench. Glass and gold and copper flew all about the room, but seemed to make no sound as they fell because whatever noise they made was drowned out by the howl of the wind. It was delightful, to slay him. Do you know, I imagined I was slaying the whole batch of obscenity that has mauled our family? Is it not obscene that a pregnant woman should attach herself like a barnacle to our father? Is it not obscene that a father won't grieve for his son? Is it not obscene that our mother was ruined by silly beans, and are beans themselves not the seeds of obscenity? Now what a comfort, to let it all fall to pieces.

Poppy must not grieve for his mechanical son. He is in that Summerland, frolicking with all the other mechanical children. Is this my madness? Now I break his crystal eyes. Now I pluck his copper hair. Now I smash his glass limbs, and I undo him. I imagined that I was undoing it all: your death; Miss Suter's arrival; Poppy's madness; Mama's madness. I undid it all until, sitting amid the shards and pieces, I was in a place where none of it had happened, where we all still lived in Boston, where Miss Suter's belly was unoccupied by spirit or flesh, where there was no war. I think that was my madness, that murderous rage. Rob, I have killed our little brother. But you see, don't you, how he was a success? How he made a sort of peace in me.

2

"IT'S A TERRIBLE THING, NOT TO MARRY," HER AUNT AMY LIKED to say. Maci understood her to mean that it was in fact the worst thing, worse than madness, worse than war, worse than the death of a brother, mother, or even the death of a husband. Aunt Amy's husband had died when they were just a few months wed, having contracted a particularly virulent smallpox during a trip to Morocco. On the journey back, his skin came off him in great black sheets, until he was all livid, denuded muscle. Aunt Amy told the story without a trace of self-pity, or even with too much sadness. "We were *married*," she'd say of him, with a happy sigh. And then she would look at Maci, twenty-four years old in the summer of 1870, and say, "It really is a terrible thing not to marry."

But Maci thought she could do without marriage. The well-dressed, well-heeled, well-educated young gentlemen to whom her aunt introduced her were unbearable somehow. In conversation with them, her mind inevitably wandered. She'd think of how their wrists were thin and hairless, or else they would inspire in her gruesome flights of fancy. "Don't you think the Germans a people more clean than the Irish in their personal habits?" one might ask her, and she'd imagine him mortally wounded, with bullets in his spleen and shrapnel in his eye.

Aunt Amy inhabited her widowhood with grace and something that seemed to Maci like satisfaction. They were the best sorts of husbands, the dead ones. They covered you with respectability, but their feet were not on your neck. Maci found it very easy to imagine herself a widow. Private Vanderbilt had died at Chancellorsville. She still had his portrait, folded up into squares and hidden away in a large rosewood box which she kept under her bed. Once a month, she'd unfold all his pieces, spreading them out on the floor of her room. Inevitably, Aunt Amy would come by to knock. She mistrusted a closed door, hated a locked one, and she always seemed to sense when Maci was engaged in private business. She'd call out, "My dear, what are you doing in there?"

"Writing," Maci would say. That was now her profession, or her vocation—she felt called to it, but it didn't really pay. She contributed articles to the occasional weekly newspaper, most notably and most often to *Godey's Lady's Book*, whose editor, Mrs. Hale, had formed a distant attachment to Maci from Philadelphia. It was almost acceptable to Aunt Amy, to write articles on perfumes or French dresses for *Godey's*. "Everything in moderation," she'd say, encouraging her niece to put away her pen for weeks between articles, warning that intellectual stimulation had the effect of souring a woman's disposition. Reading was acceptable, if the book was the Bible or something written by a Beecher, preferably Catharine. Maci preferred Mr. Greeley's *Tribune*, or even the *New York Times*, papers that were not merely trade publications put out to refine the seams or cherry pies of their subscribers. If Aunt Amy happened to find a contraband item, she never mentioned her discovery, but instead quietly confiscated it and threw it away. Maci never protested when her papers or books disappeared from behind a curtain or from under a rug. Emerson, Browning, Tennyson, Lowell, Bryant—every last great man was cast into oblivion by Aunt Amy's ignorant hand. Maci figured it for a condition of her aunt's boundless generosity, this gentle but outrageous tyranny. Anyhow, her aunt never looked under her bed, the obvious hiding place, and the one where Maci kept her dearest treasures.

"What are you reading, my dear?" Aunt Amy asked. They were sitting after dinner in a rear parlor, a comfortable room with decidedly inelegant furniture, a place where guests were not welcome. After meals, Aunt Amy liked to sit in silence with her hands folded in her lap, concentrating fiercely on her digestion. She'd done this for an hour a day all her adult life, and credited the practice with her absolute freedom from dyspepsia. Sometimes, Maci would sit in the near-perfect quiet and listen to the gentle murmur of the light, but more often she'd read.

"An article on the history of muslin," Maci replied, but that was a lie. She had an issue of *Godey's* in her hands, but slipped inside it was the June 2 issue of *Woodhull and Claflin's Weekly*. She was reading an article exposing police involvement in the business of prostitution in New York City. It would seem that the police got free go-rounds with whichever girl they pleased. Clearly, this publication was not a trade paper. It was a women's paper and a political paper and a financial paper, whose motto was *Upward and Onward*. Maci liked it very much, and she liked Mrs. Woodhull, not least because the lady had declared herself a candidate for President. This thrilled the would-be voter in Maci. She liked the paper even though the articles sometimes went exploring in ridiculous territory. Mrs. Woodhull's *Weekly* had spiritualist sympathies, and Maci, because she felt compelled to read the whole thing, suffered the articles on medical clairvoyance and thought of her father, still living on the cliff with his Heaven-sent paramour. In all the years since she left his house, he had sent her just one short letter, unsigned and written on a smooth piece of wood: *Garrison was mobbed, Birney's press was thrown into the river, and Lovejoy was murdered; yet anti-slavery lived, and those who were oppressed now are free. So shall it ever be with truths which have been communicated to man. They are immortal, my dear, and cannot be destroyed.*

Reading the *Weekly* always inspired her. Maci would excuse herself and go upstairs to her desk, where she'd sit, often chewing pensively at the tip of her pen, so Aunt Amy would scold her the next morning for staining blue the corners of her mouth. These were not articles for Mrs. Hale, the ones she worked on late into the night with a sheet stuffed into the bottom of the door so Aunt Amy would not see light spilling out and know Maci was awake giving herself wrinkles and overheating her brain. They were for the *Weekly*, for the remarkable Mrs. Woodhull, for whom Maci had written many articles but sent only one, a history of women in newspapering. It praised Maci's heroes: Elizabeth Timothy, the first lady publisher in the country; Mary Catherine Goddard, who'd been supplanted as editor of her Philadelphia paper by her brother; Cornelia Walter, who so hated Mr. Poe; and, of course, Margaret Fuller. Maci called for more of these ladies to come forth from her own generation. She wanted there to be as many females in newspapering as there were males.

She had sent the article in May of that year, and had an acceptance two weeks later. *My magazine is a storehouse for ideas like yours*, Mrs. Woodhull wrote. *You must come and visit me*. Enclosed was a little picture of the beautiful lady, signed on the back *Victoria Woodhull, Future Presidentess.* Sometimes, at dinner with Aunt Amy, Maci daydreamed of joining Mrs. Woodhull in New York, but the thought of actually doing such a thing seemed as likely as her sprouting wings and flying about over the Back Bay.

Though she wouldn't run off to New York, Maci could still contribute to Mrs. Woodhull's paper, and it was while she was preparing another article for *Woodhull and Claflin's Weekly* that her hand first rebelled against her. It was very unexpected—one minute she was writing some animadversions on Catharine Beecher's *Treatise on Domestic Economy*, and the next she was writing something else entirely, and entirely against her will. Her left hand stole the pen from her right and began to scribble.

Her legacy of madness was something Maci thought less on, since she'd been living with sane, stable Aunt Amy. Long before, in the months and years just after she had fled Rhode Island, she was certain insanity would come to her as soon as she grew complacent. So, for a long time, as they sat together in the comfortable parlor she would consider madness while Aunt Amy considered her digestion.

Maci would think how it might be voices talking in her head, and how that would be terrifying, to hear a voice that berated you, or commanded you to lick the floor, or eat filth. Worse yet would be a pair of voices, the sort that might offer a constant commentary, one saying, "Do you see what she's wearing today?" and the other saying, "It does not surprise me." Or strange beliefs would creep into her mind. One morning she'd wonder how it might have been to be Mary Magdalene or Jean d'Arc, and the next she'd believe that she *was* Mary Magdalene, or Jean d'Arc, or both combined conveniently in a single body, a lady who gave herself to men, repented of it, then led them successfully in battle.

But years passed, and her inevitable mental decline seemed less and less imminent, until Maci began not to think of it so often, and then not very often at all. Later, she would think that it was precisely when she had finally believed herself safe that she was suddenly not safe, and she would curse carefree, naive Maci, who had stupidly abandoned her vigilance. It came like her father's, all of a piece. Her left hand jerked once, then leaped from the desk, springing off on its fingers like a jumping bug. It hung a moment in the air, then swooped down to take the pen from her unresisting right hand. It drew one dismissive line through her paragraphs on Catharine Beecher, and then the words came, written carelessly with her own hand, but in a hand that was not her own:

Sister, dear sister,

Know that you are not insane, and forgive me, please, my silence. Time is measured here, not in seconds, hours, or days, but in uncountable units of desire. And it is so difficult to pierce the veil, which is composed of God's indifference and the unbelief of the bereaved—thick things. Understand that I have been trying forever to come to you, a messenger whose news is all good.

* * *

Maci thought it was sensible and just, how she was being punished for destroying the Infant, for a crime worse than fratricide, for the murder of her father's hope. Her hand—she'd not call it brother, because it was her and not him, it was the part of her that would rather sacrifice reason and sanity than accept how he was gone—reassured her, *You're not insane*. But that was like the rain telling you you are not wet. And now this not-Rob had a new admonition with which to close his letters, *Go to New York. Go to her*. "Don't you tell me what to do," she'd whisper in reply.

It was very easy, Maci thought, how all her most childish desires were written out by this renegade appendage. She wanted, did she not, to get away from Boston? Life was boring there. Aunt Amy was cool and dull, and, living with her, Maci would settle into widowhood without ever marrying. There was a lifetime of comfortable sameness waiting for her in that house. One day Aunt Amy would die, and Maci would put on all her fantastic dresses, one after the other, a new one for every day of the year. It was hateful to think of, so her hand urged her to flee. *Go to New York. Go to Mrs. Woodhull. You must go*. "I will not," she said, holding up her left hand to her face and speaking to it, just like a madwoman.

The hand didn't belong to her anymore. She could move it like her other one, but it seemed to oblige her as a favor, not because it was naturally subject to her will. It wrote letters, spinning out ridiculous fantasies of a war in Heaven, fought by contentious spirits, who wanted to return to the earth, against conservative angels. It told stories about Mrs. Woodhull, and about her sons, two boys from Ohio separated by the war and by death. Her hand made rude gestures behind Aunt Amy's back. And it drew beautiful pictures: a falling-down shack at the top of a hill; a clearing in an orchard; a hawthorn bush. It drew an enormous house in a city she knew to be Manhattan; a greenhouse; an iron door. It drew a striking woman who Maci knew from her photograph to be Mrs. Woodhull; a careless-looking, smiling fat girl; a worried-looking fellow with a neck fully as thick as Private Vanderbilt's; an angel in stately robes with a tiara of stars floating around her head, and a little pugnacious angel, with only one wing. And it drew a portrait of two boys with the little angel's face—her hand groped for blue ink with which to color their eyes. She didn't hang them on her wall, these pictures. She liked them all very little. They ought to have gone into the garbage, in fact, but instead she put them under the bed, motivated, she supposed, by affection for even the delusion of her brother.

> Heaven is cold and white. It is not a place where I would care to reside, though some spirits are drawn there by pleasures so rarefied they are, in fact, empty. I am in the Summerland, a place as warm and green as the garden at Uncle Phil's summer house. Do you remember it? We chased rabbits there, when you were only two years old. You were still learning the names of things, then. I told you how the creatures were called, but you would not believe me.

"How do you like this one?" asked her aunt. Maci's hand had been in rebellion for weeks, and she was giving up hope that her affliction would prove to be temporary. It was the third Wednesday of the month, the day the dressmaker always came to deliver new creations. In the evening, Aunt Amy would model them for her niece.

"It's very pretty," Maci said.

"Is it too busy?" Aunt Amy was wearing an outfit so complicated Maci could only take it in in pieces: a striped overskirt with fringes, bows, and ruffles; a Chantilly lace jacket; a brooch and matching pendant earrings; a velvet neck ribbon with a dependent cross; a large fringed hair bow; a fan. Elements from her aunt's outfits would stay with Maci like annoying snatches of song; she knew she'd struggle all week to forget that fringed hair bow.

"By no means," said Maci. "I think it is altogether reserved."

"It's fortunate that you like it because . . . I've one for you also!" It was always supposed to be a surprise when Aunt Amy had two hideously complex dresses made instead of just one. Maci went to her room to put hers on, too, and then she struggled downstairs, caparisoned for a supper less solemn than usual. Aunt Amy would smile as she talked about the latest wave of fashion to come out of Paris, and Maci would think how it was like a disease, fashion, spreading from woman to woman, making them deranged. When she was younger, fine dresses had given her pleasure, but now all she longed for was a set of Bloomers. So many times, in her imagination, she'd come downstairs for dinner attired in trousers, skirt, and tunic, and, laying eyes upon her, Aunt Amy fled to the kitchen to wash her eyes with lye.

After dinner, Maci went back to her room to write. Earlier in the week, she'd had bad news from Philadelphia. Old Mrs. Hale was retiring, and who knew if the next editor of *Godey's Lady's Book* would be as fond as she was of Maci's writing? She had a special relationship with Mrs. Hale, who'd dealt her a compliment just a few months after they began working together: "Why, you go on so naturally and make so little fuss about your work that I sometimes forget you are a woman." She might have become a mentor to Maci if she had not always been proving herself a backward thinker—Mrs. Hale insisted, for example, that the vote would be ruinous to the happiness of women.

Hoping to send a big bunch of fatuous articles for the lady to purchase before she retired, Maci kept busy. Night after night, she sat at her desk composing with her right hand, and she found she was able to ignore how her left hand wielded its own pen, sketching, writing, and admonishing. "I'm not looking," she'd say aloud as she worked. "Scribble all you like, I shan't cast a glance on it." But she always did look, eventually. And she'd ask questions, too, when curiosity finally overwhelmed her. "Who is he?" she'd ask, as her hand drew another picture of the ragged little angel, and her hand would write the answer alongside the bizarre-looking wing, *Somebody's brother.*

If I told you I was in Hell, suffering eternal punishment because the war made a killer of me, then I know you would believe me. If I predicted that Aunt Amy would die horribly, killed with burning, acid poison by a scarab hatched of eggs dormant in her best cotton dress, I think you would embrace that news. But when I say that the sun will shine tomorrow, you pout and shake your head. When I say we are all undying, that love and grief can bridge the measureless space between us, you think it must be false because it is good, or because it might comfort you. So let me reassure you: I am in a sort of Hell, like every other spirit who has not forgotten the earth, who remembers that we are all creatures afflicted with unremitting desire.

It was the same way that her father had got her to eat new things when she was a child. "Just try it," he'd say, "and if it is not, after all, to your taste, then you do not have to eat it." So Maci's hand told her, *Just go, and if it does not suit you, if you find, after all, that their work is not your work, then you may return here to this dreadful life, and I will leave you alone forever.* So she left Aunt Amy's house with the money she'd saved from her articles (faithful Mrs. Hale did, indeed, buy a fat bunch of them), and rode the train to New York, suffering the advances of strange men. It wasn't enough to keep you respectable, traveling with your dead brother, who lived in your hand.

Maci got a room at the Female Christian Home on East Fifteenth Street. Her first evening there she sat on her bed and thought about her aunt. Maci had sneaked away from the house like a coward, leaving a note that really explained nothing. *Aunt, I have urgent business in Philadelphia*. She'd thought she would write again from the train, to explain. But she found she was not inclined to write, not on the train, and not in the room she shared with another Christian female, a shovel-faced, opinionless girl named Lavinia. I am wicked, Maci thought to herself, because she was certain that she never wanted to see her aunt again. It made her happy already, just to be away from Boston. But then she would think how she was away at the bidding of her own lunacy, and how she had only enough money to last her for a month or two, and she'd become angry at herself, and she would think, I am wicked and stupid.

On the morning after her arrival in New York, she walked along Broad Street, looking up every so often to meet the disapproving stares of birds perched on the telegraph wires that ran everywhere overhead. She paused outside Number 44. After a few moments, her left hand reached to open the door. She followed along after it, up the stairs to the office of Woodhull, Claflin and Company. Inside, she was met by a man with immense whiskers who sat examining a telegraphic stock indicator where it chattered away near a north window. Maci could hear a similar one running behind a glass-and-wood partition at the back of the room. "May I help you?" he asked.

"I would like to see Mrs. Woodhull," she said. "My name is Trufant."

"Ah," he said, and he smiled. "She's been expecting you." Maci hid her surprise, thinking the man had confused her with someone else, because she hadn't written ahead to announce her visit. The man, who introduced himself as Colonel James Harvey Blood, escorted her to the back. The office was just as it had been described in the *Weekly*. It was luxurious, with thick rugs thrown over the floors, bushy ferns under the windows, and elegant statuary scattered here and there. Stern Minerva and luscious Aphrodite inhabited two corners of the office, and a third corner was occupied by a piano, atop which sat a bust of Commodore Vanderbilt. Maci stopped in front of it, reaching out to touch Mr. Vanderbilt on his cold, beakish nose, and thought of his son. Against the bust lay a tiny painting, which depicted three little cherubim floating in a rosy sky, holding up a winding parchment upon which was written, *Simply to thy cross I cling.*

In the back, Mrs. Woodhull and a red-haired lady Maci's own age were sitting behind twin walnut desks, with gold pens stuck behind their ears. They were talking to a reporter.

"If I were to notice," said the red-haired lady, "what is said by what they call society, I could not leave my home except in fantastic walking-dresses and ballroom costume. But I despise what squeamy, crying girls or powdered, counter-jumping dandies say of me. We have the counsel of those who have more experience than we, and we are endorsed by the best backers in the city."

"Do you mean Mr. Vanderbilt?" asked the reporter, a young man with a face so fat and white that Maci had to resist an urge to gather it in her hands and knead it like dough.

"It is very possible that I do," the lady answered. From a platter on her desk she picked up a strawberry dipped in chocolate and bit into it with abandon. She looked up at the ceiling while juice ran down her chin. The reporter turned to Maci.

"Are you a customer?"

"This is Miss Trufant," said Colonel Blood. "She's come to see you, Mrs. Woodhull."

Maci had composed a statement. It was brief, and perhaps a little elegant, a plea for employment. Here she was, a woman who wrote for newspapers, and there was Mrs. Woodhull, a woman who published one. Didn't it follow that Mrs. Woodhull should have work for Maci? Maci's hand had dictated a different statement, something about being a messenger of the spirits of the air. But Maci forgot both statements when the lady looked up and met her eyes. There was something breathtaking about her. It was not just her beauty. She had the sort of grace, Maci decided in that very instant, that arises from absolute independence of mind. Maci found herself unable to speak, but she didn't have to say anything at all.

"There you are!" said Mrs. Woodhull, jumping up and taking

Maci's hands in her own. "Tennie, here she is! Here she is at last!" Maci's right hand was limp as a dead fish, but her left hand squeezed back fervently, and trembled with nervous joy.

The lady called Tennie hauled the reporter up by his elbow, pushing him out past the partition and declaring the interview at an end. Then she threw both her arms around Maci, and kissed her on the neck. Maci wanted to ask her to stand back, to scream for her to keep her wet kisses to herself, but when she opened her mouth, Tennie covered it with her own, at which point Maci was too stunned to make any noise at all.

"There she is, real as can be!" said Tennie, pinching her as if to make sure of her flesh, then kissing her again.

"We've been waiting for you," said Mrs. Woodhull.

Mrs. Woodhull is a great and good woman, a lady celebrated by spirits. There is a grand plaza here dedicated to her and to her wonderful sister. There are colossal statues made—can you picture them in your mind?—of quicksilver desire. They stand back to back, giantesses looking with a supreme clarity of vision over the whole Summerland. Everybody here labors under a burden of enthusiasm for Mrs. Woodhull, but really her living son is more significant than she, and the small garden dedicated to him, while very beautiful, does not do justice to his importance.

Does it surprise you, that the dead build monuments to the living? Sister, the whole Summerland is stubbled with such monuments. We go to them, as you go to yours, to remember and to mourn.

It was an extraordinary welcome. Mrs. Woodhull said she had known Maci would come to New York, and hinted that her spirit guide, Demosthenes himself, had promised to deliver her, but Maci chose to believe that Mrs. Woodhull was expecting her, and welcomed her so warmly, because she believed that *Woodhull and Claflin's Weekly* must draw enthusiastic young women inexorably to her side.

She insisted that Maci be her guest, and took her to a beautiful house on Thirty-eighth Street, where Maci was given a room adjoining Tennie's on the second floor. Tennie was almost Maci's age exactly; their birthdays were just a week apart. "We are almost twins," Tennie said, convinced that they must become the best of friends. Tennie was like Miss Suter, in a way, except where Maci had always suspected Miss Suter of being a liar, Tennie was brazenly honest. Certainly it was another punishment, for Maci to have delivered herself into the hands of devoted Spiritualists. Yet these ladies did not share the quality of fear that Maci had sensed in Miss Suter. They were not hiding under their beliefs from the cruelty of the world.

Mrs. Woodhull challenged Maci to help her "abolish hypocrisy and transform the social sphere." Listening to her, Maci found her delusions easy to overlook. Mrs. Woodhull claimed wisdom from the dead, not through their books, as other people got it, but from direct personal interviews. Yet this was not to say that she did not read books. All through dinner they talked of *Woman in the Nineteenth Century*. Mrs. Woodhull had a clipping book with seventeen pages devoted to articles by Margaret Fuller. All evening she and Maci sat in a third-floor study, underneath a dome of green glass, and talked. Maci confessed her plan to write something very large—a vindication of Wollstonecraft's *Vindication*. "All that obvious truth, written over a hundred years ago," Maci said. "I look around me at the world and it's as if she never made a peep." She brought out her animadversions on Catharine Beecher, and told how she planned to dissect and refute every argument she could find in print which advocated anything but that women should have absolute power over their own lives.

"Yes, yes," Mrs. Woodhull said excitedly, and paraphrased the

Countess Ossoli. "I mean to vindicate the birthright of all women, to teach them what to claim, and how to use what they obtain." Then she yawned. It was close to midnight. "Perhaps we've talked enough for an evening. There's work for us to do in the morning." Over dinner, she had made Maci an assistant editor on her *Weekly*, just like that. It was a thrill to have employment, but Maci controlled herself, not crying out or giggling with joy, only nodding serenely and saying, "I will be very happy to accept your generous offer."

Tennie took Maci to her room. Mrs. Woodhull's house was so big she was grateful to have a guide, because she was sure she'd have lost herself among all the stairs and the halls full of doors. Maci was tired, but Tennie wouldn't let her go to sleep just yet. Maci sat on a stool in Tennie's room, which featured prominently a silken tent set up in one corner. "My Turkish corner," Tennie called it. "When we are more intimate, I'll take you in there and tell you confidential things." Now she wanted to trace Maci's silhouette, to add it to a collection. Maci sat very still in the darkened room while Tennie traced her shadow on a piece of paper pinned to the wall. On an opposite wall there were a dozen other silhouettes, framed and hung in orderly rows. "There they are," Tennie said, when she saw where Maci was looking, "the rest of the family."

"I'm really rather sleepy," said Maci.

"We're nearly done," Tennie said, and cursed the candle when it flickered. When she was finished she had a wavering outline of Maci's profile drawn on black paper with white chalk. "There," she said. "I waste no time obtaining these. Now, let's prepare for bed." She groped at Maci, undoing buttons and ties even as Maci tried to direct her hands away.

"It's something I do for myself."

"Nonsense!" said Tennie. "It's what a sister's for." When they were both in their undergarments, Maci saw that Tennie wore a thing she had never before encountered: a combination of chemise and drawers.

"Do you like my chemiloon?" Tennie asked, turning around to

model it. Maci nodded, because she did like it, and she was immediately presented with one from out of Tennie's wardrobe.

After she had bound Maci's and her own hair up in rags to maintain their curls, Tennie began to prepare her night-cream, which, she said, she made fresh every night from a recipe of her mother's. It would keep a lady's skin soft, and also drive away evil spirits. Maci watched as she mixed equal measures of white wax, almond oil, and cacao in a small blue porcelain bowl. Tennie painted it on Maci's face with a sable brush, and did the same to her own face.

"We'll bounce for a while," she said. "It makes for a good sleep." She took Maci's hands and dragged her up on the bed. Then she started bouncing, insisting, when Maci only hopped a little, that she bounce vigorously. Maci's rag-bound hair flopped in her eyes.

"Now I'm weary!" Tennie said. "Are you weary, too?"

"Entirely."

"Well, if you have trouble sleeping, if you wake in the night feeling agitated, you may have a ride on my pony." Tennie pointed to a rocking horse big enough for an adult, with a piece of red silk thrown over its saddle. "He's for sharing, that fellow. Indeed, everything in this room is for sharing." She opened the door between their rooms and ushered Maci through. Someone had already turned down her sheets and fluffed up her pillows. "Good night, sister!" Tennie said, turning down the light and retreating to her room. She shut the door only halfway.

Maci lay in her new bed, smelling like a macaroon. It was true that she was weary, but she could not sleep. She stayed awake watching the blowing white shapes of her curtains as they moved in the breeze. Her left hand was twitching, walking up and down the bed like a scrabbling crab, and pinching at the flesh of her belly. "Stop it," she said, but it would not stop. There was a writing desk already set up for her, as if to provide for her affliction. She turned up the light and sat down.

Didn't I tell you they'd be waiting?

"Why now?" she asked. "Why did you let me feel safe, first, before you began this torture?" If her hand had rebelled back when rebellion was popular, five years ago or more, then she might have been better prepared to put it down, stronger and more able in her dealings with it. Complacency had made her weak, and reflecting on the very agreeable time she had spent that day with Mrs. Woodhull, she feared it would only be a matter of days before she succumbed to delusion and declared herself the Apostle of the Left Hand.

The veil was thick, the walls were high. Soon the work will be done, and then, Sister, we will be together again. What is in you that you will only believe in despair and think hope only the comfort given by the weak to the weak?

She had no answer for that question. She rose from the desk, though the pen was still in her hand, and lay down again in bed. When the pen wrote on Mrs. Woodhull's fine sheets she ignored it, but she saw the message in the morning, smeared by her tossing body: *not insane, not at all.*

> Benjamin Franklin is here. Thomas Jefferson is here. Vergil is here—this place is stuffed with virtuous pagans. It is said, of Heaven and the Summerland, that everyone is here, and everyone will be here. But a change is coming. We mean to make the here and there a single place, to make a marriage between Heaven and Earth. Try to imagine that, a world free of the distinctions made by death, where immortals are mortal, and mortals are immortal. Glorious wedding! Mother is here, still desirous of beans. Margaret Fuller is here. She sees you and loves you.

By September, Maci was firmly installed at the Park Row offices of the *Weekly*. She was almost hidden behind the tall stacks of daily and weekly newspapers, received from all over the country, that were piled on her desk. She'd had the idea of clipping items about women and printing them for the weekly's readers. She had a nice little collection of them already: *Miss Hoag is the pioneer freshwoman in the Northwestern University; Miss Amy M. Bradley has been appointed Examiner of Schools for New Hanover County, North Carolina; Miss Louisa Stratton of Johnson County, Iowa, challenges any man in the state to a plowing match with her, and proposes a two-horse team.*

"Are you in there?" Mrs. Woodhull asked, peering over a paper tower that reached just to her nose.

"I am," said Maci.

"I want your opinion on this." Mrs. Woodhull handed over a sheaf of papers, and walked away. Maci leaned back in her chair and read what she had been given, a little treatise on the Fourteenth Amendment, and how it trumped the need for a Sixteenth, for which brave ladies like Mrs. Stanton and Miss Anthony had been unsuccessfully campaigning. Because women were citizens, they were already guaranteed the right to vote by the Fourteenth Amendment. All they need do was assert that right. The argument was brilliant and simple. "It makes perfect sense," Maci told Mrs. Woodhull, when she returned to Maci's desk. "Such an elegant, transparent solution. No wonder it has remained so long invisible."

"So you'll admit it?" said Mrs. Woodhull. "You will grant that I see the unseen?" Maci laughed.

"In this instance alone, Mrs. Woodhull." Maci insisted that Demosthenes would have to sit down with them at dinner before she'd believe in him. Mrs. Woodhull kept a place for him at her table, with a wineglass from which her drunken sister Utica stole nips. Maci kept all her own impossible strangeness a secret. She didn't tell how her dead brother commanded her hand. It wouldn't do to tell, because to tell would be to join them in their delusion, to embrace her own madness and to afford it a measure of respect which she preferred to deny it.

Mrs. Woodhull endorsed silliness in public; she'd deliver a learned argument on the politics of the ancient Egyptians, then make herself stupid by saying she had it all direct from the ethereal lips of Demosthenes. Maci wondered how much more the woman could already have accomplished if she could only keep a few choice things to herself. But it was a virtue, too, how she hated hypocrisy, how she would not lie even by omission, but always told the whole truth as she saw it. She was like her paper, sublime and a little ridiculous. She'd assign Maci to investigate a stock swindle, and the next day ask her to write a phony letter from Paris, full of fashion and gossip, under the name Flor de Valdal. Her politics, at least, were serious, and a few powerful men were taking her seriously.

At a party in September of 1870, Maci walked among the omnipresent roses in Mrs. Woodhull's parlors, talking with Benjamin Butler, a person whom she'd never dreamed of meeting. They were waiting to honor Steven Pearl Andrews, who had asked Maci to call him Professor Pearlo when they met for the first time, and had talked for an hour about his conviction that before the twentieth century dawned, a trans-Saharan railway would relieve the burdens of the camel.

"I think smart girls are ruined by marriage," Mr. Butler said at the party. "Energies that could be spent improving the world are instead wasted on the pursuit of a husband."

"But Mrs. Woodhull is married," said Maci.

"Yes, and rather more extensively than most. But she is a special case."

"I think I must agree with you," Maci said. *You are in love with her*, her hand had accused. "I do admire her," she said to it, and wasn't that reasonable, after all? Could a woman start with nothing, in a rickety shack in a place called Homer, and in the course of a decade become a stockbroker, a publisher, a writer, a candidate for President, and not demand a little admiration?

"Sometimes," said Mr. Butler, "I think a celestial accident occurred at her birth, and that a male soul must have been allotted to her body." He really was extraordinarily ugly.

"Yes," Maci said. "Isn't that easier to believe than that she could have a woman's soul, and still have a greater purpose than merely to gratify the senses of man?"

"Well," said Mr. Butler. He reached down to a tray on a table and gathered up a few carrots, cut as small and fine as the fingers of a baby. Eating them by the handful, he looked about the room at length, as if considering his response, while Maci looked over his shoulder at Tennie's friend Dr. Fie, another man she had offended that night. Her mind turned to Mrs. Woodhull's accomplished young son, a boy who had made such an early success of medicine that he was able to keep a house even larger than his mother's. Maci had seen him once or twice, small and furtive, always in the company of Dr. Fie.

"Ah," said Mr. Butler, at the sound of the doorbell. "Here is Mr. Andrews." He offered her his arm, to walk her to the crowd that had gathered around the door, but Maci informed him that she was quite capable of seeing herself across the room without assistance.

> If woman is capable of being a mother to those who make the laws of nations, if she is capable of training the young mind up to mature age, and shaping its physical, social, and intellectual destiny, then surely she is capable of taking part in politics. Death has leveled us all, Sister. Coke and Blackstone (here too!) say it also: everyone is equal in death, and when the dead live again they will bring perfect equality back with them to wash over the earth.

In January of 1871, Maci wrote a letter to Aunt Amy, the most sensible person she knew.

> *Aunt, I know what I believe. I know what is foolish and what is wise. I know the symptoms of madness, and I know that I am florid with them. I know that I have, by your judgment, run*

off quite unexpectedly to join a community of Free Love in a capital of wickedness, and that this must seem queer payment for your generosity. But please understand that every day I rise and work. I often have ideas very late in the evening. In the space of three days I see them in print, and in the space of three more days those same words, that late-night notion of mine, have gone out in twenty thousand copies all over this country, with a few copies to Britain and France and one copy—can you believe it?—to St. Petersburg. And Aunt, Mrs. Woodhull will deliver a memorial to Congress this next week. Can your dresses give you satisfaction, can the memory of your husband keep you content when such a thing is about to happen? Mad or sane, where should I be but with her? I know you worry about me. I know you think it is a scandal, to associate with such a woman. I know you think that madness has sucked me up as it sucked up your sister, that my family is come at last to absolute ruin. But I promise you, Aunt, that my hand can babble as it may, but I will never believe it. I will never succumb to that sweet belief, that the dead are not dead, because it seems obvious to me that to believe this would cast upon them the most atrocious dishonor, that to reduce their loss to nothing is to reduce them to nothing, that to indulge madness to save yourself pain for them is the work of a coward. I go forward, Aunt, as radically and sensibly as I dare.

Maci never sent this letter, or others that she wrote. It pleased her, sometimes, to imagine Aunt Amy in a fret over the disappearance of her niece, but she knew that Aunt Amy was not likely to fret over her. Finding Maci gone, Aunt Amy would have been angry, then relieved, and then fallen back into the comforts of quotidian sameness which Maci's disappearance had briefly interrupted. Maci collected the letters in a bundle, and put them away in another rosewood box, her fourth, stuffed like the others with pictures and correspondence.

Maci rode down with Mrs. Woodhull to be with her when she delivered her memorial. It was Maci's first time in Washington. "Mrs. Woodhull," she said, peering out the window of the carriage when they rode by General Grant's house on their way to their hotel, "when you are President, you'll have to live in that big white barn."

"Not if I move the capital to New York, my star." That was Mrs. Woodhull's pet name for Maci, inspired by the pseudonym, Arcturus, under which Maci wrote her articles, and by a certain spiritual radiance which, she claimed, hovered around Maci's body, especially when ideas were hot in Maci's head. Sometimes, as they worked together late into the night in the house on Thirty-eighth Street, Mrs. Woodhull would suddenly shield her eyes from Maci and say, "Oh, you are too bright, too bright!"

But it was Mrs. Woodhull who burned up the little room in Congress that day in January. She held the entire audience spellbound with her lucid argument. Maci's lips moved along during the speech—she and Mrs. Woodhull had been over it so many times that Maci knew it by heart. Maci took great satisfaction in looking around the room at the rapt, attentive faces of all the powerful men and giant women. Only Mrs. Woodhull's son, the younger Dr. Woodhull, spoiled the perfect attention. He'd brought a child with him into the room, a pale boy named Pickie, whom he claimed to have found in the snow in Madison Square Park a few weeks before.

The boy giggled whenever Dr. Woodhull whispered to him. A reporter standing next to them made hushing noises, but was ignored. Even Mr. Whitman, who Maci understood to be a friend even closer to Dr. Woodhull than was Dr. Fie, failed to quiet them when he tried. It didn't really matter that they were whispering and giggling—no one was distracted from Mrs. Woodhull—but Maci found it outrageous that the lady's own son should be so disrespectful towards her in her great hour. It irked Maci, how he did not act like her son, how he was not respectful towards her, how he showed her no affection. Maci's mother was dead of a madness much less sublime than Mrs. Woodhull's; her father was huddled uselessly on a cliff in Rhode Island. She wanted to rearrange fate, to effect a parent swap with him, and then she would see if he did not appreciate having Mrs. Woodhull for a mother. She wanted, at least, to take him aside, to scold him. "Don't you know," she would ask, "that your mother is extraordinary?"

There was something about him, though, which repelled her. Tennie described him as heavily electritized, and revealed to Maci, as if it were a precious secret, that he and Mr. Whitman were the two poles of a love-magnet. Maci did not know what that meant, and did not want to know, but she wondered, sometimes, if there were not a strange force in him. Whenever she went near him, on the rare occasions when he visited his mother's house, she felt herself pushed away by something almost like panic. *He is the Magus,* her hand wrote. *He is working to bring us back. What a celebration we would have here, if you would only speak to him. I tell you, there would be a parade! Sister, he needs your assistance.*

"Brushing his hair, perhaps," Maci replied, because it was always in a tangle.

It was after his mother's memorial that Maci, compelled by her rage, finally spoke to young Dr. Woodhull. She found him outside the Capitol, watching Mr. Whitman play in the snow with the boy, Pickie. She stood behind him where he leaned on a stone railing, and gathered in her breath to shout at him. "How dare you!" is what she wanted to say, surprising him with a bombardment of fury. But she found she wasn't able to shout at him after all. She let out the breath she had gathered, making a noise that sounded like a sigh.

Dr. Woodhull straightened up and turned around, stared a moment into her face, then turned back to watch his friend and his ward. Saying nothing, he stepped aside to make room for her to stand next to him. He began to gather up snow from off of the railing. Maci stared out at Mr. Whitman and the boy where they were frolicking around the ridiculous statue of General Washington. The boy climbed on the statue, kicking snow off of Washington's lap and into Mr. Whitman's face. "You rascal!" Mr. Whitman said. Her rage forgotten, Maci laughed at them.

"When I was a child," she said, "my nurse discovered a copy of *Leaves of Grass* in my bed and beat me with it. She said it was a naughty book, and that I was a naughty child to read it." Dr. Woodhull did a thing with his face—it might have been a smile or it might have been a grimace. He handed her a perfectly shaped snowball, then put his hands over his stomach.

"Are you ill?" Maci asked him.

"No," he said. "Don't ever tell Walt you got beaten with his book. It would make him sad." He looked for a few moments at her shoes, cleared his throat, sniffed in the cold air. "Over there," he said, pointing across the grounds to a building on the other side of Second Street. "Did you know that's where they hung Mrs. Surrat?" Before she could reply he ran off to play. Maci considered her snowball, thinking she'd never seen anything so thoroughly round before in her life. It seemed like a sin to destroy it, but still she threw it against the wall of the Capitol, imagining it a perfect ball of fire, not ice, one that would set the place ablaze, and bring down the old order so she and Mrs. Woodhull could build it up again better and more just. The snowball behaved oddly, bouncing whole to the floor of the terrace before it exploded into a cloud of snow.

She watched the three playing for a while longer, until Mr. Whitman paused to stare at her. She thought for a moment that she should wave to him, but it seemed like an overly familiar gesture to make towards a stranger, so she turned and walked away.

I saw you. The veil is thick, but not obscuring to vision. We all see you. We see all of you. We watch you rend your clothes and pull your hair at our absence. You are destroyed because we are not with you, but do you ever consider how we are destroyed because you are not with us? Do you ever consider

> our grief? Selfish, selfish! O Sister, do you see what small sympathy exists on earth for the dead?

There was a time after Rob's death when Maci went about in her aunt's house with her hair in disarray and her dress torn, when she borrowed rituals of grief and devised her own—covering mirrors and putting out food for her brother to eat; standing for hours in the foyer in case a spiritual postman should come scratching ever so lightly at the door with a letter from him; saying a prayer every night for his sake—Lord bless him and keep him eternally in light and please tomorrow let him be alive. She'd lie in bed waiting in vain for sleep to come, and scenes from their life would play out in her head—hiding under Aunt Amy's bed when she visited their house on Mount Vernon Street, and grabbing at her toes as she sat getting ready for sleep; dressing the dog; teaching the cat to swim in the washtub. Over the course of months she played out their whole lives, going back in time until she wrecked her little boat of reverie upon a first memory. She was two years old, taking a nap under the piano—a place she was fond of until she was seven—when Rob came and woke her. "Get up, you," he said. He was unfriendly, back then, because he had wished to remain an only child. He hadn't asked for a sister, and hoped at first that she might just go away without any fuss. She remembered hearing his voice, then opening her eyes and seeing him, and because it was her first memory, it seemed to her sometimes that it was he, not their parents, who had called her into creation, that she entered into life at the sound of his voice. In the weeks and months following his death, she ruminated on such strange notions. Back then she'd thought madness would be a blessing. It would be better to think constantly on beans than to think on him in his last moments, than to think on the wound in his throat, sucking and whistling, throwing out a spray of blood with every breath.

But she had not grown fascinated with beans, not with roses or budgies or with the patterns made by the grain in a wood floor, though she had given all these things the most thorough consideration, and opened herself up to them, inviting them to rule her. Instead, she had straightened her hair over a period of months, sewn up the tear in her dress, and traded her acute misery for something more sensible and less exhausting, a cruel and hard sort of wisdom that said people die, and a person can do nothing against that. It's the greatest open secret, that death will take everyone, that every person is as transient as a shadow. Embracing this knowledge, she came to realize, was how sane people managed their grief, and she thought it had served her pretty well for as long as she remained sane. *It's me it's me it's me*, her impostor hand would write all through the winter, and all through the winter she'd reply, "How dare you say that?"

And all winter long she had terrible dreams. They featured young Dr. Woodhull, a person who was expressly not invited to invade her sleeping mind. She'd lie awake, fearing sleep as she did when she was a girl, back when nightmares were always springing out of the crevices of her agitated brain. "Not tonight," she'd whisper, praying for dreamless sleep, or at least for the sort of dreams she used to enjoy, in which she healed the split between the New York and Boston factions of the woman suffrage movement, or in which Private Vanderbilt's big hands closed, over and over, about her waist.

Despite her prayers, she'd find herself in the moonlit orchard, up to her ankles in rotting windfall apples and pears. She'd look up and see a child's dress blowing in the branches of a pear tree. Dr. Woodhull would step out from a pool of darkness. "It's a shame," he'd say as he put his hand on her, "how it must pass away. Even something as beautiful as this." He'd hold her breast in his two hands, lifting it up as if for her inspection, and as she watched it turned the color of ash. His touch was reverent, but everywhere it left purple blotches of rot in the shape of his hand.

"Not much room to roll around in here, is there?" he asked her in another dream. They were together in a coffin meant, like all coffins, for just a single occupant. "Why don't they make them bigger? It's not as if people always die one at a time."

And in another dream, the worst, Maci stood with him looking down into her mother's casket. Louisa Trufant was a wasted thing, shriveled away to bones, tendons, and skin by her diet of beans. But her hair was thick and shining as it had never been in life. Even as Maci watched, it grew, filling the casket until her mother seemed to be bathing in it, and indeed it made a sound like rushing water as it poured from her head. "Look," Dr. Woodhull told her. "Look at her. Keep looking. If you keep at it she will give up a secret to you."

Maci would wake, quieting sobs with one hand while her other pulled her across the room to the desk. *We are creatures, like you*, it wrote, *made all of sadness and desire, only a thousand times more so. We share want like water, here. Sister, do you know how you are missed by strangers? We want to come back. Please, we want to come back.*

In April of 1871, Maci went along with Tennie to Number 10 Washington Place, the home of Mr. Vanderbilt. Maci had been working on something for the *Weekly*, an article in support of the late Mr. Lincoln's wife. *Mrs. Lincoln*, she wrote, *is thrown over on the assigned ground that the widow of the murdered President is not in danger of actual starvation. We have no affection for pensions in public allowance. Every honest worker is as much a servant of the state and a public benefactor as any duly appointed official. In the case of accident or sudden death the laborer's widow or child gets no State assistance. But if there be any such principle as public gratitude and any such way of testifying it as pension or pecuniary gratuity, Abraham Lincoln's widow is the woman to receive it—her husband killed on account of public duty with a record, beyond the doubt of selfish motive—if that be not a claim on the nation's bounty, what is?*

It was typical of Mrs. Woodhull's new direction. She had been courting the labor movement for months, and had instructed Maci to write pieces favorable to it. Maci complied as best she could, but always she found herself writing articles that endorsed the perspectives of the working class while simultaneously rejecting them. Maci thought it ill-advised for the *Weekly* to embrace Communists. She tried to tell this to Mrs. Woodhull, but the lady was dogged in her conviction that Communists, like Free Lovers and Spiritualists, were all decent and righteous and good.

The article was giving Maci a headache when Tennie came by and offered to take her away to visit the Commodore, a benefactor and intimate friend. Tennie had offered before to take Maci to his house, but Maci had always declined, because she was certain there would be a great awkwardness involved in visiting the father of the man she'd practically married in her imagination. But that day in April, Maci went because small, peculiar George Washington Woodhull was still sneaking into her dreams, bringing her strange gifts now: a lump of cold iron, a double handful of ashes, a bouquet of broken glass flowers. She wanted to drive him away, and she thought a visit to the Vanderbilt house might help to do it.

Her left hand denied coincidence, maintaining that it was a sign that Tennie was cozy with the Private's father. It was clear to Maci that the relationship was not exactly a coincidence, but it wasn't a magical arrangement, either. Mrs. Woodhull had told how she had sought out Commodore Vanderbilt when she'd first arrived in the city. She'd given him advice, that she claimed to have from the spirits, on the future behavior of certain stocks. He'd repaid her in kind, and she'd built her fortune on those first stock tips. "We're kindred souls," Mrs. Woodhull claimed of the Commodore, but it was her sister to whom he'd proposed marriage, and who had rejected him. "Marriage is the grave of love," Tennie said simply, when Maci asked why she hadn't accepted his offer. At Number 10 Washington Place a winking servant let them in a back door and led them through the house.

In a study full of empty bookshelves, Maci and Tennie had a visit with Mr. Vanderbilt. He greeted Maci in a very cordial manner, but soon grew cold when it became clear to him that she would not sit on his lap. Tennie did sit there, and they smoked from the same cigar, and drank whiskey. Their intimacy was routine and not shocking to Maci, who laughed now when she thought how she had been shocked by her father's behavior towards Miss Suter. Maci pretended to sip from a glass of wine while she stared at Mr. Vanderbilt, looking for his son in him but not finding him there. She'd heard it said that a bride could look to her husband's father to see the man with whom she'd spend her old age, and as she sat listening to Tennie and Mr. Vanderbilt talking of the virtues of cigars, she tried to imagine being old with someone who looked like this, a man with giant white whiskers, a hard face, and hawkish eyes. She failed at it. He was too coarse and grabby. All she could think was how her frail old bones and papery skin would never withstand his pinching and poking.

"I'll show you around the house, Maci," Tennie said suddenly, sliding off Mr. Vanderbilt's lap. She kissed his cheek and said, "You don't mind, do you, old goat?" She didn't wait for his answer, but took Maci's hand and led her out into the dark hall.

"We must be quiet," she said. "If we wake Frank we might be sorry for it." Frank was the new Mrs. Vanderbilt, the daughter of the lady whom Mr. Vanderbilt's surviving children had put forth, after their mother's death, as an acceptable bride. She was the lady he'd settled for when Tennie refused him. Maci followed Tennie as she tiptoed down the hall to a staircase, which she ascended in slow, cautious steps, pausing every now and then as if to listen for sounds of alarm.

"Where are we going?" Maci asked.

"Upstairs," Tennie whispered. On the second floor, Tennie led her to a bedroom. She opened the creaking door very slowly, and after she had turned up the gas, touched Maci on the hand and said, "I thought you would like to see it."

"Where are you going?" Maci asked, as Tennie left. Maci would have followed, but as soon as the light came up she recognized that this room belonged to her brother's friend. She had confessed her stupid conceit late one night in Tennie's Turkish corner, had unfolded Rob's portrait of Private Vanderbilt while Tennie praised the art and the man. "He's a big handsome beast," she'd said, and they'd worked each other into sentimental tears for the lover Maci never had. Maci had been deeply ashamed the next day, and because Tennie had not ever spoken of it except to ask her if her friend Dr. Fie was not the same beastly size as Private Vanderbilt, Maci figured she'd forgotten.

Maci explored the room quietly, after briefly acknowledging to herself that she ought just to leave without disturbing a thing. It was as he must have left it years before, except his uniform was folded on the bed. There were a few pictures on the wall, big oil paintings of steamers, portraits of his father's property. She opened a wardrobe to look at his clothes, oversized sack coats and shirts into whose sleeves she imagined she could easily fit her whole leg. When Maci lay down on his bed, her head found something hard under the pillow: a Bible. She put her face on the uniform, thinking to discover his secret, personal odor in it. But it had been too long since he'd worn it, and now his uniform smelled utterly blank. With her face in his shirt she considered how it was very bad, what she'd done, so grossly assuming that they might have been friends, and imagining him her husband in various domestic scenes. She was embarrassed for herself, to be sneaking in a stranger's house, sniffing at a stranger's clothes. And she was embarrassed because, lying here at last in Private Vanderbilt's abandoned bed, as close as she would ever get to him in this life, she felt very little. In fact, she felt nothing at all, not love, not grief, not desire, just a great empty space where a ghost did not live, where there was nobody and nothing, after all.

Do you remember the day our mother died? Do you remember how it was beautiful, bright, and warm after two cold days of rain? It put me in mind of Easter, because I had never seen it rain on Easter, or fail to rain on Good Friday. There was something that I wanted to say to you, then, but like you I was dumb in my mourning. I wanted to tell you that I was so sad I felt as if I might be happy, or in love, simply because such powerful feelings can appear the same to the naive. I was mighty with grief, and I thought I should be empowered by it. I thought my hands should shine with a yellow light, and that should I reach out to touch our mother on the head, I would call her back from the place she'd gone. I felt so very powerful. Later I thought, Fool, you've never been more powerless in your life. And it seemed so stupid, to think I could have called Mother back to life merely with the strength of my sadness. But Sister, the ridiculous fallacy is to think that grief cannot bring us back. You must believe me when I say that it certainly can. If only you grieved more and better, we would be back with you now. If only you did not forget us, we could return to you.

Maci tended to arrange all the Claflins but Tennie by their bad habits, and in her mind she often referred to them by their chiefest sins instead of their names. So big, hairy Malden Claflin was Gluttony. Sinister, one-eyed Buck, who'd come pawing at Maci one night in her bedroom, and was dealt a black eye by her left hand, was Avarice, because his greed was even more prominent a feature in him than his lechery. Miss Utica, drunk and jealous of her sisters every hour of the day and night, was Envy. Worst of all of them was Anna Claflin, Mrs. Woodhull's demonic mother, a lady who embodied a sin Maci had no name for. It involved a quality of being murderous in intent if not in action, of being a contemptible liar and a relentless hater, and of trying to own every person around you, even strangers.

"How do you rise, with such weighty hangers-on?" Maci had

asked Mrs. Woodhull, because she did not understand how she could have accomplished all she had with such a persecutory chorus always trailing after her.

"My family is my strength," Mrs. Woodhull replied confidently, but they almost destroyed her in May, when Anna Claflin swore out a warrant against Colonel Blood, whom she hated because he had appropriated a portion of her daughter's love that Anna thought was due all to her. May was anniversary month, when a person could not open a paper without seeing accounts of the annual meetings of a half-dozen societies. Societies bent on reforming or deforming the nation; associations for the advancement of the street urchin; bands of veterans; amateur devotees of the botanical sciences; the River Pirates' Orphans' Benevolent Circle—everyone met in May. Mrs. Woodhull had a bright moment at the convention of the National Woman Suffrage Association at Apollo Hall, but even as she was speaking her mother was slouching down to Essex Market police court. There Anna swore out her warrant accusing Colonel Blood of beating her and threatening to kill her with an iron dog similar to the one used to murder the distinguished Mr. Nathan nearly a year before. She hinted that it was very possible, to her mind, that Colonel Blood, not Mr. Nathan's son, was the still-at-large fiend who had gleefully bludgeoned that esteemed man to death.

"You awful creature!" Mrs. Woodhull shouted at her mother, after the trial was over, after her magnificent speech had been eclipsed in every New York paper by the misleading fact that she had two husbands living in her house. "You false thing!" Mrs. Woodhull put her face in Maci's shoulder and cried, and Maci brought her arms up to embrace her. Anna Claflin was shrieking curses, but Maci barely heard them. She felt suddenly transported out of the elegant parlor, out of the beautiful house, and up into the sky, because greatness had chosen her arms in which to weep.

Anna and Buck were ejected from the house on Thirty-eighth Street, but they came back in June, recalled by some familial gravity that baffled Maci. By then Maci had other worries. Ever since Anna's trial, it had become fashionable to insult Mrs. Woodhull, and every day, all over the country, some editor would hop on the slander-cart and write an editorial that called her immoral for sheltering her broken-down former husband in her mansion. The most humiliating attacks came from Catharine Beecher who claimed that Mrs. Woodhull was the pinnacle of five thousand years of accumulating indecency, and from Beecher's sister Mrs. Stowe, who caricatured Mrs. Woodhull in the pages of *The Christian Union*. In Mrs. Stowe's frankly stupid serial novel, Victoria Woodhull was a carousing lady called Audacia Dangereyes, who owned a paper called *The Virago*, who swore and had multiple husbands, and in whose wake Free Love circulated like a stink.

"This will stop their fat mouths," Mrs. Woodhull said as she and Maci worked on a letter to the *Times*, a veiled threat to expose Henry Beecher as an adulterer. *Because I am a woman*, Maci wrote while Mrs. Woodhull stood with a hand resting on her shoulder, *and because I conscientiously hold opinions somewhat different from the self-elected orthodoxy which men find their pride in supporting, self-elected orthodoxy assails me, vilifies me, and endeavors to cover my life with ridicule and dishonor. This has been particularly the case in reference to certain law-proceedings into which I was recently drawn by the weakness of one very near, and provoked by other relatives.*

My opinions and principles are subjects of just criticism. I put myself before the public voluntarily. But let him who is without sin cast his stone. I do not intend to be the scapegoat of sacrifice, to be offered up as a victim to society by those who cover up the foulness and the feculence of their thought with hypocritical mouthing of fair professions, and who divert public attention from their own iniquity by pointing their finger at me. I advocate Free Love—in the highest and purest sense, as the only cure for the immorality by which men corrupt sexual relations.

My judges who preach against "Free Love" openly, practice it secretly. For example, I know of one man, a public teacher of eminence, who lives in concubinage with the wife of another public teacher of almost equal eminence. All three concur in denouncing offenses against morality. So be it, but I decline to stand up as the "frightful example." I shall make it my business to analyze some of these lives and will take my chances in the manner of libel suits.

Maci had delighted in the letter as she wrote it. But later, after it summoned Theodore Tilton from across the river, she regretted it. He came from Brooklyn to silence Mrs. Woodhull with pleas and promises and threats from Mr. Beecher. Tilton was supposed to convert her to silence, or cow her into respecting his and Mr. Beecher's secret. Instead, he fell in love with her.

Surely, Maci thought, love could not be more Free than this. Mrs. Woodhull suddenly quite forgot Colonel Blood, who in his turn blithely ignored her frequent outings with Mr. Tilton. Maci, however, could not ignore them. She felt compelled to follow the two as they went to the park to ride in pleasure-boats, to Coney Island to play in the surf, or to the top of the Croton Distributing Reservoir to walk around and around the promenade, with their heads close together, sheltered by Mrs. Woodhull's parasol from the sun but not from common view.

She wasn't the only person following them. The younger Dr. Woodhull and his ward also trailed after his mother and her intimate friend on their outings. They'd both remove their hats and bow to Maci, whenever she caught sight of them. But he never spoke to her until the day in June that would see Anna and Buck Claflin return to their daughter's house. That day, Maci had tracked Mrs. Woodhull and Mr. Tilton down to the corner of Fifth Avenue and Forty-second Street, and thence up to the top of the reservoir, where she paced them as they sauntered underneath a sky so deeply blue it was nearly purple. On such a lovely day, the reservoir was crowded. Mrs. Woodhull looked back every so often and nodded at Maci. She found Maci's fretting laughable and sweet.

"Miss Trufant," Dr. Woodhull said, startling her where she was standing at a corner of the reservoir, and nearly causing her to leap clear into the water.

"Dr. Woodhull," she said, overcome immediately with the familiar, panicked feeling.

"Did you know," he asked her excitedly, "that this reservoir holds twenty million gallons of water? And did you know that we are a full forty-one miles from Croton Lake? The water flows all that way! Have you seen the bridge and aqueduct over the Harlem River? It is a marvelous piece of engineering. But the great bridge to Brooklyn will be even finer." His face was flushed, and he was breathing as if he had just subjected himself to great exertion. She stared in his face for a moment, and he looked away, up into the air. His eyes were perfect mirrors of the dark blue sky.

"Is science your religion, Dr. Woodhull?"

"No," he said, shifting his gaze to his mother, who, standing a few hundred feet off with Mr. Tilton, had begun to walk again. Dr. Woodhull offered Maci his arm. Not taking it, she walked with him. "I do believe, however," he continued, "that science can change the world. I think it will make a better place for us to live in."

"My father thought so," said Maci. "He was wrong." They walked for a while, stopping again when Mrs. Woodhull stopped. Maci noticed the boy, Pickie, kneeling by the water, where other boys were racing toy sailboats.

"I think science is not your religion, Miss Trufant. But tell me what you do believe in."

Maci said nothing at first, thinking how her hand was always accusing her. *Sister*, it wrote, *you believe in nothing. That is the most debilitating of sins.*

Mrs. Woodhull's vigorous laugh came drifting to them. Maci's silence stretched on.

"Yesterday," said Dr. Woodhull, "my mother was described in a Philadelphia paper as 'The Dark Angel of Divorce.' "

"I believe," Maci said forcefully, "that all existence is crossed by sorrow." A little green sailboat came racing towards them across the water. All the boys were encouraging it, except little Pickie, who was sitting down on the ground now and crying. Maci went and knelt by him.

"What's the matter, little fellow?" she asked him.

"It's my brother," he wailed. "He is unborn!"

"He means he is lonely," Dr. Woodhull said behind her. "Be quiet, Pickie. Watch the boats. See how they are carefree? You should be like them."

"There now," Maci said, holding the boy close while he sobbed. She found herself admiring his long, lustrous brown hair. But then it brought to mind the dream of her mother, and she shuddered. "This boy needs his hair cut," she said.

Dr. Woodhull shrugged. Pickie stopped crying and returned Maci's embrace with such strength that she gasped.

"Mama!" Pickie said, then laughed.

"Forgive him," Dr. Woodhull said. "He hugs dogs, and calls them 'Mama.' Trees, too."

"Not my mama," Pickie said, "but my brother's mama." He broke away from her embrace and went back to watch the boats.

"He has a volatile temperament," Dr. Woodhull said apologetically. Maci looked all around for Mrs. Woodhull, but failed to find her.

"She's escaped me," Maci said.

"She's gone home," Dr. Woodhull said. "To prepare for the party."

"Which party is that?" Maci asked him, but he'd already walked off to retrieve Pickie. The two of them made a formal bow to her and walked into the crowds.

Maci would have liked not to celebrate the return of the nasty prodigals, but Mrs. Woodhull insisted that she participate in the groundless festivities. We ought to be mourning, Maci said to herself, and sat at the far end of Mrs. Woodhull's table, away from the revelry, working on an article that profiled and condemned Madame Restell. *She is seen every day*, she wrote, *a pale lady riding fast in her gorgeous carriage. Why does she drive so fast? Is she flying from herself?*

"Sweet, sweet forgiveness!" Anna Claflin shouted at the other end of the room. Engrossed in her work, Maci didn't notice how the old lady was sneaking up on her. She'd smeared her lips with honey, and meant to give Maci a sugar-kiss. Maci looked up too late to duck away. But young Dr. Woodhull's hand came between them before Anna's lips could connect with Maci's. Anna kissed his hand lovingly, then went back to the other end of the table. She took a knife and began to stab at Colonel Blood's shadow where the light threw it on a wall.

"Thank you," Maci said, watching Dr. Woodhull wipe honey from his palm. Marking his deficit, she stared too long.

"My eighty-percent hand," he said.

"I am rude," she said. "Please forgive me."

"There's nothing to forgive."

"Was it an animal? Did an animal bite you?"

"A congenital deformity," he said. "You'll notice that I share it with my grandmother. But won't you come down and celebrate, Miss Trufant?"

"I prefer not to," she said. "In fact, I am sleepy. Good night, Dr. Woodhull." She gathered up her papers, shook his hand—the whole one—and went upstairs to her room. By the time she came to her room she'd become so weary that she lay on her bed without undressing and fell immediately into a dream, in which she and Dr. Woodhull were back at the reservoir, sitting with their bare feet dangling in the water. He had an abundance of hair on his toes.

"Do you believe in love, Miss Trufant?" he asked her. "Do you believe it is more than a gratifying delusion?"

"Free Love?" she asked.

"Any kind," he said.

"Well," she said, getting up from where they were sitting and walking away rapidly on her wet feet, suddenly remembering that she had to find Mrs. Woodhull. "In fact I do not," she said softly. Dr. Woodhull had hurried after her and was walking with his face very close to her own. "I do not believe in it at all." Mrs. Woodhull dropped down out of the sky to land in front of them without a sound. Maci reached out and touched her face, and woke to her voice.

Mrs. Woodhull and Mr. Tilton were on the roof. They had a bower there, to which they retreated nightly. Mrs. Woodhull was berating Mr. Tilton for going on about how his wife and Mr. Beecher had wounded him. They began a spirited argument, but just as they seemed ready to start screaming like Claflins, their voices cut off, and presently Maci heard Mrs. Woodhull crying out in a high voice, and Tilton shouting, "Praise, praise!"

Maci had gotten into the habit of listening, rather than closing her window, just as she listened sometimes at Tennie's door when she was entertaining her large friend Dr. Fie, or some other friend, large or small. Tennie seemed to take them in all sizes. Maci pretended that she was exploring a mystery with her shameful listening. She'd write down the words she heard, the cries that sounded plaintive, frustrated, angry, relieved, and then arrange them together in sentences of strident lust. And, sometimes, when she had been lying in her damp sheets for an hour listening to the lovers on the roof, she'd consider finally taking a ride on the pony, which Tennie had solicitously moved into her room, insisting that Maci had greater need of it than she did. Maci had sat on it once, the little bump put just in the place it was meant to go, and taken a few exploratory rocks. She'd dismounted immediately, covering the thing up again with its slip of silk, and then with two wool blankets on top of that, to hide it completely. She never got on it again, but on the hottest nights, when she could hear the lovers so very loud on the roof, she thought of riding the pony to a strange, new place, with her book open in her hand, reading aloud as she went.

Is it because Adam sinned to keep company with Eve? Is it because intelligence can only become perfect through suffering, as the earth can only reach a perfect state through storms as well as sunshine, and the soul can only reach a perfect state through storms of sorrow and despair? No, I think it is for no reason, or, at the least, for no good reason. I do not believe that we are hallowed by sadness. I do not believe it is sufficient answer, to say we are justly punished by death, or to say that we die because we die.

Maci kept busy, all through the summer of 1871, organizing Victoria Leagues. They were Maci's own idea, associations, formed all over the country, whose purpose would be to promote Mrs. Woodhull's bid for the Presidency. Maci recruited members from out of Mrs. Woodhull's parlor parties, from subscribers to the paper, and from brokerage clients. And, sitting at a table in the third-floor study, she wrote an anonymous open letter to Mrs. Woodhull, care of the *Weekly*.

Madam, a number of your fellow citizens, both men and women, have formed themselves into a working committee, borrowing its title from your name, and calling itself The Victoria League. Our object is to form a new national political organization, composed of the progressive elements in the existing Democratic and Republican parties, together with the Women of the Republic, who have hitherto been disenfranchised, but to whom the Fourteenth and Fifteenth Amendments of the Constitution, properly interpreted, guarantee, equally with men, the right of suffrage. This new Political organization will be called The Equal Rights Party, and its platform will consist solely and only of a declaration of the equal civil and political rights of all American citizens, without distinction of sex. We shall urge all women who possess the political qualifications of other citizens, in the respective States in which they reside, to assume and exercise the right of suffrage without hesitation or delay. And we ask you, Madam, to become the standard bearer of this idea before the people, and for this purpose nominate you as our candidate for President of the United States, to be voted for in 1872, by the combined suffrage of both sexes.

Across the table from her, Mrs. Woodhull wrote back a long, elegant, and somewhat demure letter of acceptance.

Maci had by this time understood completely that nothing would come of Mr. Tilton's association with her employer except the fatuous biography he had written, a fawning, spineless thing that damned Mrs. Woodhull with abundant praise. It was widely mocked because it detailed all Mrs. Woodhull's spiritual transactions, telling how Demosthenes was her mentor, how Josephine was her spirit sister, how all Mrs. Woodhull's utterances were dictated under otherworldly influence.

Not concerned anymore about Mr. Tilton, Maci exercised her organ of worry on Mrs. Woodhull's Communist enthusiasm. Mrs. Woodhull had thrown herself into the leadership of Section Twelve of the International Workingmen's Association, not caring if she was lumped together with the Paris revolutionaries, who were widely regarded as repulsive monsters. Maci reminded Mrs. Woodhull repeatedly that no one but a Communist likes a Communist. It was to no avail.

In August, just when she was afloat on a tide of hot, Communist distress, Maci received an invitation from Dr. Woodhull. *We must discuss my mother's situation*, he wrote to her. *We are not alike, she and I, but I have always known that she will achieve great things, if she is not brought down by her wilder sympathies. Come and meet with me at my house, No. One E. 53rd St.*

Mrs. Woodhull's house was very noisy, so Maci was glad to leave it for a while. Because Tennie was campaigning for a spot in the New York State assembly, the house was full of prospective German constituents, who in the weeks previous had serenaded Tennie outside her window. Now they played their brass instruments inside the house, and there was nowhere a person could escape the splattering music, which was silly as Tennie was silly, and as her lighthearted, completely unserious campaign was silly. Maci went out into the dreadful heat without even telling anybody goodbye.

The younger Dr. Woodhull lived way up towards the park, where enormous houses were popping up with ever greater frequency. Maci's hair was hanging wet and stinging in her eyes when she rang the bell, but when the door opened she shivered in the rush of cool air that poured out onto the marble steps. Dr. Woodhull stood in front of her with a pair of ice skates in his hands.

"You've come!" he said. "I wasn't sure you would."

"It was serious business in your letter."

"The letter!" he said. "Come in and we'll speak of it. Mind your way." Maci slipped when she stepped into his unnaturally cool house, but he caught her arm and held her up. "That meeting has been canceled, after all," he said. "It has been postponed in favor of a skating party."

Maci might have reminded him it was August, except she could already see how the floor was covered with ice.

"I thought it might please you," he said, "because it is so hot, and because you are from Boston. Don't they all love to ice-skate in Boston? Come and skate with me, Miss Trufant. The ball is up. It's a private pond. Nobody will disturb us."

"You have deceived me," Maci whispered. It occurred to her that she should be angry at him for drawing her into his house with false pretenses, but she was wonderstruck at the ice, and it was all she could think about. "How did you do it?" she asked.

He tried to explain about the copper pipes under the ice, and how liquid ammonia, as it expanded to a gas, could steal heat from water. "It's really very simple. It's how they make ice in the factories."

The drapes were drawn all over the house. She could see very little besides large, dark shapes that leaned in the corners. Maci thought they might be furniture. She and Dr. Woodhull glided from room to room, through open doors into a dim parlor where a hundred mirrors reflected her shadowy, floating image, into a dining room where the table was pushed on its side against the wall, and where Maci caught her skate on a frozen apple. They didn't talk, except when Dr. Woodhull pointed out an obstacle. She collided with him repeatedly. Even when they stopped to rest, standing in a wide, blank room whose purpose, before it became a skating pond, Maci could not figure, she drifted towards him and collided with him softly. "Excuse me!" she said, backing away.

"It's the floor," he said. "It slants."

On her third pass through the mirror-parlor she skated closer to a large shape to investigate it. It was partly sunk in the ice. When she got right up by it she could see that it was a giant gear, like what might turn a house-sized clock.

"What is this?" she asked. "Why do you have this?" Dr. Woodhull was not in the room to answer her question, though he'd been skating at her side just moments before. She went looking for him, thinking she might have dreamed this already—searching for him in a dark, cold house, floating like a ghost—but knowing that she hadn't because this was stranger and suddenly more terrible than any dream she'd had. She wandered through his house, tottering awkwardly, once upstairs, with the skates still strapped to her shoes, going from room to room, discovering old furniture, tall stacks of moldering books, and everywhere gears and rods and pieces of shaped glass, machine-spoor the sight of which made her stomach twist up in a knot. With the sense that she was wandering at her own peril she went up and up, compelled to open every door until she reached the top floor. She stood in the abandoned conservatory, and made the mistake of leaning against a withered potted tree, which tipped and fell, and broke in half when it struck the floor. She hurried clumsily from that room, and went through the only other door on the hall. Then she was in Dr. Woodhull's bedroom, where she found him sitting quietly on his bed.

"Why are you crying, Miss Trufant?" he asked her, after he'd thrown open the other iron door and brought her in to see the sprawling thing he kept behind it.

"It is too, too much, Dr. Woodhull," she said. "Too, too much." Because it really was too much, for such a thing to happen once, and too, too much for it to happen twice, for her brother to introduce her again to an unsuitable boy, and for somebody else's life to be wasted in the construction of an impossible and useless machine. It was clear to her then that she should sit on the bed and calmly remove her skates, then run frantically out of the room, down the stairs, and out of the house. She ought to run right back to Boston, because she would proclaim herself an irredeemable fool if she stayed and ignored the lessons of her ridiculous life. *Dear Aunt Amy*, she wrote in her mind as she stood there, *Here I come!* But she didn't go anywhere except deeper into the room, following her left hand as it yearned towards the machine, closing in a fist around a hot section of pipe. Something beat through it like blood.

"Do you like it?" he asked her.

"I despise it," she said, but her hand would not come free, and she feared, in that moment, that it never would.

3

YOUNG DR. WOODHULL INVITED MACI TO AN INDUSTRIAL EXPOsition in September of 1871. She went, though it was obvious to her that there was nothing she should like less than a festival of machines. Tennie rushed to accompany them when she learned Mr. Whitman was to be seen and heard. As they stood together in the little crowd at the Cooper Institute, listening to Mr. Whitman read a poem, Maci thought she understood why the poet and Dr. Woodhull were friends. Mr. Whitman was another engine-lover. He'd even imagined a muse for their new mechanical age, a dame of dames who would supersede Clio and her sisters. How she must clank when she moves, Maci thought, and stink of oil and coal smoke.

Mr. Whitman, with his big gray beard, reminded Maci of her father, though her father had the voice of a man used to giving sermons, and Mr. Whitman squeaked his poem like a mouse. On the stage, the poet waved his thick arms in broad, warm gestures of invitation, and spoke:

"I say I see, my friends, if you do not, the illustrious émigré.
Making directly for this rendezvous, vigorously clearing a path
for herself, striding through the confusion,
By thud of machinery and shrill steam-whistle undismay'd,
Bluff'd not a bit by drain-pipe, gasometers, artificial fertilizers,
Smiling and pleas'd with palpable intent to stay,
She's here, install'd amid the kitchen ware!"

It went on and on, as laborers abandoned the work of putting up the exhibits and came over to listen. Maci liked it much less than the poems she'd read as a girl. It's Gob Woodhull, Maci thought, whose acquaintance makes people less than they were. He's poisoned Mr. Whitman's muse, altered her so smoke pours out of her ears and she leaves wet oily spots wherever she sits. Gob, Gob, Gob, she'd say to herself sometimes, thinking how it sounded like the noise made by irritable intestines. She would have preferred not to think of him or his machine, but despite those wishes she spent many hours in consideration of both.

"I cannot," she had replied, when, standing in front of his machine, he had asked her to help him complete it. She had laughed in his face when he told her his ambitions for the thing, when he claimed it would abolish death. She thought he would cry, and this pleased her during those furious, confused moments after she was introduced to his secret. But the laugh was directed at her own life, and not at him. She hadn't meant to be cruel. With her left hand still fastened to the pipe, she considered that she might be able to help him, after all, though not in the way he suspected. Here at last was not only punishment, but penance suitable for Infanticide: she might save Dr. Woodhull from his delusion, and show him how the complicated assemblage that he revered was only a pile of stuff.

Maci went among the industrial exhibits arm in arm with Tennie, while Dr. Woodhull and Mr. Whitman walked ahead of them. "See how he goes like a bear?" Tennie asked her. "But he is as gentle as a deer."

"Gentler, I think," Maci said, because Mr. Whitman seemed to her eminently gentle and sad, not at all the stomping, shouting fellow suggested by the poems for which she'd suffered a beating so many years before. "As gentle as a plant," Maci said, as they passed into a stand of rubber furniture.

"It's not bouncy," Tennie said, sitting down in a hard, ornate chair. "Still, I like it very much. It's just the sort of thing I'd like to have in my corner." She refused to walk any farther. Maci left her there, amid a crowd of workmen who'd been drawn to her as if by a scent. Walking on, Maci overtook Mr. Whitman, who'd paused, and seemed to be admiring Dr. Woodhull as Dr. Woodhull admired a candy vat.

"I think science is his religion," Maci said.

Mr. Whitman turned to her and looked earnestly into her eyes. It was rare for Maci to be unable to meet a gaze, but she found herself compelled to look elsewhere. She considered how Mr. Whitman's shirt, open at the neck, allowed white hair to curl out at her.

"What is *your* religion, Miss Trufant?"

"The religion," Maci said, "of earthly reform."

"I think you made that up just now. One day this spot will be holy. 'Here Miss Trufant founded the religion of earthly reform!' " He laughed, and Maci found herself laughing with him.

"Very well, Mr. Whitman. Let me clarify. I do not hope for Heaven, except as we can approximate it on earth. I am not religious."

"Your life must gape like a hole," he said. Maci thought this a harsh accusation to make to a practical stranger. Yet he laughed again.

Dr. Woodhull had turned his attention to a mechanical thresher, and was touching it affectionately. Maci said, "I say science is his religion because I think he is overfond of machines. Don't you think it is possible to be overfond of machines?"

Mr. Whitman said nothing for a moment. Thinking he might be a little deaf, Maci was about to repeat her question when he spoke. "Has he shown you his . . . thing?" he asked.

"You mean his engine? He has. I think I must have been the last person in the world still ignorant of its existence." *Now it can be told!* her hand had written, when she went home that night in August, and had proceeded to bore her with the particulars of its construction. Maci discovered, in the next few days, that every Claflin knew about the engine, though none of them would talk much about it. Tennie would only say that she thought it was wonderful and sad.

Mrs. Woodhull said it was her son's work to build, as it was her own work to reform. Even Dr. Fie knew about the thing. Indeed, he was assisting in its assembly.

"Then you are not fond of it, Miss Trufant?"

"It is a functionless machine. It is, as you say, a thing, and not to be liked or disliked." Maci was tired, suddenly, of engine-talk, and decided to alter the course of their conversation. "But I did like your poem," she said, though she hadn't really.

"Then you should take it." He held out his copy to her, folded up to a square the size of his palm.

"Oh, I couldn't," she said. "I certainly couldn't. I'll get a copy from out of the papers tomorrow."

"No, please," he said, his voice rising. He angled his head to meet her eyes again, his stare rude and intense. "I want you to take this, too." He reached for her with the paper, pressing it against her hand, then letting it go.

It fell to the ground. Dr. Woodhull, returned from his close examination of the thresher, picked it up and presented it to her silently. "Walt," he said, "come and see the sewing machines!" He ran off, scampering like his boy, Pickie. Mr. Whitman followed him, and Maci looked down at the dirty old piece of paper he'd made a gift to her. It was full of writing, front and back, used and used again until every inch was covered with ink. She unfolded it and brought it up close to her face to read the poet's script. On the front was the poem, on the back, a list: *John Watson (bed 29), get some apples; Llewellyn Woodin (bed 14), sore throat, wants some candy; bed 14 wants an orange.*

Dear Aunt Amy, Maci wrote in another unsent letter. *I am doing well here in New York, proceeding sensibly from day to day and living a good honest life. I know, Aunt, that you worry about me, and that to your casually observing distant eye it may seem that my urge towards free thinking has plumped into actual vice, and that I am engaged in foolish, scandalous, even dangerous behavior. Let me reassure you that this is, in fact, not the case.*

He is a magus, her left hand wrote, creeping over with an extra pen to crowd her right hand off the paper. *And though he is small, his hips are handsome.* She pushed the hand away.

Yes, I associate with him. Yes, I am alone with him in his house. Yes, we are awake till very late in the evening. We discuss science and mortality and politics. He has got a keen interest in his mother, for all that he pretends indifference. He hates her, I think, because she is not like him, because she does not spend her whole life stretched on the grave of his dead brother. She works in the world to change the world, while he cloisters himself in a decaying mansion and wastes his obvious talents making his grief for his brother manifest in iron and glass and copper. I tell him as much, and he says, "I like how you are honest with me, Miss Trufant."

I cannot make you believe in his work, but he can make you believe in his work. You believe in his mama as she changes what can't be changed, why can't you do him the same favor?

How comforting it would be, Maci wrote to Aunt Amy, *to believe that the whole war happened for reasons more cosmic than political, to believe that all the war's deaths could be undone, that Rob and all the others died only so they could come back to us. But Aunt, comfort is a clue to falseness, and the ease of a thing can make it not so.*

Sister, you don't believe in anything good.

"I will create a distraction," Mrs. Woodhull told Maci, "while you do the deed." They had a plan to cast a vote in the November elections of 1871. A whole contingent of women, accompanied by a few male reporters, marched down from Thirty-eighth Street to the polling place for the twenty-third district of the twenty-first ward, a furniture store on Sixth Avenue. While Mrs. Woodhull, with Tennie by her side, made what came to be known as her "Rats and Spiders" speech, Maci made a lunge for the ballot box. Her shooting hand felt to her like a bullet, and she suspected it would kill any man who got between her and the vote that day. But the attendant—a Tammany thugee, Maci was sure—slapped her hand down, scattering her tickets whole feet from the box.

Maci thought, later, that if she'd only had both hands functioning at the time of her attack on the ballot box, she might have performed some dexterous switcheroo to confuse and defeat her adversary. But for weeks her left hand had been immobilized in a split and wrapped in thick white bandages. The senior Dr. Woodhull had indulged her when she claimed to have sprained it. "What injury there is, is not severe," he said, turning her hand over in his skeleton claw. But he did as she asked. "Please," she said, "would you bind it up a little more? The bandages are a comfort." Three times he tried to stop when her hand was still not sufficiently wrapped, but she urged him on. She liked to put the hand on the desk, next to the paper and the pen. It would flop and twitch. "Is there something you wanted to tell me?" she'd ask it.

"Next year, my star," Mrs. Woodhull told Maci, after her failure, "I know we will succeed." Mrs. Woodhull led the voting party back to her house, where she fed and liquored everyone while they waited for news of the returns. Maci sat by herself on a bench secluded by ferns. A reporter found her there.

"What have you got to do with all this?" he demanded. Maci decided to lie to him.

"My mother," she said, "is a leader in the woman suffrage movement. I may not tell you her name—suffice to say that she is a member of the Boston Coven. Do you understand my meaning? What I am saying is that she may be Lucy Stone, or she may not! Anyhow, Mother is a great and secret admirer of Mrs. Woodhull. She has called her an apotheosis and the Jean d'Arc of Woman Suffrage. Yet publicly she excoriates Mrs. Woodhull for her social theories, even as she embraces them in her private behavior. Is this fair, sir? I think it is not, yet family loyalties keep me from speaking out. I know only too well how blood is thicker than water."

"Are you an admirer of Mrs. Woodhull, then?"

"Is the sun a round ball of fire?" She asked him for a glass of water, hoping to sneak away while he fetched it, but he returned in an instant with champagne for her and whiskey for himself. He interpreted Maci's exasperated sigh as an invitation to sit next to her. It was Tennie's fault that the male reporters of New York expected a kiss from any lady who resided at Number 15 East Thirty-eighth Street, because Tennie was always drawing them aside for kisses.

"Clark is one hundred to Bradley's sixty-five," the man said.

Maci thought, Next he will ask me to show him my ankles. Two times before, reporters had asked her that, thinking she was Tennie. Once, on a whim, Maci had obliged, but she could not master Tennie's maneuver, a standing skip and hop that flashed the ankles so briefly men were left wondering if they had been revealed at all. Maci had merely lifted her hem. The reporters had gone away from her disappointed, and, she thought, a little embarrassed for her.

"I'll dash your hopes," Maci said.

"Pardon?"

"A dash of hope. Perhaps Tammany is doomed, after all."

"How did you injure your hand?"

"It's a casualty of our war. I bruised it assaulting the walls that imprison my sex."

"Let me kiss it, then. To speed the recovery."

"Please do not," Maci said, but he was already bending toward her big white mitt, which twitched and knocked him in the nose. He straightened up with his hand over his face.

"You are hard, Miss Stone," he said, walking off, and not bringing her any more returns.

"If I let you out," Maci asked her hand, "will you behave?" If it gave any sort of answer, Maci missed it, distracted by abrupt cheers that broke out all over the house. News had come from Rochester that Susan B. Anthony had successfully cast a ballot.

Until January of 1872, Mrs. Woodhull always had just as many New Year's visitors as were due a lady who was famous, beautiful, daring, and consistently more interesting than anyone else, male or female, in a city full of daily distractions and ever-hatching novelty. The previous year, Maci had barely been able to walk through the house because it was so crowded. But now no one came to eat from tables set in magnificent style, to drink the brandy and whiskey and lemonade and punch. Mrs. Woodhull seemed to have driven away all her friends with the lecture she'd given two months before at Steinway Hall, or all except Mr. Andrews (who could never be shocked or out-radicaled by anyone, even Mrs. Woodhull). Maci, sitting down next to Mrs. Woodhull and listening to clocks ticking all over the quiet house, thought back to that wet, disagreeable night in November.

"Yes, I am a Free Lover!" Mrs. Woodhull had exclaimed. She hadn't been supposed to say that. It was an unfortunate departure from the text Maci had written, a reasonable discourse on social contracts which meant to demonstrate that freedom in the social sphere was no less desirable, and no more immoral, than freedom in the political and religious spheres. Mrs. Woodhull departed from the text after her sister, drunken, despicable Utica, heckled her from a box where she leaned against her escort, a man in green spectacles who hissed like a furious kitty all during the lecture. Hissing and boos came like that from the smaller part of the audience. Mrs. Woodhull ignored them. But when Utica stood up and demanded to know how Mrs. Woodhull would like it if she was a bastard, then asked if she was a damned Free Lover, she stirred her sister's passion. Mrs. Woodhull got such an awful and majestic look on her face that the first five rows fell absolutely silent. Just with her gaze, Mrs.

Woodhull seemed to fling Utica back into the recesses of her box. Then she spoke some words which delighted the reporters, but distressed Maci.

"I have," Mrs. Woodhull said, loud and clear, "an inalienable, constitutional, and natural right to love whom I may, to love as long or as short a period as I can; to change that love every day if I please, and with that right neither you nor any law you can frame has any right to interfere. And I have the further right to demand a free and unrestricted access of that right, and it is your duty not only to accord it, but, as a community, to see that I am protected in it. I trust that I am fully understood, for I mean just that, and nothing less!"

For the party, a New Year's hair artiste had given Maci an enormous hairdo to match Tennie's and Mrs. Woodhull's. It made her head feel very large, and gave her the shadow of a monster. Maci stared at her hands where they lay folded in her lap. She'd freed her left hand two weeks before. It seemed a little shriveled up now from disuse, though it was vigorous as ever, if more polite, when it wielded a pen.

"Was that the door?" Mrs. Woodhull would ask, every so often.

"No," Tennie would say. Colonel Blood and the senior Dr. Woodhull were playing chess. Once in a while, Canning Woodhull would bemoan a loss, but otherwise it remained silent. Maci almost wished she hadn't arranged for all the noisemaking Claflins to be sent away for the day. She went often to the window, where she could see little crowds of people passing from house to house, some of them already drunk on whiskey and punch, stumbling on the ice. Many passed by, but none stopped.

Maci had quite given up hope of there being any callers at all when the bell finally rang. Mrs. Woodhull leaped up and shouted for a servant to open the door. But it was only Gob Woodhull, with little Pickie in tow. Dr. Fie was not with him. Maci was certain he must be back at the house on Fifth Avenue, building on the machine. Was it noble to share your friend's delusion, or merely foolish? Maci didn't know. Dr. Fie was sullen and grim, very much the opposite of Tennie, yet Maci was sure those two would have married if Tennie had not considered marriage a terrible sin.

Mrs. Woodhull's son was not surprised at the empty house. "You have frightened people away from you," he said. "The timid and the hypocritical, who do not understand how your notions are refined, indict you with your own words. You ought not to have strayed from your text." It was a sign, Maci thought, that he was concerned for his mother, that he scolded her for being too bold. It was Maci's aim to make him an ally in his mother's cause, and to lessen the distance that seemed to stretch between the two of them. She'd imagined a scene between them, in which, fully reconciled and truly loving, they embraced, and in which Mrs. Woodhull would say, "Come into the world. There is so much work for us to do, here."

"Oh, you are like a croaking bird, with that refrain!" said Mrs. Woodhull to her son. But Maci, too, had been telling her all month how she had made a mistake at Steinway Hall. And Maci had been telling her, also, that she should not have marched at the head of the December parade protesting the execution of M. Rossel, one of the Paris Communards. Mrs. Woodhull had walked behind a black-draped coffin, while Maci and Tennie had followed carrying a banner that read, *Complete Social and Political Equality for Both Sexes*.

It was the most self-evident of facts, that there was no profit in associating with Communists. Maci knew that, and yet she had marched anyhow with Mrs. Woodhull, because she couldn't refuse her anything. Maci had been constantly afraid that they would spark a riot, that by evening bodies would be piled on all the corners of Manhattan, and the city would be in flames. But the march had wreaked a different sort of havoc—the two sisters' participation alienated Commodore Vanderbilt. Free Love excited him, Spiritualism comforted him, but Communism was anathema to him. Tennie announced one morning a few days after the march that he wouldn't see her anymore. "I knew it would happen," she told Maci. "But oh, it still hurts!"

At her guestless party, Mrs. Woodhull shook her head at her son, then went to sit down between her two husbands, who had given up their chess game and retired to a sofa. "It's a hot January for us, isn't it?" she said. "Well, I am inclined to make it hot for somebody else." It had become a reflex with her, to threaten Henry Beecher whenever her fortunes dipped. She'd come to blame him for most of her troubles, though, as far as Maci could tell, he hadn't actually done anything to hurt her. It was Mrs. Stowe and Catharine Beecher who wanted to destroy her. Mr. Beecher had, in fact, made an attempt to rein his sisters in, but, frenzied with hypocrisy and vituper, they would not be silenced.

"We have the fixings already for a celebration," Gob Woodhull said brightly, closing the curtains and hiding the stream of visitors passing the house by. "And today happens to be Pickie's birthday. What shall we do?"

"It's not my birthday," said Pickie.

"Certainly it is. I found you on this day one year ago. My boy, you are one year old today!"

"It is not my birthday, and it is not my brother's birthday," the boy insisted. Nonetheless, he had a happy party, eating his fill of white cake and red punch. The house became as joyful and carefree as it had previously been sad and nervous. Mrs. Woodhull seemed to forget that Mrs. Grundy had brought a fist down upon her that day. Standing on a chair, she proclaimed how 1872, the year of her predestined election to the Presidency of the United States, would be the greatest year of her life, and the greatest year of all their lives. "This is *my* year!" Mrs. Woodhull said.

She took Maci aside to confide in her. "My star," she said. "I know it looks dark now, but don't give up hope. We'll bounce back, and bounce higher than anybody expects. I've never told you this. I've been waiting, and now I am inspired, in this dark hour, to give you the news I've been husbanding. I mean to give you a cabinet post, if I arrive in Washington in my destined capacity."

Maci was flustered. She didn't think at all how it was almost impossible that Mrs. Woodhull would be elected, or even get very many votes. All she felt was honored, but this soon passed as Mrs. Woodhull distributed promises like party favors. Everybody was a future secretary. Colonel Blood would be Secretary of War, her son the Secretary of Building, and Tennie C. Claflin would be Secretary of the newly established Department of Good Times, from which she would dole out budgets of fun to every despondent citizen.

Maci's hand drew a picture of Gob Woodhull, a life-sized masterpiece of foreshortening—if she squinted at it she almost believed that his hand, detailed down to the split nails, was reaching out of the paper. She'd lie back and consider the picture, wondering if he and Private Vanderbilt would quarrel if she put them side by side on the wall. Little Dr. Woodhull was stronger than he looked—she'd seen him lift boilerplate as if it were china plate. Her hand attributed that strength to what it called a demispiritual nature, but it was Maci's belief that the strength of his obsession found its way into his muscles and bones. How many times had her mother lifted up her bedstead in search of a stray bean?

Maci found she could complain to the picture as she could complain to nobody else. Mrs. Woodhull, Tennie, her hand—these all talked back. They all tried to convince her that sanity was unreasonable, but Gob Woodhull's picture never did that. He smiled, he held out his hand, and that was all. "Isn't it a burden?" she said to him. "Isn't it unfair, how I am afflicted with lunacy from the outside and the inside?"

Here are his hands, her own hand wrote on them as it drew, *to touch you. Here are his eyes to see you. Here is his mouth to speak you.* Tattooed with this primer, he was not clean. *Here is his heart, to love you.* Maci groaned and looked away when her hand wrote this last thing, fearing it would draw his heart popping out of his chest, as in those gruesome Catholic icons. But her hand only drew a black shadow in his breast.

"Tell me," he'd ask her, whenever she visited at his house. He'd say it both playfully and plaintively. "I know you can tell me." He remained convinced that she could help him build up his folly. Maci suggested that a bit of raw iron might be decorated with blue or yellow paint, or suggested arbitrary revisions: "Shouldn't these three inches of wire be gold, and not silver?" He seemed not to realize that she was mocking him. They were playing like children, piling up stuff into a heap of nonsense. It gave her a wicked sort of pleasure, to think how it was all a waste, and to think how it would gratify her when the giant apparatus failed at everything but being a giant apparatus. But sometimes it made Maci sad, for his sake, to think how he would fail. And, most rarely, she'd think it would be wonderful if this thing could cough out the dead, after all, if even one dead soul could be born again out of its chimney-stack. She even tried to believe this, closing her eyes and straining to see the triumphant spirit of her brother being born back into flesh. But, try as she might, all she could see was darkness.

"Oh, sir," she said to his picture. "You refine my sense of the ridiculous and the tragic."

Maci went with Gob Woodhull down to the foot of Roosevelt Street, where the New York tower of the great bridge was going up. Across the river, the Brooklyn tower was already one hundred feet high.

"Isn't it beautiful?" he asked her. They were there on an errand. Mrs. Woodhull had asked Maci to write an article for the March 8 issue of the *Weekly* on the progress of the bridge, with an eye to uncover any corruption in its financing that might yet be lingering despite Mr. Tweed's downfall. Dr. Woodhull had offered to escort her, as the bridge was understandably fascinating to him. He had friends there, and could get her into the bowels of the construction. They walked onto the top of the rising tower, among the workmen with their wheelbarrows, hods, picks, and shovels. Dr. Woodhull put his arms out towards a huge steam crane lifting stone off a barge at the side of the dock, and Maci got the impression that if only his arms had been long enough, he might embrace it lovingly.

"Are you ready to go down?" he asked her, after they had been introduced to their escort, a man named Farrington who was so efficient he shook Maci's and Dr. Woodhull's hands simultaneously. He had them put on ankle-high rubber boots.

"Of course," she said. Dr. Woodhull had offered to go down alone and give her a report, if the thought of doing it herself was too frightening. She went first down the ladder. They were crowded together in a little room lit from above by glass in the iron ceiling.

"This is the air-lock," said Mr. Farrington. "You'll be uncomfortable, soon," he added bluntly, "but do as I do and you'll come out all right." Outside a worker was tightening down the roof, and when he was done Mr. Farrington put his hands over his ears. Maci copied his motion too late to block out the piercing shriek that filled the room. "Just the air coming in!" Mr. Farrington shouted.

"A curious sensation!" Maci said, because her head felt as if it were sinking underwater. The sensation was curious, then painful—the pressure felt as if it would crush up her head to the size of her fist. Dr. Woodhull showed her how to relieve the pressure by pinching her nose and trying to sneeze. The sound stopped, all of a sudden, and a hatch in the floor dropped open. The feeling of disagreeable heaviness in Maci's head had not passed altogether, and as she went down another ladder into the caisson she felt dizzy and a little breathless. Her pulse was racing in her ears, and when she spoke her voice sounded unnatural. Dr. Woodhull's voice was high as a child's when he spoke. "Are you well?" he asked.

"I'm well," she said. "Are *you* well? I fear you may be too delicate for this place!" She turned away from him to look around at the room into which they'd descended. Her first impression was of flame and shadows and a great noise that managed somehow to sound very loud and very distant; hammers and drills striking rock. Half-naked men were walking everywhere in the steaming light between shadows, and breaking rocks. It looked very much the way Maci expected Hell to look.

They started their tour, Maci walking carefully along planks that ran across the sucking mud, but giving up in seconds on ever rehabilitating her dress. Mr. Farrington explained how there were five other chambers like this one. "We are seventy feet below the river surface," he said. "And even now, as the men clear away more rock and mud, we are descending ever deeper." When they came to a wall he pointed at the boilerplate that covered the whole interior and told how it had been installed as a precaution against fire, which had nearly destroyed the caisson on the other side of the river.

"Fascinating!" Maci said, but she wanted to leave, and she wished the tour would end. She had gathered all the information she needed in the first moments, and she felt confident that she could convey to the readers of the *Weekly* a sense of the hot, close horror of the place. Mr. Farrington was called away. He left them standing under a blinding calcium light.

"Do you like it down here?" Dr. Woodhull asked her.

"It's charming," she said. Then she cried out because she got a pain in her ears as if someone had poked them each with an awl, and the pain distracted her from the great blast of air that almost knocked her into the mud. The lights were all extinguished. The workmen were groaning and cursing. She heard Mr. Farrington shouting for them to mind their language for the sake of the lady journalist.

"It's just a blowout," said Dr. Woodhull, explaining how the edge of the caisson, because it hadn't sunk far enough into the ground, was prone to lift a little as the tide shifted, sending a burst of air out into the river. "The lights will be out momentarily," he said. "But all's well."

"No," she said. "No, I think that all's less than well." They were knee deep in water so cold it hurt her bones, and she was sure the water was rising. "I think we are going to die."

"Nonsense," he said. "You will never die, Miss Trufant." Her eyes were opened as wide as they'd ever been in her whole life. They were opened so wide they were burning and tearing, so she thought she should have seen him coming closer to her. But she didn't know he was there until he'd already pressed his lips against hers. What was he doing? Was she one of those Portuguese ladies who when left alone with a man are mortally offended if he does not at least try to be grossly familiar with their person? The thought flashed in her mind that she should scream and push him away. Bright as lightning, it flashed in her eyes, but it passed in an instant, and then the darkness, which somehow was sweet now, returned. Maci grabbed at his lips with her own. Grab grab grab, she thought. Gob Gob Gob. She knocked a tooth against his.

> We are motivated strictly by love or by fear, and it is better to go the way that love pushes you, than the other way. I think I climbed off the earth on that thought, the way the pious dying climb off on a prayer. You, with your rich vocabulary of motivation, will find this a silly, simple idea. But isn't it rightly said of the dead, that they are wise? I'll give you this advice, and plead with you to accept it: let him enter you and obsess you, as I have entered and obsessed you.

"Spiritualists are all so serious," Maci said to Gob, as they took another turn on top of the Distributing Reservoir. "There are trance-speakers, trance-healers, trance-levitators. But why are there no trance-comedians?"

"There's no humor in death," Gob said.

"Isn't there? I giggled at my mother's funeral. To any observer it seemed a sob, but I know what it was. Hideous, perverse giggling, because my mother died of bean-love. I thought of them spilling from her mouth even as she lay in her coffin, and I felt I'd have to laugh, or else die myself right there."

"A terrible story, Miss Maci."

"Yes. But don't you believe, Dr. Gob, that a person ought to be able to laugh at death? I think that's how we bring him down."

"Did your mother come out of her grave, when you laughed at her?"

"Of course she didn't. You deliberately misunderstand me."

"I understand you very well," he said, slipping his arm into hers. An urge to pull away flailed and died in her, then she leaned against him.

"What a ridiculous assertion," she said, though just that morning she'd stood in her room with all the curtains flung open, and the lights turned up to a blaze, looking in the mirror and examining herself in the flood of light. She turned her head and brought her eye almost close enough to touch the glass, peering into her own pupil because she was sure that if only her vision could penetrate through the tiny black hole, she'd see him there, sitting comfortably inside her head. "Get out," she'd whispered. They'd shared one deep breath—in and out—down in the caisson, and Maci was sure he'd put something in her, a part of himself that inspired in her a relentless desire to be near him. She liked to think that another woman had come out of the air-lock that day, one who hurried out before she could get kissed, one who went on without need of this strange person, who went on with a life not afflicted anymore with ghosts and rebel hands and machines. Every day that passed after the kiss, Maci made sure to set aside a little time to be happy for that girl.

"There is a secret world, Miss Maci," Gob Woodhull said, taking her to lean over the edge of the water. "Hidden in plain view of this one, it is invisible to people who truly believe that hurling giggles at death will ameliorate mortality. It is full of grieving people and grieving spirits. See? Here are two citizens of that world." He nodded his head at their reflections.

Maci disengaged herself from his arm and stepped back from the water. "Morbid fancy," she said.

"Look here, I have something for you." He took off his hat and reached into it, bringing up an ordinary flower, a humble daisy, mashed and sweaty from being under his hat. He held it out for her. She took it with her right hand.

"Thank you," she said, and put it to her nose. It smelled of his hair.

Do you remember playing Troy? I was Helen bound up with our mother's scarves, high on their bed, which we'd pushed into the middle of their room. You had to be Achilles, splendid in your fury, dragging the cat around the bed by a string, and calling it dead Hector. Such a cruel game; only children could play it. Around and around you went, deaf to the protests of the cat. I had to shout for you to hear me. I wanted to be released. "Let me go," I pleaded. "I'm uncomfortable." "Wretched creature," you shouted, never slowing, "there is no comfort in this world!" You were five years old. I was ten.

Now, any spirit will grant that the comforts of mortality are small and fleeting, but that is no reason to spurn them. Sister, I urge you to take a portion of happiness for yourself.

Maci confided to the senior Dr. Woodhull that she believed herself to be the victim of some infective illness. "There was an invading process," she told him, describing her symptoms, "and now there is a dissolving process." Dissolving was not actually the appropriate term. Whatever had been put in her with the kiss had exploded, and shattered her into a confused, fractious being. Wasn't that the function of time, to keep you from being more than a single person at once? But Maci was at present a crowd of contrary opinion and indecisiveness.

"I have just the thing for you," said Canning Woodhull. He left the kitchen to go to his room, and came back in a moment bearing a lovely yellow bottle marked with painted flowers and eyes. "Believe me," he said, "this will help you." It only made her drunk.

If Maci had learned anything, living in Mrs. Woodhull's house, she had certainly learned that marriage was not an exalted state, or even a necessary one. A husband could be merely a courteous appendage, like Colonel Blood, or, like Canning Woodhull, a broken thing deserving of heaped charity. So why did Maci wake one morning convinced that marriage was the only remedy for love, and why did she wake one morning believing herself in love with Gob Woodhull? She did not believe these things—it was the others who did. The rebellious other Maci Trufants who jostled inside of her, who staged a coup and overthrew her reason.

"Now you will be my mama, too," little Pickie told her. She tried to imagine mothering this strange child, who curdled all her maternal instincts. He was listening at the door when Maci went to Mrs. Woodhull, to ask for the hand of her son in marriage. Maci wanted so badly to agree with her employer, when she argued against the idea of Gob and Maci's binding themselves in conventional union. "Did you know that the Colonel and I are divorced?" she asked Maci. "Just after we were married, we obtained the divorce. As a protest, my star, against Sunday-school mentality. And didn't you just review a novel called *Married in Haste*?"

I'll be with you, her hand promised, *I'll give you away*. Maci went down the aisle alone, a bride without need of her father. She had not invited him or her aunt to the wedding, though she felt compelled to write a brief message to Aunt Amy, which she actually mailed to the lady: *Aunt, it is indeed a terrible thing not to marry*. Maci had wished, anyhow, for a wedding so private that there'd be no one there but her and Gob and some unifying principle. They would join their hands and cleave to each other. They did join hands at the behest of Mr. Beecher's subordinate, but when they did it brought her no mystical feelings of union. As she held his hands she wondered how she could possibly be marrying someone who dismissed the *Vindication* as "chatty."

It was the least private function she'd ever attended, crowded with guests, all Mrs. Woodhull's, people who came out to show their support of her. Her friends had flocked back to her since January—it turned out that no one could stay away from her for long, no matter how the scarecrows of so-called morality shook their pumpkin heads. But they had not really come for the wedding. They hoped for a speech that would preach brilliant, exciting reform at the same time it wished her son a happy future with his bride. There wasn't a speech, but Mrs. Woodhull threw a brilliant party, paid for with her son's money. Mrs. Woodhull was getting poor.

"You must adore the first night," said Canning Woodhull, one of many people who accosted Maci with advice. "It will be the very best of your life. Everything that follows will be misery, my dear."

Colonel Blood said, "Do not try to pin his heart to the wall of your bedchamber. It will only bleed, you know."

Tennie scolded her. "You broke your promise, didn't you?" They'd had an anti-marriage ceremony, almost two years before. Maci had stood with Tennie in the Turkish corner, dressed in white, and shared a golden cup of wine. "Marriage is the grave of love," they had intoned together. "I will never enter the grave of love."

Maci wanted to say, "You're right!" And she wanted to take Tennie's hand and flee with her to Paris or Berlin, places Maci remembered from her childhood tour, where they could lead unmarried lives of complicated pleasure. But some other Maci was in charge of her limbs, in that moment, and she could not flee. Still another Maci was trying to push her heart out of her chest, towards Gob where he stood talking with Dr. Fie underneath a mural depicting the loves of Venus: Adonis, Ares, and Anchises. From across the room her new husband looked very small. She wanted to gather him up in her hand.

Maci refused to live in his house, with his engine. They took rooms down at the Fifth Avenue Hotel, where their windows looked out on the trees of Madison Square Park. They had a parlor, with a marble fireplace big enough for little Pickie to stand up in, and red curtains that Maci could close when she did not wish to see the telegraph wires, when she thought they were making a noise like many conversations. Little Pickie remained at the house, under the care of Dr. Fie, but he was a frequent visitor at the hotel. Maci and Gob each had a study, hers filled with a big desk upon which she could lay out proofs, and his stuffed with moldering books. They were on the fourth floor, reached by means of a mechanical elevator, a thing Gob loved. He'd pay the attendant to take him riding in it for hours.

"Would you like to dance?" Gob asked her on their wedding night, when they'd both made themselves ready for bed. Maci had a satchel full of creams and perfumes and washes that Tennie had given her, each with five minutes of advice on its function. She'd not used them, and thought that must be why she felt awkward and homely as she sat on the bed. So she was glad to dance. They danced without music, and they talked, until Gob said he was very tired. He lay down in their bed and fell immediately asleep. Maci lay down beside him, watching him breathe and snore. He groaned, and ran in his sleep like a dog. She considered putting her arm around him, but in the end she did not. She was surprised at how quickly she fell asleep, when she tried.

"Maci," he said later, shaking her awake. "Did I ever tell you about the time I saw Mr. Lincoln's funeral procession? He came to New York, you know, on his way back to Illinois. He left this city escorted by sixty thousand citizens and soldiers. They passed under my window, and woke me up with all their noise. I put my head out and watched them go by for hours and hours. The very last mourner was a snuffling dog, a great big gray one. He looked like a ghost." They were both silent a moment, and then they sat up, each on their own side of the bed, and had a passionate talk, shifting from topic to topic—from Mr. Lincoln to Mrs. Lincoln to madness to insane asylums to Margaret Fuller to shipwrecks and on.

Every night they'd do the same thing. They would dance, sleep, talk. It went on for days, then weeks. Maci wished for absolute darkness because she was certain that would inspire her husband to kiss her—there could be no other reason for his shyness but the light, for hadn't he been rude and bold down in the caisson? But light from the streetlamps in Madison Square came in their windows, even when the curtains were closed, so Maci could see Gob's face as he talked, and she knew he could see hers.

She never asked Tennie for advice, but she always credited Tennie with the course of action she took, because it was by pretending to be Tennie that she solved the problem. One night, Maci put her hand over her husband's mouth and said, "It's enough." She kissed him, and grabbed at him everywhere. When he ran from her, she pursued him, grabbing and kissing though he cried out for her to please stop. He ran to a corner and bent down in it, hands over his head, making a crooning noise. She stood over him, staring down. He peeped up at her through his arms. They stood a little while like that, until she put her hand out to him. She had to wait a long time before he took it. She remembered the things that Mrs. Woodhull had shouted from her roof for all of Thirty-eighth Street to hear. Maci shouted these, too, because she thought the noises would encourage her husband, and for a little while she was brutal with him, slapping at his head and his chest, shaking him, and staring fiercely into his lustrous, dilated eyes. "Praise!" she cried, imitating even Mr. Tilton in her desperate excitement. Gob was silent until the end, when he shouted so loud in her mouth she thought her lungs would burst.

She woke up just at dawn with a twitch in her hand. She thought it wanted to congratulate her on the consummation of her marriage, that her left hand might walk over her chest to shake her right. But it wanted a pen, same as always. There weren't any words, just drawings, not of people or places, but of the thing. For an hour before dawn she watched as her hand drew a profusion of gears and cogs and struts and pipes. She kept on drawing into the morning while Gob slept behind her, waiting and wanting for him to interrupt her, but she didn't stop until one of the hotel staff came to their door with a telegram announcing that Canning Woodhull was dead.

The Magus, who is beloved of every spirit, cannot see us or hear us. We cannot reach him, and his brother cannot reach him. Heaven loves cruel ironies, but we hate them here. We cannot offer him our wisdom, so we offer it to you.

Maci knew it must be inappropriate, to think of children and their making, while at a funeral. But at the white celebration of death held in honor of Canning Woodhull, she did just that. *Dear Aunt Amy*, she'd written in another unsent letter, *Even as he goes into me, I go into him, and fill him with doubt to topple his delusion. I think he will give up building on his machine in favor of building on a family. Isn't it how married people manage their mortality, with children?*

The children would come, one, two, three, four, another with every year, so she would barely have time to know what it was not to be pregnant. Yet it would be a delight, even the agony, because with every birth a little more of the machine would go away. Five, six, seven—the thing would be reduced to a shell. Eight, nine, ten—it would be scraps. Eleven, twelve—they would sell the house on Fifth Avenue to a man who made his fortune in pessaries.

"A sad day, Mrs. Woodhull," Dr. Fie said at the funeral. They were wandering together among the monuments, like all the other white mourners who went in groups of two or three over the lush grass.

"My name is still Trufant, Dr. Fie."

"But you will always be Mrs. Woodhull to me." He nodded at Gob, where he was still weeping by the grave with Mr. Whitman.

"They have a special friendship, those two," he said.

"Do you envy them?"

"No," he said. "But I think I envy Canning Woodhull. Think of it, Mrs. Woodhull, a place where you can dip whiskey out of rivers, and there are ladies whose breath is a gas of peppermint and morphine."

"One hears that Heaven is white and cold and pleasureless."

"Well, I don't think he went to Heaven," he said. "What a strange occupation it must have been, to be an ex-husband. There goes Miss Claflin." He put his arms behind his back like a schoolboy and sang:

> "She's sweeter than the flowers in May,
> She's lovelier far than any;
> I care not what the world may say,
> I pin my faith on Tennie!"

"Dr. Fie," said Maci, "I think you are deranged with grief for your former colleague."

"He was a wise man. I never appreciated that until I'd lost the opportunity to learn from him. And you can see that your husband feels the same way." They walked along in silence for a while. When they came upon a sad-looking tree that drooped like a willow and hid three graves in its shade, they walked under it to inspect the headstones of a Mrs. Sancer and her children. "Recent departures," said Dr. Fie. "We'll have you back soon enough."

Maci thought of the lady's children. Were they buried with her in the same coffin, snuggling through eternity? She had forgotten, it seemed, that children could die. Now that she remembered again, it was a terrible surprise.

"Do you really think so?" Maci asked him. He plucked down a spray of leaves from the tree and gave them to her.

"Of course I do," he said. He plucked another leaf from the tree and, taking a piece of charcoal from his pocket, bent to take a rubbing from one of the children's headstones. Maci leaned against the trunk to watch him. "It puzzles me," he said as he worked, "how you are a helper, but not a believer."

"It puzzles me, too, Dr. Fie. And it puzzles me, that such strong minds could subscribe to such an easy, candy-coated belief."

"But what if it is true, Mrs. Woodhull? What if they are all around us? What if they are all around you now?"

"Books are immortal in the world, Dr. Fie. Not people." Maci closed her eyes.

"Are you well, Mrs. Woodhull?" he asked her in a little while.

"Just sleepy," she said. In the silence, she'd been naming children in her mind: John, Jacob, little Victoria, Arthur, Corwin. She loved to name them. "Why don't you walk on," she told Dr. Fie. "I'll join you in a moment." He looked at her with an inscrutable expression, but then he nodded and walked out. Maci shielded her eyes against the flash of sunlight that came through the hanging leaves as Dr. Fie parted them. Little Tennessee, she thought, Polly, Christopher, Isabella, Constance, William.

> I was surprised. Everyone is surprised. But why are we surprised? Haven't we known, all our lives, that this would come? Such a quiet, subtle poison. Those who complain at how death ruins their days, they are called weak, or morbidly sentimental, but really they are prophets, who rail against the despair that every person practices, but none will acknowledge. Can you imagine, Sister, a world not poisoned? Once or twice in your life, you might truly forget—say, when, thinking yourself incapable of love, you find it, after all, or when your baby hangs dependent on your breast, and you think it must live forever because it feeds on pure, powerful love. But can you even imagine a world in which immortality is fact, not fancy or suspicion, a world in which the worm has departed from the rose? Can you? Can you even?

"What is equality?" Mrs. Woodhull asked, at the May convention of the People's Party. "And what is justice? Shall we be slaves to escape revolution? Away with such weak stupidity! A revolution *shall* sweep over the whole country, to purge it of political trickery, despotic assumption, and all industrial injustice!"

"Wake up, my love," Gob said to Maci, moving her head where it rested on his shoulder. "You're missing the speech."

"I wrote it," Maci said. "I know it." She opened her eyes and saw Mrs. Woodhull on the stage in Apollo Hall, in her red cheeks, white rose, and her blue dress. "Now you must admit she is a great woman," Maci said sleepily.

"Who will dare," Mrs. Woodhull asked, "to unlock the luminous portals of the future with the rusty keys of the past?"

Who indeed—it seemed everybody in the hall was willing to have a try. The whole place was on its feet and screaming for her, "Woodhull! Woodhull, Woodhull!"

Colonel Blood stepped up from the crowd, dressed in a fine black suit. He nominated Mrs. Woodhull to the Presidency of the United States of America, then cried out for all in favor of the nomination to second it, and the hall shook with ayes. Women wept and kissed each other. Men wept and kissed women. A fat man next to Maci jumped up and down on his chair until it broke under him, and then he lay laughing on the floor. "Woodhull!" he shouted.

Gob leaned close to Maci and said, "Look at her. She doesn't even remember that someone has died. Woodhull! They think they're shouting for my mother, but really they're shouting for *you*. She is the Mrs. Woodhull who will be President, but you're the Mrs. Woodhull who will bridge Heaven and Earth."

"My name is Trufant, sir," Maci said. She wondered if he might not be putting something else in her besides the stuff that makes a baby. Maybe it was an acid to erode her disbelief, something that went into her soul and her mind to make her weak and gullible. It was a terrible thought, and she always banished it when it came, but it was true that she felt weaker as the days passed, that she became ill sometimes with nerves. It was something different from madness, softer, sleepier, and harder to resist, this smothering, nervous fatigue.

"You are the most important person in the world," he told her, while the crowd continued to scream for his mother. "Others will help me, but no one else can help me as you can, I need nobody as I need you. Who else is there but you in the world? I look around every day and the whole vast city is empty but for you. I look up above the roofs and see your face flashing in the sky."

"Flatterer," she said.

Two weeks later, Mrs. Woodhull had another triumph when her nomination was ratified at a second meeting of the People's Party, which had renamed itself the Equal Rights Party. Frederick Douglass was selected to be her running mate. In the grasp of their considerable enthusiasm the members of the Equal Rights Party neglected to inform Mr. Douglass that he'd won their nomination, and when he did discover it, he didn't much care. Maci thought his male pride must have been bruised by having a lady put over him on the ballot.

The month, which had started with a funeral, got gloomy again as it closed out. Maci found it startling, how there were people who took seriously Mrs. Woodhull's bid for the Presidency, how all the work on the Victoria Leagues had borne fruit. Maci thought they were inflating a glorious trial balloon, making a brazen, powerful statement, and it was her conviction that even a score of votes would be a triumph in November. But the largely imaginary Victoria Leagues had turned entirely real. This was a miracle equal in Maci's mind to the one Gob hoped to accomplish. For roughly a week, she truly believed that Mrs. Woodhull would make a very serious bid for the Presidency, and for a few moments of that week she believed that Mrs. Woodhull actually would be President. Then Mrs. Grundy sat on Maci's cake.

Maci didn't know who precisely all Mrs. Woodhull's enemies were. There were the obvious ones: the Beecher sisters and their devotee, Governor Hawley of Connecticut; Mr. Greeley, who had always vilified Mrs. Woodhull in the *Tribune*, and perhaps thought her candidacy somehow devalued his own; the entire editorial staff of *Harper's Weekly*. These were the people who spoke publicly against Mrs. Woodhull, and though they were all giants, they were slayable because Maci could fight against them in the pages of her own *Weekly,* addressing every charge they printed or spoke and specifically refuting it.

But there were other enemies, large, nebulous, and inchoate. There were unknown persons who were possessed of such power that they could have the rent raised on Mrs. Woodhull's home and place of business by ten thousand dollars a year, all payable in advance. In May alone, advertisements in the *Weekly* fell off by seventy-five percent, and clients abandoned the brokerage in droves. Mrs. Woodhull was forced out of her beautiful house, and no one in the city would rent to her. Maci came home one day to find the Claflins crowded into her rooms at the Fifth Avenue Hotel. "It's just for a while," Mrs. Woodhull said, but Maci, looking at Anna Claflin lying in her bed with her shoes on, suspected it would be for a long while, indeed. Yet it was a pleasure to give Mrs. Woodhull shelter when she needed it, even if the Claflins trailed after her like a persistent infestation. Maci was rarely at the hotel anyhow.

For all that she had sworn not to live in Gob's house, she practically did live there. Her hand ached from making the drawings her husband used as fast as she made them, and she could tell now how his machine was beginning to take its shape from her madness. *From your brother*, her hand corrected her. *From an association of spirits millions and centuries strong. From the accumulated longing of all history's dead.*

In July, Maci sat at a table in Gob's house, drawing with one hand, writing with the other, while Dr. Fie and her husband wielded sledges to knock down walls, making room for the fattening new Infant. Little Pickie approached her, wearing an apron of pockets, each one holding a different tool, wrenches and hammers and things that looked very much like surgical instruments. "Mama, would you like to make an adjustment?"

"No, thank you," she said.

"Damn you, then!" he cried, his standard response to her refusals to play at building. He said it more with an air of exuberance than condemnation, and always with a smile. Maci continued with her writing, an open letter to the *Times, Herald,* and *Tribune,* in defense of her employer: *Mrs. Woodhull is a great and good woman, assaulted by men who hate and fear her because they recognize her as the lady who will steal their fire and make of it a gift for her own sex. No one would ever think of calling her a Romanist because she says that everybody has the right to be Catholic, but transfer the question from religion to sexuality, and because she advocates the same theory for this that she does for religion, she is denounced as an advocate of promiscuousness.*

Maci jumped in her seat as a piece of wall fell with a crash. She looked at her left hand as it drew, undisturbed by the noise or the floating plaster dust that settled over the page. It finished a picture, a gentleman's hat pierced with a corona of glass spikes, then pushed it aside to start another on a fresh sheet. Sometimes she imagined herself drawing and drawing, as her hand stiffened with age, until she was an old lady buried under twoscore of years' worth of mechanical illustrations. And still, she was sure, her crimped hand would move the pencil.

By summer's end, Mrs. Woodhull had quite run out of money. The *Weekly* suspended publication, and the brokerage had no clients anymore. Maci and her husband had their first quarrel when Gob refused to give money to his mother. Everything he had he needed for building, he said, though they were welcome to shelter and feed as long as they wished at the Fifth Avenue Hotel. Maci might have carped at him like a Xanthippe, but whenever she considered this injustice, it made her more sleepy than furious. And Mrs. Woodhull, who Maci had thought capable of taking money from anyone, seemed horrified by the prospect of taking money from her son.

Instead, Mrs. Woodhull exhausted herself lecturing—the more scandalous her reputation became, the more people all over the country wanted to hear her for themselves. But even at the annual convention of the National Association of Spiritualists, who had elected her their president the year before, the audience was just as hostile as it was curious. She went to Boston in September to speak to them, and nearly lost her office. She was challenged on account of her reputation as a Free Lover. She'd always insist it was Demosthenes who prompted her to defend herself with an extemporaneous exposé of Mr. Beecher. In the open summer air, she addressed the soft-minded thousands who sought to impeach her, detailing Mr. Beecher's infidelity with Elizabeth Tilton. They were all won over. The Spiritualists elected her for another term, and would have proclaimed her Queen if their charter had permitted it.

"There's nothing left for us," Mrs. Woodhull told Maci when she returned to New York, "but to do the thing." She meant to expose Mr. Beecher in print, a move that Maci discouraged at first, because she was sure it would bring nothing but a crushing retaliation. "My star," Mrs. Woodhull scolded, "you are a frightened innocent!" She gathered Maci into her arms, shouting that Mr. Beecher would fall like a giant into the East River, and send up a wave to soak Manhattan from South Street to West Street. Mrs. Woodhull, temporarily as bouncy as Tennie, held Maci tight and jumped up and down with her, as if trying to launch them both into the sky.

Through September and October, Maci worked with Gob and his mother, and sometimes she was so tired that she confused their projects, so she thought that Gob was building a machine to expose and destroy hypocrisy, and that Mrs. Woodhull was writing an article that argued so powerfully against death that nature, shamefaced after reading it, would revoke mortality. It made sense, after all, to conflate these tasks, because they were equally impossible. But by the time she and Mrs. Woodhull had finished with the Beecher article, when all the facts were gathered, sorted, and transcribed, Maci had a feeling that this thing she'd helped make was so powerful that it couldn't help but wreak some great change out of its destructiveness. It was a bomb that would burst over Brooklyn and rain down burning, phosphoric reform on the pleading, hapless population.

When she and Mrs. Woodhull were done, when all that was left was to wait for the paper to come back from the printers, she went to Gob's house to rest. Maci had the feeling that she'd been running for weeks, building up speed to lend to her spear when she hurled it, and now that it had left her hand she was too tired to care where it landed. "Good night," Gob said to her by way of greeting, when she went to his house on the last day of work on the November 2 paper. She sat down in one of his dusty parlor chairs and fell promptly asleep.

Here is New York after the change, her hand wrote beneath a drawing of a city that seemed to be made all of glass. Crystal bridges leaped off towards the horizon; Maci could only guess where they rested their other feet. Different bridges ran between buildings so tall Maci wondered if the ground would even be visible from their roofs. Three concentric suns hung in the sky.

And here is our family after the change, her hand wrote beneath another picture, this one a crowded group portrait. *See how happy you look? See how everyone looks happy?* Maci wanted to think that the occupants of the portrait looked merely smug, or simpering, but it was true that their faces and eyes seemed blessed with radiant joy. There she was, standing with Gob on one side of her, and Rob on the other. Her mother was there, looking composed and sane, holding up a book so Mrs. Woodhull might read the title off the spine. There was Private Vanderbilt, stooping to kiss Tennie as she held the hand of a man Maci did not recognize, a long-faced fellow in the uniform of a Union soldier. Dr. Fie was standing with his hand on the shoulder of a smaller man, who resembled him in the face. Maci's father, Miss Suter, Aunt Amy and the man Maci knew must be her husband—these were just the people in front. There were rows and rows of people behind them, and even those whose features were made indistinguishable by distance managed somehow to project great happiness. Everyone was happy except Gob, who knelt with his head bowed, weeping at the feet of a soldier boy that

Maci knew was his brother. The boy had a bugle in one hand. The other rested on Gob's head.

Dear Aunt, Maci wrote. *I am a fugitive from justice. There is a man named Anthony Comstock who perceives me as having committed a grave sin against him. He's taken offence at our* Weekly, *greater even than Mr. Beecher, who maintains what seems to me an embarrassed silence about his exposure as an amative hypocrite. I know how you love the Beechers, Aunt, and I feel obligated to say that we never really meant him any harm. It wasn't out of spite for Mr. Beecher that we burst our bomb over Brooklyn. Mrs. Woodhull herself said she has no fault to find with him in any sense as that in which the world will condemn him. The fault and the wrong were not with him, or with Mrs. Tilton, but with the false social institutions under which we still live, while the more advanced men and women of the world have outgrown them in spirit. Practically everybody is living a false life, by professing a conformity which they do not feel and do not live, and which they cannot feel and live any more than the grown boy can reenter the clothes of his early childhood. So you see I had no malicious intent against Mr. Beecher, and certainly none against Mr. Comstock (though I know for a fact he shoots dogs for sport). Yet that man is determined, if he can find me, to put me in jail, where he has put Mrs. Woodhull, her husband, and her sister. But Aunt, you mustn't worry that I'll rot in the Tombs waiting for a trial at which justice will no doubt prove elusive, or that I'll flee to Boston to make unreasonable demands of our relation, and compromise you with my fugitive presence. I am well hidden here.*

Maci went about outside disguised as a man, with her hair under a hat, and a beard made of real man-hair that Gob pasted on her face in the morning. On warm days it slipped a little after a few hours of wear, but on cold ones it stuck fast till evening. She registered to vote in her disguise, and voted under Rob's name on November 5 of 1872. She'd never believe the reports that came later, that Mrs.

Woodhull never got a single vote, because Maci cast hers for the lady, and she knew that Gob had, too.

"How are things on the outside?" Tennie asked her, when Maci went to visit her and Mrs. Woodhull at Ludlow Street Jail. There were difficulties with the bail—every time a supporter provided the money to free the sisters, they'd be arrested again. Maci wrote outraged letters every day to five different papers.

"Dull," Maci said, though really she was caught up in an excitement of writing and building. Her days were structured—agitate in the morning, go out in the city in her disguise during the day, build at night. She wandered in a mixed state of belief and disbelief. Sometimes when she was walking alone she'd look at her passing reflection in a shop window and not believe it could possibly be her under those clothes; other times it seemed the natural fruition of the past two years' events, to be walking the city as a man. Likewise, she'd wander in Gob's house, not believing it could be her hand that helped shape the machine that was growing every day until it was no longer possible to distinguish it from the house itself. "What are you doing?" she'd ask her reflection, a lady in men's clothes with glue on her face, her hat off, her hair down, a pencil in her left hand and a pen in her right. Sometimes she would just stare and stare, wondering if she shouldn't break the mirror that showed her such a thing. "I don't believe it," she'd whisper, but it was getting harder to say that. "Why not?" she'd ask, experimentally, of her reflection, and a voice in her mind—her own voice, the voice of murine sanity—would say, Simply because it is never so, and never has been so, and never will be.

"It's a poor likeness," Gob said. One day, after visiting the jail, Maci and Gob came to a museum on the Bowery where all sorts of sensational persons and things were on display: a three-hundred-pound lady, tattooed over every inch of her massive body—she was called the Mystic Bulk; a man who could swallow half his arm and spit it out again; and a woman who juggled with her feet the body of her amputee husband, a distinguished veteran who had lost all his limbs at Sayler's Creek. Mrs. Woodhull's likeness was featured in a display of wax figures called "Dante's Inferno." Here you could see personalities writhing in eternal torment. Mrs. Woodhull's figure had recently been added. It really was a poor likeness, obviously executed from Mr. Nast's cartoon, the one that portrayed Mrs. Woodhull as Mrs. Satan, who beckoned to downtrodden wives with the promise of salvation through Free Love. Her hair was done up in horns, and she sported a cloak that flared out behind her like bat wings. In such an outfit, Maci thought she'd more properly be depicted as an infernal administrator, but she was suffering just like any other of the damned, writhing with her hands lifted up in a gesture of supplication, and a look of weakness and horror on her face such as Maci had never seen on her, and knew she never would.

Mr. Beecher was writhing beside Mrs. Woodhull, and Mr. and Mrs. Tilton were there too, all of them licked by flames fashioned from orange and red cotton. It was a depiction of Hell less convincing than the scene in the caisson, and Maci said so. She took out a pad of paper and pencil from her coat and began to sketch the thing inexpertly with her right hand—Mrs. Woodhull had heard about the display, and wanted to know what it looked like. Her left hand plucked away the pencil and took over the work. "Thank you," Maci said politely. Her eyes and her attention were free to wander. She watched her husband standing at a recreation of Mr. Lincoln's funeral catafalque, which had been on view in City Hall seven years before. Gob stood peering down at the wax face. "Another poor likeness," he called back to her. She walked after him, still sketching, and she paused before a set of twisted mirrors that tortured her reflection. She was short and fat in one, immensely tall in the other.

"More poor likenesses," Gob said when he was next to her again. He lifted his head to talk into her ear, telling her how every person was a poor likeness of herself, how death holds the best part of us in a prison of fear, and how his machine would reverse this, so all the undying people who walked the earth would be perfectly themselves. Maci tried to laugh.

"Don't give your machine too much work, sir," she said. "You'll make it nervous with exhaustion."

> Such wings! They spread over the whole Summerland, and the gates are as high as the clouds. We could sigh forever over the beauty of this engine. It is almost alive, here. When the Kosmos steps into it, when he takes his places as its heart, then it will breathe and speak. Come to me, it will say, the walls are falling. You have torn them down with your brilliant grief, with your love, your desire. Come to me, the way is open.
>
> Goodbye, Sister. You'll hear from me no more, until we meet again in the changed world. Farewell, I am coming to you!

Maci tried to cheer as Mrs. Woodhull threw off her coal-scuttle bonnet to reveal herself to the people who'd gathered in the Cooper Institute in the hope of hearing a forbidden lecture called "The Naked Truth!" But all Maci could manage was a weak little yelp. She was very tired—not sleepy, but so weary she ached. Months of building had done this to her. As the weeks passed it seemed that every drawing took something from her, as if she were using her own vital stuff for ink, and that in putting it on paper her hand made her a little more fatigued. She knew she ought to be excited, that she ought to be cheering for Mrs. Woodhull, free at last from Ludlow Street Jail and actively resisting attempts to return her there, and that she ought to be cheering in her heart for the machine, because it was all finished, the ink in Maci was dry. The last strut had been installed, the last glass negative put in place, the last glass pipe filled with a curious liquid fetched by odd little Pickie. She might at least muster the energy to curse the thing for a folly, but when she tried, sometimes, in a fit of sanity, to shake her fist at it, the result was the same as when she tried to put her hands together for Mrs. Woodhull. All she seemed able to do was raise a hand to her eyes, to cover them up and press on them until they ached.

"You're tired, my love," Gob had said to her. "You ought to rest." He had wanted her to stay home and await the arrival of Mr. Whitman, who, he insisted, would come to the house on Fifth Avenue now that the machine was ready to receive him. That seemed unlikely to Maci, because she was sure that Mr. Whitman had absented himself most purposefully from her husband's life. "He will come," Gob had said.

"Hooray," Maci said softly, at the Cooper Institute. She looked across the crowd to where her husband was standing with Mr. Whitman, cheering and applauding. Mr. Whitman looked tired, too. After the speech had reached its dramatic conclusion, and Mrs. Woodhull had surrendered again to the marshals, Maci went back to the house on Fifth Avenue with Dr. Fie. Little Pickie was in a fury of polishing and preparation. Maci sat down on a cold pipe the thickness of her whole body, and the cool brought to mind the private skating party Gob had arranged for her fourteen months previous. She closed her eyes and remembered gliding through the dark, cool house. It was all she could think of for a little while, but even as she enjoyed this pleasant memory, another thought kept crowding into her mind.

It was a thought that had been coming and going in her head over the past few months, the thought that she needed to destroy this thing, that she ought to have been undoing it every night, a Penelope faithful to her reason. "I ought to smash it," she said, "before it can disappoint him." Her left hand crossed to her right, and took it by the wrist, holding it down against her leg. "I wasn't going to," she said.

She wouldn't do it because she thought it was necessary for her husband to put his friend in the thing, and then see how nothing came of it. And she thought it was necessary because she hoped sometimes that something might come of it after all, the sky might crack open, and all the departed might rain down like feathers. She had been trying so hard to believe, for his sake, and it was to this that she really attributed her weariness, not the days of being a fugitive, or the nights of work on this strange, monstrous Infant that made her father's Infant seem like a puppy. Maybe unbelief was her madness, since she didn't believe when her hand spoke to her with love, when it spoke like Rob, when it drew like Rob, when it knew what Rob knew, and told true stories that were other people's lives—when it did all these things and she still could not call it brother. When she saw little Pickie rolling a giant lens down a hall in Gob's house; when she saw the machine grow so huge and complex that it looked to be sufficient engine to drive Manhattan out to sea, so the island could anchor halfway to Europe and become a new Atlantis: still she didn't believe, and wasn't it madness to ignore the evidence of your senses, even when they said you must believe the unbelievable?

"Here they come!" Pickie said, bouncing elastically on his feet. He rushed over to where Maci was sitting and pulled her up by her hands. He pulled her around in a little dance. Just for a few seconds, Maci shuffled around in a circle, then he let her go and went to the door. She would have fallen if Dr. Fie hadn't caught her. "Steady," he said, looking at her but not smiling.

"Is it right, what we're doing?" she asked him, but even as she asked, she knew it wasn't the proper question for the situation, and it was only something she asked to distract herself from the more pressing question of whether or not they would succeed, and the still more pressing question of why she could make no room in her heart for the possibility that they might.

"God bless you," she said to Mr. Whitman, when he came in, and she called these words after him when he fled, hoping that God would bless him, after all, and keep him from such situations as the one he'd just escaped. She had a rush of energy at the thought that now they must begin a work of disassembly, for she knew that if Mr. Whitman wouldn't play, there'd be no game, tonight or ever.

"He'll return," Gob said. Maci thought he meant he'd be back in days or weeks, but he was back in moments. Maci smiled at him again. Gob and her hand had told her how it would be uncomfortable for him, how his body would articulate the formless grief that saturated the world of the living. But it would do him no lasting harm. He was a kosmos, Gob said, who had the qualities of everyone and everything. The grief would pass through him, but not hurt him. "Are you sure?" she'd asked, when her hand drew the spiked hat that was painful just to look at.

"Absolutely," he said.

"There it is," Gob had said, speaking to Mr. Whitman before he fled. "The engine. It's complete, except for you. There's a place for you in it, Walt. I need you to go in it, and then it will bring them back, all the six hundred thousand, my brother and Will's brother and Maci's brother and your Hank, too. All the dead of the war, all the dead of all the wars, all the dead of the past. We'll lick death tonight, Walt, if you'll help us. I'm ready. Will's ready, and Maci is ready. Pickie is ready and the engine is ready. Are you ready?"

Am I ready? Maci asked herself. She tried again to believe, an effort of will that was like trying to get her bones to step out of her body, but when she looked at the thing all she saw was failure, and it seemed to her that it was a great curse and a punishment, not to believe, that after all it was the people who could believe in nothing but death who got nothing but death for their lot. And she worried for the first time that her doubt would poison the working of the thing, as she feared that her doubt in her father's Infant had poisoned it and killed it even before she beat it to death with a wrench.

"I should go," she said aloud, but Dr. Fie was already directing her to her work, to the switches that needed to be thrown, the valves that needed to be turned. There were a hundred different tasks split among the four of them, and every one had to be done in an order that was as precise as music. "Bless you," she said again to Mr. Whitman as she settled the spiked hat on his head.

As the gears started to turn, she thought her doubt would fall away. When she saw how it looked to be doing something, how the steam engines steamed and the lights lighted, she thought that mechanical competence would indicate supernatural competence, and her doubt would shrivel. But the thing was roaring away gloriously and still she thought it was folly, just an enormous monument to Gob's grief that was beautiful and complex, but no more likely to raise the dead than an ordinary lever. Maci found herself planning a future for herself and her husband. Her neurasthenia would remit, and she would be strong for both of them because he would collapse in a wreck of disappointment. He'd be so weak and sad he'd not be able to speak for months, but she'd take him away to Europe, and fortify his ailing spirit with a tour of great museums. Slowly he'd come back to life, and they would return to America in time for Maci to help Mrs. Woodhull organize her next bid for the Presidency in 1876.

Even when the impossible light came on, so bright it seemed to shine through them all, she didn't believe. But then she thought, Maybe somewhere tonight in this city a dog will die of loneliness and neglect, and then in the next moment it will rise again. And then she thought, Maybe it will be a child who gets up out of his deathbed to kiss the face of his mother. She heard a keening, which she mistook for the noise of a grieving mama, but it was Mr. Whitman, crying out from within his crystal house. As he screamed more forcefully, her belief grew, until it was three babies, ten men, a hundred women who would rise from death that night. As he writhed and screamed, making the most horrible noise she'd ever heard in her whole life, Maci believed and believed and believed. It was like a muscle in her, swelling as she flexed it over and over. Her weariness evaporated—she thought she saw it pass away, a little wisp of gray smoke that bled out of her eyes with the tears. There was the other thought still in her, dwarfed by the joy of faith, that she had come all this way to wreck this machine, too, that it was her sacred responsibility to smash it. Hadn't crude fate let her practice one such destruction? But she paid very little attention to this thought.

Instead, she considered how it was wonderful that a machine could manufacture faith and put it in you, how it could abolish doubt, and that this was perhaps more miraculous than the abolition of death. She held on to a pipe that was hot on one side, cold on the other, while the whole house shook and her husband cried out exultantly. With her right hand she raised her left to her cheek and cried out, "Rob!" and there was a picture in her mind as perfect as a photograph, a scene in which he was alive again, marching through the gate in the machine with Private Vanderbilt at his side. "They're coming!" she shouted, because she believed it.

Gob was standing outside the gatehouse, chanting words Maci could not understand. His hair was standing up ridiculously on end. Maci put her hand to her head and discovered that hers was doing the same. She heard breathing, and singing, a beautiful sound of plaintive voices, and over that Mr. Whitman's terrific screaming. There was another sound, too, a rude knocking, as if someone was at the door trying to disturb them in this exquisite moment. She had a notion it must be Mr. Comstock, come to arrest her, but actually it was Dr. Fie, who, having tried to open the door to Mr. Whitman's crystal house and found it locked, was banging his fist on its walls. Every time he struck the noise changed—now it was like a knock on wood, now it was like a brass gong, and now it was the delicate chime of two glasses struck together in a toast to success. Gob walked slowly towards him, and when he was close he shouted a question at him. In answer, Dr. Fie pushed him away, and when Gob came at him again Dr. Fie struck him in the face.

Pickie came clambering down off a scaffold and leaped on Dr. Fie. They struggled a little, and Gob came rushing again at them, shouting words that Maci thought she could see leave his mouth as gusts of wind to knock Dr. Fie back against the glass. He shook his head, holding Pickie at arm's length. When Gob reached him, Dr. Fie pummeled him with the boy, hitting him as if with a big stick. Maci came to them just in time to see him smash Pickie against the glass wall. It cracked with one blow, shattered with the next. Pickie seemed not any worse for the abuse. He clawed at Dr. Fie's face, and cursed. Dr. Fie threw him across the room.

"Help me," Dr. Fie shouted at Maci, over a new noise, a disharmony in the singing. Mr. Whitman was still screaming, louder now that his voice wasn't contained by the house. "It's killing him!" he shouted.

Maci shook her head. "Dr. Fie," she said incredulously, "don't you understand that there is no more death?"

"Oh, Mrs. Woodhull," he said. "There is for *him*." She put her hand on Dr. Fie to stop him when he tried to go in, and he thrust her back as he entered, so that her head knocked into Gob's head as he was coming up behind her. Gob was saying "No!" again and again, and Maci had the thought that he must have looked just this way, weeping and protesting, at the grave of his brother. There was a surge of breathing and singing. The light flared from the giant lens, and Maci heard a popping in her head, similar to what she'd heard in the caisson, as if there'd been a precipitous shift in the pressure of the air. She felt nauseated, and fell to her knees, thinking she would vomit.

"Will," Gob said softly—Maci picked his voice out among all the great noise as if it had been spoken in a quiet room. "You'll ruin it all." Pickie Beecher ran into the house, only to be ejected. He bounced on the floor like a ball.

Gob went into the crystal house after Dr. Fie, and there they grappled over Mr. Whitman's body. While Mr. Whitman arched and screamed in his chair, they pounded each other in the head and face. Maci shouted, "Stop! Stop!" but they paid her no heed, or didn't hear her at all. Dr. Fie brought his two hands together, cranked them back, and struck Gob in the face with such force that blood flew and coated the wall of the house with perfect round drops. Gob staggered, and fell, and Dr. Fie took that opportunity to wrest Mr. Whitman from the chair.

All the noise stopped suddenly, started again and stopped. The floor lurched, and the great lens fell out of its supports. It came crashing down on the gate, splitting it in two. In the quiet before the machine noise started again—a coughing and choking sound in it now—she realized that Mr. Whitman was no longer screaming. He came out of the house, leaning against Dr. Fie, who draped him against Maci and said, "Take him out of here." When Maci tried to push Mr. Whitman back into the house, Dr. Fie shoved her roughly aside, and hurried away with the poet even as Maci called for him to return.

Her balance was off, or the floor was heaving like liquid, or both—she could barely guide herself through the door of the house, to where Gob was slowly rising to his feet. His nose was crooked and bloody, and blood had stained his teeth and his mouth and his torn lips. "Come away," Maci said to him. His hands were slick with blood. He pulled them easily out of hers and shook his head.

"To where?" he asked. With great calm and precise deliberation, he set himself down in Mr. Whitman's chair and set the hat on his head. "You may go out, but there is no other place for me." Something crashed very nearby, and a moaning sound started up amid all the choking and coughing and intermittent singing. The floor threw her into him, and he pushed her away, an expression of terror and hatred now on his face from which Maci nearly fled. He shouted at her then, without any words she could make out, or perhaps he was shouting because he was feeling the same agony as Mr. Whitman had. She thought his yelling blew her back and forced her away from him, but really it was Dr. Fie, his big hands tangled in her dress and her hair, who dragged her back through the open crystal door, through the crumbling spaces that used to be parlors, over the nubs of walls. As she receded from him, she saw Gob begin to writhe and kick in the chair. She saw little Pickie, trapped under a giant gear, wriggling his limbs like a bug and shouting for his brother. Dr. Fie would not stop to assist him.

Dr. Fie dragged her outside, held her tight by both shoulders and shouted in her face, "Stay here, I will bring him out!" But before he could pass through the door again they were sent flying down the marble steps by an explosion. Maci lay on Fifty-third Street with her leg twisted beneath her, obviously broken, but somehow not very painful. Dr. Fie and Mr. Whitman both lay near her, neither of them moving. There came another explosion, and another, and fire came bursting out of a whole row of windows. A piece of stone came flying down—she watched its whole journey from the house to her head. As she slept she dreamed of a night when her husband had put his finger on the same place the stone hit her and named it for her. "Glabella," he'd said, and she'd thought how it would be a beautiful name for a daughter.

When she woke, Dr. Fie was sitting on the steps, weeping into his hands. Mr. Whitman had opened his eyes, and was moving his lips, but not making any sound. Maci raised herself on her arms and looked up toward the house, where a figure stood just outside the flaming door, looking indecisive and confused. "Down here!" she called to it, thinking it was Gob. "Come down!" The figure turned at the sound of her voice, and did start down the steps, too slow for a person fleeing a fire.

"Stop your crying, he's alive!" Maci said to Dr. Fie, but he only wept harder, and as the figure came nearer, she saw that it was not her husband, or even little Pickie. It was a boy older than him, one who wore Gob's face. Entirely naked, he stepped close and peered at her, trying, she could tell, to recognize her, and then he flinched away, as if he had never seen a lady scream or weep before. "Let me go!" he pleaded. But she held him fast.

"THOMAS," HIS WIFE CALLED OUT FROM THE OTHER SIDE OF their bed, "it's past your rising time."

"I know it," Tomo said. "I'm on my way." But he lay in bed awhile longer. His knees and his elbows and his shoulders were so stiff these mornings that he liked to loosen them up some in bed before he tried to rise. He was old for his age, and his joints seemed to be the oldest part of his body.

"Don't be late," she said, because she thought he had an appointment across the river, a weekly obligation to teach a class at the medical college. She went back to sleep. Tomo felt blindly for his cane, and when he found it, slowly moved his legs off the side of the bed, and rose with all the speed of a growing plant. He'd slept in a hunch, and now his back did not wish to unbend itself. He walked a little around the room, leaning on furniture as he passed it, and paused by the window to look out at the bridge. Half the windows in the house had a view of it—it was the reason he'd purchased the place. He'd put out his clothes by the window so he could dress there, so he could see the bridge and think how he would soon be on it. It was a weekly ritual with him. Every Saturday he'd take a walk over to Manhattan.

Tomo was one of the first to cross over, when the bridge opened at midnight on May 25, 1883. He was twenty-one years old, still a student and still living with Will, who had taken him in even before his mother and Tennie went away to England in '76. "Aren't you coming, Will?" he'd asked, but Will wouldn't go out of the house that night. "Eventually," Will said, but Tomo was sure that he never even looked out his window at the incredible display of fireworks.

"I sent my mama a telegram," he said the next day. "Datelined 'Brooklyn Bridge.' "

"She'll be glad of it," Will said. "You ought to have sent one to Walt."

"I'll send one to him, too," Tomo said, though he did not intend to do that. When he was still a boy, Will would take him to Camden to visit the old poet, a man who pinched Tomo every time he saw him, and demanded kisses like a bearded, bad-breathed aunt. Will went down to see him every year in January, on the anniversary of the stroke that had made an invalid of Mr. Whitman, half-paralyzing him.

They had their breakfast—steak for Tomo, apples and toast for Will—and Tomo talked excitedly of how the bridge was magnificent, of how he had jumped up and down in the middle, expecting it to bounce under him.

"Of course it did not," Tomo said, and then continued to eat in silence. Moody Will was crying again, and it was best to let him alone when he got this way. When Tomo had returned earlier that morning, Will was sitting in a battered chair and looking down at the crowds walking home underneath the paper lanterns on Fulton Street. "No one remembers," he said as soon as Tomo came into the room. "Not even you. I think that is the worst thing about it. Walt'll kick off soon, and then it will be just Maci and I. He never forgot *you*, did he? He remained inside, when he might have come back out into the world. Why don't you remember? Shouldn't you be ashamed, to have forgotten him? And shouldn't you be ashamed, to have forgotten what he did?"

"I don't know what you're talking about, Will," Tomo said. "Are you talking about Sam? Are you talking about Gob?"

"You should remember," Will said sadly.

"But I do," Tomo said. "What sort of person wouldn't remember his own brother?" He pulled a chair closer to Will's and put his hand on Will's knee, thinking of their respective brothers, both dead in the war. He cried a little, too, thinking of Gob's abbreviated life, but he could not keep up with Will, a champion mourner, and Will's snuffling sobs turned to voices in Tomo's head as he drifted to sleep in his chair, thinking again of the illuminations over the bridge.

He had stood under the millions of flashing stars, listening to every ship in the harbor blow its horn, and thought how Will must be standing with his face to a wall, so as not to see even the glimmer in neighboring windows. Next to Tomo, a little boy in a black suit and a porkpie hat was clapping his hands and laughing at the display, at the fountains of gold and silver stars roaring off the towers, and the hundreds of Japanese shells bursting in rapid succession into blue, red, white, and emerald sparks that fell, still incandescent, into the river. "Isn't it sad?" the boy asked Tomo. "Isn't it so terribly sad?"

Tomo was always very slow going up the stairs to the promenade. Sometimes he'd stop and lean casually against the rail, unfold the paper that he carried under his arm, and pretend to read. In a little while he'd be able to go on again, up to the top of the stairs, where he always found himself thinking of the people who'd died on the bridge during the big stampede. Every May he'd bring a little wreath over and lay it down to get trampled, too.

It was his custom to stop in the middle of the bridge and look down the river. It was pretty rare, these days, to see anybody jump, or even to read about it in the papers. But Tomo had been there when Odlum made his leap in 1885, and he still remembered very well how he jumped, with one arm raised up over his head, and how his fall was so easy to follow because of the startling red shirt he wore. Tomo had missed Steve Brodie's supposed midnight jump, which had probably not ever really happened, anyhow, but he had been there in '87, when a man named Hollow had leaped off wearing a pair of giant canvas wings. Tomo watched as the man glided down to land gently on the surface of the river, just in front of a friendly-looking tug. It plowed over him, crushing his wings, but he lived through that abuse.

"He's dead!" the little boy had said, next to Tomo. He'd hauled himself up on the railing, and was looking down the river, his face all twisted up in dismay.

"No, child," Tomo told him. "See there, he's swimming away in the wake. It's only his wings that have been injured."

"He's dead!" the boy wailed. "He has died, and nothing can bring him back!" Tomo reached out to console him, but the boy dropped off the rail and ran away.

"What do you remember of your youth?" Maci would ask him. It was a question she reserved for her rare solemn moods. A friend also to Tomo's wife (she'd introduced them to each other), she was often a visitor at their house. She'd been visiting Tomo all his life, with such frequency, when he was younger, that she had been nearly a constant presence. Now her visits were more rare. Five or six times a year she'd take time off from her career of political agitation and come to Brooklyn.

"Not very much," Tomo told her again at her last visit, the same answer he always gave her. "When we were small, Gob and I used to play in a clearing in the orchard behind the house in Homer. He liked to play games called Fredericksburg and Chancellorsville—we had scarecrows dressed up as Confederate soldiers at whom we would shoot with toy muskets made from apple boughs."

"Yes," Maci said, and was silent a moment. "My friend," she

said, "I don't think memory is to be trusted. I used to think that madness was the chief enemy of joy, and then I thought it must be hypocrisy, and then it seemed very clear that it was mortality. But in my late days I think it is memory that keeps us all ever from being happy."

"My dear lady," Tomo said. "Learn from me. I am very happy." It was the truth. Her visits made him happy. From the next room his wife threw off happiness like heat from her person. And yet, thinking of the orchard in Homer, he suddenly remembered how he had hurt his brother, how he had been a coward and refused to go along when Gob ran off to the war. Tomo closed his eyes and inhabited that moment, with Alanis Bell's warbling ringing in his ears. Over and over he sent his brother off to die without him.

"Why are you crying?" Tomo asked the boy. He was three-fourths of the way across the bridge, and about one-fourth of the way to his destination, when he saw the boy, leaning against the railing and sobbing. Every other passerby seemed completely unmoved by the boy's display. He was about seven years old, with long, shining brown hair that fell past his shoulders and down his back. He wore a neat, old-fashioned black suit. In that moment, he was not at all familiar to Tomo.

"He's gone!" the boy said. "Gone forever!"

"Who?" Tomo asked. "Did somebody jump?"

"Who?" the boy asked him back, looking up at him with black eyes that had more anger than sadness in them. "Who do you think? They're all gone. All of them, never to return, and before them all my brother is gone, gone for always."

"There now," Tomo said, reaching out to touch the boy on his head. "My brother, he died, too." He leaned down slowly, sure he heard himself creaking, to better comfort the little fellow. "It is a difficult thing, the death of a brother," he said. The boy smiled, then, and darted forward like a snake. He kissed instead of biting, a dry little peck, but it burned horribly where he planted it on Tomo's cheek.

"It's a difficult thing," the boy said, and Tomo felt dizzy. He had a falling sensation, and he was certain he had managed somehow to tumble off the bridge. He raised his arm up over his head in the attitude of Odlum, and prepared to meet the water.

"Goodbye, my love," he said, speaking to his wife. He heard a noise like the ocean, or the breathing of a giant, and he was overcome with desire—he opened his eyes and wanted the whole far shore of Manhattan and all the tall buildings on it; he wanted the bodies of every person passing him where he stood with his arm up over his head, still feeling as if he were falling through endless spaces of air, he wanted to put his hands under their dresses and shirts, to grab at their flesh with his dry old hands.

"Excuse me," said a lady walking by, because her dog had nipped at Tomo's shoe as they passed. He took down his arm and looked around. There was the boy, standing a few feet off. Tomo could not remember what they had been discussing. He tossed the little man a coin, because he knew every child likes a nickel to buy a bag of candy with, and every child liked how Tomo could make a coin spin in the air. The boy caught the coin in his mouth and seemed to swallow it.

"I only wanted to see you, Uncle," the boy said, and then he ran off towards Brooklyn, ducking between pedestrians. Tomo turned and walked on, thinking, just for a moment, that the boy was very familiar, after all, because he suddenly knew how the boy had been haunting him all his life—Tomo had seen him all over Manhattan and Brooklyn, far away in London and Paris, in Cuba, Hong Kong, Portugal, and Morocco. There was no place where he was not. Tomo kept walking, thinking that very soon he would remember why the boy was so sad, and why he never got any older, but as Tomo got closer to Manhattan he began to forget about him. Walking up to the terminal he stepped over the shadow of a streetlamp and paused to read a sign far ahead—though his joints were ruined, though his heart was weak and his bladder was nervous, his eyes were quite sharp. "If the baby is cutting its teeth," it advised, "use Mrs. Winslow's Soothing Syrup."

"What baby?" Tomo asked aloud, and then he walked on.

"Would you like to go faster?" his mama asked him. They were driving in a speedy Talbot-Darracq, her latest automobile. She kept a chauffeur, but always put him in the passenger seat, insisting on driving herself at high speeds all over her estate at Bredon's Norton in England.

"No," Tomo said, knowing she would go faster anyway. His wife didn't like automobiles. She had remained at the house to eat strawberries and doze in the sun while Tomo and his mother went out for a drive. She thought there was something obscene about automobiles. Tomo thought they were intriguing, though he would not ever drive one.

"It's a shame they don't make them any faster," his mama said. She drove every day for an hour because she insisted that in doing so she was putting a little more distance between herself and death. Since her third husband, the banker Mr. Martin, had died, she'd become obsessed with her own mortality. "Not too close," she'd say, if a person tried to kiss her, because she feared the pollution of touch.

"You quick widow!" Tomo called out to her, but she was half deaf, and could not hear him above the engine.

Often, by the time he'd reached the other side of the bridge, Tomo would have had enough of walking, so he'd take a cab to the church, struggling with his paper to pick out the address to give to the driver. It was a different church every time, and he was sure that by now he must have visited every one on the island. On that day in 1927 he went to a Catholic church on East Twenty-fifth Street, to a funeral, one that was especially dolorous and grim—that was how he liked them.

It was a sin, he knew, to lie to his wife, and probably also a sin to masquerade as a mourner. And yet wasn't he sad for this person, this man who had died of a bleeding stomach, who was survived by a wife, seven children, and a full score of grandchildren? Tomo might go to the hospital tomorrow or the next day and fail to save a person like this man, a balding Irishman whose skin was too big for him to fit into anymore. He might go to that funeral, too, because he was drawn to them, because he had always been drawn to them.

Tomo sat in the back, and watched quietly, not crying until the end, when he approached the casket and looked in to see the face of the man. He put a hand over his mouth and wept, sure that all around people were wondering who he was, this well-dressed, hobbling old man who grieved so dramatically. A pair of girls led him back to his seat. They were sisters, he could tell. "Are you twins?" he asked them loudly, and they both told him to hush. One of them stayed with him, standing while he sat, her hand placed gently on the back of his neck.

"Listen," he said to her. "Do you know how you are undying? Do you know how Heaven waits for the faithful? It's the good news, that a person is such a piece of work that there can be no end to her."

"Hush," she said.

"Do you doubt it?" he asked. "Do you?" He held her wrist, finding her pulse and reading her perfect health in it. "You do doubt it, don't you? You callow, doubting girl! You are afraid to die!"

"Stopper it up, Gramps," she said, placing a soft hand over his mouth, but Tomo pushed it away. He stood up and left the church, not caring how his slow, heavy tread rang out in the air and marred the lovely, sad music.

"Was it a good day?" his wife asked him. It was the question she asked every night as they got into bed together.

"Good enough," Tomo said. He'd spent the afternoon in Central Park, eaten ice cream on Madison Avenue, and bought an armful of daisies for his wife, enjoying, for a while, how they drew the stares of everyone who passed him.

"My feet are aching," his wife said, after they had been lying side by side for a while in the quiet dark. They had been dancing, that evening. They were neither of them very good at it, so they did it in the privacy of their home, in the empty bedroom that had once sheltered their second daughter.

"I'll heal them," Tomo said, sitting up and peeling back the covers so he could get at his wife's big feet. They were very pale, and as he massaged them they seemed brighter than any other thing in the room.

"Shall I reach under the bed?" she asked him, after he had been rubbing on her for a while, and after his hands had started to wander up her body.

"I think you had better," he said. Even as he worked her with his hands, she reached down under the bed and brought up a little porcelain bowl. It was too dark for Tomo to see it clearly, but he knew how it was painted in blue with birds, tall herons and egrets. It made a grating, ringing noise as his wife removed the top. Age required her to augment her natural charms with petrolatum.

With his creaking joints and his crooked back, his cloudy brain and his obstipated bowels, it always seemed to Tomo that physical love should be beyond him, but it was not yet, and sometimes, as on this night, it took a supreme effort of will to keep from spending himself like a naive boy. He did surgeries in his mind as he kissed his wife and whispered her own name into her face. It made him think of hernias, what they were doing, of organs invading cavities that were not their usual homes, and so to keep himself in order he went through the Bassini repair, sewing, in his mind, the conjoined tendon and the iliopubic tract into a forbidding wall that said to the protruding viscus, Stay where you belong.

When his time came, he imagined the futile sutures bursting, the tendons ripping and breaking to release a tumbling mass of bright confetti that ignited in his brain, becoming the millions of stars that had fallen around the bridge on that distant past night. He called out his wife's name, "Phoebe!" It was a distinct and equal pleasure, to shout it as loud as he could, in a house emptied by time, where no one could hear the name but him and its owner. His wife, a singer, answered him with a perfect C in an octave that told him he was doing well for her this evening.

He got a terrible pain in his left eye, and if his arms had not been locked around his wife, he would have clapped a hand to his face. It was painful, like being stabbed, and painful because it brought with it searing, lucid remembrance. Just for an instant, Tomo knew it was not Gob who had died at Chickamauga. His wife, he was sure, must take his screaming as a manifestation of unbearable pleasure.

But the knowledge, like the pleasure, passed in an instant, and he collapsed, still crying out softly, against his wife. There was a confused mess of flame where his mind ought to have been, and he did not know why he was crying. "There now," his wife said, putting her hand on the back of his neck, and stroking him there. "It wasn't all that bad, was it, my love?"

"No," Tomo said. And then he said it over and over, "No, no, no."

"Go to sleep, now," his wife said in reply to his continued

protest. Tomo became quiet, but the word still echoed in his head. He rolled onto his side and held her even closer, thinking how she was undying, and how he himself was undying, how Heaven waits for the faithful, how a man is such a piece of work that there can be no end to him, and how he wanted to believe that.